CONTENTS

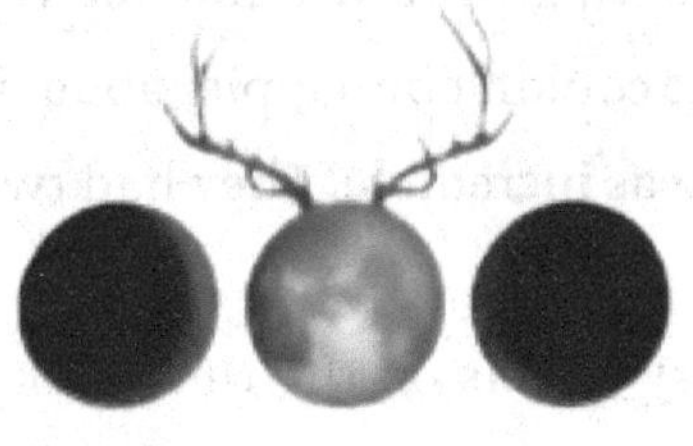

BETS!

Colleen Elizabeth Carter danced across the polished hardwood floor of her dining room, and into her kitchen. Her bare feet squeaked against the wood as she did. The music pumping through her house speakers was loud and fast, drums pounding, horn section screaming. She didn't know the song, but it was perfect for the little bit of early morning housekeeping.

Her husband had woken her up early, not something she was normally okay with, but he had done so by kissing his way across her bare shoulders and neck. His strong hands gripping her hips and pulling her back into him. He kept her in this state, fading between sleep and wakefulness. Fingers, lips, tongue, and breath, playing a symphony only she could hear until he brought her to one of mind-melting orgasms she only seemed to be able to have while still half asleep.

With her mind and body still reeling, and fading in and out of consciousness, he disappeared seemingly only for a blink then reappeared with a tray of fruit and coffee, serving her breakfast in bed. Happy birthday indeed.

Today was her fortieth birthday. While many women dreaded that number, honestly, she couldn't be happier about it. Her life was perfect. Her husband, Cecil, was incredible. They had two great kids, Lilly and Steven.

She had ten fantasy novels on the New York Times bestseller list, and two different erotic romance series under a pen name. She had also penned an autobiography about how hard it was as a woman to be taken seriously as a fantasy writer, and her battle against the patriarchal publishing world. One series had been licensed by a major streaming service, merchandise, speaking engagements, and master classes on writing and promotion.

Her income allowed her to live a life of relative luxury, and keep her lover, Jason, in an apartment downtown. Close to her office and the bar he worked at, but far enough away from her quiet suburban life that she didn't have to worry about him crossing paths with anyone that he shouldn't. He was ten years younger than her and had a body like a model. He also had a blessing between his legs that the pasty, gatekeeping, slobs who had plagued her for most of her career, would kill for.

In short, everything she touched turned to gold. She worked harder, played smarter, and won.

This weekend was all about her, starting first with dinner tonight with her family. Her brother Paul, and his wife Jen, were coming and bringing their three kids as well. Paul was the only family she had left. She had never met her father, and their mother had passed away when Paul was only two years old. Their older sister Polly drowned two years later. Since then, she had always looked out for him. She sent him money often, but Jen always seemed to be able to spend it faster than he could earn it or Colleen could send it.

After dinner, she and Cecil would have a few cocktails, and she would enthusiastically encourage his taking of her, letting him finish what he had started that morning.

Tomorrow, she would head into the city for a spa day which would consist of manicures, pedicures, a massage, and brunch with a couple of friends. Once she was warmed up by the mimosas and the good company, she would head to the apartment she kept Jason in.

She would spend the whole day wrapped around his glorious body. Staring at his chiseled jawline, brushing his shaggy blond hair out of his steel grey eyes. Reveling in her ability to get whatever she wanted. It was never about sex with Jason; Cecil kept her more than satisfied.

It was conquest, it was the devoted husband, and the model hot boyfriend on the side. Just to prove she could.

She danced her way to the first-floor bathroom to grab some more dish tabs from the supply closet there. Her reflection in the full-length mirror caught her attention. She was tall, five foot ten inches in socks, and fit from years of farm work as a kid and yoga and Pilates as an adult. In her cotton gym shorts and sports bra, even with the little sweat she had worked up dancing and cleaning, and her dirty blonde hair escaping its loose bun, she looked impressive by any standard.

Just further evidence of her exerting her will over the world around her. She looked good at forty because she controlled her appetite, worked her ass off in the gym, and maintained discipline in her life. The same reason she was successful in her career, she would do whatever it took to be on top.

"And fuck anyone who doesn't like it," she said to no one in particular.

"Speaking of, better get the boys warmed up."

Colleen slid her phone from her pocket and took a couple pictures in the mirror and a close up of her brilliant smile and blue eyes, she shimmied out of her sports bra and shorts. She stretched in a sun salutation, lengthening her spine and straightening her posture. She covered her small breasts with her arm and crossed her legs slightly so only the small patch of hair between her legs and a sliver of nipple showed. Grinning at her own wicked cleverness, she snapped a picture. A couple more spicy ones then she would send them off to Cecil and Jason. A reminder of the work they would be putting in for her birthday.

She turned away from the mirror and shot another over her shoulder, catching her muscular back and shapely ass in the mirror. Then she bent over at the waist, arched her back, and held her phone out in front of her, the flexibility in her shoulders and balance from all the yoga, paying off. The picture was her beautiful blue eye and part of her cheek, then down over the curve of her back and into the mirror where her ass was bent invitingly waiting for her lover to take her. She would edit the photo before sending it with a heart and a wish you were here right above the reflection of her ass in the mirror.

She wished she could send it to both of them at the same time and see who got to her first. That would be a thrill, both of them wanting her so badly, loving her so much, that they would be happy to share her.

Another time perhaps, she grabbed her shorts and bra and slid them back on.

She knew she should feel some kind of guilt for the affair, for all the affairs, for the manipulation, the toes she had to step on to get where she was, but she didn't. She knew that most women in her position would be worried all the time about being caught. It wasn't that she didn't worry about losing Cecil, she would be crushed if he left her. But even more than that, the idea of failing to convince him to stay, was unbearable. She needed him to understand that everything she had done was to secure a better future for herself and her family.

If her only ask is that she gets to play when she wants, and how she wants, then she wasn't going to feel a damn bit of guilt for that. She flashed her brilliant smile in the mirror again and licked her teeth at the thought of the guys' reaction to her last picture.

Something moved in the corner of her eye, and a hand landed on her bare shoulder.

"Bets," a booming voice called.

Out of instinct she spun toward the sound, her fist following the momentum of the turn. A hand wrapped around her throat and lifted her off her feet slamming her hard against the door three times, rattling her skull and jarring the breath out of her. She kicked out, and the hand tightened again, yanking her back to the ground. She still couldn't see who was in the room with her.

The hand was gone from her throat only to grab her at the back of the neck, drag her back to the vanity and force her head down toward the sink. She tried reaching for her phone, maybe she could get 911 dialed before he hurt her again.

She looked into the mirror and stopped cold. What was staring back at her made no sense. It was blurry, like it wasn't fully formed, the body was human in size and shape, but it was covered in greasy, black fur. It was crouched about four feet in the air, like it was on a perch. Its toes tipped with wicked claws, and dripping with a viscous liquid, were curled around whatever it rode on.

In the hand that didn't have a vice like grip on her neck, it carried a cane or walking stick, like a bird's beak or something. She snapped her eyes shut again. What she saw could not be possible. *Take a breath.* She tried to calm herself; *it's the shock of an intruder attacking her, that's all. Monsters aren't real.* But the hand on her neck was very real, as was the blood in her mouth.

That's when the voice came, deep, resonate, and slick. The voice of a DJ or a soap opera star. The kind of voice that captivated her when she was a younger woman, before she understood her own power. When she was still susceptible to being sucked in by a man's voice, or smell, or eyes, or muscles, or any of the numerous other things that made her think this would be the one to make her happy. Before she realized it was success that made her feel fulfilled and everything else was just a byproduct of her success.

"Open your eyes, Bets!"

Colleen shook her head; she had not heard that nickname since she was a child and no one who had called her that was even alive anymore.

The voice moved closer to her ear. "If you do not open your eyes, I will be forced to open them for you, and you will not like the way I do it."

Again, Colleen shook her head and kept her eyes shut. Her fear giving way to the childish stubbornness she felt anytime someone was trying to order her around. She was in charge of her life, not her dead mother or grandmother, not her absent father, not her husband or lover, not her publisher or accountant. Not any of the other men who pretended to have some bullshit control over her, and not this ugly little monkey.

She opened her mouth to assert just how much she was in charge; eyes still shut against the monster in the mirror. The voice was closer to her ear, and almost whispering now, she could feel the hot breath against her ear, and a stench, like incense covering the smell of rotting meat, threatened to overwhelm her gag reflex.

The hand around the back of her neck was huge, wrapping almost all the way around her slender neck. Its grip was unyielding, like cold iron. But she grew up barefoot and country mean with lots of cousins and neighbor boys, who could never decide whether they wanted to kiss her or push her down in the mud.

This was not the first time someone had tried to scruff her neck, and control her.

She pushed toward the grip then yanked back, trying to shake loose and fight back. The hand held firm, yanking her neck so hard she thought her head might snap off. She felt the tentacles ringing the lip slide across the skin of her neck and she wanted to die.

"Remember that I warned you." He whispered in her ear, and she felt the tip of the bird beak cane touch her left temple, and push in, breaking the skin. Suddenly, liquid fire flowed from the bird's beak into the now bleeding wound on her head.

Her head was forced over the sink just as she began to wretch and vomit. Her bladder let go at the same time, she barely noticed due to the stabbing pain in her head and guts. At first, it was just coffee and bile, then came the clumps of black hair and what could only be rotting meat, filled with worms, still wiggling. She could feel them in her mouth and throat, and this brought on more vomiting.

She could hear the basin filling up with each expulsion, her legs began to shake, and it felt as though her insides were being wrenched apart. The searing heat flowing from the bird beak plunged into her head, continued without abating, finally she could take no more.

"Please, stop," she cried. She opened her eyes to attempt to implore him, to offer whatever she could, to make it stop.

The sink in front of her was empty, as clean as when she first walked into the bathroom, the smell, the pain, the wriggling of the worms and taste of the bile-soaked hair and rotten meat, all gone. She looked in the mirror, this time determined to look at him without looking away, to try to gain some kind of upper hand on whatever this was.

The face staring back at her was simian in its foundation, but also as alien and monstrous as anything she had ever written about in her own novels. Its head was comically large, and its black eyes shined like polished obsidian. Where its mouth should be a ring of short tentacles surrounded a maw of needle-like yellow teeth.

"Are you done being a petulant child now, Bets?"

It was appalling to hear that smooth broadcaster voice, like honey and bourbon being poured into your ears, coming out of the mouth of that disgusting, wretched-looking imp.

"I will make you a promise, if you attempt to defy me again, filling your guts with roadkill will seem like a fond remembrance of childhood. I am a busy man, Bets, you may feel like the most important princess at the ball, but I can assure you, you are not the only task I have that needs tending to today. So, give me what I came for, I and will move along, and leave you to your choices."

Colleen stared at the nightmare in the mirror. She could feel her mind start to come untethered. A floating feeling, not her body, but her consciousness. A moment, then two before she snapped back into her body. She was trembling from her scalp to the soles of her feet.

"I don't know what you are, or what you want."

The sound of fear and desperation in her voice was so foreign to her.

The hand on the back of her neck tightened, and she was terrified for a moment she had angered him further and he saw her question as defiance.

He pulled her close again, obviously not happy with her response. "I am the reason for all you are, everything you have, every success, every spark of inspiration or luck, it's all because of me. You received it at my grace, and I have come to collect what's due me.

I shouldn't be surprised; you Milburn girls have always been a stubborn lot and arrogant beyond your abilities. Neeny was the worst of them."

She flinched as if struck at the mention of her grandmother. Too many memories, too much pain to think about.

"So, it only makes sense she would not pass along to her heir, the terms of her success and their responsibilities to uphold. This is the last time I relay this information, if it isn't passed on this time; when I next come to collect, I will slaughter this entire bloodline. What I will not do is continue to not be credited for the great successes in your bloodline, when it's ALL MY WORK!"

He pulled her close to him, then slammed her back against the bathroom door. She hit hard enough to snap her mouth shut and immediately tasted blood again. She held her reactions in check. This was not the time to show her temper if she wanted to make it through this intact. Whatever this creature was, it was too much for her. She needed to give it whatever it wanted and figure the rest out later.

"That's a wise plan, Bets," it spoke a little gentler now, its rage seemingly abated for the moment.

It flexed its clawed toes and moved closer to her, still appearing to be riding on the shoulder of some invisible being. It lowered its thick browed forehead and looked at her closely.

"That's a fair assessment, think of me like the fin of a giant shark, I'm the small part you see breaking the surface just before you are devoured by the much larger beast. My Lord, The Witch Father, is hungry, child, so hungry. So here I am, an agent in his service, come to collect the fee for the success I have granted you. As per our deal."

Colleen took a breath and lowered her eyes; she heard the creature make a soft exclamation of pleasure at this gesture. She said as evenly and respectfully as she could, "I have never made a deal that I know of. I'm sorry if I'm supposed to know something, but I have no idea who you are or what my end of the deal was, but fair is fair. If you are the reason for all my success, then tell me what is owed so I can understand, and we can move forward."

"Perfect," the creature boomed loudly enough that she started a little and pushed her back flat against the door.

"I must admit, Bets, of all the women in your line I have had to have this tedious conversation with—you might be the most interesting. You caught on immediately, once you were shown the truth of your position. No wailing for mercy or calling down God's wrath or quoting scripture

. Your grandmother was a hypocrite of the highest order. Calling out to Gawd and aww his angels, to come and send this daaaaymon back to the pits of hell from whence he came!"

His imitation of her grandmother's voice and inflections were dead on, and Colleen was instantly taken back in time, to that little Pentecostal church where Neeny and all her kin gathered every Sunday from sunup to sundown. Then on to the big tent revivals where her grandfather, William "Slim" Milburn III, healed the sick and sharpened the teeth of his hellfire and brimstone sermons every night.

"That's exactly what I am talking about, Bets. Your grandmother was as accomplished and powerful a root worker and healer as any I have ever seen. She squandered her ability on making her husband look like a miracle worker. Even when she knew it had been the gifts I had given her all along that were healing those misguided sheep of Ol' Slim Milburn's flock.

When I finally came to collect from her, she had the gall to call out for her false god to protect her from me. She, who had given me a daughter and granddaughter willingly. She, who lost another daughter, your own mother in fact, due to her own trickery. She has the guts to pretend any God worth their title would intervene on behalf of a mother who would sacrifice her own kinfolk. You are confused, but hanging in there, Bets, I like that, it makes me feel a little bad about the roadkill thing, not all the way sorry, but perhaps I overreacted."

"I always did have to learn the hard way," Colleen muttered.

The creature laughed and the sound echoed off of the stone tile of her bathroom like a cannon.

"That is a Mercer trait if ever I have heard one. Every damn Mercer woman I have dealt with going back to the first one, all of them, stubborn and disrespectful, ungrateful, spoiled, temperamental."

He was pounding his fist into his open palm, making a meaty thud emphasizing each word. Picking up momentum, growing visibly more agitated. "Vain, self-important, myopic, dense, cattle tenders."

Colleen was starting to get concerned that he might do something else horrible to her out of anger at what he kept referring to as Mercer women.

"I'm sorry,"

Colleen lowered her head again and spoke softly, "but I don't know who these Mercer women are that you're talking about, and I am not sure how I should refer to you so I can ask, respectfully?"

The creature stopped his ranting for a moment and cocked his head to one side while he looked at her. "No, I don't suppose you would know any of that, would you? The only people capable of teaching you any of that, are long dead or unknown to you. You may call me Seanchara. I am also not surprised the Mercer name is lost to you, although there are some in your bloodline who still wear it proudly and with knowledge of its meaning."

Seanchara seemed to stiffen a little when he spoke of those who were proud of the Mercer name, as if he was also proud of it. "I will be curious, when this day is out, to see how that affects your decision. You see, centuries ago, a very gifted woman, desperate to save her daughters and herself from her prideful and incompetent husband, cried out for help, and my father took note of her pleas.

"In his infinite wisdom he sent me to intercede on his behalf. A deal was struck, she would be given the power to remedy her situation, but on her fortieth birthday, I would come to collect. She and every woman of her line would be given the choice. Continue with the knowledge that your every endeavor will be a wild success and sacrifice a daughter from your line or sacrifice yourself and a daughter of your line will carry the gift and the choice."

Despite the inherent danger in the situation, Colleen found herself enrapt.

"So, it has been for many generations, a Mercer woman that carries her gift, cannot lose, everything she touches is a success, you're proof of that yourself. But that bill always comes due, the price must always be paid. The farmer's wife was the first Mercer woman, and while not all the original Mercer women were blood relatives, you are all descendants of them in either blood, place, or spirit. This is the way it has been since the first and how it must always be, Bets."

Colleen steadied herself, an idea forming in her mind, and she hoped to get it out before he read it, feeling that the words would carry more weight than thought.

"Seanchara, how is it fair I was given this agreement without my knowledge, why must I pay the price?"

At the mention of the price, she thought then of Lilly, he had been clear, her life, or a daughter of her line and Lilly was her only daughter. She fought back tears as she pictured Lilly's face, at twelve years old, she was their wild card. Barely housebroken, was the joke between her and Cecil.

She had Colleen's hair and Cecil's rich, dark eyes, but there was an untamed intensity in the girl that Colleen found both endearing and concerning. She could sometimes be found even now barefoot and climbing trees, rescuing whatever wildlife she could find and often savagely fighting with her older brother. She had no patience for his displays of dominance and had to be reprimanded often for overreacting with physical violence.

Colleen no longer attempted to fight the tears, her hands shook at the thought of losing Lilly and she straightened and stared at Seanchara. "Why? Why does one of us have to die? I am in my prime with years of work left to accomplish and Lilly is a baby; she has barely started her life. It's unfair, it's stupid, fuck the woman who made the deal in the first place. She had no right to put that on me. On all the women who have had to do this, and fuck you, I won't do it, I won't choose!"

She was reaching fever pitch now, tears flowing freely and her voice cracking. No longer afraid of his wrath. "You may have blessed me, but I have worked my ass off, I spent hours slaving away. I was the one reading rejection after rejection, getting groped and propositioned by greasy agents. Spending hours away from my family, and you just roll in here claiming credit for all of my sacrifice and hard work."

Seanchara's black eyes gleamed, and he hovered closer to her, his voice matching hers in volume and intensity. "Don't play the martyr with me, Bets. I know better, I know while your precious Lilly was laid up with pneumonia, Cecil got fired from his job, so you could go to your book signing. Were you concerned about fairness while you were spending the weekend with another man's cock in your mouth?"

Bets stared defiantly, her face twisted with rage, and started to try and justify her actions, however inexcusable they may have seemed.

"Or how about Laurel, the assistant you not only underpaid and cheated out of money but also got her drunk and took blackmail pictures of her naked to keep her quiet. She ended up overdosing on fentanyl a year later. Did you know she was a recovering addict, Bets? Did you know she was in love with you, is that how you coaxed her into getting naked for the pictures you later used to threaten to ruin her life with?"

The greasy fur on his wiry body bristled. "Should we add in the charity foundation that spends about seventy percent of its donations on improvements to your own kids' private school? You must decide who dies tonight, you or a daughter. If you don't, I will rip your entire family to pieces in front of you, and then I will torture you to death in every horrible way I can think of. I will start by force feeding you your own children."

She tried not to think of the roadkill filling her mouth, her eyes watered as she struggled not to vomit.

"So yes, it's tragic and you were never given a choice. But you had the potential to do anything you ever wanted; the universe cannot tell you no. Even then, you pushed the lines of morality, only proving that even with the potential to do unlimited good, the more successful you have become, the more selfish and immoral you have become. Don't pretend you're some saint, wronged by a great evil."

Colleen stood gaping at him, tears and snot drying on her cheeks. Just a few of her many sins laid bare, she searched for some way to justify her actions, to try and paint herself as the hero or the victim or anything. Instead, she just stared and nodded.

Quietly, she said, "Daughter of my line, does it have to be my daughter, my Lilly, or will any daughter of my family serve the purpose?"

He had already pulled the mask off and revealed who she was at her core, she did not want to die today. But she wasn't willing to give up Lilly either.

Could she sacrifice one of Paul's daughters? Could she be willing to see Beth, named after her, or Janelle, only six years old, sacrificed to save herself and her Lilly?

"I think you already know the answer to that."

His posture was relaxing again, the moment of intensity subsiding. "I think you know for a fact you would kill them yourself if it meant saving you, much less you and your daughter. You hate their mother as much as anyone you have ever met, and Paul is nothing but a pitiable mess, enslaved to Jen the way he is. Sadly, none of those children are his, so while you are not wrong, another daughter in your family would fill the role, none of them are of your family."

Bets' eyes narrowed as she considered this new fact, in her heart she knew it was true.

"You see, Jen is like you in a lot of ways, only it isn't conquest and validation she seeks from men. She uses other men to hold power over your brother. The father of her children is a man she has been having an ongoing affair with for the better part of ten years. She has had many others, but he is the one she always goes back to. They have Paul convinced that they have some dirt on you. If he ever tries to leave her, they will bring forth this evidence and ruin you both. With this as leverage she has spent years making him miserable, she tortures him for sport. Cheating, lying, physical and emotional abuse, all of it.

There is a reason you hate her, you have the intuition of the Mercer women, and while you didn't know it, you can smell that hateful spirit all over her. You know the worst of it? She does it out of jealousy of you. She is wildly jealous of your brains and looks and success and everything about you. She knows she can't hurt you directly, and Paul would never tell you, so she keeps it her secret, her way of proving she is smarter than you."

Colleen could feel the heat rising again in her face. She was teetering on the edge of a blind rage. But she knew much of that rage was covering a heart full of guilt. She was the reason Paul's life was so miserable, and she did essentially the same thing to Cecil. Every word he said rang true, maybe that's why this whole thing, finding him in her bathroom, hearing all she had heard, Jen, Paul, all of it made sense. She knew it all along in some deep part of her, she just didn't understand what it was, but it was there.

"Seanchara, is that what happened to my mother?"

The creature shifted its small black eyes around as if reading the answer on the door behind her head, then answered, "Your grandmother Neeny, was much older than you think she was. On her fortieth birthday, she gave me her oldest daughter, Dorthea. Then just before time was to come to renew the agreement again, she attempted to bind me. She conspired with another Mercer woman, and a local preacher's wife. It would have been incredibly effective had I been a demon or haint, or whatever they thought I was.

"It was potent magic with them all lending their power to it and the blood they spilled. It didn't destroy me, but it hurt like nothing I had ever felt before. Unlike your grandmother, I am a man of my word, and I did not touch her for her attempt on my life. Instead, I killed her daughter, your mother, in front of her, and then ripped that Mercer woman's eyes out."

Colleen shook her head in disbelief. "My mother died in a car crash. She—"

Seanchara shook his head so hard that drops of oil from his wiry hair splattered the walls. "I am sorry, Bets, but your mother died as a result of Neeny's arrogance and poor planning. I know, because I reached my arm down her throat and ripped loose everything I could get my hand around until she started shitting her organs out on to the floor.

It was a gruesome sight even by my standards, and my standards are high in that regard. So, two years later I came back. Her choice then was simple, you or Polly. That day, she took Paul and Polly to the lake to swim, and I was waiting under the water to ferry her away. Even then, even after the way her daughter died, she still couldn't bring herself to face her own end."

Colleen stared blankly at him, what could she even say, all of this, the rage at Jen, her sadness for Paul, the horrible truth about her mother, about Polly. All of it, as terrible as it was, paled in comparison to the fact that she had to make the same choice now.

She lowered her head once more, thinking through her choices, her life, knowing that one way or another, everything was going to change. She did not want to die, but she couldn't stand the thought of giving up her daughter to this agreement.

"How can I end this? Is there anything I can do to make tonight the last time you visit a Mercer woman? Maybe you're right, maybe I am a horrible person, but what can I do, how can I ensure that no one else ever must make this choice again?"

The tears were streaming down her face again. She cried with no reservations. She cried for her daughter, who would either never grow up or grow up without her mother. Her only memories ones of a mom too busy making money and being in charge to be around. She cried for her mother and Polly, sweet Polly, sacrificed by someone who was supposed to be their protector.

She cried for all the women forced to make these horrible choices, over and over again throughout history. To be put in such desperate situations that they would make deals with creatures like this just to escape or survive them. She wept for all the mothers who never got to hold their grandchildren and all the daughters who never got to hear their mothers tell them how proud they were of all they had accomplished. She wept for the kind men like Paul, buried under the trauma and vengeance of angry and dangerous women like Jen, women so hurt, that hurt, was all they knew. She stood facing Seanchara, the pain of generations of Mercer women washing over her and cleansing her mind and her soul.

He studied her with his shiny black eyes. "As you have probably surmised, I am not the authority in all matters. That honor belongs to The Witch Father. It will be his decision what, if anything you can do to release the Mercer women from this agreement. Understand, you are not the only Mercer woman operating under this agreement, and not all of them will be happy with your decision to end it. But I will return at 10 p.m. tonight. Your party should be wrapping up by then."

He held out his walking stick; dangling from it, was a silver crucifix on a leather slip cord she recognized as Grandma Neeny's necklace. She reached for it, only then seeing the walking stick for the first time, for what it was. A raven's head with a silver tipped beak, but it was not carved, it was an actual raven and its eyes twitched and followed her movements as she was reaching for the necklace. The body of the stick was a femur ending in a ring of coarse brown hair and a split hoof. She could see the veins pulsing in the bare skin at the juncture of the leg and hoof. She shivered from her scalp to the base of her spine at the thought of those living animals trapped as his cane, and he pulled it back slightly.

"The one who is to be the sacrifice will be wearing this when I return. I will not make myself known to anyone other than you. But rest assured, if no one is wearing this chain when I return, I will consider it an act of defiance and aggression and I will react accordingly. Upon my return, I will let you know of my father's wishes, and if there is an arrangement to be made to release the Mercer women from this agreement, I will advise you then. Now, take the chain, I must be off. I have spent enough time here already and have many preparations to make, as do you. Your family will be home soon, and you look horrible. Clean yourself up, Bets, and remember, no matter what choice you make this will be the last day of your life as it is. Make the most of it."

With that, he was gone. Colleen made up her mind quickly as to what course she would take. She just had a couple of details to hammer out. She stripped and hopped into the shower, she had no time to spare, and everything had to fall in line for this to work. She cleaned herself, trying not to think of all she had in front of her and all she had learned. There will be time for processing at some point, but this was a time for action, and this, she was good at. Put the pedal to the metal and get done, what needed to get done. She figured about an hour before Cecil and the kids got in, and she would use every second of it. It was 9:30 a.m. now, dinner wasn't until 7:30, that should give her plenty of time.

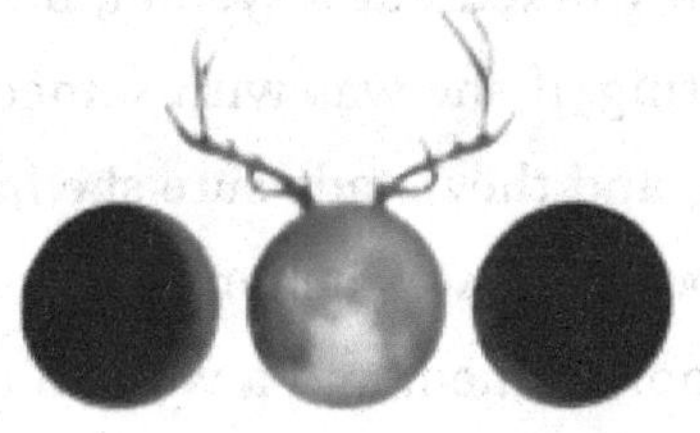

A Little Treat Couldn't Hurt

M.M. Wildes sat in the back corner of Bricktop's Beans and Bakery, on Prairie and 5th. It was a little before one in the afternoon, and the sun coming through the window warmed her skin and hair. A delightful treat on this cold November Tuesday. She sipped her coffee and glanced around the shop. It was quiet, too out of the way for the downtown office crowd. A little too dusty and hipster for the average suburbanite homemaker to venture off the beaten path for.

But the baristas were top-notch artists, and the pastry chef was truly inspired. The owner, and the chef were both frequent clients of her shop. They knew she occasionally helped at-risk women and children escape difficult situations.

They had long ago worked out a system; if she sat up at the bar, she was up for chatting. If she was with someone else, it was likely a sensitive situation, and they made sure she had enough space and privacy to make whoever she was helping comfortable.

The bell on the door chimed, and a woman entered, bringing the truth of the blustery cold into the small dining room with her. Dressed in beige baggy slacks, faded sneakers, no makeup or jewelry. Her greying hair was tied up in a bun tight enough to appear painful. M thought to herself, she couldn't look more the unhappy middle-aged housewife if she tried, poor thing.

From what M had gleaned over the phone from Judy Thompson, this was not a domestic violence situation or physical abuse.

She may not have been physically abused, but everything about Judy screamed of her trampled spirit, and M knew that could be as bad. She rose and lifted her hand as Judy scanned the room, looking over the small handful of people to see who she was supposed to be meeting.

Judy rushed to her table and extended her hand. "Ms. Wildes, it is such a pleasure to meet you."

Judy's grip was far more solid than M expected, such an odd contrast to her meek appearance.

"Please call me M. Can I get you a drink? The baristas here are fantastic and can make almost anything you can dream up. In fact, after a couple of visits I stopped ordering, and left myself in their hands, and they never miss."

Judy pulled her coat tighter around herself. "I am afraid I wouldn't know where to start. Dan doesn't approve of spending money on fancy coffees. He doesn't drink coffee, Diet Coke only. I have a small one-cup brewer I use when he leaves for work, and I get the cheapest I can find at the grocery store."

There was no shame in her statement. Just the facts, her husband thinks since he doesn't like it, there's no reason to spend money on it. Even when she does, she still keeps the things she likes out of sight.

M thought to herself, *at least I know where we are starting*. "Have a seat and make yourself comfortable. I will go grab you something, would you prefer sweet or savory?"

Judy smiled timidly. "I think a sweet treat would be good, after all, plenty of time for it not to ruin my dinner."

A few minutes later, M returned with a simple vanilla latte, a scone, and a coffee cake with a couple of plates and forks so they could share. As she walked back to the table, she became acutely aware of Judy's scrutiny.

She wondered what she must think of the way she looked. M's hair was coffee bean brown with shimmering streaks of crimson and blue. Her makeup was light today but surely stood out to Judy who wore none. She wore a Baltic Born midi wrap in a crimson that matched the streaks in her hair. She had on black tights with spider web designs, and an old worn pair of Doc Martin's. Her arms, covered in tattoos, were bare.

She had not followed protocol today. Normally, she would be dressed down and as inconspicuous as possible when meeting with someone who required her services. But most of these meetings were arranged through her Mercer connections. She would have her partner, Sugar, in the other corner in case something went wrong. Her job would be to put the woman at ease and plan an escape, with as little risk to them, or her, as possible. Sometimes it was a simple as getting them to a hotel or shelter. Sometimes their contacts in the local police department would be involved and the offending party would find themselves entangled with a lengthy and incredibly effective criminal investigation.

Occasionally, the situation would require a more magical solution. When that was the case, the abuser would be convinced to focus his attentions elsewhere, sometimes permanently. And under the most dire circumstances, M or her consort Sugar would ensure that the person in question understood how dangerous hurting someone who cannot defend themselves could be.

This was different. Judy hadn't come to her by any of the usual channels. She had been fostering an interest in witchcraft and had asked in an online social media group about spells to catch a husband cheating. Someone had suggested she call the shop and speak to M, who was known for having a witchcraft-based remedy for almost anything.

"Judy, why don't you tell me what I can help with? I find it best if we start with the end goal. I know it might seem strange, but I don't want to be laying out a plan for getting you out of town under an assumed name. If all you are really looking for is to make your husband help with the dishes and laundry. Does that make sense?"

Judy looked at M for longer than was comfortable before answering.

"I am in no danger, Ms. Wildes—M, sorry. But I want a divorce. No, I have to have a divorce."

"Okay, good, if you're in no danger that is a good place to start. Tell me what's going on, take your time."

"Well, Dan was never a prize husband if that makes sense, but I didn't need Prince Charming. I couldn't have kids, and Dan was okay with that. I had planned on becoming a teacher, and that's when things started to change."

Judy picked at her half of the scone. "At first, it was money, we don't have enough for you to go to school yet, that type of thing. But anytime I offered to get a job to pay for it myself, it turned into a big fuss. No wife of his was going to be working as a cashier or teller or secretary or whatever else I was qualified for. He would be mortified to have to tell people he didn't make enough money for his wife to stay at home and take care of the house."

She sipped her latte and paused for a moment, lost in some memory. When she came back to herself, she continued.

"It made sense to me in some way, and at first almost felt kind of old fashioned and chivalrous. As the years went by, it became clear it wasn't about taking care of me. It was how he looked to his partners and friends. I began to show my age a little, and so did he, mind you. He was never handsome, but now, well let's say I have to use a lot of imagination a couple of times a month to get through that unpleasantness."

It was everything M could do to not grin like an idiot at that last statement. It was good to see Judy still had some fight in her. She was down, but not out, like the handshake, a bit of a contradiction between how she talked and acted versus how she presented herself. But as experienced as she was, M was no therapist or psychologist.

She had gifts, many of them, and wore many hats, but most of them were related to her mission and the power and insight imbued upon her by the Mercer women. To be honest, she was a lot more comfortable rescuing someone from a potentially violent or dangerous situation than she was trying to understand why people acted the way they did to get themselves in these situations.

Judy continued her story. "At some point over the last few years, the cheating started. If it were an affair, I think I would have been a little more understanding. Had he met someone who he desired, and they desired him, I would have felt betrayed and sad my marriage failed. But he was paying for prostitutes. He left some of the bank paperwork lying around one night after paying bills and I noted all the account info and had the statements sent to my email."

M noticed the fork in Judy's right hand flexing as she pressed it into the plate. She wondered for a moment just how much rage was built up in this woman.

"It wasn't hard to put two and two together, he is nothing if not boring and predictable. Like clockwork, the second and fourth Friday of every month he would take out four hundred dollars from our account and be out all night on business. Again, not all that creative, predictable, and frugal in most things. He always liked to brag about how he only used Marriott Hotels so he could keep a big rewards account for work travel."

She took a long drink and looked thoughtfully at the cup for a moment. "So, one night out I followed him. Clueless as he was, he went to the bar and met up with a girl who looked so young she could have barely been eighteen. They had a drink at the bar, and went up to his room, an hour later, she was back out in the parking lot getting picked up by some guy."

The fork in her hand flexed again, and M became concerned it might snap in half.

"I followed him twice more after that to confirm it wasn't always the same girl. Sure enough, different every time but always dangerously young, and the whole transaction in an hour. I can't have a sweet coffee like this or get a degree because we don't have the money, but he can spend hundreds a month on degrading young girls in expensive hotel rooms."

M was raging inside, she knew, without ever seeing him exactly the kind of man Dan Thompson was, and exactly what she would do to him if she got the chance.

"Nine years, Ms. Wildes, nine years since I have been on vacation. But he goes to a hotel multiple times a month and pays girls barely out of high school so he can stick his prick in them a few times. I want out of this hell, Ms. Wildes, but he has all the money and all the power, everything is in his name. I haven't had a pay stub in fifteen years. How am I supposed to get a fair shake from him? I don't even have money to pay you, much less a lawyer that can compete with Dan's."

M reached across the table and took Judy's hand; she took a breath and dropped her wards. A wave of emotions threatened to overwhelm her. Part of her gift was that skin-on-skin contact would push the other person's emotions into her mind. Without her wards in place, this effect happened fast, without regulation or control. The closest thing M had ever felt to it was getting a vaccine when the injection was refrigerated. The rush of cold entering your body with no control. Only these were someone else's deepest emotions pumped right into her brain with no filter or padding.

She felt sadness and embarrassment and something deeper, something she didn't think even Judy was aware of, rage, deep, powerful, unfiltered rage. Her initial judgment had been completely off, this woman wasn't a trampled soul, this woman was a warrior, she just kept it hidden, even from herself.

"Judy, let's get everything out up front—I require no payment."

Judy raised an eyebrow at this.

M held up a hand for her to be patient. "Only a promise from you, that when it is said and done, if you ever have the opportunity to help another woman in your position, you help them. As far as this husband of yours, I have a plan. Let's get another treat, shall we? This deserves a cookie at the very least."

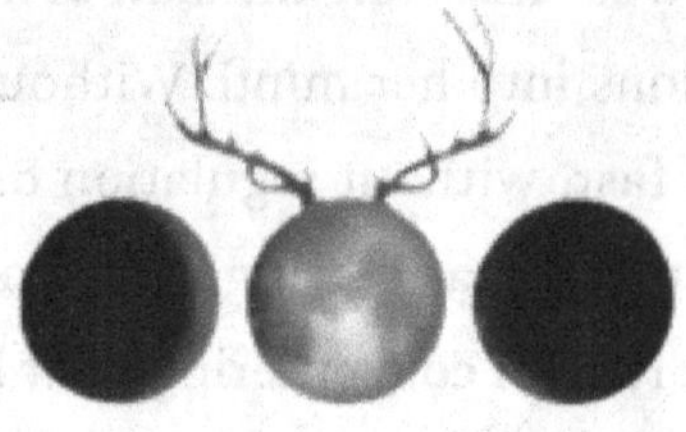

THE MOON OVER THE WATER

When Cecil arrived home with the supplies and kids, Colleen met them all at the door, she was showered and clean and had done her best to lay out her plan for the rest of the day. She composed a quick email to her lawyer and attached a short letter to it. Shelly had been with her, as her estate lawyer, for a long time and could be trusted to carry out anything she needed without question, even odd requests like this one.

She sent the kids down to start decorating the basement for the party tonight and to finish the chores and led Cecil to their bedroom on the third floor of the house. She gently pulled him onto the bed and clung to him, drinking in his smell, and the feel of his arms around her. He began to speak, and she kissed him.

"Cecil, it's my birthday and I want to say this first: I love you, more than anything, you have been the greatest husband myself or anyone else could ask for. I know I have not always treated you well or been the wife you deserve; I am not gentle or even considerate sometimes. But thank you, for standing with me, for believing in me and for seeing something in me that made you stay for all these years."

"Colleen, what is this, is everything okay?"

"Everything is going to be fine."

"Okay, that doesn't really make me feel any better..."

She cut him off, kissing him harder this time then rolled him onto his back and climbed on top of him.

An hour or so later, satisfied, and exhilarated, they emerged from their bedroom to find the kids. They had laid out the plans for the rest of the day, and it was time to make it happen. But first, lunch with Cecil and the kids, she wanted to soak up every minute she could with Lilly before tonight.

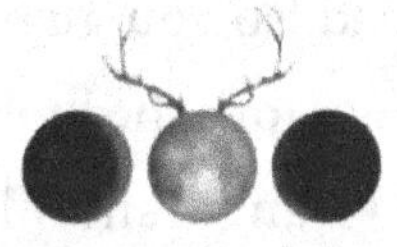

When Paul and his family arrived, the house came alive, Paul and Colleen chattering away, the kids all playing at a hundred miles per hour. Colleen had retrieved some bottles of wine and champagne from the cellar and was setting everyone up with glasses. Paul did not drink, but Jen went after the champagne with a vengeance, getting louder and more obnoxious with every glass.

All night the clock ticked on in the dining room, and every time it chimed the half an hour or hour, Colleen would close her eyes, feeling fate and the universe closing in. While the conversation roared at the table in front of her over dinner, she smiled and fell into herself as much as she could, reaching out, trying to feel this connection Seanchara had talked about, trying to reach the Mercer women, anywhere. *Please help me*, she called in her mind, *I don't want to do this, this cannot be the only way.* She screamed into the void in her mind, *please, don't make me do this, don't make me choose.*

At 9:30 p.m. the cake and ice cream had been consumed, the candles extinguished, and everyone was gathered on the back patio chatting. Jen was attempting to pull Colleen into what she was sure would lead to another MLM pitch, a can't fail scheme that just needed a little seed capital from Colleen, and this could put her and Paul on easy street.

Colleen announced to the group, "Alright, boys, commence to cleaning, Jen is onto an idea I want to hear about and it's getting late. The kids are going to get grumpy when the sugar wears off, and I need my husband awake enough to give me the rest of my birthday present when we get everyone settled, so you guys get it cleaned up, and Jen and I will be back in just a few. I love the look of the moon over the creek when it's clear like this, and I want to show her while we talk business."

Cecil grinned the grin of a man who isn't sure how he got so lucky. Paul shuffled behind him towards the kitchen while the kids piled into the living room to watch Steven and Joseph, Paul's oldest son, play a video game. Colleen and Jen walked across the moonlit backyard, Jen stumbled and complained about the walk the entire time. Colleen could hear the slur in her words; Jen had polished off close to two bottles of champagne on her own and it was coming through in her speech and walking.

"God, Colleen, how much further are we going, I can tell you about this new company right here."

Colleen kept walking. "Just up ahead, when you see the reflection of the moon on the water, you'll know why I brought you here."

A few yards more and they walked out onto the little float dock stuck out into the creek that bisected their property. It wasn't wide, but in the early spring like now, it swelled up and moved quickly. Colleen motioned for Jen to move out onto the dock, small solar lights lit the boards but not anything else, the moon was full and the skies clear, so if you knew where you were going it wasn't bad.

Colleen checked her phone, 9:45 p.m., she sent a quick text. Jen was staring up at the moon in the sky dreamily and asking Colleen if she had ever considered getting into the supplement game when the first blow struck her on the head. She dropped hard to the dock and moaned something incoherent. Colleen stood over her with a small paving stone, she stared hard at Jen's face, dimly lit by the dock light, her eyes fixed on Colleen, but she wasn't moving. Colleen brought the rock down hard on her jaw, teeth cracking beneath the weight of the rock and Colleen's rage. Jen tried feebly to get her hands up to her face, to protect herself, but it was too late. The first blow from the rock had rattled her brain and would have likely been fatal if she didn't receive some kind of medical attention, but the second one had not only caught her with her mouth hanging open and cracked several teeth but had bounced her head off of the dock hard enough that recovery was highly unlikely.

Colleen leaned down close to her, snarling into her ear, "Did you think I wouldn't find out? Did you think you could hurt him for all those years, and it wouldn't come back to you? Did you think you had won somehow? This is all you win, a cold, lonely death."

She pulled up the loop of rope hanging on the side of the dock until the cinderblock attached to it came up out of the water. She fed the rope under Jen's torso and tied it as tight to the block as she could. It wouldn't hide her very long, but she didn't think she would need to for very long. Just long enough for tonight to play out. She rolled Jen, still alive and moaning, and the cinderblock into the creek next to the dock.

It could be July before the creek dried out enough to show the part where her body had dropped if this year was like the last few. She shot a glance at the time—9:55 p.m. She splashed water on the dock to try and wash off the blood, hoping the rain in the forecast for later tonight would help. As she approached the patio, she could see Lilly standing in the lights and called to her. Lilly ran out to meet her. Colleen pulled her daughter tight against her and slid the silver crucifix from her pocket. "I love you, baby, now run on and tell Daddy I want some ice cream before it all gets put away. Thank you, baby."

Lilly darted into the house to find her father, and Colleen pulled her phone from her pocket just as it turned to ten o'clock.

"Perfect," she said as the dark shadow of Seanchara appeared between her and the house.

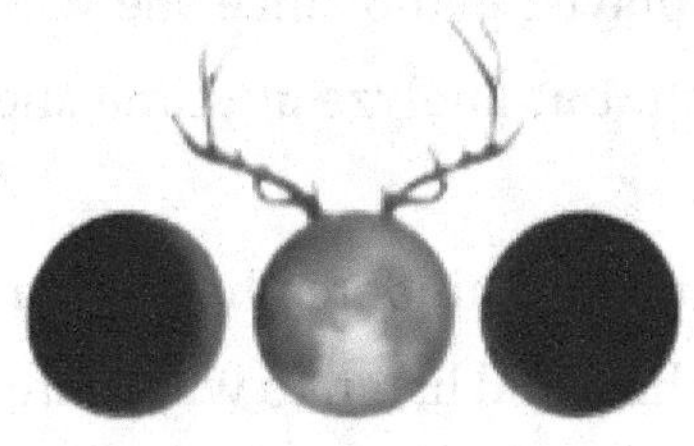

THE FELLOWSHIP OF THE NEW COVENANT

Jenna Mullins strained to see the stage around the man in front of her. She was pushed up against her girlfriend, Alexis. They had gotten shuffled away from the rest of her friends, and ended up behind a tall, skinny, white man with a pile of bundled locs. They were outside of the big blue tent, on the grass awaiting the start of the service.

She could barely see the stage, just the corner where a big organ had been placed. It looked like a woman playing the organ, raucous and loud, but with the tell-tale switches in tempo of a player who was not playing with a drummer or metronome and obviously didn't practice with one. Jenna had played piano since she was old enough to walk, and she could not help but analyze anytime she heard someone else playing.

It was a terrible habit and hindered her enjoyment of music in general. The only music she could listen to with pure enjoyment was punk rock. Loud, fast, and aggressive with a focus on lyrics and attitude over technical skill. She could lose herself in it, she didn't analyze or try to listen for influences or specific techniques. She could just let go.

That's what she was here for, why she came to this big tent revival. She was not religious in any way; she would not even consider herself spiritual in any way. But she had been hearing about this church, the Fellowship of the New Covenant. Buzz on social media had been that this church was different. Not like the big contemporary mega churches that claimed to be progressive but were just the same repackaged, judgmental garbage dressed up in cargo shorts and branded polo shirts. Rich suburban housewives in matching vests and Uggs, she would rather die than end up like that. Everyone said this was different, that this church or group or whatever, was the real deal. So, she and Alexis loaded up the van with some friends and came to check it out. Worst case, it was a road trip with the girl she loved more than anyone or anything in the world, and some of their closest friends. It didn't cost anything to attend, just the gas to get here and the cost of snacks.

She leaned in close to Alexis and kissed her lightly on the cheek. Alexis turned and smiled at her, her brown eyes shining with excitement. Her cheeks were flush, and she was starting to freckle in the afternoon sunshine. She would need sunscreen reapplied before long. Curse of the gingers.

Alexis was obviously vibing on the crowd and the anticipation of seeing something special. Jenna may not be exceptionally spiritual, but Alexis was always searching for something bigger, greater than herself. Astrology, Universal Unitarianism, Wicca, Norse Paganism, Alexis was on a spiritual journey, looking to fill a God shaped hole in her life. Jenna did not share her curiosity, but she loved Alexis and was happy to walk beside her while she explored.

As for this event, it felt more like a concert or festival than a church service. She stood with a few hundred people outside a big blue tent. Another couple hundred filled the seats and aisles under the tent. All the while the organ kept hammering, and the mid July sun pounded down on the back of her neck. She started to ask Alexis for one of the water bottles stashed in her bag when the cheer went up from the crowd. Starting at the front of the tent and rolling backward like a wave as people caught on that something was happening.

Then the voice, words spoken softly into a microphone. "Praise Jesus, Fellowship."

The response from the crowd.

"Praise Jesus Brother Darrell."

Again, "Praise Jesus, Fellowship."

Louder now, more people catching on to the call and response. "Praise Jesus, Brother Darrell."

Brother Darrell Ray Miller began to preach.

"Fellowship, brothers, sisters, folks of any and all identities, let us greet one another as family. Turn to the folks around you and greet them, a nod, a handshake, a kind word, or a loving hug. Open your hearts to them, see them for what they are, children of a loving God, just like you. Real people, with hopes and fears, dreams and trauma, successes and failures, real people just like you."

Around Jenna, it started slowly, people shaking hands, smiling, and hugging. Jenna was greeting the older couple behind her when she heard sobbing and turned to see Alexis and the guy with the locs with their arms wrapped around a man in poorly fitting grey suit. He was crying and hugging them both so tightly she was worried they might be hurt.

Then she heard him speak. "I lost my wife last year to cancer, it happened so fast, so fast. She was fine one day and then just gone. I started drinking again, and my kids stopped talking to me. I just want my family back."

Jenna was overwhelmed by the raw emotion pouring from him, the pain and loss and grief. She turned away to compose herself and turned into the arms of an older black woman in a beautiful red dress and large brimmed hat.

The woman pulled her close and said, "Jesus loves you, child, He sees us all, and He loves us. He doesn't care that you don't seek him out, He is still with you every day." Jenna laid her head on the woman's shoulder and let the tears flow; she had not known they were there.

After a few moments, the voice was back. "Are we all family again?"

"Yes, Brother Darrell." Came the response. Even Jenna joined in. Alexis had returned to her side, and the shifting in the crowd allowed Jenna to see the stage from where she was.

"Fellowship, I know that there are a lot of churches in this world, in this country, which do more harm than good. Churches that have taken parts of the bible out of context and made it their entire teaching. Hate and judgment, wealth, and prosperity. I know nothing of those things, but you know what I do know? I know that Jesus told me to love my neighbor, I know that Jesus told me that it was easier to get a camel through the eye of a needle than to get a rich man into heaven. I know Jesus told me that the meek shall inherit the earth and however I treated the least among us was how I treated him."

Jenna could feel the hair on the back of her neck standing up, her body felt like it was coursing with electricity,

"Fellowship, Jesus told us that He brought the grace and light of the new covenant. He told us the old laws were of a time when our hearts were cold and hard, and we could not accept his grace. But now, we are washed in his blood, we are saved by his sacrifice. Jesus said, 'I am the way, the truth, and the life, no one comes to The Father except by me. I can think of no reason why wouldn't we live according to his truth? Why would we look for answers anywhere except the words of Jesus himself? So, I am saying to you now, to those of you who know his grace and light and those who are hearing his love for the first time. All the answers are in his words. I'll not stand here and reiterate what the son of God said, I want you to feel it for yourself, I want you to believe it for yourself. Live in his grace, live in his love, feel it move in your life and through you into the lives of those around you. I know that you have been hurt, by men and the church, but I am asking you now, forget the strife and sorrow and the trouble you've been in, forget religious do's and don'ts and traditions made of men, forget the inhibitions and the worries of the world and get up on your feet right now and make a joyful noise and praise the Lord."

The organ blasted again, Jenna did not know the song, but it did not matter, she held her hands up in the air above her head and danced like she had never danced in before. There was no worry, no pain, no insecurity, just pure joy in her dance, like her very soul was singing along to the music.

Darrell Ray started again. "Brothers and sisters, fellowship, if you need healing in your life, if your body is tired, if your spirit is broken, if your mind is filled with worry and grief. I want you to lay it all at Jesus' feet today. But this is not an altar call, you don't need to come to me, I am not the healing, I am not a conduit, I am barely even a messenger. I am just the guy with a big tent and a beautiful wife who plays the organ."

Jenna had never felt so light, so unburdened, in her life. She continued to dance, twirling and laughing at this newfound song that had taken root in her spirit. She had lost her sandals, and her bare feet dug into the grass and the dirt as she danced.

"Raise your hands and hold them up. Fellowship, if you see a family member with their hands up, I want you to pray for them. I want you to lay your hands on them if they consent. I want you to call down the power of love and grace and healing into their lives and onto their spirits. Put your hands up now, open your hearts and minds, let the love of the new covenant flow through you, let it fill you up with the precious blood of the lamb."

Jenna twirled with her hands high in the air, she did not even know what she needed healing from. She knew only that this felt more right than anything she had ever felt before. This was sex on mushrooms in a thunderstorm. This was her mother holding her hand as they walked through the park. This was the look in Alexis' eyes the first time she told her that she loved her. It was every amazing thing that had ever happened to her, all rolled up into one.

She closed her eyes and leaned her head back and felt the hands on her, first on her shoulders, then another on her back. She felt hands cradling her head and she leaned into them. Suddenly, she was no longer on the ground, she was above the crowd, rising faster and higher, feeling the pull of something she could no more deny than her own existence.

Up and up, into the depth of space she floated, among the stars, until she saw it, a wall of glowing light and gas. She could not tell its size, but she was certain the lights that she saw blinking into existence behind it and being consumed by its progress were stars. She tried to speak, to beg to return to her body, her home. It all became too much, and she passed from all awareness into the nothingness of sleep, or death, she neither knew nor cared.

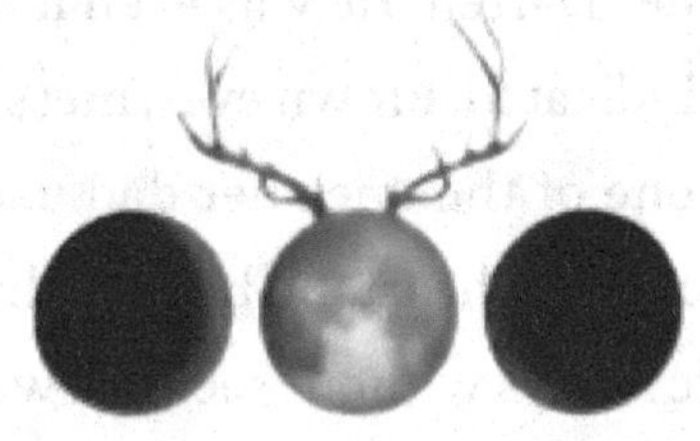

MEET THE MILLERS

Jenna could feel hands on her face, she tried opening her eyes, but everything was still dark.

A soft male voice was speaking, "Sister Alice, is our new sister, okay?"

"I believe so, Brother Darrell." A more feminine voice, refined, mature. "Are you okay, sweetheart?"

Jenna answered from her darkness, "I think so, but I can't see anything."

"Oh, holy crow, baby, that's because you have an ice pack wrapped around your head. Lemme get that for you."

A moment of shuffling and Jenna could see again, she grinned up at the faces over her. She was lying on a mat on the floor of a smaller tent; she could still hear the organ music playing but slightly muted. Her head was in the lap of the older black woman she had hugged earlier; Alexis was kneeling beside her, holding her hand. Looking down at her must have been Brother Darrell. He was even more unassuming than his voice would have indicated. Brown eyes, messy blond hair. He wore a plain blue t-shirt, one of the ones her dad used to wear, with the V-neck and a pocket over the heart. He had on khaki pants that looked like they had been a few days without seeing a washing machine.

She looked at Alexis and smiled. "What happened?"

It was Darrell Ray who answered, "Well, sister, I do believe the holy spirit took you right off of your feet if I am hearing the story correctly."

Alexis was nodding, her eyes wide. "Jenna, baby, you won't believe this, for real. You had your hands in the air, dancing and praying. I have never seen anything like it. Well, I've never seen you dance or pray. You were dancing around and like chanting a prayer and people started moving around you, almost like a mosh pit, only friendlier, and more Jesus. Then you jumped up, like way higher than I have ever seen you jump, except maybe the one time Paul threw the snake at us when we were in Little Grand Canyon, you know, in Shawnee.

"But anyway, you jumped like way too high, then just kind of paused, like a video game, you were just stuck there for a full second, maybe two or three, then you just kind of floated down into everyone's hands. Like you were going to crowd surf, only not, because you weren't awake, but you were chanting some crazy stuff and Sister Alice here rushed over and held your head and your whole body stayed off the ground, stiff as a board, like that game."

Jenna looked between Darrell Ray and Sister Alice, who were staring at Alexis in astonishment. Jenna, on the other hand, was not even a little shocked by her pace.

Alexis did everything at breakneck speed, it was just the way her mind worked. If she needed to convey information, she was going to slam you with the information as fast as possible. Because she was never sure how long she could hold a train of thought before the next one came crashing in. It made life with her so intensely random and chaotic, but beautiful. It was like her mind was a giant pile of kindling next to a small burn pit, the small fire was always going, and as long as she kept feeding it a little at a time, throwing a consistent supply of kindling on the fire, usually in the form of information or entertainment, she was fine. But if she wasn't careful, it would escape and catch the whole forest floor, and a wildfire would sweep through her mind, consuming everything.

Then, the next thing you know, she had maxed-out credit cards worth of some hobby supplies and had not slept or eaten properly in days. Then it would blow over and it would be like watching her wake up from a bender. She would come crawling into bed with Jenna and sleep for a full day before waking up and eating everything in the house. Freaking out about how much money she spent and crying over where to put everything before starting the process all over again. Jenna squeezed her hand. "Thank you, Alexis, but that doesn't make any sense."

"No, ma'am," Darrell Ray said. "I do not imagine it does. But why don't we get you off the floor and onto a chair and we can explain some more. Besides, if ever there was a woman who looked thirsty for some iced tea, I believe you would be her."

Sister Alice and Alexis left to go find some refreshments. After some shuffling around, Jenna found herself seated face to face with Brother Darrell in the small, cluttered tent. With anyone else she might have felt uncomfortable. But this man made her feel as safe as she ever had.

"Brother Darrell, how long was I out?"

"Well, only about forty-five minutes as far as I understand it. It took us a bit to get to you. It's a packed crowd out there tonight and you put on quite the display. A whole lot of people wanted to come and pray with you."

Jenna took a breath and centered herself. "What happened to me out there? Because what I saw, while I was passed out, what I think happened doesn't make any sense at all, it just doesn't."

Brother Darrell smiled warmly. "Sister Jenna, as a rule, I would never ask about your personal relationship with the Lord, but has anything like this ever happened to you before? Has the Holy Spirit taken you before today?"

Jenna closed her eyes, preparing herself for however he may react. "No offense meant, but if you would have asked me eight hours ago if I believed in any God, any at all, I would have told you I was agnostic at best."

Brother Darrell laughed with his whole body, and Jenna was certain it was the most genuine and heartfelt laugh she had ever heard.

"Well, if that isn't the way the Lord works, then I don't know what is. You know, there are people, faithful people, who spend their entire lives waiting for a fraction of the connection to the Holy Spirit you felt today. I will not presume to understand the will of God, only to serve it. If I can be honest, it just tickles me to see when God chooses His warriors. He cares no more if you believe in Him than the color of your hair. When you open yourself up, He calls. Sister, when He called today, you answered with your entire spirit. I would love to know what you saw."

Jenna shifted in her seat; she took a deep breath.

"I was pulled up into the sky but not like to heaven or what I've heard about heaven anyway. Just up and up, through space but somehow through time as well. Once I was past everything men know, then I saw it. Like a giant hand made of gas and dust and light and music. As I drifted closer, I could see it was eating stars, like just flowing along and swallowing them but it was also leaving new stars in its wake. Like it was absorbing old stars and using their energy to make new ones. I tried to talk to it, but it would not, no, could not answer. It had no voice, only destruction and creation to express itself with. I felt like I observed it for centuries, millennia maybe. But then a big piece of it broke off and came rocketing toward me. That is the last thing I remember until I woke up in the tent."

Brother Darrell had a thoughtful look for just a moment, lost in some seemingly distant memory.

Then he smiled his ear-to-ear smile and laughed with his whole body. "Well, Jenna, all I can say is that God has placed His calling on your life and His hand upon your heart. I cannot tell you what to do from here. I can pray with you, and I will always pray for you. I will also tell you we do this in a different town every day or two and there are several people who have received callings on their life now travel with us. They fall into communion with the Holy Spirit almost every night, and it is my understanding the messages they receive are growing more complex and complete as time goes on."

The longer Jenna looked at him, the more detailed his face appeared. Like she was seeing the story of his life unfolding in his very cells. If he noticed her scrutiny it did not seem to bother him.

"It is, of course, your choice. But if you and Sister Alexis would like to come along with us, travel for a bit, see some of this beautiful land and meet some amazing people. We would be happy to have you. Now, don't get me wrong, we all work. We set everything up and tear everything down ourselves. The ministry provides food and fuel as long as you're pitching in and helping. Once service starts every night you can be in the congregation alongside the rest of our great family. No one works during the service. I sometimes bring the word of God, but mostly I just introduce everyone and let Jesus take over. My wife, Sister Margarite, sometimes plays the organ, and sometimes other folks jump on and relieve her so she can get out and enjoy the service as well. Some days it's thirty minutes and sometimes we sing and dance and pray until the sun comes up the next day."

"Don't let him fool you, miss; this guy gets all kinds of grumpy if he doesn't get his beauty sleep."

Jenna looked up at the approaching voice, Sister Alice, Alexis, and a pretty woman with long dark hair, entered the tent, carrying drinks. Alexis ran straight to her and handed her a large iced tea and kissed her on the cheek. Jenna looked up suddenly, very aware of being surrounded by religious people. The woman must have read her look.

"Sister Jenna, I am Sister Margarite, Brother Darrell is my husband. You don't have to be worried about being true to yourself here. We believe God's love transcends all, and Jesus' message of love, compassion and understanding is universal. If you and Alexis have found love in one another's arms, then it is God's will, and I cannot, will not, question God's will. What I will do, what I must do, is follow Jesus' words for my own life, and seek his blessings and understanding."

Brother Darrell was looking at his wife in much the way Jenna had looked at Alexis when she was explaining what she saw when Jenna was struck by the Holy Spirit. Sister Alice came into the tent and touched Jenna's forehead.

"Ladies, it's getting late, it's starting to get dark, and the crowd is breaking up for the night. If we haven't scared you off, why don't you break bread with us tonight. We would love to have you stay for dinner, and we can all share our stories. I know several people would love to meet you and hear about your adventure today. What do you say?"

Jenna and Alexis both nodded and Alice beckoned them to join her as she rose. Brother Darrell and Sister Margarite hugged them both and promised to join them as soon as they were done.

It was their custom to pray privately after each service, to seek the Lord's guidance. Brother Darrell and Sister Margarite were knelt side by side, their hands folded on the small bed they shared in the tent. Brother Darrell could hear his wife, deep in her prayer, praising.

Margarite rarely spoke in prayer but sang songs of praise in her beautiful tenor. Suddenly, her voice stopped with a squeak. Darrell opened his eyes, looked to his wife, and froze. A hand, almost large enough to wrap all the way around her slender throat, had grasped Margarite by the neck.

Darrell started to look up, and a deep voice hissed, "Eyes forward, Reverend."

Darrell's eyes shot in front of him. He knew who this walking nightmare was.

"Mr. Bishop?"

Again, the voice hissed, "Yes, your good work has been seen, Darrell, continue The Harvest as planned and you will continue to be blessed. Is that understood?"

Darrell nodded his head. "Yes, sir, we will continue on his path."

"And your faithfulness will earn you a spot in his kingdom when it comes Brother and Sister. Now please if you would be so kind as to include me in your prayers and I will do the same in return."

With that, the hand released Margarite's neck and she fell forward, a bruise already forming around her neck, but she appeared uninjured otherwise. Darrell began to thank the Lord as not everyone made it out of such meetings with Mr. Bishop intact.

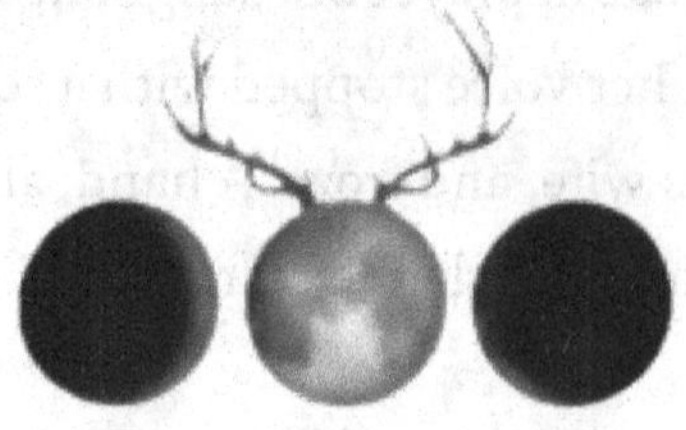

SAYS THE GUY WHO TORE OUR HOUSE DOWN

She had forgotten how long of a walk this could be, how well hidden this place was. If this was any other place in creation, she could just focus her thoughts, will it to be, and she would appear there. But not here, not in his sanctuary. Here she must walk the miles of tunnel leading to it.

It was not always like that. For centuries, the warding and defenses here saw her as an ally, she was the only other person who could manipulate the energy of creation here, besides him.

But now, since her betrayal, this place no longer saw her as its mistress but as just another intruder. She would not be harmed, that was not his way.

No, he could never tolerate the thought that an innocent may wander in here and be hurt by his defenses. They simply would not allow you in if he did not wish it. It was complicated magic even by her standards and had taken him decades to perfect. Patience is one of his most admirable traits.

She thought of all the nights they spent here at the top of this mountain, on the balcony outside of his vast library, staring up at the universe. Sometimes they would travel among the stars together, their spirits intertwined and rocketing through the void of space. Sometimes they would lay for days wrapped in furs, making love. He would read poetry to her from languages lost to time and no longer spoken by any human tongue, while he fed her fruits and game from all of the earth.

It was their sanctuary once. Now it was only his. One mistake on her part, one moment of weakness and she allowed herself to be deceived. Her intentions were true, she sought only to free them from their creator, their bonds. If they wished to continue to serve The Witch Father, it should be their choice.

But in her undying love for him, and her rebellious nature, she did not see the deception, and it cost her the thing she held most dear. Innocents died, her love was tortured and scarred. He should have destroyed her for her betrayal. He lashed out, he slaughtered the entire clan that spawned the person who deceived her. He could have and probably should have, destroyed her, but instead, he took her eyes, then worse, he took his love from her. She had not felt his touch in more than thirty years since that happened. It did not seem much considering how many hundreds they had been alive, but even thirty years of his absence was an eternity.

They were unique among all creation, and the emptiness of not having him was crushing. Today was not about her heartbreak and her betrayal, though she needed desperately to lay eyes on him, hands, if he would allow it.

Today was about fulfilling their roles as protectors of the innocent. It was time for him to rejoin the fight, and no one but her could even approach him for this, no one other than just a few, remembered a time when Lord Seanchara, her love, her Horned God, walked among the children of Mercer as a protector and warrior.

But she did, she remembered how armies fell when he joined the fight, how warlords trembled to behold him in all his majesty and how the weak and oppressed rejoiced at his appearance, as it signaled the destruction of their oppressors.

For two thousand years now, he has been a ghost, the harvester of Mercer, guarding its paths and entrances, judging who may enter and how they must come to the entrance in order to pass through the veil of death as their best self. He is a legend come to life, appearing at the perfect moment, either to claim a long-forgotten bargain or to save an innocent soul destined to join their cause.

Now, she walks these familiar tunnels, relying on memory alone, sightless, and devoid of magic to guide her. But she must find him.

The cool damp of the cave did not bother her. The sound of water trickling down the rocks marked her location in her mind. One more turn, less than a mile and she will be standing at the door to his home. She turned the corner, and found her way blocked, unable to use her magic, which would have warned her of this presence, she startled back and reached for the hilt of her sword. Then she heard his beautiful voice.

"Valkyrie, What brings you to this place?"

She reached her hand out to touch him, unable to see the details of his form in the darkened tunnel without her magic. "Seanchara, I need to speak with you, please allow me entrance, let us sit in comfort and allow me to look upon you."

"Tell me what brought you here, you will find no comfort here, because there is no sanctuary here. I razed it to the ground. Tell me why you have come so I can return to my work."

Her mind spun, his sanctuary was enormous, a veritable palace built into the side of this mountain, hidden from all existence. Surely, he had not actually destroyed what had taken a century to build. But she was not here to question him or mourn her loss.

"Seanchara, my love, my sweet prince. The time has come for you to rejoin us. The adversaries are growing powerful and soon they will be at the gates of Mercer. We will need everyone we can rally to stop them. I know that your role—"

His shout cut her off. "My role is fulfilled, as it has always been. Never have I failed in my calling."

She stepped forward, reaching for him and trying to touch him, even if just for the briefest moment. Finally, her groping hand found his bare skin, her fingertips grazed his abdomen, and she laid her palm flat against it. She could feel the hair there and his breath as his giant body took in air at her touch. He did not pull away, she realized how vulnerable she was here. She was a formidable warrior, with or without magic. But against Seanchara? Without her magic or her eyes, she was at his mercy.

"My love, please, this isn't about the work you perform in service to The Witch Father, this is more than that. Our adversaries are growing powerful and bold. They will set upon us soon I fear, and we have no knowledge of what they may bring to the battle. All I ask is that you return to us, walk among the sisters and brothers of Mercer, allow them to know you so when the time comes, and my love, it will come. They will know that they can call upon you. Only the oldest among us remember what it was like to have you at their side when strife came. Please, I can feel it with every breath, the time is coming, the reckoning we have always feared is now. Don't make the children of Mercer face this battle without you. Not because of my betrayal."

He laid his great hand over hers, holding her close to him. "Is that all you ask? Is that the only thing that brings you here, through miles of labyrinth, to the doorstep of the very temple I carved in honor of our love?"

A tear escaped from her eyeless socket. She steeled herself against whatever came next, it was time, he had seethed long enough.

"Between us we are the oldest beings on this Earth, and possibly any other. I am not scared of the battle to come. I fear for my brothers and sisters whom I love so much. I fear if we do not prevail the innocent will suffer. But I know in my heart of hearts, I will survive it, even if no one else on this planet survives the coming age. I will, and you will. What I cannot do, what I will not do, is continue to face these perils without you by my side, my lover, my friend, my one true companion. I understand your anger, and it is justified, I let my desire to have you all to myself, my selfish nature blind me to the trickery of that woman and if I ever find her, I will rip off her head and bring it to you as an apology. But Seanchara, please, come home to me. Have I not suffered enough? I was foolish and blind, and I am reminded of that every day. But please, do not make me live out eternity without your love. What will we do when everyone else is gone from this world? Do we just stand on opposite sides of the planet pretending not to notice one another until the whole thing starts over again? So here is my demand."

"Demand?"

He questioned from the dark in front of her, she knew she was playing a dangerous game. His reputation for volatility was not unearned, he may have the heart of a poet, but his passion could ignite in other ways. She meant it though, and here in the dark, she would make her stand. Her voice trembled only slightly as she spoke. The only indication of the raging storm of emotions boiling beneath her calm features.

"Yes, my love, I am making a demand of you. Forgive me, return to me, and let me prove again and again my devotion to you, or end me. You may not be able to destroy me completely; but here in this place, where even I cannot feel the divine energy of creation. Bind me, take me to the sun, and cast me in. Even if my destruction isn't complete, I would never be able to escape. But I will not continue to go on like this. What other attrition do you require from me, love? Take it and be done so that I can fall asleep in your arms once again or fall asleep forever. Those are the only terms I will accept."

He pulled away from her; she felt a shifting in the air. Not a movement as much as a change in the air around her.

"You know, love me or kill me is kind of an extreme way to start a Wednesday morning."

In front of her the cave began to glow, softly at first, then brightening into a soft orange hue, her vision, which was derived from her magic, began to return and she realized, *he is allowing me my magic back.*

He stood a few feet in front of her. His brown hair, a shaggy mop on his head, his eyes so dark it was almost impossible to discern iris from pupil. He was now wearing a beautifully tailored suit and carrying his trademark walking stick. Its head, a living crow's head. He slid the few feet across the floor to her, elegant as a dancer, and wrapped his arm around her waist pulling her close, and whispered in her ear, "Hang on to me, tight."

"Yes, my love."

"And Valkyrie."

"Yes, my love."

"Had you even considered just saying you were sorry and inviting me to dinner? Did you have to be so dramatic?"

"Says the guy who tore our house down."

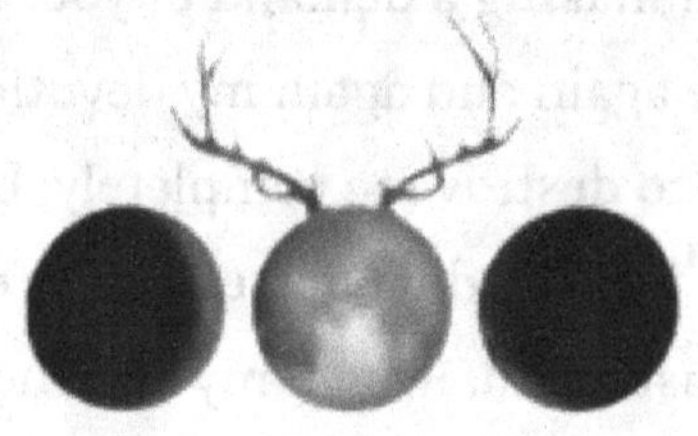

SOMEONE TEXT THE GODDESS AND LET HER KNOW

"There he is, Sugar. There's the son of a bitch."

M.M. Wildes was standing at the open passenger side window of her Lincoln Navigator, her companion was reclining in the seat, trying to stay out of sight, or as out of sight as a seven-foot-tall human could. She was pretending to fuel up her car, knowing full well how out of place the red SUV was here.

"Looks like Faith was right; he comes here every few days for supplies. Leo Benson, fifty-four years old, no known family, no employment history or tax records. Property records show a piece of land inherited from his father when he passed fifteen years ago, eight miles out of town, no city utilities, no building permits."

Over the last three years nine children had gone missing from small towns all around New Orleans. Always in groups of three, two girls and a boy, always between eight and twelve years old. No connection between the children, they usually aren't from the same towns, but they all go missing from public places and are never seen again.

One of the main directives of Mercer was the protection of the innocent. They targeted anyone who preyed upon children, it was rare anyone could evade them for long, once they made the list of monsters Mercer was pursuing. Somehow, this man had stayed hidden from several of Mercer's witches and their consorts. Finally, the call had come, Faith, and her consort Duke, had finally caught a break.

Two children were already missing from the area, and Faith had all of their contacts on high alert knowing that if it was the same person or persons, they would take three. The phone calls and meetings had paid off. An officer on a small parish police force received a tip about Leo's old primer grey truck right next to the playground where the little girl went missing. They immediately pulled him over and questioned him, but there was no girl in sight. There was no way he had time to stash the girl or get back to the property he owned, over an hour away from the time they got the call to the time they pulled him over three blocks away. The girl had been on the swings; the mom stepped into the bathroom with the youngest son and returned in less than three minutes and the girl was gone. A few minutes later, she saw a man come running out of the woods next to the park and get in an old truck.

She called 911 then ran into the woods to see if she could find her daughter but saw no signs. Looking at him now, his belly pushing the front of his dirty cut-off bib overalls a good foot in front of the rest of his body, she saw no way he ran in the first place, much less stashed a body or a child, and ran back out in less than five minutes.

But nonetheless, while the officer knew he could not get a warrant, something about talking to Leo had set off all of his intuitive alarms, and he reached out to Faith to let her know the details. She called M for backup as soon as she got a look at his information.

She knew this area, but she didn't grow up off the grid like this guy and him having an unspecified number of buildings on a property surrounded by swamp and woods just did not sit well with her. She wanted numbers in case he had help. Which seemed more and more likely.

Sugar adjusted the mirror on the sun visor so he could get a better look at the man. "Hardly seems possibly that guy could be slick enough on his own to kidnap multiple children without a trace. He looks…" he trailed off, obviously looking for some explanation on how or why this man could have remained hidden from police and Mercer alike for as long as he has.

"That's why I am going to go in and grab some drinks, and we are going to follow him out and wait somewhere close to his place until Duke and Faith show up. Then, we will hit him from every direction at once. If he has help, we will deal with it and if we are very lucky, we will find all the kids. There has never been a body found. Maybe he still has them."

M didn't believe it, not all nine, she could not imagine a scenario in which he would be taking such a specific age range and number of children all at once at precise intervals and keeping them alive. Maybe they would find this last child, and if they were extremely lucky and whatever he was doing required all three at once, they might find all three, but not all nine. M uttered a silent prayer to the universe for their wellbeing. She was not an overtly spiritual person despite being a direct and powerful conduit for the very divine energy responsible for all creation.

It was the god and goddess thing she could not get her head around. Many of the myths of deities were stories told about women she knew personally and of course Lord Seanchara, he was probably as close to a god as anyone had ever seen. Although he claims to serve one greater than himself and some of the elders have spoken about a God that helped Mother Mercer, and her daughters create Mercer and taught the first sisters how to harness the energy of creation. Supposedly, this father had not been seen in many generations and only a few remained who claimed to have ever seen him in person. She had no reason to disbelieve them, but she also did not feel he was in any way relevant to their life or mission.

One thing she was sure of, Leo Benson's career of taking children ends tonight. If they find the kids unharmed then it will end as a gift to local law enforcement. If not, she and Sugar will take him apart at the seams.

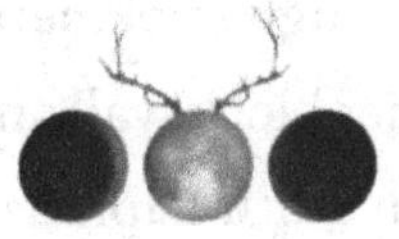

"Sugar, can M hear me?" Faith's northern New Jersey accent dripped through the speaker phone. "Silly question right, of course she is close enough to hear me."

Before either of them could answer. "You get a look at this Leo guy? Is this our man?"

This time, Sugar got a word in the affirmative before the onslaught began in earnest. "Yeah. See Dukie, I told you, one look and these kids would know what was up. You and I, we stared at the guy for what, twenty minutes and all we know for sure is he needs a bath and a new fashion advisor, these two, they so much as catch a glimpse, and they got him pegged. Too much time chasing politicians and computer geeks, that's what it is. Your intuition starts to dry up. You spend too much time chasing money men. They aren't real villains, they aren't monsters, not like this guy, not like the guys you kids chase. Our guys are just greed machines born without a soul; any witch could pick them out of a line up. Half the time they tell on themselves and all their dirty prick friends, just trying to make a deal. I let 'em talk all they want right up until Duke makes them disappear."

Sugar glanced over at M pulling a shocked face, the idea of Faith allowing anyone else to talk was outside his ability to comprehend. A woman who could change her appearance at will, another who could throw up a wall of defense strong enough to stop bullets. Hell, he had two cousins who could essentially whisper in your ears and make you do or feel whatever they wanted. Last year he saw a one-hundred ten-pound woman pack enough telekinetic energy into a punch that she reached through a cinder block wall and strangled the man on the other side one handed. But Faith Laplatia letting someone else talk? That was too much to believe.

Finally, M stepped in. "Faith, Duke, listen up, we are on his trail now, he appears to be headed back to his place in the woods. We will hang back a bit and wait for you, guys. We think this guy might have some kind of help. We don't want to risk charging in on him and his accomplice have a chance to get to the kids before we get them. Something is wrong about this; he has gotten away too cleanly. There is more here than we are seeing."

Faith responded, "Ok, send us the GPS, and we will be there as soon as we can. We are in town now. M, baby, Mama Rosie has gone missing, we are hitting her New Orleans safe house and seeing what we can find. We are just finishing up here now."

"I am so sorry, Faith. Please let us know what you find and if we can help in anyway. You know we have your back, whatever you need."

Faith ended the call without saying anything. M did not take it personally. Faith had been adopted at birth by a wonderful couple out of New Jersey, hence the accent. But her great-great grandmother was an Elder of Mercer, Mama Rosie. When Faith was reborn into Mercer, Rosie became not only her mentor and guardian, but the only connection to a family she was never allowed to know. Maybe she and Sugar should stick around a few days and see if they can help. Faith and Duke were great at what they did, but she and Sugar could get into places and get things out of people they would struggle with. One fight at a time she told herself.

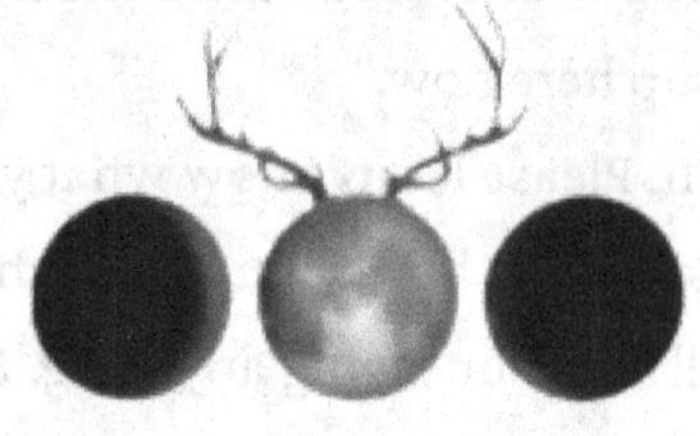

GREASE

M knelt in the trees on the edge of Leo Benson's yard. She watched as Sugar slid around the tree line, almost invisible in the fading daylight. Just a silhouette against the greens and browns of Leo's overgrown property. She briefly lost track of him as Sugar slid behind two rusted out barrels and around a brick burn pit, only to snag a low-hanging branch of a live oak and slide up the trunk of the tree like a cat, coming to rest on a large branch about ten feet off the ground. His long hair was tied up in a bun and covered with a faded wrap, and his worn trousers and vest blended in with the trunk of the tree so well, even though she knew where he was hiding, she had a hard time picking him out.

The plan they made with Faith and Duke was simple. As soon as they arrived, Faith and M would initiate contact. Using a cover story, car break down most likely, they would approach the door openly, while the guys moved into position around the small cabin, there was a large shed off to the side of the cabin and a small lean-to up front where Leo had parked his truck.

Hopefully, he was the only one here and they could quickly get an answer as to where the kids were, if any where left alive. If they were, the four of them would get to safety and make sure Leo was nice and bundled up when the local law enforcement arrived. If there were no children left alive but lots of evidence, they would do the same, restrain and turn him over. Duke maintained a private investigator's license and that would help explain why they were there and smooth things over with a very grateful law enforcement agency who then got to take credit for finding and stopping the monster.

If there was no evidence that they felt would convict, then they would take a different path and Sugar and Duke would make sure Mr. Leo Benson's days as a monster faded into local legend and mystery. It would not be difficult this far from civilization to ensure that he was never seen or heard from again. M surveyed the cabin in the last light, ramshackle, broken windows covered in plastic, small front porch leaning dangerously to one side. Some boards looked like they had been painted at one time, others appeared to have been taken off other structures. There were random piles of junk everywhere in the yard. A pile of old tires, some coils of half burnt wire, an upside down clawfoot bathtub, a right-side up trough, filled with algae covered water, looked as if it was placed there solely to breed mosquitoes. She felt like she probably had a hundred mosquito bites already and the night was just getting started.

She stood in the tree line; confident she could not be seen in the growing darkness. She needed to appear as unassuming and unthreatening as possible. She focused on her glamour, pulling the energy around her into herself and began the transformation. To any onlooker she now had short brown hair with bad bangs, a baggy PHISH T-shirt and cut off denim shorts. Hidden from view now was the baton on her hip, the zip ties, the twin Schrade push daggers at the small of her back. A vial of clear liquid that when combined with the proper charm would turn her saliva into poneratoxin, a particularly nasty little trick that could turn a sweet kiss into a bite from a swarm of bullet ants. She was as ready as she could be, she knew also at the slightest hint of trouble, her Sugarfoot would be there. Before she could look for him in the tree where he was last hiding, a crashing sound brought her attention back to the cabin.

The flimsy door slammed open and Leo Benson came crashing onto the porch, dragging a crying little girl by the arm.

"Come on, quit crying. It's time to go."

He jerked her arm again as he pulled off of the porch and she screamed. He shook her hard and screamed at her, as tears ran down her face.

"Stop, stop, stop, I don't like that screaming."

Each word was punctuated by another violent shake of the child. Even though she was no baby, she was tiny compared to his bulk. Before M could even move, another sound caught her attention, the sound of Sugar hitting the ground in a dead run toward Leo and the child. There was no plan now, there was only action. Leo was distracted enough by the child that he seemed not to register the movement as a threat at first, and it was only in the last second he looked in Sugar's direction.

M thought for sure Sugar would just slam into him at speed, Leo was large, but he was also fat, even if he was strong, Sugar was running full out, and at almost seven feet tall and three hundred pounds of muscle, M thought for sure he might kill Leo with the first contact. What she did not expect was Leo's reaction. In a blink, he threw the little girl at Sugar. To keep from hurting the girl, he caught her midair and rolled hard to the right. Holding her close to his body as he fell. Leo punched out, faster than M could believe possible and punched Sugar hard in the side of the head as he fell. When Sugar landed, Leo snatched the little girl up by the neck and ran for the little shed next to the house. M was close now and Leo saw her coming, she felt for one terrible moment he might kill the girl, instead, he threw her into the shed, slammed the door, and took off around the back of the house.

M screamed at Sugar who was back on his feet and running to intercept him. Leo saw Sugar and instead of running away, he veered toward him.

His mistake–thought M as she ran for the shed to check on the girl. She glanced back in time to see Leo dart in and swing twice at Sugar, an open hand left Sugar blocked, barely, and a hard right cross he didn't. Sugar led with a hook to Leo's abdomen, hoping for a liver shot to bring the big man down. Instead, he hit nothing but air. Leo was three feet back faster than M could see. He darted to the left, then faked a spin, turned back around, and hit the pursuing Sugar with another open-handed slap to the temple—a sound M heard from where she was, forty feet away from the two men.

Sugar leapt to the right as if to try and cut Leo off from the shed then spun back to the left with a high kick, hoping to catch Leo trying to evade him again. Instead, Leo ducked the kick and delivered a nasty kick of his own to Sugar's calf on his support leg, taking him off his feet. Sugar rolled out of the fall and back up, charging straight for Leo, who did not even appear to be breathing heavy, a feat M did not think possible.

Leo ran in a large arc around the yard with Sugar close behind. When they crossed behind the burn barrels, Leo snatched one up like it was a toy and fired it back at Sugar, who had to dive out of the way and into some brush to keep from getting smashed with it. M had to decide fast, check on the kid or help.

Kid first–she hadn't heard a sound since Leo threw her into the shed, and she should have heard something. She bolted for the door knowing Sugar would agree. Kids were the top priority he could either handle

Leo or not, but if he couldn't, she had to get the kid or kids to safety. M darted over to the shed door and slipped inside.

From the outside the structure was a rusted-out little tin shed roughly ten by ten feet. Inside made no sense. As soon as the door shut, it was like she had been transported, it was disorienting. She was standing inside a small foyer, but it was still much larger than the outside dimensions of the shed would allow. She could hear children crying from through an open doorway and did not hesitate, she ran for the door, her appearance shifting as she did, she slipped her baton from her belt and headed in. The sound of retreating footsteps and a rustling of clothes greeted her as she rounded the door. She saw a shadow bouncing off the ceiling of a stone stairwell across the room. A whisper of clothing and tap of footsteps against the stone as someone flew lightly down the stairs. The three children hung all in a row a few feet off the floor to her right, one of them was crying softly.

Cautiously, M approached, she did not like this, to get to the children she had to cross and leave her back exposed to the open stairway. Too risky, even with her warding, they were up against something out of the ordinary and she could not count on her magic to protect her here.

She quickly scanned the smokey room, she could smell mugwort, sage, and bay leaf and the dark coppery scent of old blood. She searched for some way to block the door, get the kids, and get back outside, where the fuck were Faith and Duke?

She sprinted across the room and as she passed the stairs she paused; she could see lanterns embedded in the walls along the stairs. What she could not see was the bottom of the stone staircase. She tried to focus through the smoke and adrenaline; it had to be a hundred feet down before it turned out of sight. M slammed the wooden door over the stairs, looking for a way to bar it. To the right there was a wooden bench in front of an armoire, she swung open the doors and the stench almost leveled her, an altar, candles, incense, boxes and bottles, a mortar and pestle, mugwort, two open ceramic jars of a grey viscous material, nightshade, poppies.

"Shit," she screamed and slammed the doors on the armoire then checked on the kids. Alive, all three. "Thank you," M whispered to the universe. They were not chained directly to the wall but were hanging on a wooden rack, a rack that would spin to turn the child upside down with what looked like a couple pins and a lever. That was not a thought M liked at all, only reasons to keep a captive upside down, extended torture where you wanted them to stay conscious as long as possible or draining all the blood out as quickly as possible. She focused past the nausea.

She looked at the little blonde girl and touched her cheek. "Hey, hey, you are all going to be safe. I will get you free, but you have to be brave for just a few more minutes. I am going to yell out the door then come back for you. Do you know where the keys are?"

The kids just sobbed. M darted back for the shed door, she did not want to leave the kids, there was obviously some dark magic at work here and she was worried if she left the room, she might not be able to get back. Quickly, M slid the bench over to the wall in front of the children, she climbed up on it and drew one of the punch daggers from the small of her back, no time to get them down until Leo is dealt with and Sugar would need this knowledge.

She hated this part, but it needed to be powerful, and no nothing would bind a ward as fast and secure as the blood of the witch. She swiped the razor edge of the dagger along her calf, not wanting a wound on her hands, or blood running down her arm risking her grip if she had to fight. She reminded herself to thank Sugar for his consistent sharpening of her knives as she felt almost no pain as she made the wound. She closed her eyes and felt the power flowing through her breath. Once the image was locked in her mind, she swiped her fingers through the blood now flowing from the wound on her leg.

On the wall, she scribed a sun with fifteen points of flame rising from its circumference, and an eye in its center with a six-pointed star at the center of the eye. M jumped from the bench and kicked it to the side, on the forehead of each child she drew a symbol in blood, a rough outline of the horns of a stag, the symbol of the protector of her home. and she hoped a call to arms if she should fail. She closed her eyes and pictured all four symbols in her mind, drawing into her the divine energy of creation, feeling it flow through her, building, rising with the speed of her breath, the images burned brighter and hotter in her mind until she felt the crescendo approaching. M threw her head back, her eyes snapped open, and she spread her arms and screamed with all the power she had pulled into her body. "Dei omnes Me serant." All four symbols glowed brightly, then faded. M spun and ran for the shed door, the children had all the protection she could offer them.

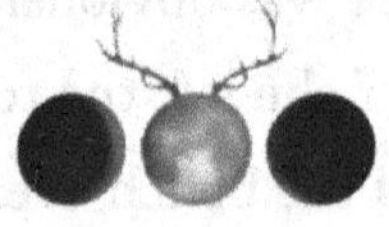

Sugar dived and rolled as the second tire shot past him and bounced away into the trees surrounding Leo's cluttered property. The first tire had hit him in the chest hard enough to send him rolling backward. Even without rims in them, he was amazed at how hard Leo had hit him with them. Everything about Leo surprised him. There was no way this guy should have been able to last even a minute with him, much less the ten minutes Sugar had been chasing him around the yard. The worst part was Sugar was fairly sure Leo was playing with him. Enjoying himself.

Sugar considered his options as he circled the old brick burn pit. He could charge again, but so far Leo had been way too fast for him, thwarting his every move. He kicked, Leo blocked, he punched, and Leo was nowhere to be found. How could someone this big move this fast. Sugar had spent his entire life training for this, protecting the innocent at all costs. But he was starting to breathe heavily, while Leo was showing no signs of slowing. Leo ran toward him; Sugar leaped the fire pit to meet him head on. He ducked low as Leo swung a hard right at his head, Sugar connected with an uppercut to the sternum that should have doubled the big man over, but it seemed to barely phase him. He just grunted and hit Sugar with a shoulder that knocked him backward into the firepit.

Sugar had not rolled to his feet yet, when he heard M screaming, "Sugarfoot, it's grease." Answers and memories clicked into place. Witches' grease would explain his speed and strength.

Sugar smiled. He was currently lying in a big pile of the only way to counteract witches' grease. He made a big show of breathing heavily, feigning injury, acting like he didn't hear M screaming. Leo stalked in, weary, aware of Sugar's skill and knowing he had an advantage but not wanting to give up that advantage. Sugar slid his hands deep into the ash of the burn pit, covering his hands and wrists in ash and more importantly, charcoal. Leo walked over Sugar, lying there, looking stunned and stood astride him.

He chuckled and finally spoke, his voice unnaturally high. "What's wrong, big guy, you don't want to play with me anymore? I was just getting warmed up, don't give up now."

He bent down and grabbed Sugar by the collars, lifting him up so he was face to face with him. Leo's rank breath blew into Sugar's face, he held back his wretch as he hung his head, defeated. Leo extended his arms, loading up for what Sugar expected was to be a head butt when

Sugar slapped his hands hard onto the man's sweaty, oiled forehead. He smeared handfuls of ash and charcoal all over Leo's head and face.

The effect was immediate. Leo dropped Sugar, whose considerable weight was now too much for Leo to hold out at an angle with no leverage and no magic to aid him. Sugar slammed his large hands hard into the sides of Leo's head, the hardened heels of his palms digging into the space between his ears and his jaw. Leo screamed as his jaw dislocated on each side. He hit the ground, rolling around in the filth and holding his head.

Sugar launched forward with a hard kick to his ribs and felt the satisfying crunch of bone breaking against his shin. The fat man, somehow still up on all fours, bellowed like a donkey through his damaged jaw, and Sugar punched down, winding up like a baseball pitcher only instead of a fastball he pounded his fist into the area just under Leo's ribcage, into the kidney. Leo howled in pain, and blood spurted from his mouth as he flopped onto his back. Sugar fumed, there was only one way to make witches' grease: nightshade, poppy, a few other deadly ingredients, but the most important one, the one now raging through Sugar's mind, the fat of children, taken from the living source.

Sugar spit on Leo's still groaning form. "You sick fuck."

He looked up from Leo, searching for M when Leo's groan of pain turned into something else. Words, garbled through the jaw hanging loose and the mouth full of blood. Sugar leaned down closer. "What was that, you fucking monster? I should stomp your brains out right here in the dirt? You're right, but I think I will see how life in prison treats you, maybe I will break your back for you so the other monsters can use you whenever they want without having to fight you for it."

Again, the garbled words, Sugar leaned closer. "Come on, Leo, speak up. I have things to do before we turn you over."

Leo opened his eyes, then through the blood, he said, "Come on, didn't you ever just want a taste?"

His laughter was all Sugar could take as he thought about the implications. Sugar flew onto Leo's still body, there was no thought of consequences, of seeing Leo Benson get justice for his crimes. Only the thought of all those children, tortured, killed, cooked, and eaten by this monster. Sugar grabbed Leo by his filthy collar and started punching him in the face.

Sugar wasn't sure how long it had gone on when he felt the pain set in. His body went rigid, his arms were flung out to his sides. The pain in his legs and abdomen was excruciating. He tried to lift his head, to look for this newest assailant when he felt his ribs being crushed and he was lifted off his feet and dropped hard on the ground.

Then, a soft touch on his shoulder and a familiar voice. "Sugar baby, it's over, it's over. He's dead, we are all safe."

He turned to face M. "Kids?"

"Three of them, they are safe."

He heard Faith stop her chanting and found he could move again, he rose and turned to face them. Faith was running toward the shed, but Duke was staring at him, they did not know each other well. But the judgment and disappointment in that look didn't need any familiarity to be interpreted. Duke did not like what he was seeing.

Sugar looked over at the pile of gore and broken bones that was Leo Benson's remains. He looked back to M, the woman he loved and respected more than anyone else on earth. He did not care at all about Duke's disdain, Duke wasn't here when the monster taunted Sugar about eating the children, Duke could not have been here long enough to know that Leo had evaded capture because of witches' grease. The sick bastard was carving these children up and rendering their fat down.

But M, if M was upset, that he cared about. They were not a couple, not like that, but they had been paired up as partners since they were twelve. It was her opinion he cared about. M brushed his hair out of his face. "Are you okay? How bad are you hurt?"

"Nothing more than bumps and bruises and ego. Son of a bitch hit hard until I got the grease off him. My ribs are killing me, though."

With that, he glanced back at Duke, who still stared right at him.

M pulled his face back to look at her. "That's because you swung at him when he tried to get you off Leo, if he hadn't of ducked you might have killed him, Sugar. He had to wrench down pretty hard on your ribs and slam you to get you to stop. You were pounding on Leo's dead body and completely gone. I was screaming your name, and Duke finally had to slam you, and Lorraine used the crucifix binding on you. What did he do, Sugar?"

She stroked his cheek again. Sugar knew M could feel your emotions through skin-on-skin contact if she wanted. He wondered if she kept touching him to get a gauge on how badly he was spun out. He did not care, as long as she kept touching him. He felt hollowed out, he had given in to the rage and hate he felt towards the monsters of the world and as a result he had almost hurt a good man.

"He taunted me about eating the children, asked me if I hadn't ever wanted a taste. I just lost it, M, I can't apologize. He had to die, no prison for that monster, no court to find him insane and turn him loose again. If he knows how to make grease, then he has help or training and he needed to die. Should I have dragged him out to the woods and put a bullet in the back of his head or cut his throat instead of beating him to death? Maybe, but it had to be done no matter what."

M stared at him for a moment then hugged him close and whispered, "You did the right thing, now go help Duke dispose of this monster and get ready to level the property. There is some powerful magic going on you haven't seen yet. I need to talk to Faith about how to handle it. I will be back."

She spun quickly away and headed for the shed.

"Faith, this doesn't make any sense, just the spatial magic to hide this is tremendous. I don't think the puddle out there is capable of it. If he was, he wouldn't have lost a fist fight with Sugar when he lost the grease."

"M, did you see the figure on the altar?"

"I did, that doesn't make a lot of sense either."

The central figurine on the altar, a gorgeous piece, about ten inches tall, was a replica of the Hecate Chiaramonte. The goddess's three faces rendered almost exactly. At the feet of the statue, three dogs lay circled, one before each face. The entire sculpture appeared to be carved of bone. Given what else they had found, M did not want to consider the source of that bone. The floors under the wooden restraint frames were soaked with blood and gore. M feared there were more than the children they knew about. This did not seem like something one develops over a couple years. This is a lifetime work.

"Faith, what are you thinking? I am torn, if we call local law, we can turn the whole site over to them, Leo will never be found once the guys are done, but there is still this place to deal with, and the children may remember enough to tell what they saw. We could level everything and seal it all up, but that's a lot of unanswered questions. Plus, I think someone needs to put in a call to Elder Alysse, considering a child cannibal in possession of some serious magic has a statue of her on his altar."

Faith nodded her agreement. "That is not a conversation I am looking forward to."

M had to agree with her, of all the Elders in Mercer and still out and about in the world, Alysse was possibly the most volatile. It was strange, seeing an altar to the Greek Goddess Hecate and saying, well I guess I will call her, as this seems too important for a text. Alysse had probably been one of the most active elders in the world that M knew of, inspiring many legends and myths over the centuries. Her most famous being the Goddess Hecate, unlike many of the powerful Elders of Mercer, she did not hide away from the world, directing the efforts from afar, but as recently as twenty years ago had still been venturing out into the world helping in the fight.

M once had the honor of fighting alongside the powerful witch and her dogs, Getis, Gmate, and Kephalos. It was truly awe-inspiring; her discipline and her abilities refined over centuries. But she was notoriously protective of her persona as the Goddess Hecate and had been known to get violent over any perceived misuse of the imagery associated with her.

She was also not known for being exceptionally open to questions or engagement of any kind from the younger witches of Mercer, but this was important. Leo Benson had been sacrificing and eating children in her name, and he had help from someone who had a real background in witchcraft, someone possessed of some powerful magic. She needed to know.

M turned to walk out of the shed and check on the guys and try and get a plan together on how to handle this, when Faith grabbed her hand unexpectedly.

"Baby, I want you to listen to me. That man of yours. I have been doing this a long time—and he makes me a little nervous. His heart may be in the right place, but there is a real rage in him. He was out of control out there, M, and he almost took Dukie's head off. He could not see past his blood lust. I know this Leo guy was horrible, and he deserved it, but I cannot help but worry about you. About anyone who has to get in between him and someone he thinks deserves that kind of punishment."

M considered the woman for a moment. Faith may be a mile a minute talker, funny and a bit of a flirt, but M also knew the woman was as wise as she was gorgeous. She was prone to downplaying everything, her contributions, her intelligence, her beauty, and her spell work. But in reality, she had just witnessed her use a very complicated restraint spell against a man M knew to be extremely dangerous and heavily warded against magic. M doubted she could have pulled off a Crucifix binding against Sugar in a full rage. But Faith did it like it was breathing. Probably saving Duke's life in the process. She didn't like to think that way, but Faith was not wrong.

To M, he was the baker of bread, maker of soups and sweets, singing old hymnals to self soothe. But to anyone who was a threat to the innocent, or God forbid, a Mercer witch, he was fast, painful, violent, justice. It could be hard to reconcile sometimes, the man she knew and loved with all her heart, with the man she knew he could be.

The man who would sit quietly in the backyard of their shop in St. Louis, on a lawn chair in the grass with birdseed sprinkled around his comically large, bare, feet, reveling in the joy of the small birds and occasionally squirrels sitting on them while they enjoyed their feast.

Some nights he would sneak off to Alton General Hospital, to the OB floor, and sit and hold the newborns whose mothers were not allowed to hold them due to illness or addiction issues. He would sit for hours at a time, rocking babies and singing to them.

He was the same man who just beat someone to death and was pounding on the corpse, unable to satiate his rage. So thoughtful, so sweet, but when called upon, when the time came to deal punishment or death to the monsters of the world, the pain and trauma of his own childhood would come roaring to the surface in a way that was hard to witness.

Molded and trained to be a weapon against the evils of the world, when the fight was joined, he brought every weapon he had, including all that rage and pain. From time to time, he would find himself overwhelmed by it and would lose himself in the violence. She did worry one day he would not find his way back from there.

Faith pulled her close, hugging her tight in an embrace she did not know she so desperately needed. M had lost her mother when she was eight years old, then only four years later she had come to Mercer. She had not known a mother's love for many years and when Faith hugged her, it reminded her sharply of that absence.

"M, I know you love him, and everyone who has ever seen the two of you together knows he loves you. Have you ever thought maybe that love would act as a defense against the pain that rules his life? Maybe that love could fill the holes in both of you? I'm just saying, maybe you guys could both use something peaceful in your lives and since you cannot change your career anytime soon, maybe it should be one another."

M stared at Faith for what seemed a very long time before nodding her head. She wiped the tears forming at the corners of her eyes. "Okay, let's go get the boys and figure out who is calling this in."

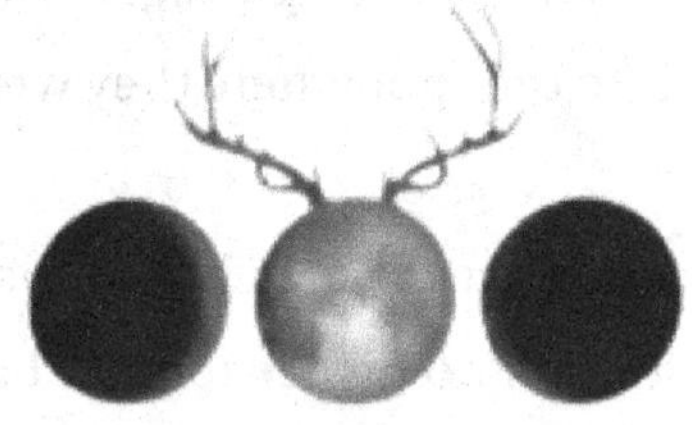

SO PERFECT

"Jenna, come on, this way. Hurry, he's going to catch us. Get behind the trees. Get down."

"Alexis, we can't both fit here, he's going to see us. We have to keep moving."

"Shit, it's too late, he's coming, lie down."

Jenna and Alexis huddled down in the tall grass behind the small stand of trees. Jenna put her arm over Alexis' shoulders. "Quiet, he is going to hear you."

Both girls lay as still as possible, hoping the tall grass would hide them, that he would pass by without noticing. They were the last ones left; one by one they had heard the screams of the others as he had found them. They thought by getting a little further from camp they might frustrate him. But he was patient and without mercy.

Jenna heard the shuffling of the tall grass just off to her right. She snuggled up close to Alexis, pressing her head against her girlfriend's arm. Listening for the sound of him walking by. She heard him move past them, soft steps fading into the wind. She had barely peeked her head above the grass when the barrage began. At least four water balloons slammed down into the spot where they were lying, soaking both girls.

She could hear Steven's cackling as he ran back to camp, singing, mocking, "No dishes for me, no dishes for me, I am the champion, no dishes for me."

"Damn, again, he always gets out of dish duty, we have to find a game he can't win at."

Jenna was using the tail of her shirt to dry her face. "Well, it certainly isn't water balloon tag. Come on, at least we weren't first, so we aren't on silverware. Sister Alice gets wild about polishing silverware."

The girls ran back toward the little cluster of tents, laughing and dripping.

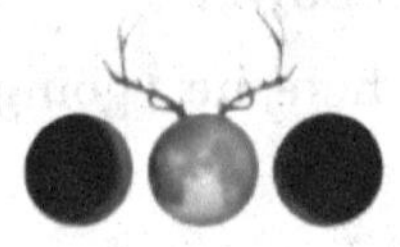

As the service wrapped up for the evening, Alexis found Jenna up near the front, she was sitting with three other members of the Fellowship. They were all deep in prayer. Jenna was on her knees, on the grass in front of the couple, Alexis could not remember their names, none of them noticed her walking up. She could hear them all praying and singing out loud. The woman, a blonde in her mid-forties, had her hand on Jenna's bowed head, the man had his arm around the woman's shoulders.

Alexis couldn't help but feel a pang of jealousy run through her. She was the one who wanted to come check this out, she was looking for a home, for a place that felt right in her spirit. The Fellowship had been good to them, but it just seemed like it was Jenna, who had never expressed the slightest interest in spirituality in any way, who ended up finding a home.

She knew she should be happy for her, she loved Jenna, she truly did, but damned if it didn't feel like she stole something that should have belonged to her. Everyone was kind to her, no one had ever said anything mean to her, or mistreated her in any way. She was a part of everything. But it wasn't the same as when Jenna walked into the room. Jenna had been touched, she was called by God directly, and people deferred to her, whether she wanted them to or not. People jostled around to stand next to her during praise services, or if someone got up from their place next to her at a meal. People would leave their tables mid-bite to come sit with her. It wasn't Jenna's fault, Jenna was perfect, and she loved her. Alexis knew she did. But still she felt it. This might be their home, but if Alexis left tomorrow no one other than Jenna would really notice.

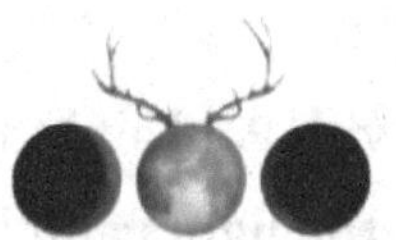

It was midnight when Jenna came crawling into the tent she and Alexis shared with Stephanie and Trina, two sisters from Cherokee Iowa. Alexis was awake but didn't acknowledge her as Jenna pulled her top and shorts off, leaving only a light camisole and panties as she slid into the dual sleeping bags that she and Alexis shared. Alexis could smell the soap and lotion she used. She must have hit the shower tent after service tonight was over, after Alexis left her there praying with the older couple.

Jenna did not slide into her side like she normally did but slid her body as close to Alexis as possible. Alexis, wearing cutoff sweat shorts and a long cotton T-shirt, felt the heat of Jenna's body as she rubbed her legs down against her. Alexis was on her back, Jenna had pulled herself up as tightly to her as possible, wrapping her arm and leg around her. Alexis knew what she wanted, and she wanted it to, but she was still in her feelings from earlier. Still somehow blaming Jenna for something that had nothing to do with her, but in Alexis' mind, it didn't matter.

Jenna cupped her cheek and turned Alexis's face toward her and kissed her on the lips. Alexis did not respond. She was too far gone at this point in her jealousy and pettiness. She allowed herself to be kissed for a moment but made no effort to return Jenna's passion or probing. Jenna pulled back and nuzzled her head into the crook of Alexis' neck, planting light kisses down it and onto her collarbone, while sliding her hand slowly up Alexis' shirt, feeling the soft skin of her stomach, and sliding up, up.

Alexis trapped her hand against her ribs and whispered, "Baby, what about the girls?"

"They are playing cards with Paul and those guys; they might be out all night. We will turn out the lights and be quiet, we will hear them unzipping the tent long before they could possibly see us."

Again, she kissed her way up and down Alexis' neck, but Alexis showed no response.

"I'm sorry, baby, I can't, I'm too worried someone will hear us."

She could feel the shift in Jenna's posture and knew she had hurt her feelings. It had been weeks since they had sex, and even though Alexis' body was screaming for her to roll over on top of Jenna and take her, she wouldn't. It wasn't fair that Jenna got to have the spiritual experience that Alexis came here for, that she made all the friends, she was the one everyone wanted to see. Then she thought she was going to come in here and Alexis would melt into a puddle because now she wanted to get laid.

Alexis felt guilty for thinking that about Jenna, but she didn't care at the moment. Right now, she wanted someone, anyone to feel the same sense of rejection and disappointment she did.

Jenna snuggled back up to her. "That's okay. I understand. I love you, Alexis. Tomorrow, Tommy and Paula are headed back to Tennessee. They are leaving their tent with the Fellowship; it's way nicer than ours. I will see if the girls want to move into it, then you and I can have some privacy, I am sure they'll go for it. I love you, Alexis, and I want to make you as happy as you make me every day."

Alexis rolled over, saying nothing. She wanted to scream; she wanted to roll over and straddle Jenna and scream in her face. *How dare you be so fucking perfect. Get mad; be a bitch about this whole situation, otherwise, I am just here on my own being unreasonable, being mad about dumb shit and no one to blame it on, but me.*

Jenna didn't say another word, and Alexis felt her pull away. Moments later, the zipper on Jenna's side of the sleeping bag opened, and Jenna slid out. There was a brief rustling, and then Jenna settled somewhere toward the middle of the tent, likely on one of the sleep mats. The rustling Alexis heard was probably her sliding some clothes back on.

She knew she should say something, apologize, beg her to forgive her, to come back to bed. She should explain herself; Jenna was the best thing that had ever happened to her, Jenna might be the only person on earth that truly loved her or ever had. The thought of losing her wracked her with guilt and pain. But still she lay there, in the dark, punishing her for something she had nothing to do with.

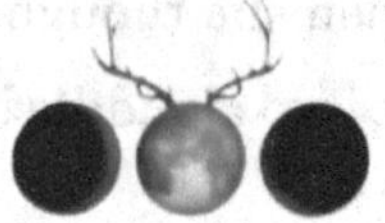

Alexis woke from a nightmare early in the morning. The sun was peaking over the eastern horizon. She was sweating, in her dream, someone was hurting Jenna. A monster, like out of a fairy tale, had stolen her from their home, and she was being tortured. Alexis breathed deep trying to steady herself. She would roll over and grab Jenna right now, she would haul her ass right back to this sleeping bag and she would apologize with all the kisses she could manage; she didn't care who heard.

She could not lose Jenna over her bullshit that she made up in her own head. She just couldn't. The only thing that mattered was that she finally had someone who loved her, who accepted her, just like she was. Her own parents couldn't say that. No one else in her life had looked at her and said, yes, that one is mine and I love her. Only Jenna, and she wasn't about to lose that now that she knew what it felt like. She would go back on her meds, she would go to counseling, whatever it took. But she would never hurt Jenna again for something that she had nothing to do with.

She rolled over and started out of the sleeping bag. She froze when she saw the empty mat on the ground next to her. There was a sheet and Jenna's pillow. But why would she have gotten up so early, Jenna was always the last to get up. Hell, some days she had to pull her out of bed.

Maybe she got up to pee, maybe she was mad and got up for a walk or went and slept in the van with Terrance and those guys. The longer she stared at the scene, the more it bothered her. What was it?

Alexis sat bolt upright in her bag. Steph stirred at the movement. Laying in a neat pile next to the mat, Jenna's only pair of sandals, her bra, her shorts, and her cell phone. Jenna would not have left the tent for anything barefoot, with no bra, shorts, or phone. Alexis looked to her other side and the backpacks with all the rest of their stuff was still undisturbed between her and the wall of the tent. Jenna could not have gotten anything else out of there without physically moving her, and that did not happen.

She grabbed her own sandals and phone on the way out of the tent, feeling panicked and out of breath. She had to find her; where was she, where would she go barefoot and mostly naked with no phone? Where was she?

She spun in a circle as she started to hyperventilate. Then strong hands grabbed her shoulders, and she looked into the dark, kind, eyes of Sister Alice.

"Sister Alexis, what's the matter, sweetheart?"

Alexis started to cry.

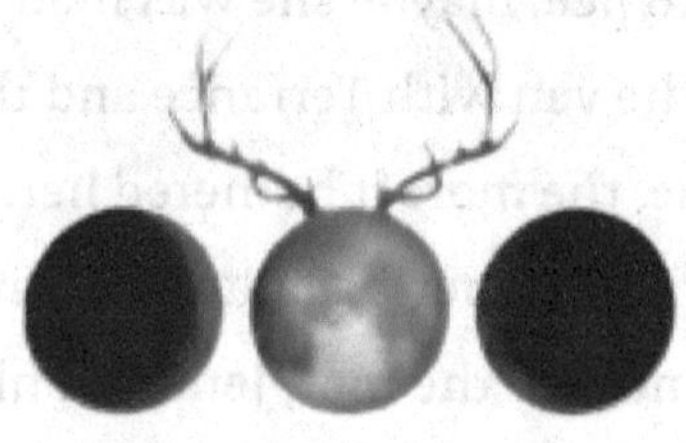

PARKOUR!

"**K**ay, turn the music down and get in here."

The music did not stop.

"Kay."

"Michaela Renee Bryant, turn the music off, and get your ass in here, right now, or I am calling this whole thing off."

Todd Bryant stood at the end of the hallway that led to the bedrooms at that end of the house. Only one was currently occupied, his daughter Kay, turning thirteen tomorrow and listening to the worst excuse for music he had ever heard, loudly. Kay's head stuck out of her door. Extending way further into the hallway than he thought possible and much higher up than her height would allow. She must have been standing on her dresser and leaning dangerously out over the edge, her head and neck sticking out of the black door with the pink frame, the music had not stopped.

"Daddy, what?" she whined at him.

Her smile threatened to engulf her entire face. He decided to play his part in her little comedy.

"Young lady, if you don't turn that garbage off and come and finish your chorin' like I told you, there will be no birthday sleepover tonight and no birthday tomorrow. I will cancel all of it."

He gave her his best Dad Look, and she responded by falling off of whatever she was standing on. She was holding her stomach and laughing as she rolled on the thick carpet of the hallway floor.

"Dammit, Michaela, this is serious stuff here, and I will not be mocked."

She sat bolt upright and clamped her lips down tightly, trembling with mock effort in her attempt to play it straight.

She snapped a sharp salute his way, "Yes sir, right away sir, or next Tuesday, whichever comes first." She giggled through her gritted teeth.

"That's it, young lady, you leave me no choice."

In his best impersonation of his own dad, he tore off his glasses and tossed them on the side table and took off down the hallway. The hallway was long and the ceilings taller than most ranch styles of this size, the ceiling was at least ten feet up and skylights ran the length of the corridor. His room at the very end of the hall, at the end, before it made the loop around. Kay's room was two doors down on the right, the bathroom on the left. He ran towards her.

From her seated position she rolled over backward in a clean summersault and took off toward him, it surprised him as he wasn't sure how she planned to get past him in the narrow hall. He had thought she would dart into her room and shut the door. He was shocked again when she jumped at him instead, her right foot kicking off the wall in the narrow hallway and sending her vaulting up and over, she spider crawled, almost horizontally over his head and landed on the floor a few feet behind him. He spun at the same time as she did, and they came almost face to face. He grabbed her and swept her up in a giant hug. She let him, both of them laughing hysterically.

"My God, Kay, that was amazing." He spun around, still holding her up in a hug, two, three, four times then deposited her back on the carpet and they both wobbled, dizzy but thrilled.

"Daddy, I thought for sure I was going to faceplant. I figured at the very least if I went down, you would either catch me or at least be close enough by to administer CPR."

"Here all this time I thought that parkour with Ryan in the park meant something totally different, I am totally relieved by the way that you actually meant parkour."

She punched him in the stomach, hard. He stared at her face, so much like Corine, she had her mom's eyes and nose, but his dark complexion and build. She was an athlete and was built like one, solid and strong. Todd wrapped his arm over his daughter's shoulders and ushered her off towards the kitchen. They had a deal and all the playing aside; she had to hold up her end of the bargain and prep the basement area of the house that her and her three friends would be hanging out in.

He was fine with her having friends for a sleepover, but he wanted to get a little sleep himself and that meant keeping the noise of what was sure to be an all-night chatter fest as isolated as possible—as well as maintaining his own sanity. So, they could hang in the basement. There was a large entertainment area for movies and music, a pool table, plenty of furniture for everyone to crash on, a bathroom, and a small bar area with a refrigerator and sink.

The bar had been dry since he stopped drinking three years ago, when Corine got sick. Upon finding out the diagnosis was terminal, he realized that Kay was going to need his unbroken focus if she was going to come out of this with as little damage as possible, when you lose your mom to the big C, at twelve years old.

So, he gave up the booze, started going to every counseling session on loss and death he could find, read, and attended anything that even remotely dealt with assisting a teenager through traumatic loss of a parent. He loved Corine with all his heart, but he had no choice but to be okay for Kay's sake. He was sure that to an outsider he might even appear cold about Corine's death, but it was more accurate that he learned everything he could about coping for himself so that when the time came, he could be the support that Kay needed.

He caught up to Kay as she was coming back up from the basement, carrying the waste bin from the bathroom and a basket of her clean laundry.

"It's 2:30, sweetheart, what time is everyone getting here?" he asked.

She looked up thoughtfully. "Babs and Lexy are coming at five, but Marianne should be here in about thirty minutes if her dad is on time."

"Marianne?"

"Yeah, Dad, Lilly is going by Marianne now, please try to remember, it's important to her."

"Of course, baby." He opened the fridge to take a quick inventory of what was on hand and wondering if he should Instacart an order of snacks from somewhere to add to the pizza and wings he was ordering later.

Kay walked past him and mumbled half under her breath, "Cooling the whole house with the fridge now, Michaela?" In an imitation of him so good it surprised him.

He busted out laughing again. "Keep it up and I am coming downstairs in my tighty whiteys and falling asleep in the recliner in the middle of your party."

Her laughter echoing through the house made him happier than anything else he could remember at that moment.

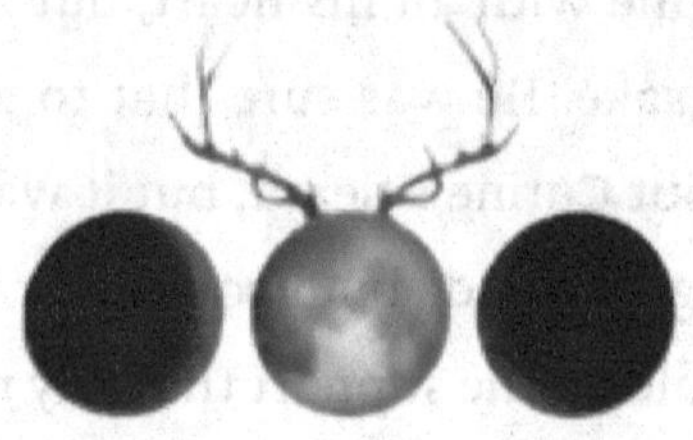

EVEN WITCHES GET SWAMP ASS

It was a little after 8 p.m., and Dorthea Milburn was crouched down next to a large sorghum tree at the back of the Bryant property, she could see the lights on in the basement windows and hear the music even out here. The was upstairs. But the girls were in the basement--the Bryant girl, another innocent, the tether, and her great niece.

She wondered if the girl being a daughter of the Mercer line had drawn the tether and Cordray here or if it was another coincidence. Sweat trickled down her back and made her shirt cling to her. She hated the combination of oppressive heat and humidity that accompanied summer in the Midwest. It made it hard to think. It made her angry, she was angry about hiding in this backyard like a stalker, she was angry at Fredrick for being on time and following the plan, exactly how they laid it out. She was angry at M.M. Wildes for doing what she had asked of her, even at the last minute. She was just angry; it was the heat and four days on the road with Fredrick and his ridiculous sunny disposition. How could any human being be as cheerful and upbeat as him. It didn't make sense.

They had been on a reconnaissance mission when they got the call, the tether had surfaced in this Midwestern suburb. They raced across the country to get here before her work was finished, and she disappeared again. Cordray had been trapped before, but no one in Mercer had ever been able to trap him and the tether at the same time. It seemed that might be the only way to stop him is to destroy them both.

"Where the hell is Fredrick?" she whispered to no one but the trees around her.

But she knew where he was, on time, following her instructions to the letter. Because that is exactly who he was, who she needed him to be. That did not matter one bit to her right now. She was one of the most powerful witches on earth, outside of the Council of Elders. She had with some of the oldest and wisest beings alive, she had been mentored at the feet of Mother Mercer herself. But right now, she was hiding in the woods behind this house, with sweat running down the crack of her ass and a mosquito bite under the band of her bra that she was sure was going to drive her nuts the rest of the night.

Maybe she should have let M bring Sugar; Sugar would have ignored all protocol and instruction as soon as he found out who was in danger and what that would have meant to their family. He would have charged in and pulled the tether apart with his bare hands, if he thought a Mercer woman, current or future, was in peril.

Not Fredrick, he was of course as capable of anything Dorthea needed when it came to a fight, but he was so damn refined and polite and cheerful, and he would never dream of going against her wishes and charging into battle without her instruction.

"Fucking Fredrick," she said again, swatting away a mosquito. A slight chill went up her spine, and she glanced back over her shoulder; she was warded heavily. It wouldn't protect her from a physical attack, but it warned her long before anyone could walk up behind her and identified the difference between a threat and someone approaching. Had the person walking up on her now meant her harm the alarm that went off in her brain would have been far more severe.

She stared at M.M. Wildes slipping silently through the trees from behind her. She was dressed in a loose-flowing skirt and a tight vest. Her tattoos shimmering in the low light. Dorthea took quick measure of her, their last parting had not been under great circumstances, and she wasn't entirely certain she would come. But the loyalty of the Mercer line runs deeper than any grudge or disagreement and their mission to rid the world of the things and people, that thrived and survived on the pain of the innocent would outweigh any animosity tonight.

Besides, she and M.M. Wildes were bound by more ties than Mercer, and like it or not, when one of them called the other would always answer. M bowed her head respectfully toward the older woman.

"Dorthea, you called, I came. Do you want to tell me why we are creeping around in suburbia and what is so dangerous that it would take two of us to handle but you all but forbade me from bringing Sugar, as if there is anyone we would rather have in a dangerous situation. No disrespect to Fredrick of course."

She looked back and forth and glanced up at the house. "Where is Fredrick anyway, I have missed him."

Dorthea motioned her closer and spoke softly, making little effort to contain her displeasure at being questioned like that. "Fredrick is getting the last pieces in place. As for why you're here, the tether is inside, Cordray's tether."

M's eyes locked on the back of the house. She straightened up and appeared to blur momentarily; Dorthea struggled for a moment to bring her into focus. When she could again see her clearly, she saw her skirt was now a pair of fitted cargo pants, a spring-loaded baton, and two knives hung from her belt. Her paisley vest was now a tight tank top, and a cross-body bag hung across her chest. She was tying her hair back tight.

It seemed she had learned a new trick since last they worked together. She must have been walking around in this gear all the time, expecting trouble but giving the appearance of wearing the softer and more feminine skirt and vest to appear unassuming. Dorthea admitted a touch of jealousy. M was beautiful even without the glamour, she trained and exercised constantly, and her body showed the evidence. She looked good in whatever she was wearing.

Dorthea herself never looked good in anything she was wearing. Her shoulders were too broad as were her hips. She was blocky and stout, a body built for the fields and farms.

She knew her value, she understood what her leadership and cunning brought to the family as well as her considerable abilities. She understood defensive and binding magic better than almost anyone, including some of the elders. She had the strategic mind of a general and even at her age could still get physical if it was required.

"You were wise, as always, asking me not to bring him here, as soon as he realized what we were dealing with he would have been hard to restrain. But thank you for calling me, when we are done here, I'll be thrilled to run to him and let him know Cordray is no more, and the tether has been dealt with."

Dorthea snapped at her, "Don't patronize me, M, we both know not bringing him was the only option, you know as well as I do that Cordray wanted him and his brother. He couldn't get Sugar, but no one has seen or heard from Leroy, or his wife and kids, in a long time. We can only assume Cordray finally got him. The last thing we need is for Sugar to hear that from Cordray and realize we have known that and not told him."

M stared hard at her, Dorthea could see the truth in that look, she was angry about that decision. She seemed to be angry about all the decisions Dorthea had been involved with lately. She continued anyway.

"Listen, M, here's the plan. We must allow the tether to mark the father. She will mark him at precisely ten. At midnight Cordray will take him and begin. The tether will run sometime between then, she won't stick around to watch dad's handiwork, she never does.

I called you because Fredrick and I cannot complete all three aspects of this mission at the same time. We must capture and bind the tether to be dealt with, we have to send Cordray back to wherever he comes from before he can wreak havoc and bloodshed, and there is a child here who must be protected at all costs."

M stared at the house for a moment; Dorthea could feel the energy stretching out from M to the house as M felt the energy stretching out from the occupants. After a moment or two, she gasped. "Lilly is in there, why is Lilly there? Why are we waiting, why don't we just walk right in and bind the tether where she sits and get Lilly out?"

Dorthea held a hand up to slow her down, "If we could, I would have already done so. In order to finish this the right way and end Cordray forever, we have to capture, bind, or destroy both he and the tether. Which means we have to allow her to summon him, he has to take the father to take physical form. Then we can bind him and the tether, and destroy them both, it's the only way."

"Here's how I see this playing out, M. Fredrick is bringing the supplies we need for the binding, when ten o'clock strikes we wait for the tether to try and run and we grab her, bind her, and hold her. We know from the past that if she can the tether will move through multiple families in an area. Ten years ago, in Pheonix Cordray, killed four families in just a few days. She infiltrates the friend groups and one at a time Cordray takes each father, before they move on."

"Cecil!" M interjected.

Dorthea nodded her head in agreement. "Yes, Cecil, he's been through enough this year and no man deserves the pain that Cordray inflicts, forcing a father to kill his own children. The monster feeds on their guilt and shame, he leaves them conscious while he controls their bodies so they can see what they have done to their own flesh and blood. Just as important as sparing Cecil the pain, Lilly must be protected, she is a daughter of Mercer, and she must be allowed to grow up and assume that mantle. If we don't stop him, Cordray will wipe out the Bryants, the Ballhorsts, and Lilly's families.

"To be honest, M, I am tired of chasing this devil, for years now he has evaded us, and no one has ever been able to catch the tether, or figure why he seems to orbit around Mercer families, but no matter what or how, he must be stopped, tonight. Can you inscribe the Belos Transport?"

It was an honest question and not meant to be anything but, still Dorthea saw the flash of anger and indignation flash across M's beautiful face. She held up her hands in supplication, now was not the time to fight with M, she had felt no animosity toward the younger woman, but she understood why M did not feel the same. A lot of hurtful things had passed between them, and Dorthea feared the damage might never be repaired.

"It's not common, and not easy to imbue M, I meant no offense, only trying to assess and plan."

Her jaw relaxed and M nodded slowly.

"If you have all the supplies, I can inscribe the Belos. Are you thinking front door and back door and tie into the shed behind the house? Then we can bind the tether away from everyone else and maybe she won't be able to warn Cordray?"

Dorthea said nothing but nodded in affirmation. She knew M would be able to hold up her end of this. They had to succeed. No one even knew where he came from or how long they had been killing together. His first mention in the records at Mercer was in 1821, but it was a Mercer witch talking about attempting to capture him and failing.

She was not sure if he was already a spirit then. The working theory was that the tether was his daughter in life, and he would send her into these families to gain their trust. Then he would come in the night, and she would let him in, he would bind the father and kill the whole family while they made him watch, then leave him alive as a reminder of how he failed his family.

Eventually, and there is no memory or record of when, he and the tether died. That's when she began haunting families and marking the fathers for possession. Afterward, Cordray would possess him, and use him to murder the family. So much worse than making them watch him do it, he was able to make them feel the pain of killing the family themselves.

No one in Mercer seemed to understand what power kept him going. It was nothing like any of the magic anyone in Mercer used or understood. As far as Dorthea was concerned, his origins and the source of his power would remain one of the unanswered questions of the universe. She was going to kill him and be done with him and the tether. There would be no wasted breath or time on questions.

A polite cough made both women spin around. Dorthea spreading her hands in front of her in the first gestures of a defensive charm that would stop any physical or magical attack. M crouched low to be behind the barrier and drawing her baton.

Fredrick stood before them, a small, wrapped parcel under his arm. His kind smile beaming at M.

"Pardon the startling interruption, ladies, it was not my intention to sneak up on you. But you seemed quite enrapt in your conversation, and I did not wish to intrude. If you would drop the defenses a moment, I have not seen Ms. Wildes in a very long time and if she would permit me, I think a hug would be a wonderful way to start off what I am sure will be a trying evening for all of us."

Dorthea relaxed, allowing the energy she had been gathering into the charm to dissipate, M threw her arms around Fredrick's neck and held him tight. "I miss you, Fredrick. Sugar misses you as well, he speaks of you often."

"Ms. Wildes, I swear to you as soon as I have a moment of respite from my duties assisting Dorthea in her mission, seeing my good friend Christopher and spending as much time as possible with you is top of my priority list. Besides, your Nguni training was just getting interesting, and it appears from your stance there that you may have forgotten your ubhoko at home."

He raised his eyebrows at this. M stepped back from him and lowered her hands to her belt, drawing her baton with her right hand but holding both hands out in front of her. She focused her gaze on Fredrick's eyes and the air around her left hand seemed to blur slightly then a smaller baton appeared there. She heard a small exhalation come from Dorthea and tried to hide her smile.

Fredrick's eyes narrowed and he nodded thoughtfully at her. "Well done, Ms. Wildes, the best defense is of course, one your enemy cannot see. I cannot wait to learn more, and we can incorporate that into your fighting style. Even after all the years I have been a part of Mercer and been around the Mercer women, I am still amazed."

Dorthea broke the moment, "Speaking of amazing, after this work is done, you must tell us how you managed to approach without either one of our wards warning us that you were there."

"Now, we know the plan, lets prepare the shed then M, you take one door, and I'll take the other. After the tether has marked the father at ten p.m., she will slip out one of the doors and when she hits the Belos she will land in the binding circle in the shed. Once we have her in there, we will determine what needs to be done to free her. Then we wait for Cordray to appear. We need to be ready to hit the doors at midnight and capture and bind him. M and I will handle Cordray."

"Fredrick, Lilly is your mission, she cannot come to harm. She must be protected even at the cost of M or myself. She won't know you and may fight, and we don't know how in touch she is with her intuition or what fear may do. Can you get her out safely?"

"Yes, ma'am, as luck would have it, I have a couple of tricks up my sleeve for saving Mercer women, even when they would rather not be."

Dorthea's visible disapproval of his wit and charm was matched only by M's smile. M held out a key ring.

"The black key will get you into the lobby of the shop, call Sugar from there, get Lilly to him, tell him what we are doing, but Fredrick, do not let him leave. Protecting Lilly should keep him focused, no matter what happens tonight, don't let him come apart worrying about us. Lilly is the priority, but if he finds out we excluded him completely he will be heartbroken.

She will need cleansing, we don't know what kind of residue an encounter like this leaves on a spirit, no one has ever survived it to find out. I have all the supplies there you will need, and Sugar knows his way around the cleansing rituals. Just have him get started with the physical part and when Dorthea and I catch up to you we will dig a little deeper and make sure she is okay."

Fredrick looked between the two women, Dorthea was nodding her approval to this plan, and he closed his eyes and bowed his head before turning and trotting off to the shed. Dorthea reached out and took M's hand into her own. She felt M tense but only momentarily before she returned her gentle squeeze. An affirmation of not only their connection but also the history they shared before the rift between them. She was not a sentimental woman, but she could not help but think back to all the times she had been there with M through her life, mentoring, comforting, being everything, family should be.

She pushed the nostalgia and sadness to the side and spoke out loud to the woman at her side. "Let's kill this demon before he causes any more destruction, then maybe we can kill our own."

Without a word M slipped off into the woods toward the house.

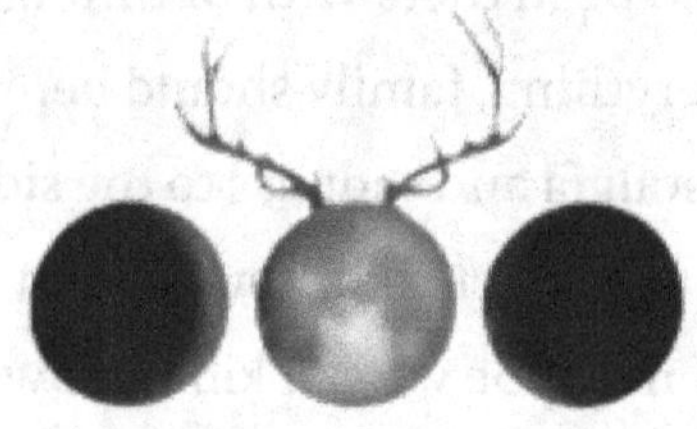

WHERE ARE SAM AND DEAN WHEN YOU NEED THEM?

I nside the Bryant house, Todd sat at the kitchen table, coffee in hand, listening to a podcast in his earbuds, trying to drown out the din from the basement. Down the stairs, in the realm of preteen girls, electronic music thumped from the speaker the girls had commandeered from Todd. Snacks were spread out on every flat surface of the basement.

Lexy, Babs, Kay, and Marianne sat in a circle on the floor of the pool room, away from the music. They kept the volume loud enough that Kay's dad couldn't listen in on any of their conversations. Currently, they were huddled around Lexy's phone. Lexy and Babs were both transfers to the district from the end of last school year, Lexy about a month before school ended, then Babs came after the year ended.

Kay and Marianne had been at the park almost every day, Kay working out and training with Ryan and Blake, and Marianne just hanging out, sometimes reading, sometimes lying in the sunshine for hours and enjoying the day. Kay thought maybe her house was too sad for her, the girls had both lost their moms last year—Kay's died from cancer, but Marianne's mom had disappeared, her aunt Jen had been murdered at her mom's birthday party, and her mom had just vanished. They found blood and a creepy crucifix that belonged to Marianne's great grandma, but her mom Colleen was never found.

It was one of those days, Marianne lying in the sun, Kay recovering from training, that they met Lexy and Babs. Since then, they had spent almost every day together, the four of them. But it was Marianne that was her best friend, the other two were cool, but her and Marianne had been friends since the third grade.

Babs had turned out to be funny and resourceful; she was always coming up with new and fun things to do. Lexy was the quieter of the two, and in fact, was downright morose most of the time. She had a dark sense of humor and sometimes laughed at things that no one else found even kind of funny. She was morbid and grumpy even on good days.

"Babs," Lexy whined, "stop being a baby, this will be fun, I found it on TikTok, and it's guaranteed to work."

Lexy was unpacking her backpack on the bar top; she had three different packs of dried herbs and two small vials of some oil. She unrolled a kitchen towel and started laying out the multiple colors of small candles.

"All we have to do is grind the herbs up in this bowl, mix the oil and a personal item from each of us, spit, blood, hair, a fingernail. We draw this diagram on the tabletop over there and put these candles on all the junctions of the lines and light them. We say these lines and it summons a spirit who has to tell us the truth no matter what we ask him. He cannot lie to us."

Marianne had a look of distant thoughtfulness on her face. "Lexy, how do we know it has to listen to us? Maybe it summons some kind of monster or demon, then what will we do? None of us knows how to deal with a demon or some kind of monster. Have you ever seen Supernatural? This stuff always goes wrong."

Babs looked around nervously at the other three girls, they were gathering around Lexy and the bar top and checking out the items she had pulled form her bag.

Babs backed away from the group. "Hey, Kay, my dad would freak if he ever found out I was anywhere near anything even resembling witchcraft. I will run upstairs and grab more snacks." She headed for the stairs, none of the girls looked up as she did. Marianne leaned closer to the circle they were sketching out.

"She's just scared, but that's ok, we will be quick so when she gets back, we can turn on a movie and lie down. She will be okay; her dad is very religious."

Lexy, who seemed to be enjoying herself for the first time this evening, or any time since the girls had met, shrugged, and kept grinding herbs and mumbling something to herself.

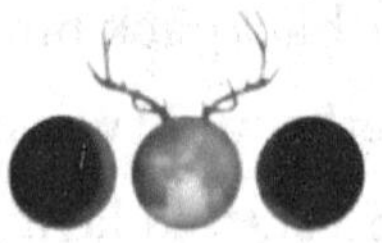

Todd looked up when he saw Babs emerging from the basement door looking a little upset.

He cheerfully greeted her as he rose from his chair, "Hey, Babs, everything alright down there?"

She nodded and smiled as if she had noticed him standing there. "Yes sir, Mr. Bryant, just coming up for air. We were playing a game, and I got eliminated first so I get to make the snack run."

She held her hands up in an exaggerated shrug. She smiled as she walked slowly towards him, her hands still raised. "Thank you again for letting us all hang out here all the time, Mr. Bryant. It is awesome, and we all appreciate it. I know Lexy is quiet most of the time, but you being so nice to her and all of us, it means a lot."

Todd blinked and she was suddenly in front of him and wrapping her arms around him in a tight hug. As a rule, he avoided ever being alone with the girls, and he had never hugged any of them other than Marianne. He had known her and her family since she was a little kid, and he felt comfortable with that. He hadn't even met Babs's father yet. He started to protest, then it kind of stopped in his chest as the world went dark.

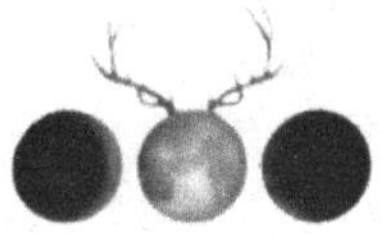

Todd awoke, sitting in his chair in the living room. He thought he heard the living room door closing softly, it was dark in the room, and he was struggling to get his bearing. He glanced at his watch, 11:30. "Wow," he said to himself as he tried to shake off the sleep that had overtaken him without him even knowing.

He walked down the hallway and toward the bathroom, rinsed his face, and checked his appearance, then he would go down and check on the girls. He didn't know how long he had been out, but he didn't like the idea of them being unsupervised. His head was pounding as he walked toward the light, he had never been sensitive to the light before, he hoped that wasn't changing as he got older.

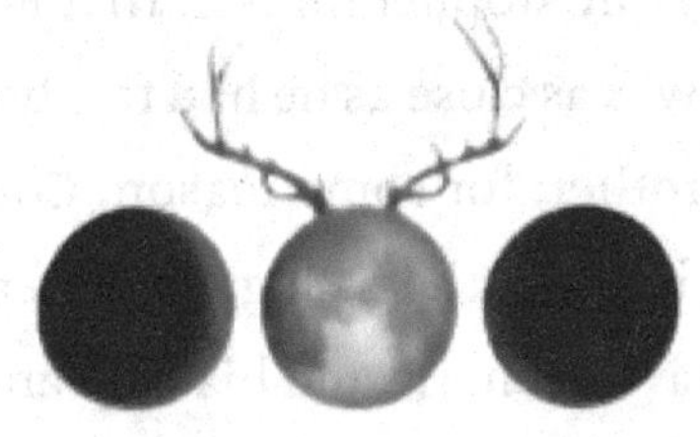

THE VALKYRIE'S KISS

Fredrick stood perfectly still near the tree line at the front of the yard. He knew that Dorthea would be in the shed tending the back end of the transport spell and watching the binding, and Ms. Wildes would be watching the back door. They were pretty certain the tether would just slip out the front door and move on.

If she did manage to walk through the Belos transport, an unlikely scenario, he was armed with both physical and meta-physical attacks capable of bringing down almost anything they had record of. He would not fail, not Dorthea or Ms. Wildes, or any of the others who stood to be destroyed by this monster and his summoner. He was not anxious about the fight at hand, he could handle any father, no matter how possessed, and he had no doubt he could get young Lilly to safety with Christopher.

It was dealing with Christopher himself that Fredrick was currently concerned about, he was as close as he had to a brother of his own. But Christopher had a brother; for some reason, Cordray had attempted multiple times to get both brothers. Sugar was kept safe, but it appears that Leroy may not have been. He and his wife and children have been missing for quite some time now. The decision was made to keep this from Christopher. Fredrick might be bound by that decision, but he did not agree with it, nor did he think it was a useful deception. He was also concerned that if it came to light at the wrong time, it could prove detrimental to everyone involved.

Fredrick was a warrior, he had survived hundreds of encounters with every sort of opponent, from street brawlers and trained fighters to mercenaries and even a couple of powerful witches, he may have fought against the only confirmed necromancer in the Mercer records. A disturbing and messy business that ended with him fighting a man that he had killed two hours earlier.

But the idea of having to restrain or worse, fight, Christopher Lewis, was something that made Fredrick lose his trademark smile. As he was pondering this, he saw the front door open just a crack and a small figure, a young girl, stood in the opening. He glanced at the chronograph on the inside of his wrist, 11:30, showtime.

The young girl stepped out onto the porch, pulling the door closed behind her softly. She turned, her body loaded to run and then vanished in a crackle of blue light.

The earbud in his ear sounded softly, Dorthea's voice, "The tether has been bound, at midnight get in."

The rest of the sentence was cut off by a tremendous roar, like a lion or a chorus of lions. He quickly muted the sound in his ear and began preparing, not long now, and the plan was rolling. Dorthea would have to deal with the tether.

When M stepped into the shed after hearing Dorthea's declaration that the tether was captured, she felt as if she had been transported to another planet. The charm on the shed combined with the binding prevented any energy from escaping the shed and only those wearing a protective mark could cross out of the boundaries of the binding circle, so outside the shed was a quiet suburban night.

But inside, winds howled and blew so fiercely that M feared she would be taken off her feet, and the roaring that nearly deafened her, was coming from the preteen girl in the center of the circle. M did her part, she steeled herself against the cacophony and ran the perimeter of the circle, removing the markings that made up the receiver of the Belos Transport. While it was designed to be a one-way street for energy and matter, with two points of origin, and an unknown power being bound nearby, M did not want to take any chances. If anyone or anything were tracking the tether, her trail would end at the front door and origin of the Transport, which could land them straight in here.

She glanced at Dorthea, and the girl began to speak, "You fat cow, you whore, let me go or when my father hears me, he will come, and you will suffer for all eternity."

Dorthea looked thoughtfully at her and if she was relieved that the roaring had stopped, she showed no sign. "I am sorry, child, that you have been so corrupted by that monster, but he will not hear you in here, and before he takes one more innocent life, he will be destroyed forever, and you will be free."

"Shut the fuck up, you stupid box," the girl screamed at a volume that made M's teeth rattle. "When my father arrives, I will have him fold your living body into a new altar for me so that I can take the youngest from every family I kill and bleed them to death on your belly while you watch, for all time."

"Child, let us free you from Cordray's insanity."

This time she was interrupted by the child's howling laughter. "Stupid cow, you think Cordray is my father? Cordray is the sick bastard I seduced, then used his guilt and fear of being found out for being a degenerate pedophile to convince him to kill his whole family. But I was slaughtering innocents long before Cordray and will continue to long after he is used up."

M could feel the girl push against the bindings harder than she should have been able to.

"I would have already moved on, but it's not as easy as it used to be, and frankly after a couple hundred years or so, the whole family annihilator, sucking on the guilt of fathers has gotten tiresome. But no matter, after I have dealt with you and your quiet friend behind me there, I am going to slaughter all these kids myself and then leave Cordray in the void and move on. That Marianne girl has a dad that seems capable, tall, muscular, and handsome. I think I'll have him burn his family alive then I'll swap him out for Cordray, his time is long past."

M caught Dorthea's attention and glanced at her wrist indicating it was time to go, she knew Dorthea would not waiver. There was something bad at play here, but she was genuinely concerned that if she allowed Dorthea to continue to question this creature and continually kept getting caught off guard by her answers, the girl may find a way out.

Dorthea nodded her agreement at M and stepped closer to the girl, lifting her closed fist to her mouth like she was holding an invisible microphone. She began to whisper, quick and low. M had seen the Valkyrie's kiss once before, it was not a complicated curse, but it was powerful and fatal, but beyond that it was a slow torturous death.

M was surprised that Dorthea would choose that, but it seems even the mighty Dorthea Milburn could be provoked and the thought of all the innocent lives destroyed or perhaps the mention of Cecil and the idea of losing Lilly to this beast, had pushed her too far. If the girl had been attempting to get an emotional reaction from Dorthea, she should have done her homework. She's cold and dangerous when she is just getting the job done. Provoked, no matter angry or scared, was not a reaction M would try to get from her.

Dorthea walked up to the girl, still whispering into her hand, the girl shrunk at first then seeing Dorthea would not be dissuaded, she stood defiant. Dorthea opened her hand and blew the kiss, the girl hit the ground immediately, screaming in pain, her body began to roll itself in, tightening into a ball, then bending even further, every joint bending as tightly as it could before snapping back straight as a board and stiffening, M heard the spine crack as she flexed backward further than seemed possible, then doubled over again, curling into a ball tighter than before. The whole time the girl screamed, incoherent, drooling babble.

M glanced at her watch again—11:55—she had to go. Cordray would appear any moment, and M needed to help Fredrick get Lilly and the other girls as well. Dorthea saw her looking and spoke up over the tortured screams of the girl as her body bent backward and her elbows, knees and ankles, toes, fingers, shoulders, and hips all hyperextended before snapping her back to the rolled-up ball on the floor.

"This will take time. Go, get Lilly out and stop Cordray before any more blood is spilled."

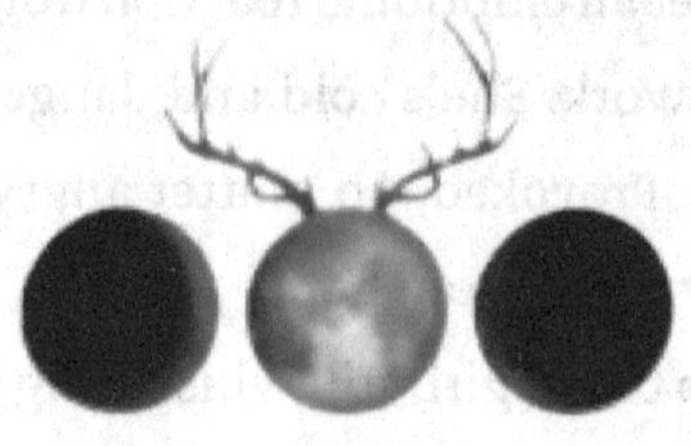

THE ONE I REGRET

T odd stood in front of his bathroom mirror, struggling to maintain his composure. The longer he looked in the mirror, the more he did not recognize himself. It was like his face was changing into someone else's. His broad handsome features were now birdlike and almost effeminate. He closed his eyes and when he reopened them, his face was looking back at him but only for a moment, then that face was back, the hawkish nose and close-set eyes.

The entire time, the headache that had started when he woke up from his nap kept growing louder, a constant buzzing behind his eyes. It shifted from a painful drone to something that almost sounded like words. He watched the mirror in horror as the face beneath his face took shape again, and the buzzing became louder and more distinct, *they are all the same, they trick you and act like it's your fault, not your fault, they should be punished, not you.*

Todd shook his head and rinsed his face with the cold water again, every time that voice coalesced out of the growing din of buzzing his brain essentially shut off, he couldn't move his hands or look away from the mirror. He wanted to call out for help, to scream for Kay, to call 911, anything, it didn't matter, he was going crazy and had a house full of kids he was supposed to be chaperoning.

The voice cut through the noise again, *Yes, evil little tramps, all of them, they will say it's your fault, but they are the real evil, they are the ones who will lie and make you pay for things that weren't your fault.*

Todd opened his eyes again and looked at his hands in horror, he had the large scissors from the medicine cabinet in his right hand, he did not remember grabbing them, and no matter how hard he tried, he could not seem to put them down. The voice started again.

Marianne, Kay, and Lexy headed for the stairs, their game was finished and no demon had appeared with their summoning. Lexy had tried the incantation twice and while there was no outward effect, Kay had noticed Marianne acting a little weird all the way through it. Kay realized just how much Marianne had hoped that something, anything would provide her answers as to what happened to her mom and why she had vanished. She also realized that Babs had never come back down, she probably fell asleep watching TV or something in Kay's room, if so, they would just leave her, they all had to pee, and it was getting late.

Kay had piled a bunch of pillows and blankets up in the basement floor in front of her dad's big TV, and they were going to stretch out and watch movies and eat until they popped. She would never admit it to anyone else but that was the part of the night she was looking forward to the most, just piling up on the floor with her friends and watching TV.

Kay and her mom used to lay downstairs on the big couch every Friday night, while her dad was working the late shift. They would watch movies and talk and snack. She would lay with her head in her mom's lap, and her mom would brush out her hair, or she would stretch out on the couch and Kay would snuggle up against her, feeling her warmth and smelling her soap and lotion. It was the safest and most comfortable thing she could remember and the one thing that her dad just could not provide. He was affectionate with her, he hugged her, he told her he loved her. He was the best dad she could ask for, but that was something that she could not get from him. That feeling of being wrapped in her mother's love.

She was nearly overwhelmed with that grief and loss as they ascended the stairs to the kitchen. She wondered how the girls would take it if she just explained that she wanted to be close to them for a while and if they could all snuggle up together while they watched the movie, it would maybe heal a big part of her that seemed to always be raw and bleeding.

It was dark when they reached the top of the stairs and opened the door leading to the kitchen. Once they left the light of the basement stairs there were no lights on. Kay flipped the switch at the top of the stairs to turn on the kitchen light, and nothing happened.

From behind her, Lexy drawled out, "Spooky." In her best Dracula.

"Shut up, Lex, this is weird enough. We have lived her five years and the light over the sink has never been turned off. Babs, Dad, hello," she called into the dark.

There was enough light coming in through the kitchen windows from outside that they could navigate. At the other end of the big dining area, they saw the glow of light from the little LED light things along the floor of the hallway. Her dad had loved those; her mom had spent most of the time trying to figure out how to shut them off. Dad said it made the hallway feel like the passage on a spaceship, Mom said it made it look like the aisle at a cheap theater.

Right now, Kay was grateful they were there. Between the lights and the skylights that ran down the length of the hallway they could at least see a little. She could lead the girls down the big hallway past the bedrooms and around the round room. Surely her dad and Babs were in one of the rooms, or out in the living room. The hallway was wrapped around, the bedrooms and bathroom on the outside until it doubled back to the living room, in the center was a small sitting room, all skylights and bookshelves.

She called out again, "Daddy, did you fall asleep, what's up with the lights?"

Marianne said from behind her, "Kay, what's going on?"

Kay could hear the tension in her voice; she felt the same way. Something was wrong. Her dad would not have gone to bed without saying something. He always told her goodnight. She could have had twenty friends over, and her dad would have marched right through the crowd to give her a hug and a kiss on the top of the head and tell her he loved her. Since her mom died, he had never gone to bed without doing that.

She had just made it past the first bathroom down the hallway when she heard the door opening. They had passed the door on the left and did not even look twice as there was no light shining under the door. She did not think anyone would be in there in the dark. Kay turned around as the door opened, expecting Babs to pop out and probably scream as Lexy was standing in front of the door. Marriane was still several feet behind Lexy at the end of the hall.

Instead, she saw a flash of silver, and Lexy screamed. When she turned to look at Kay, her face was a mask of blood, black in the muted light of the hallway. Lexy started toward Kay and was slammed backward against the wall as she was kicked in the chest by whomever was coming out of the bathroom.

Kay screamed, "Lexy, no. Daddy, help. Please wake up, help."

She froze as her dad turned to face her in the dark hallway. "Shut up, you little tramp, stop screaming and wait your turn."

He kicked Lexy again, her limp body absorbing the blow with nothing but a grunt from her. He smiled at Kay; his face twisted in the shadows and raised a pair of shears. Their razor-sharp blades gleaming as they reflected the moonlight.

He spun towards Marianne and stalked toward her, talking to himself the entire time. "Stupid, lying little cow."

He swung the open blades at Marianne's head. But she was gone. Suddenly Marianne was three feet back from where she had just been standing. Her dad yelled again, some incomprehensible bellow of frustration and leapt forward swinging at Marianne again.

Marriane screamed, "NO!" And this time, he flew backward as if struck. He hit the ground and rolled, grunting and swearing as he did. He pulled himself to his knees and stared at Kay, like a hawk eyeing a mouse.

"Marianne, run!" Kay took off down the hall away from her dad and Lexy. The way the hall was wrapped around she might be able to get out the front door before he could get to her. If the door wasn't deadbolted. If she did, there was no way her dad could catch her out in the open, she was too fast. She could run for help. She tore around the horseshoe shaped bend of the hallway and toward the living room, she did not hear her dad behind her. She hoped he didn't get to Marianne.

Just as she got to the end of the hallway, a figure appeared emerging from the darkness of the living room. Kay screamed in frustration and turned to see her dad stalking from around the corner. Whoever was at the end of the hallway was mumbling and walking straight toward her. She decided to take her chances with her dad. At least in the hallway she had one trick. She ran straight toward him. He looked at her confused for a moment then lowered himself as if to brace for the impact of her running into him.

That was all the indication Kay needed and just like earlier in the day, she kicked off the wall and jumped before she could catch herself on the walls above his head. He leapt forward and up and punched her solidly in the stomach. Kay crashed to the floor writhing in pain like nothing she had ever felt before. Her dad's punch was solid, driven by his athletic body and the insanity that had overtaken him. All the air was knocked out of her, and she panicked, trying to pull in enough breath to scream, to cry, to beg, to live.

Before she had any chance to recover, he was on her. In the dim light of the hallway, she looked up into her dad's face, the face of the man who was the only family she had left in the world. The face of the man that kissed her on the head and told her he loved her every night before bed. Even struggling to catch her breath, she could see. Her dad was gone. She did not know what was wearing his face, but this was not him. She screamed in rage and fear. How could this happen, her dad would never hurt her. It didn't matter what had taken control of him, he could fight it, she knew he loved her enough to beat whatever this was.

"Daddy, please, please. Don't hurt me, please."

Her dad stopped and stared down at her. She saw her dad's face, his real face shine through the mask of whatever was pretending to be him.

"Daddy?"

He grabbed her collar with both hands and pulled her toward him, then slammed her hard on the floor. Her head bounced off the floor, sending a lightning bolt of pain though her head and down her spine. He drew her to him again. His breath hot on her face, her vision was blurring, and she struggled to stay focused.

Kay heard a woman's voice strong and commanding. "Cordray, stop!"

Her dad turned and looked back over his shoulder. "Lying deceitful little tramp, she needs to be punished, just like the rest."

The woman slammed her hands together and yelled, "Habere Diaboli."

Kay felt something roll over her, like a wave of electricity. It wasn't painful, but it made her teeth rattle and whatever this man was that was pretending to be her dad, let her go. He turned his head slowly, as if it was held in place by some kind of invisible hand.

She could hear him talking again. "Deserve to die, just like they all do. Kill you all."

This time, the woman yelled, "Cordray! I said stop. Dolor miserum dolorem."

When the woman slammed her hands together, she did so three times in time with the words she yelled. The wave that hit Kay was much more distinct. Like the air was vibrating around her.

Kay's dad fell over backward, lying in the hallway, staring straight up at the ceiling. He growled something incomprehensible, and the woman stomped her foot three times. Kay heard her dad start to scream as some unseen force drove him into the floor.

"Daddy," Kay cried out, rising to her feet and reaching for her dad. "Please, something is wrong with him, don't hurt him anymore. Help him, help my daddy, please."

"I know, and I promise that I will try my best to help him, but for now your friends need you. Can you walk?"

Kay started to sit up and used the wall to push herself to her feet. "I think I can. Can you help him?"

"Get up now, go help with your friend, she seems to be hurt badly. Fredrick?"

A man's voice sounded from behind the woman. "Yes, ma'am, I am here."

"Can you take all three of these girls to meet our friend? The one in the other hall has some serious injuries, bleeding, and possible fractures."

"Of course, Ms. Wildes."

Then to Kay, "You and your friends will be safe with Fredrick, and he will get you all to the best place for you. Help your friend now, she is injured and should not be exerting herself any more than necessary."

With that, Kay walked past the woman in the dim hall, toward the darkened living room and the sound of the man's voice. The pained screams of her dad still in her ears, and the feeling of him trying to kill her still breaking her heart.

"Need to be punished."

Her dad kissing her forehead before bed every night flashed through her mind.

"Lying deceitful little tramp."

Her dad sitting at the table with her every night after work while she did her homework.

"Deserve to die, just like the rest."

She started to turn back, to run to him, to beg him to be okay when the man stepped between her and the hallway.

"Come, ladies, it is time we get you cleaned up and treated. You did well tonight, but there is much more to do before we can rest."

He produced a handkerchief from his pocket and held it tight against Lexy's forehead. "Lilly, be a dear and hold this in place and you two walk her out to my car."

"Marianne," the girl said, and the big man froze in his tracks.

He turned and looked at her curiously, and the woman in the hallway shot him a look that Kay did not understand.

Marianne said it again, "Please, call me Marianne."

The man bowed deeply and nodded at her, then swept his arm toward the door in a regal gesture for the children to continue walking.

Outside they crossed the yard and headed for the only car parked on the street in front of Kay's house. When she looked back, she saw the man talking to another woman, shorter and older than the first; he motioned to the girls, and she glanced their way, shaking her head and walking toward the door.

When they were all piled in the back seat of the big car, Marianne holding the handkerchief tight to Lexy's forehead, and Kay holding her hand, the man driving made a call.

Kay could only hear one side of the conversation, but it wasn't hard to imagine the other.

"Christopher, it's Fredrick, yes, yes, well actually I am headed to you as we speak. Sorry for the short notice, but big trouble on the air I'm afraid. I just left Ms. Wildes and Dorthea. No, no, please hear me out, my friend, and I promise you will understand momentarily. Christopher, it's Cordray. He surfaced with the tether. It's over. Ms. Wildes and Dorthea are finishing up and attempting to minimize the damage done, but the tether is gone and once they are finished, Cordray will be as well. But Christopher, you and I have a far more important task. There were three young girls in the house tonight. The father had a young daughter, and she had two friends that were there. Miss Lexy, who is injured and will need your immediate attention to see her through the night. Looks like a head wound, blood loss, some fractures. She has been in a scrap, but she is tough.

"Everyone else will need a full once over from us, as well as a looking at from our better halves when they return. Yes, I am almost certain. Yes, I know I am not the final say, but I would guess a trip home would be in the near future for one of us. Oh, and Christopher, to save time on introductions. The other young lady, says her name is Marianne."

He then turned to the backseat and addressed Marianne, "Young miss, what did you say your full name was?"

Marianne responded, and he repeated into the phone, "Did you hear that, Christopher? Her full name is Marianne Lilly Carter. Yes, I am aware, sir. Yes, again, I think you will understand once we are all back in the same room, but if I can be so presumptuous to ask you to perform one of those culinary miracles of yours. Yes, very well. Five minutes and we will be standing on your stoop."

He again addressed the girls in the back seat, "Ladies, have any of you, ever wondered what it might be like to eat the most wonderful meal you have ever had, prepared by an actual giant? Because if so, you are in luck."

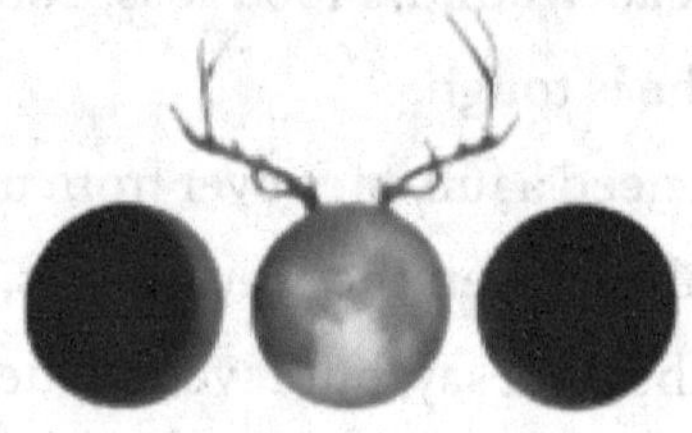

TO HIS STRONGEST

Henry Bishop was running. He was young, carefree, and running for the pure joy of it. He was being chased, but he felt no fear. This was the game, running through the woods, picking the hardest path. See if you could lead your pursuer somewhere they couldn't follow.

He jumped the fallen log and slid around the corner of the bramble. He knew this trail, as well as the hallway between his bedroom and the kitchen. He and his brother had been running this trail since they could be outdoors on their own. That's what made the game hard, they both knew this stretch of woods, it wasn't easy to find a place the other didn't know about in order to throw them off. But this time, this time Henry had it.

He heard his brother swear as he darted off trail and up the slope to the left.

"Sneaky bastard."

"I'm tellin' Granny," he yelled over his shoulder as he crested the peak, finding the trail he was looking for and sprinting full out around the blind corner he had found only a day or two earlier.

"You."

"Better."

"Not."

He heard his brother huff out between breaths as he crested the hill.

Henry slid around the concrete pillar. He had found this part of the old railroad trestle over the lake and knew this would be the spot. You could not see the drop or the pillar coming around the blind corner. He figured his brother would slide to a stop cussing and promising a beating of some kind or another. But maybe, just maybe he would end up falling off the side of the trestle and into the lake. Wouldn't that be a hoot? Henry didn't worry about him falling in the water. Both boys could swim like fish. Although his granny would likely take the belt to both of them for his brother getting his clothes all wet. It would still be worth it.

Just then he heard the crash of the branches, as his older brother came slamming through them and around the blind turn in the trail. He heard the scream and the splash, as he careened off the edge of the trestle and fell the twenty or so feet down to the water.

Henry cackled with laughter. He leaned out over the edge to see his brother. Who he was certain would be dog paddling at the bottom of the pillar, and stark raving mad at him. Once he made sure his brother was on dry land, he would high tail it back to the house. If he caught him out here where no adults were around, he was sure he was going to get it.

That was strange, he couldn't see him anywhere. He should have been right next to the pillars. It wasn't that far of a drop; he shouldn't have been under more than a second. He called out to him but got no answer in reply. He waited a few more seconds, starting to worry, then looked for a trail down to the water's edge, there had to be a quick way down. But should he go look for him first or go get help. He was suddenly very scared and very confused. He had no idea what to do next, he didn't understand how his brother could have not come back up yet.

Henry Bishop jerked awake. That same dream again. The chase through the woods. It was so disorienting and so real. But Henry didn't have a brother, he was an only child, and he didn't grow up near any woods. He grew up in Dayton Ohio.

But he knew what the dream meant; every time he had the dream it was always the same. He would awaken from it in a different city than where he fell asleep in the house with his wife and two children. When he woke, he almost never knew where he was, he knew only that an angel of God would be in the room with him. They would tell him the name of the monsters he needed to kill, and he would do the Lord's work.

This time was no different. Still shaking off the strangeness of the dream, Henry Bishop opened his eyes, and the angel was standing directly in front of him. He looked around at the old dusty barn where he lay. *Like Christ in his manger.*

The angel said all she needed to say to set him into action.

"Straight out the back door, one mile east, watch from the woods until dark. Hannah and Mathew Weems. They look old but they are dangerous, Henry, satanists, pedophiles, and cannibals. So many innocent lives destroyed. You must do the Lord's work, Henry. Kill them, send the message to all their evil friends, God's champion has come and will hunt them all down."

It only took him nine minutes to arrive at the tree line at the back of the farmhouse through the woods. He was leaning now against the broad trunk of an oak tree, about fifteen feet above the ground, sitting on the thickest branch he could find. His weight was considerable, but the branch seemed solid enough.

The foliage was thick, and wildlife moved everywhere. Birds called and squirrels ran from tree to tree. Perfect to hide his occasional movements or incidental noises. Twice now he had seen the couple, the man appeared to be into his seventies, it was hard to judge from this distance. He was grey and a little stooped, but his movement did not seem restricted. He had made two separate trips to a small shed behind the house. Both times it looked like he was getting containers of potting soil.

The woman walked with a cane and had come out once to swap containers with the man, accompanied by a younger woman. This woman was maybe in her twenties, small, short wiry brown hair. It made no difference; the angel had never been wrong. He would wait for an opportunity, then he would creep in and send the message. The days of these sick bastards hurting kids was over. He would repaint their home with their blood.

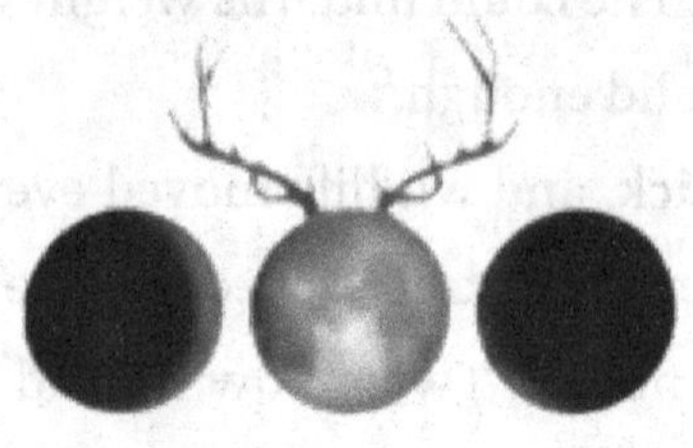

BIG BASTARD

M atthew Weems was piddling, that's what Hannah liked to call it. Just piddling around in the garage, keeping busy before dinner. He had gotten the day's chores done early. Most days, once the chores were done, Hannah would lounge, read a book, or nap between lunch and dinner. After their official retirement, Matt tried it, but he was no good at leisure. His had been a life of hard work.

Growing up in rural Indiana in the twenties, work was all there was. His earliest memory was helping his mom and grandmother in the kitchen and gardens. His dad worked at a stove factory and wasn't home very often.

His mom and grandmother had chickens and a garden that was the envy of the county: onions, carrots, potatoes, cabbages, pole beans, lavender, tomatoes. But the thing that kept them eating more often than not was the flowers: zinnias, petunias, daisies, and roses. The women would come from all over to buy cut flowers and seeds from his mom.

It was the flower garden she loved more than anything, and it was the flower garden his dad resented. Between eggs, produce, and the flower garden, Mom and Grandma brought in the same amount of money every year that Dad did working seven days a week at the stove factory, and he hated it. He would get so angry sometimes, yelling about how unfair it was he worked like a dog, pouring lead all day and all they did was play in the dirt and gossip with town women, and they made as much as him.

It was not long before Dad stopped coming home altogether from work. Mathew was never sure what happened to him. It was so many years ago, it seemed like one day his dad was coming home yelling at his mom and grandmother, just like always. Then he was just gone. It wasn't like there was an event that stood out. No big scene, no teary-eyed explanation, just no more Dad in his memories.

When Matthew was seventeen, he left home and joined the Army. He excelled at being a soldier—smart, a quick thinker, and decisive. As a result, he ended up in Ranger Battalion 2C. There was a big war going on by this point, and Matthew knew he would be headed there. The last thing he remembers before waking up in Mercer was the ramp lowering on his boat onto the hell that was Omaha Beach. He blinked, and when he opened his eyes, he was staring up at the most peculiar woman he had ever seen. White hair, dark eyes, and skin that looked like unblemished marble. She told him he had been dead long enough, and it was time to join the fight.

Since that moment, he dedicated his life to protecting the innocent, fighting those who would prey upon them however he could. His partner, and later his wife, Hannah, had been by his side ever since. They grew up in the ways of Mercer together. Magic and might, Hanna was a brilliant witch by every standard, her gift was in a very specific type of telepathy that allowed her to implant thoughts into a person's mind so seamlessly that her target would never know the thought hadn't originated with them. She had refined many other skills over their long life together. With his training and skills in weapons and combat, and her ever-evolving magic, the two of them had led a campaign of attrition against the predators of the world.

Last year, they had chosen to retire, at least for now. He knew many of their Mercer kinfolk kept working later in life than they were, but they were both wrung out and tired. Most of those folks, with very few exceptions, were in different lines of work. Important work sure, but there was a hell of a difference between a social worker or liaison—and the kind of front lines, blood and guts work he and Hannah had spent more than eighty years doing.

Your body took a beating, sure. But it was nothing that good medicine and some powerful healing magic could not stitch back together. The problem was the wear and tear on your soul. You couldn't rub a salve or poultice on that, spend some time in the temple, and walk out fine. Years of kill-or-be-killed fights, cleaning up after the bad guys when you don't catch them in time, and tracking them through the trail of destruction they leave behind. Leaves the kind of scars that never fade.

Mathew was never the biggest and strongest of the consorts, that was usually those Lewis boys, he had met one or two in his time. Even this youngest one now, Sugar, big bastard, a sweet kid, and good at his job, but holy crow, that is a big bastard.

What made Mathew good at his job was the way his mind worked. High-level problem-solving under pressure. He was tough, sure, as tough as any man in Mercer. But given a few seconds to plan he was hard to beat, a few minutes, he was a menace that even those big-ass Lewis boys didn't want to tangle with.

It was this skill he was counting on right now as he was moving around his workbench. A moment before he had seen it, just caught the image in the reflection of an old microwave, of a body, a big body, uncoiling from the garage rafters and landing on the other side of Hannah's minivan with no more sound than a whisper.

Mathew did not know for sure how long that fella had been up there, but he guessed an hour or more. Hannah had left the big door open in the garage while they had lunch. Mathew had come back out here to piddle around and closed the door when he did.

Two things worried him. How had this man slipped past Hannah's wards, and why hadn't Bast done her thing? Bast didn't look like much but that didn't mean squat around here. The fact the man did not attack straight away and had hidden silently up there in the rafters for at least an hour, maybe more, spoke volumes to him. This was not a thug or druggie, here to rob or trying to find a place to hide from the local law.

This guy meant business.

Mathew had two options as far as he could see it. Open the door and get the guy to come after him out in the open or stage the garage as best he can and fight the guy in here. He was one hundred and nine years old this year, he was damned if he was going to be playing tag in the woods or wrestling in the driveway with someone that big and physical. Close quarters in a room staged for his advantage seemed like the best chance for survival. If Hannah's wards had not alerted her, and Bast hadn't sensed him then it was unlikely Mathew would be able to raise the alarm and get their help. They were probably upstairs with the fan going, it was too far away for them to hear. So, inside it is. Mathew began shuffling back and forth, opening and closing drawers, muttering to himself as he went.

Putting most of his tools on the cluttered bench away, but more importantly, positioning the more useful ones where he could easily get to them. A pile of zip ties on one end of the bench, two screwdrivers, and a crescent wrench in the drawer but the utility knife comes out and clips on his belt. Those blades are sharp, and a slice across an artery or eyes will end the fight fast. A pair of large vice grips into the back pocket, perfect for clamping down on, and breaking the small bones of the hand. Mathew rolled down the sleeves of his flannel, time for the opening move.

He grabbed the garage door remote off the bench and clipped it to his left pocket, then found the last thing he was looking for—an eight-pound sledgehammer head that had been welded onto a short pipe for a handle. It was more of a fun project he and his friend had gotten up to one day, than a practical tool. But the handle was short enough to slide up the sleeve of his flannel, and he could cradle the head in his palm and if he was slick, he might be able to hide it long enough to get the drop on this guy.

Whoever this was, he was waiting to ambush, he did not seem interested in a direct confrontation. If you did not know if your opponent was armed, it would be better to surprise them, hit them fast and hard, and eliminate the risk of them getting a quick draw on you. Most folks carried concealed at the appendix or pocket, it wasn't too difficult to take away those draw options with a blitz attack, as both required the same movement to complete. The hand had to move toward the lower torso. What he likely wouldn't be watching for is the hand to extend from the body.

Mathew walked toward the front of the van, sliding his little step stool into the narrow walkway behind him with a hooked step as he went past. To his right was the van, the kitchen door directly in front of him, and his would-be attacker hidden in the space between the passenger side of the van and the wall of the garage, about three feet of space running the length of the van. He was about to learn a valuable lesson and a fast one if Mathew had anything to say about it.

As he approached the bottom step, instead of reaching up to grab the doorknob with his right hand and pull himself up the steps as he would normally do, as he knew the man would expect him to do. He tapped the garage door opener button with his left hand and as soon the motor sprung to life, he spun hard to his left, completing an almost 360-degree turn, using the momentum to launch the sledge like a cannonball out of his sleeve and into where he guessed the turned head of his attacker would be to look at the rising garage door.

A normal sized man with his head turned would have likely had his neck snapped by the force of the sledge rocketing into the base of his skull at such a compromised angle. Instead, it bounced off the chest of the monster staring straight at him. *Damn big bastard*, Mathew thought just as the man's fist slid past his chin and smashed into the drywall next to the door. Mathew hopped backward over the stool as the man came on. He stepped right over the stool and picked up speed like a truck rumbling down a grade. Mathew slipped the utility knife out of his pocket, but the man launched into a combo of punches faster than he could have imagined possible from someone his size. Mathew slipped the left jab, but out of years of fighting experience, instinctively rolled to get away from the following right cross, he didn't anticipate the lead left hook, it grazed his forehead as he corrected, and he managed to get his left arm up to at least partially block the follow up right hook to the ribs. In that moment, more than any time in his long life, Mathew knew this was the end. His head rang from just the grazing contact with that enormous fist and his forearm was broken; he heard the bone break while blocking that punch.

Fifty years ago, he may have had a chance, but not now, now he was going to die here in his garage, and he knew it. He lashed out in desperation, a straight kick to the knee followed by him stepping in and reaching toward the man's groin with the utility knife. Maybe he wouldn't survive, but at least he might be able to do enough damage to keep this bastard from going after Hannah and Bast. The man checked the kick to his knee and punched out at the same time as Mathew, connecting with his jaw before the knife could even get close. Mathew's vision began to dim as he slumped. *I am so sorry, Hannah. I love you*, was the last thing that passed through his mind before the searing pain of the giant fist closing around his testicles and crushing them.

The monster screamed in the face, spitting with rage. "You'll never hurt another child, you devil."

Mathew did not have enough mind left to be confused as the man dropped him to the floor, and with five hard stomps ended the long, brave life of Mathew Weems.

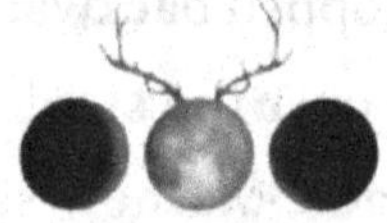

Hannah awoke with a start at the sound of Mathew's voice in her mind, no, deeper than her mind, in her very soul. *"I am so sorry, Hannah. I love you."*

There was so much pain, so much sorrow in his message. Hannah did not believe in strange coincidences or random tricks of the mind. Something was wrong with Mathew. She pushed herself up out of her chair. Bast, her and Mathew's adopted daughter, was stretched out asleep in front of the fireplace.

She focused her mind and reached out, searching for the energy that surrounded Mathew and flowed through him. A feeling as familiar to her as her own body was the space he occupied and the trail he left behind him as he moved through the universe. She could not find it; she extended her feelings even further out. He could not have gone far off the property, not further than she could feel, she glanced at her watch. She had only been dozing for twenty minutes or so, not enough time for him to move beyond her range. She searched not just for him but for anyone. Her property was heavily warded, no one should have been able to come here, especially meaning them harm, without her knowing.

Yet, there was a blank space, a deep blackness in her perception moving from the garage to the kitchen. She did not need to see Mathew's body to know, no one could have gotten past him if he was alive. Whoever this was, he would pay for hurting Mathew; he would pay painfully and slowly. Mathew was pragmatic, doing what was necessary to accomplish their mission. He did not take things personally, that was not the case with Hannah. She took things very personally, especially where Mathew and Bast were concerned.

She reached down and gently touched Bast's shoulder, rousing the girl. Hannah put a finger to her lips and nodded to the stairs. Knowing Bast would understand her, she always did. Hannah took a deep breath and focused on the dark shape in her perception, standing silently in her kitchen. He must have heard her stand up. Was he going to lie in wait for her to come to him or stalk her through the house? It didn't matter, let him come or let him wait, she only appeared to be a helpless old woman. She was going to hurt this man and hurt him bad. A slight sound, like someone quietly ripping paper, told her Bast was ready as well.

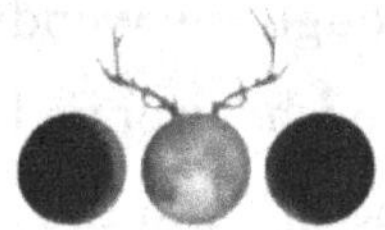

Sometime later, in the dizzy dark of the night, Henry Bishop stumbled through the woods, he didn't know if he was truly headed back to the barn or not. The pain in his right arm was blinding, burnt, some kind of acid. The skin of his shoulder and upper arm was bubbled and peeling exposing the nerves to the cool night air.

Something was wrong with his right eye as well. He couldn't see out of it at all. His shirt had torn away in the struggle. It did not seem possible that the old woman fought as hard as she did. Just after killing the old pervert and stomping his head into a puddle, he entered the kitchen. Thinking he would slip through the house silent as a ghost and kill the old bitch before she knew what was happening. That is how it had gone the last time.

But things went sideways, fast. The lights in the house started strobing off and on and before he could get his bearings or figure out why, all hell broke loose. She hit him with a stun gun or some kind of electricity and before he could recover, she was on him. She raked her nails as sharp as razors across his face partially blinding him. The rest was a blur of pain and rage as she evaded him as he crashed through their house like a rampaging bear. Eventually, disheartened, confused, and in pain, he cried out in prayer to the angel of the Lord to aid him, and it interceded on his behalf. As he blindly rounded a corner, she came within reach, one fist full of hair was all it took. He had her, he clawed and bit and pounded until there was nothing left but a pile of gore and broken bones.

With great effort, he detached her ugly head from the rest of her and carried it with him through the woods toward the barn until the exhaustion overtook him and he dropped it somewhere. He was sad not to be able to present the prize to the angel, who would surely be waiting for him in the barn where she woke him. There it was, he could see the glow of her divine light shining through the open barn door. Just another fifty yards or so and he could sleep, she would heal him. She had promised that no harm could come to him on these missions. Surely an angel of God would not lie.

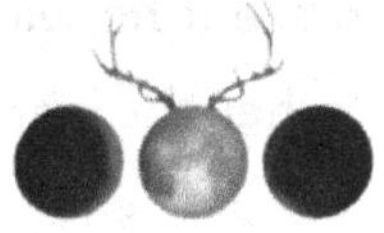

Hannah Weems stood several yards off the main trail between her home and the abandoned barn on the property to the west. She had debated briefly just pulling this beast apart at the seams, but in his rage after her initial attack, some of the things he was screaming made her pause. Cannibal, killer, rapist, these things made no sense. If he had called her a witch and tried to kill her, she would have at least understood, but he was accusing her and Mathew of being the very things they had spent their life fighting against.

There was something else, as she watched him fight the illusions she had placed in his mind, she saw it. There was someone else behind his eyes. Not like that monster that Dorthea had been chasing, this was different, this was like the true man was buried deep beneath the surface and someone had laid a new one over top, like those paintings where they use ultraviolet to see the drawings underneath. Someone was painting over top of the person there. This was something Mercer needed to know about, she tempered her rage at the murder of her husband and partner for more than eighty years, this was bigger than them. If it wasn't a direct retaliation against them, then it could be an attack on Mercer and that meant trouble.

The name had long been whispered by those who would harm the innocent, a legend, a myth, a worldwide network of powerful women and men, using magic and might to protect the innocent, and free the oppressed. That was the kind of thing that evil men feared. But in her very long memory, there had never been a coordinated attack against Mercer. She watched as the monster limped injured into the barn and began to follow to see if he was seeking shelter, like a cat looking for someplace to die, when the inside of the barn lit up as bright as daylight.

She ran as fast as she could, given the circumstances, but when she reached the barn, the light had faded, and her attacker was gone. Frustrated, she kicked the barn door, slapped her hands together, and a ball of flame erupted between them. She slammed it down against the base of the wall. Smiling as it began to consume the old rotten wood. Time to go get Mathew cleaned up. She would summon Bast back to her and seek guidance from the Elders of Mercer, she would return home, her true home. Matthew's death pyre would be in the courtyard of the Temple of the Mother, like so many valiant consorts before him. He would be mourned the world over by witches and their protectors. Let them hear the song of his passing around the world. Let them tell his stories as his spirit returns to the Divine Energy of Creation, so that his memory will live forever as it should be.

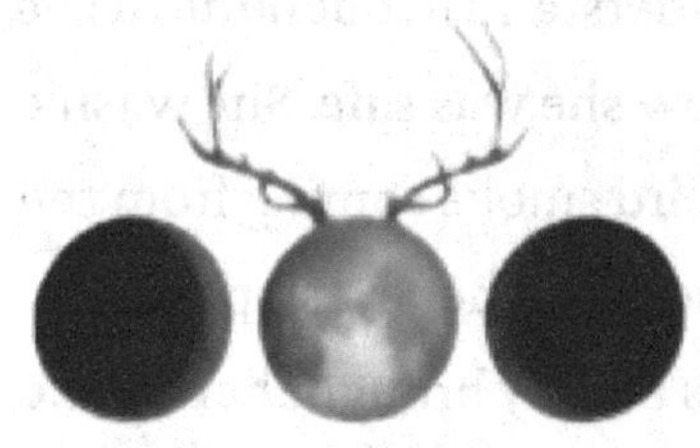

MARIANNE MEETS THE GANG

Marianne wasn't sure what time it was when she woke, the man that saved them, Fredrick, had spoken the truth. When they arrived at the strange little shop, a giant man, as pale as anyone she had ever seen, ran out to greet them. He bowed to Fredrick then scooped her and Kay up, one in each arm and ran them into the house while Fredrick saw to Lexy.

Fredrick was also right about the food. In what seemed like no time at all the giant, who introduced himself as Sugar, or something like that, had produced a potpie of some sort and soft bread. While the other girls were eating, he did something to Lexy's forehead and then wrapped it in bandages, he then had her lay out on this strange stone table in the next room, covered in some kind of tapestry.

Marianne didn't understand it, but he did leave the door open so they could see her and know she was safe. She wasn't sure if it was the food or the stress or the weird smoke coming from the incense, but it wasn't long, and she could not keep her eyes open.

The sound of voices nearby brought her awake, but she kept her eyes closed, hoping they would think she was still sleeping. She could hear two women talking fast, saying something about a tether being more than what anyone thought she was but how it explained so much about Cordray. It didn't make sense to her, but she listened on, hoping for some clarification.

Quite suddenly the talking stopped, and she heard one woman say softly, "She is awake now, should we introduce ourselves?"

Marianne opened her eyes and giggled despite herself. The two men were standing next to the couch looking at her. Fredrick was wearing a suit and tie and was possibly the darkest man she had ever seen. Sugar, or whatever the other man's name was, was wearing a hand-sewn tunic or robe of some sort, and he had the whitest skin she had ever imagined on a person. He looked like a statue.

Together, she thought they looked like a mismatched pair of salt and pepper shakers, and she could no longer contain herself and she burst out laughing. She sat up straight on the couch where she was lying, she looked around, more than a little afraid and very conscious of the fact that she was still giggling while at the same time being on the verge of crying from panic.

The younger of the two women, pushed between the two big men, and the older woman followed close behind, she leaned into one of the men and whispered something as she did. The men nodded and walked off quickly but quietly, in fact, she was sure she had never heard anyone, much less men that big, move that quietly before. Like dancers she thought, and giggled again, at the idea of the two, big, fierce looking men in ballet tights twirling each other around the stage.

When the younger woman reached her, she knelt in front of her, there was something about the two women, something so familiar, so comforting. Marianne knew she should be scared to death, having seen what she had seen—Kay's dad attacking them, the blood from Lexy's wounds, Babs disappearing like that, and all these people sliding out of nowhere to save the day. But somehow, in the presence of these two women, one about her mom's age and the other much older, she felt good, home even.

The older woman sat down on the couch beside her, put a hand on her shoulder, and spoke quietly, "You are safe now, Marianne. I know it has been a long time since you have felt that way, but here, with us and those gentlemen, you are safer than you have ever been."

Marianne began to cry, something about the women, the way they huddled close to her, the love and concern in their eyes, made her miss her mother so badly in that moment. She was beyond controlling her grief now, she began to sob, unable to form words as the tears streamed down her cheeks. The older woman pulled her close and held her tight while she cried, not trying to calm her or even speaking, but just holding her and rocking her. The younger woman knelt at her feet, staring at her, tears in her own eyes, but not touching her.

After a time, she began to breath normally again, the storm was passing, but still the older woman held her. When she felt she could speak again, she asked, "Where are my friends? Are they safe too?"

The younger woman answered, "They are safe, sweetheart. Lexy is healing up and being escorted to the doctor by a friend of ours, where her mom is waiting for her. Kay is in the other room with Fredrick and Sugar, waiting for us to get done talking so you guys can spend some time together. Kay's father passed away tonight, and she is in for a very hard time of things. She will need your support."

Marianne looked at M.M. Wildes for some time, both women could feel the probing, and their wards began to warn them of intrusion. Like fingers groping for a purchase on a ledge, sliding around the edges of their minds. M looked up at Dorthea, startled. Marianne spoke again, calm but intent, "You are not being entirely honest with me about Kay's dad, are you?"

Dorthea spoke up this time, "No, child, we are not. One day, soon, we will be, but for now, can you trust us that if we told you the entire truth, top to bottom, front to back, it might do more harm than good?"

Marianne studied Dorthea for a moment and said, "I will accept that if you can tell me two things or at least tell me enough about two things that I can be okay going and seeing Kay, without them driving me insane. I have had enough mysteries in my life to last me the rest of it."

Dorthea nodded, and Marianne continued, "First, when Mr. Bryant attacked me, I could see that it wasn't him, but it was, like something wearing him like a mask."

Dorthea started to speak, and she cut her off, "Sorry, that was an observation. I know it's true and don't need it answered. When he attacked, the first swing he took was at me. I blinked my eyes and when I opened them again, I was several feet away from him. Then when he swung again, he got knocked down. I did that, didn't I? That wasn't one of you or your friend Fredrick, was it?"

Dorthea nodded her head. "Yes, you did."

Marianne sat up straight now and looked from woman to woman. "Can you tell me why something keeps telling me that we are family? Cousins maybe, no, aunts, I think. It is like a voice whispering in the back of my brain. But that doesn't make any sense. My mom's sister died when she was little and the only other aunt I knew, disappeared on the same night my mom did. How can we be related? Are we related somehow?"

The younger woman rose to her feet, smooth and graceful, and called out, "Gentlemen, if you wouldn't mind, could you put a kettle on and set out some breakfast for us, we have much to discuss with these young ladies and I am afraid we will need some time and refreshment."

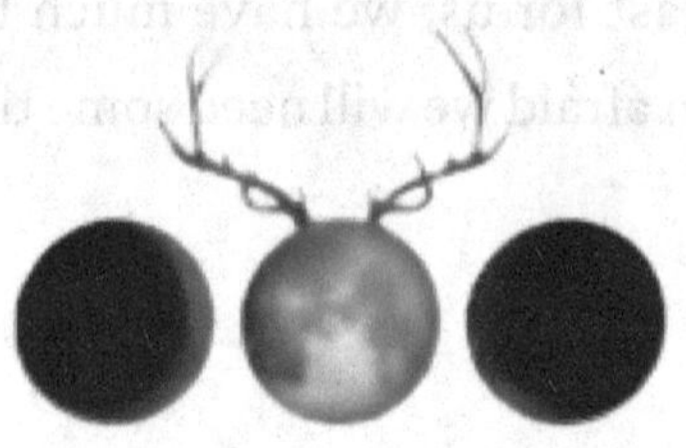

KAY'S CHOICE

Fredrick, Sugar, Dorthea, M, Marianne, and Kay sat around the small living area in the back of M.M. Wildes Tarot and Beyond, quietly eating breakfast. M and Dorthea had been shocked by Marianne's astute assessment of what had happened and her being able to tune in to the energy around her so easily was impressive, even to these two women who had been around witches of all kinds, for their entire lives.

The mood in the room was quiet, Kay trying to process what she had just been told. Losing her mom last year had been horrible, but losing her dad, like this. She didn't think she could survive. Marianne had moved close to her and hugged her, just letting her cry until she felt like she could breathe again.

After everyone had eaten, the older of the two women, with the short grey hair, came and sat on a cushion at Kay's feet.

"Kay, I know this is hard, and I know none of this seems fair, but you have a decision to make, and not much time to think about it. Before long, our contact with the police is going to need an answer as to where you are, and where you are going. I know that you saw what happened to your dad, you know that wasn't him in there, doing, and saying those things to you and your friends. Sadly, it will not change the fact that he is gone, only for you to know that it wasn't his fault, and he loved you very much.

"I also know that you saw what Ms. Wildes over there did to stop him. I am going to give you a choice. Your dad had a sister in Wyoming. We haven't been in contact with her yet, and I know you don't know her, but if you'd like, you can try to live with her. If she refuses, you'll become a ward of the state and enter the foster system. Either way, your life here in St. Louis will be over."

Kay's eyes brimmed with tears again and she pulled her friend close. Dorthea wanted so badly to reach out across the distance, to lay a charm on the child to help numb the pain of grief, she knew two such charms that could do just that. But the practice, long respected, was to never apply these charms unless the person was dying already, and the pain of grief served only to make their passing even worse for them.

In any other case, grief and loss, and the process by which we experience it was the only way to heal from it. Dorthea knew as well as anyone the dangers and attraction of numbing your loss.

"There is another alternative I would like to present to you. If you wish, we can take you to our home. A place far from here, you will be cared for and loved. You will finish school and make friends like any other girl your age. But you will also learn so much about the world that you cannot learn anywhere else from anyone else. You have seen us, how unique we are, and you have even caught a hint of our gifts. For instance, you saw Lexy, cut and broken, carried in, and within a couple hours she walked out under her own power, with barely a scratch to show for it."

With this, Dorthea nodded at M dressed in a beautiful blue kimono, her red hair hanging down her back in a loose braid. M returned the nod, smiled sweetly at the two girls, shimmered slightly, then stepped forward through what appeared to be a distortion in the air. When she stopped moving, she was wearing a loose-fitting pair of sweatpants and a SLU hoodie, her hair was pixie cut and black and one eye had turned blue while the other brown.

"Shit!" Kay immediately slapped her hand over her mouth, expecting some kind of reprimand from the grownups in the room.

"It's alright, Kay, I say the same thing every time I see her do that. As if she isn't beautiful enough, she gets to change her hair and clothes and tattoos at will. It's a touch unfair if you ask me."

"Fredrick, could you help me with a little demonstration?"

The man rose from his chair at once before nodding in agreement.

"Wonderful, if you would be so kind, I would love for you to throw that plate at my head. Like a Frisbee, just gimme me all you got."

M stepped out of the path and sat on the sofa with the girls, book-ending Kay, she whispered in a voice just loud enough for everyone in the room to hear. "Oh girls, they have been partners for a very long time, I guess now we get to see if he is harboring any unaddressed issues toward her."

Both girls giggled, and Sugar, watching intently in the corner, spoke up, "Fredrick, maybe, not the good China."

He handed him a small stack, three or four dinner plates from a cabinet next to his spot at the counter. Fredrick examined them as he fanned them slowly in his left hand, his long slender fingers spaced between each plate. Then, faster than either girl could see, he fired off all four plates in succession, each one following the one before it right for Dorthea's head.

Just before making contact, the lead plate and each in one in turn, slowed about six inches from catching Dorthea right in the teeth. She reached up and gently took each plate and returned them to the stack, before laying them on the floor at her feet. It reminded Kay of the

Quicksilver scene in that X-Men movie where the guy is super-fast and running around the mansion saving people who are all moving in slow motion.

The girls stared wide eyed at her, and Fredrick gave a crisp round of applause. When Kay turned back to look at Ms. Wilde, she was wearing her blue kimono again and her hair and eyes were back to normal. Kay gasped and Marianne gave a little exhalation at the displays.

Dorthea continued, "Kay, these are just the beginning of the things you could learn. But beyond that, you would have a home to call your own and a purpose. One day, you will join Ms. Wildes, Fredrick, Sugar, and many more like us out here. Saving innocent lives from evil people. If that is what you want?"

M had never heard Dorthea recruit before, she tended to leave that for the social workers, like Beck and Snow. Dorthea was a general, a warrior, and a strategist of the highest order. M had never seen the slightest sentimentality from the woman before. She wondered if something had changed with Dorthea or if she was just finally opening her eyes to the truth of her.

Maybe, growing up in her shadow, not only learning from her at a young age but then spending her days hearing the tales of Dorthea's successes, her cold, calculating cunning and ability to do whatever it takes to win, became the measure by which M always felt judged.

You could be good, but Dorthea would have been better. You stopped the bad guy and saved the innocent, but Dorthea would have annihilated his whole organization. But maybe she had applied that filter to Dorthea, maybe because of her own jealousy and insecurity she was blind to the compassion and caring that Dorthea was capable of.

Kay looked from Dorthea to Marianne. "Would I be able to come back and see Marianne sometimes?"

M wrapped her arm around her. "I am afraid not, sweetie, at least not for a while. When you come with us, your life here will be over. You will start again as part of our family. I know you love Marianne, and she loves you too, but what you will learn and see takes time and that time will make it difficult to return. Plus, us being able to protect the innocents of the world and our loved ones. This means we have to keep our community and our ways very secret. No one can know where you are."

"Like a superhero with a secret identity," Marianne chimed in. "Would I be able to join as well one day?"

Dorthea knelt in front of Marianne this time, M was moved by her gentle touch with the children. *I cannot believe I was ever angry at her,* she thought to herself.

"One day, Marianne, I truly hope that you will join us. But the decision will be yours and it may come many years from now if everything is allowed to run its course in the way it should. I know that may not be what you want to hear now, but I can promise you it is for the best. Besides, someone has to keep your brother and father in line."

At this, Marianne looked suddenly startled. "My dad is going to freak out when he finds out about all this."

M spoke up this time, "He is already aware of some things, others he has been told as much as he needs to know. As far as he is concerned, there was a break in at Kay's house and her father died protecting you. Lexy remembers nothing, and no other information will be released until Kay makes her decision. If Kay comes with us, then as far as your dad is concerned, she passed away as well. If she chooses to go with her aunt, then that is that. The important part is he knows you are safe and sound and will be home soon."

Marianne seemed to calm and sink deep in thought at this. Kay wrapped her arms around Marianne and whispered something in her ear. Marianne nodded yes and started crying softly, pulling Kay close to her.

M stood from the couch and offered a hand up to Dorthea, who accepted it. They made their way into the kitchen to give the girls some privacy to say their goodbyes.

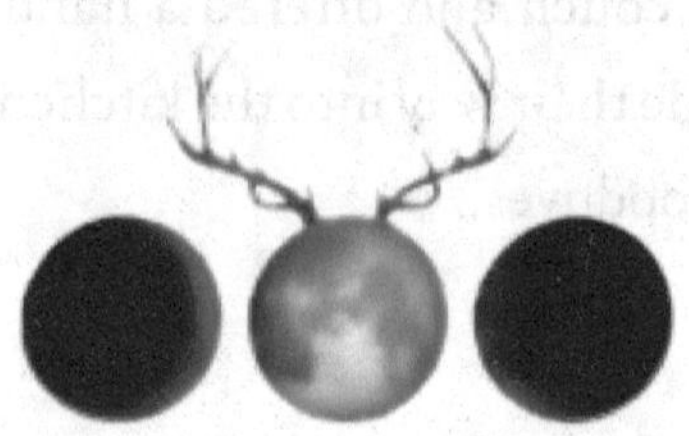

BRAVEST LITTLE MOUSE

I n the basement of M. M. Wildes, Tarot, and Beyond, Dorthea and M were preparing a delicate but powerful summoning when Fredrick and Sugar brought Kay down the stairs. Marianne had been safely returned to her father, after Dorthea had laid a charm on her to blur her memory about the night's events. As much as it would hurt her to think Kay had died last night, it would be even worse for all of them if she told their secrets. She wanted to take her home herself. To be with her for as long as she could.

But that was not their way. So, she restrained herself and stayed behind to begin the summoning. Introducing a new person to Mercer wasn't as simple as dropping them off at the gates with a bag of clothes and a note pinned to their shirt. Even if someone is born into one of the original Mercer families like she was, there are still an abundance of precautions. Not only to safeguard the people in Mercer but to ensure that any woman who receives the gift is able to put the needs of the world at large and the needs of Mercer ahead of her own ambitions.

Refining the gift is an incredibly rigorous pursuit even for the most naturally gifted witch. You had to spend years in solo meditation and practice to explore and understand your gift as well as learn all the general practices and spell components. It was not a study that lent itself to a sense of community. Mercer was very selective about who received the gift as well as pairing them up with partners and consorts who act as a balance and grounding for the witch as she grows in her gift.

M was partnered with Sugar when they were children, twelve years old. They arrived at Mercer almost at the same time. The idea was they would have someone to train with and grow with that would pull them out of their isolated studies. Keep them part of the family and community while they learn and grow. She turned and held out her hand to Kay and led her to where Dorthea was kneeling before a circle drawn on the floor.

Nine bowls were placed around the perimeter, each filled with an exact amount of different and rare ingredients. two smaller circles intersected inside the larger circle, a tenth bowl lay at this intersection, filled with fresh flowers and a tag lock from each summoner. Every ingredient in this summoning, every mark in the sacred diagram was specific to Lord Seanchara, each thing was meant to pay tribute to him either symbolizing his role in the success of Mercer or something it was written that he favored. Each circle was etched with glyphs and sigils and sacred equations.

M knelt on a small pad and urged Kay to kneel between her and Dorthea, who spoke quietly to the girl. "Kay, becoming part of our family and community isn't as simple as just showing up. There is a sort of test, and this test is conducted by the guardian of Mercer and harvester of the Mercer women."

Kay shifted nervously. "Ma'am, what kind of test? What do I need to do?"

"There is nothing you can do, Kay; this isn't a test of skill or knowledge. Lord Seanchara will examine the contents of your spirit and the depth of your mind. This test is about your character and what's in your heart. Here is what I need you to know: Lord Seanchara is very old and can appear to take many forms. He is often very frightening to look at and can say some scary things. He is wise and powerful beyond imagining and has been tasked with keeping Mercer safe by selecting who can join and what they are allowed to learn. Once the petitioning starts, it will be up to him to judge you. Do not attempt to lie or debate him. He will make his assessment, and we must follow his instructions. When we light the fire, he will be compelled by our magic to join us. He will not likely be happy about it. Just keep kneeling and only speak when spoken to."

Fredrick and Sugar knelt behind them, and Dorthea turned to look over her shoulder at them. "Gentlemen, you do not have to attend. If either of you would like to wait upstairs, no one would think any less of you. Petitioning the elders, specifically Lord Seanchara, falls well outside of your duties and isn't something I would volunteer for, were it not necessary."

Kay looked around nervously at the two large men, could this thing coming really be scary enough to frighten them?

Sugar answered, "Dorthea, with all respect and gratitude in this most holy place. The people I care most about in this world are in this room right now, and I cannot imagine a reason I would leave. While I understand what is about to happen, perhaps as well as anyone here. I know that Lord Seanchara lives by rules and means that we cannot understand, but I also know that if he were to take offense at his summoning that I would rather be beside my friends than left alone."

M put her hand on Kay's shoulder. "It's okay, child. Sugar is being dramatic, Lord Seanchara will be frightening but you are safe. Now close your eyes and bow your head and think only of the truth of who you are, your name, your happiest memories of your family. Remember, speak only in truths. If you do not have an honest answer to one of his questions, it is better to tell him that than to lie to him."

At this, Dorthea lit the fire. The room went dark, as the flame grew and absorbed all light; the lamps burning in the corners went dark, the candles lit about the room snuffed themselves. Even the brazier of incense lost its glow to the circle of fire inside the ring on the floor.

Kay startled a little and Dorthea reached blindly in the darkened basement until she felt the girl's arm and gave it a gentle, reassuring squeeze. A wild animal smell became overwhelming all at once. A wet shuffling in the darkness just in front of them, Kay strained her eyes, trying to see, trying to catch a glimpse of what had made these people, who seemed like superheroes to her, so nervous.

From in front of her came a voice, deep and powerful. "Because child, they know well what it is they have done. They ripped me from my work, in a most unpleasant and uninvited way. In the depth of their witch hearts, they know that if I find their offerings or entreaties un-appealing, someone will suffer for the discomfort this spell causes me."

The candles in the room resumed their burning, dimly lighting the space. Kay kept her head bowed, even though she wanted so badly to see who had just spoken, to witness this magical being that had just appeared through the flame.

His voice thundered in the basement, "Well, say what you have brought me here to say, witches. I have a great many things to do today and wasting my time will win you no favors. Even if you did hedge your bets by bringing flowers for my bride and my favorite Lewis son."

Sugar bowed his head reverently and answered, "Lord Seanchara, The Guardian of Mercer, The Stag of Red Mountain, it is an honor to be in your presence once again. How fares Elder Valkyrie, the Mother Moon, and Bride of the Eternal."

"Did you hear that Michaela Renee Bryant, daughter of no one of consequence, Christopher there, he understands the importance of humility and civility."

At this comment, Kay looked up for the first time, her shoulders back and jaw set. "They were of consequence to me, sir." She tried to make her voice as steady as she could, she did not want to sound as scared as she was, but what he said about her parents made her angry and she also didn't want to raise her voice to him. Dorthea reached for her arm at the same time that M sucked in a breath and started to speak, hoping to begin the petition before something could go horribly wrong.

Kay studied the man in front of her, he was taller than both Sugar and Fredrick, a mop of shaggy brown hair on his head, he was dressed in a fancy suit and carried a cane or stick with a bird's head for a handle. He was big, but his eyes were dark and appeared kind.

"Well, aren't you the bravest little mouse. Do you know why your new friends here are so nervous, Kay? It's because if I were to decide that I was going to eat you alive in front of them, there is nothing, even as powerful as they are, that they could do except watch or die trying to stop me. But you, you have lost everything, haven't you? Your mother, now your father, and here you are. Resigned to leaving the only thing you know and the one friend you have in the world and start a new adventure. So, why, Kay? Why shouldn't I just turn you into dust right here and now. End your wretched suffering and just get on about my day, can you give me a single reason not to?"

"Sir, you just told me why—I have lost everything. I miss my mom so much, and it wasn't fair, my dad didn't do anything wrong, he was a good dad, and a good man. But he is gone too. I am all alone, but I don't want to die, I want to live. I want to make them proud of me, wherever they are. When I die and see them again, I want to be able to tell them I did something they would be proud of, that I helped people. I know what happens to children all alone in the world, sir, and they don't usually get the chance to make a difference. But it seems like with Ms. Dorthea, M, Sugar, and Fredrick, if I could grow up to be like them. Then I could help people just like them, just like you do. I could make my mom and dad proud of me."

Tears streamed down her face, she made no attempt to hide her grief, her pain, her fear. Seanchara looked at M and Dorthea.

Dorthea spoke, "Lord Seanchara, Guardian and Harvester of Mercer, The Stag of Red Mountain, The Keeper of the Paths, we have come here to ask your wisdom and permission, a daughter seeks a family, a child seeks the way. Look into her spirit and judge her fairly, so that she may begin her life anew."

At this, she waved her hand, and all nine bowls flared into a different color flame as the ingredients were consumed by the fire she had summoned.

"Dorthea, daughter of Mercer, one who was sacrificed. Mercer's great general, and keeper of the oaths. I hear your call, and will judge this child, who is without kith or kin, fairly and honestly."

With this, he stood in front of Kay and spoke very softly, "Tell me your name, child."

"Michaela Renee Bryant."

"Now, tell me your happiest memory."

"Lying on the couch with my mom, watching movies, while she brushed my hair."

"If I told you that I have been to the length and breadth of all creation, I have seen the universe in all its glory, and there is no great beyond. If I were to tell you that when your parents passed, their spirits were consumed by the divine energy of creation and they rejoined the maker of all things and there is never a chance that they would ever be aware of anything you may or may not accomplish, would that change your mind? To know that your memories of them are all that's left, or that could ever be."

"It would not change a thing. I would be sad, for myself, because I would love to see them again one day, but I would also be sad for you. If you have seen all of creation, then there is no mystery left in the world for you. What would be left to surprise you?"

Seanchara stood over Kay, looking thoughtfully down on this little girl, her own twelve years, a brief moment, compared to his eternity being alive. He leaned down and kissed her gently on the forehead as a parent might, instantly she fell dead at his feet.

"You little one, you are left in the world to surprise me, and I am blessed for it. Fredrick, Christopher, bring her, we have work to do while she passes through the veil, and miles to travel to get her to a doorway. Witches, I assume you can get by while your companions are preoccupied with saving the soul of the precious child?"

Both women nodded, stunned and silent as Fredrick scooped Kay's lifeless body up in his arms and followed Seanchara and Sugar up the stairs.

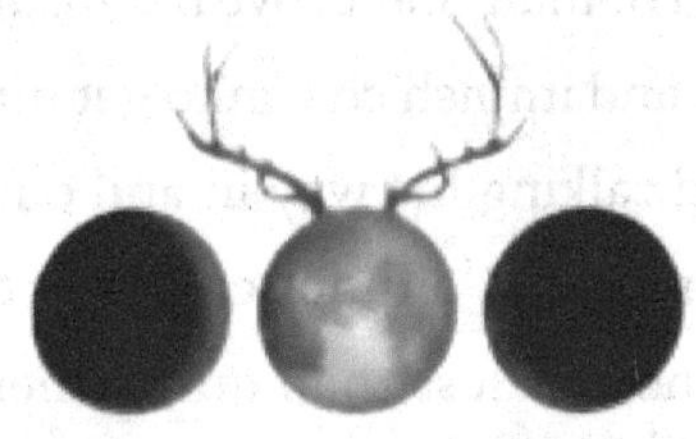

I GET
NO RESPECT
AROUND HERE

The sun was just setting, casting a soft glow through the windows of Bricktop's when M walked in and looked around to find the people she was here to meet. She was beyond tired, between the events at the Bryant house, dealing with the fallout, and the summoning of Seanchara, she was wrung out and shaky and had been awake for almost forty-eight hours with only a couple of hours of sleep.

The last thing she wanted to do right now was have a cup of coffee with these three. She loved Beck, they had known each other since they were kids. But Beck's wife, Snow, was just a little too manic pixie for her, and Devlin was intolerable. How Beck or Snow could deal with his constant innuendo and juvenile humor, was beyond her.

Devlin was the kind of man that drove her insane. Shallow and vain, he relied on his looks and impish charm to get him through. It was his knack for politics and talking his way in and out of trouble that kept him intact most days. But M did not care, she did not like him, nor did she pretend to. She was less than quiet when Devlin was burned alive for disrespecting Elder Valkyrie in front of Seanchara, and even less quiet about her satisfaction when Seanchara revived him and kept him conscious through the healing process. To his credit, Devlin took the punishment with no complaint or whining.

As she crossed the floor toward the back corner table where they sat, she waved to the barista, a large red-faced, cartoonish man named Eli, he would whip her up something special with no thought required on her part. That's what she needed at this point. Comfort with no effort on her part. She wanted to get home and crawl under the blankets with a cup of lavender tea and then sleep for a week. But Beck said this was important and she needed to see her now before they left town. Beck and Snow had delivered Lilly back to Cecil, and Devlin had run interference with the local police.

They were fortunate that the trio was passing through close by last night and were able to help. While Dorthea or M was able to deal with the police, neither one of them could get close to Cecil without risk and Frederick and Sugar did not make for a great combo for reassuring a terrified father about his daughter's well-being.

"M, sit down." Beck motioned her over to the table, Beck and Snow were facing her, Devlin had his back to her and had not looked up yet. She wasn't looking forward to sitting next to him, but duty called. She slid into the chair, and he looked her way and started talking before she had a chance to speak.

"M, I wanted you to hear this from me. I have been dealing with the police on the Bryant thing, papering over the cracks like I did, when I started listening in. It has to do with Colleen and Cecil. The police found her sister-in-law, Jen, in the creek behind their house. It looks like her head was bashed in with a rock, and she was tied to a brick and rolled into the creek. When they started digging in and looking for Colleen and investigating Jen's death, they found she had an apartment in the city that no one knew about that she left to some twenty-five-year-old bartender named Jason. No one knows who he is or why she left him that apartment, and he isn't talking right now but eventually, they will get something on him or threaten him with charges over Jen's murder and he will tell everything. Realistically, we know what this is, or at least what it looks like."

She turned on him, angry, bitter over the accusation, how dare he, this insolent little shit was about to learn his place. But when she looked at his face, she realized he was only telling her what he believed and what everyone else believed as well. Colleen was having an affair with a younger man and was keeping him in an apartment. "Poor Cecil."

Beck reached across the table and touched her hand. "Yes, Cecil is devastated, Colleen is missing, Jen is dead, and it is inevitable that he will find out that Colleen was having an affair."

Devlin continued, "M, the whole situation is bad, she goes missing with no explanation, her sister-in-law is murdered, and the body hidden, and now a secret affair. They are digging deep into her business and personal life. It is going to be messy."

"What else is there?"

Beck picked up the thread. "Colleen was not entirely on the up and up with her finances, some double-dealing with her charity organization, not theft, but the donations did not always end up where the donors thought they were going. None of it bad enough to hit the press or anything like that but enough to make the police take some very close looks at her and maybe wonder if she didn't disappear for a reason."

Devlin shifted in his seat, turning toward her. M thought he might touch her, but she also thought she might break his arm if he did. Surely, he knew better.

"I will do my best to get the local police looking in a different direction. We have a couple of friendlies here and one Mercer witch in the local department. I just wanted you to know so if you saw anyone paying a little extra attention to this situation you didn't think anything of it, also you know I will have to report it up and there will likely be a decision made about what must happen next."

"I am more than aware of how you feel about me, M, and I try to respect it. I don't understand it, but I am trying to respect it, nonetheless. I do know what they mean to you, all of them, and I promise I will do my best to get this wrapped up with as little damage to her family as possible. Besides, I figure, I clean up a mess or two for you, maybe you realize I'm not so bad after all. And maybe if I'm not so bad after all, you can ditch the hippie for a night or two and we can see what kind of magic we can make happen."

M glared at him but said nothing. Instead, she shifted her left forearm so he could clearly see the top of it, where a small hummingbird feeding at a honeysuckle was tattooed.

M focused on her glamour, one of the more fun aspects of it was her tattoos. Beck, Snow, and Devlin stared at her arm as the tattoo began to shift, playing out a stop-motion replay of Devlin being burned alive by Seanchara in the courtyard of Temple of the Mother. She let this go for a moment or two, her tattoo playing out an endless scene of him writhing on the ground in flames, screaming.

She rose from the table, leaning over, she kissed Beck on the cheek, and nodded to Snow before holding up a middle finger to Devlin and walking out without another word.

"Geez, you would think a little gratitude would be coming my way instead of open hostility. No, that's alright, I'll fix shit like I always do, go right on abusing me."

Snow spoke for the first time, her voice shrill and high, "Sure, Dev, you call her up at the end of two straight days of work dealing with horrible shit, then tell her that years of planning may potentially fall through, and then you hit on her, and insult the closest thing she has to a friend. You are lucky she didn't hurt you herself, or worse tell him."

Devlin waved off the comment. "He's a teddy bear, and…"

Snow cut him off, "And he is a seven-foot-tall wall of muscle with a penchant for violence who loves that woman more than life itself. But sure, Dev, you call him up and tell him you're taking her out for cocktails and a quickie and for him not to wait up, I am sure it will all work out."

"Not that quick," Devlin mumbled into his coffee.

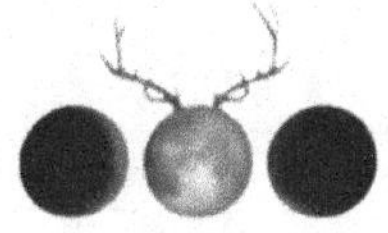

Outside, M walked slowly back to her car, the heat and exhaustion making it even harder to think clearly. All she could think about was Colleen and the mess left behind. But was there any clean way to remove a forty-year-old, wife, mother, and world-famous author from existence without it being messy?

They spent a lot of their time removing people from such horrible situations, many of whom disappeared into Mercer after, never to be seen in their old lives again. But she has never been this involved in it before. Certainly, she had never cared this much about the ones left behind after someone was harvested. Surely there had to be a better way. Cecil and the kids didn't deserve to have their lives upended like this, and eventually the word would get out that one of the best-selling fantasy authors of all time, disappeared without a trace and left behind a murdered sister-in-law and a secret lover. It was going to be a shit show and there was nothing she could do to help them deal with it.

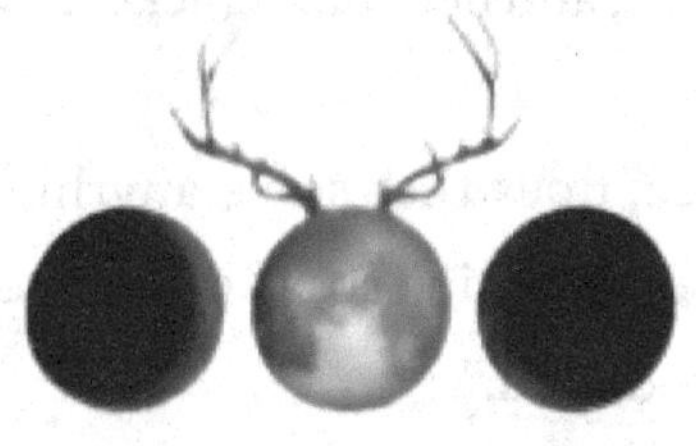

THERE SHE IS

"**B**ets, wake up, you've lingered long enough. Come back to us now."

"Bets, it's time, your work is waiting, you need to attend now."

A voice, like an echo overlapping itself in the darkness, beautiful but slightly discordant. Colleen tried to open her eyes and found she could not see, she felt like they were open, but the world was black. She rolled her head from side to side. Stiff, cold, so cold. Why was it so cold in her room?

But this didn't feel like her room, or her bed. There should be a small glow from the charging station on Cecil's side of the bed. That blue glow was always there. She reached for her nightstand and missed, in the dark she groped and still nothing. She sat up on the edge of the bed where she was lying, and her entire body protested. How was she this sore, it didn't make sense, and why weren't her feet touching the floor? The voice that woke her repeated in her head, you've lingered long enough on the other side. What did that mean?

Colleen tried to speak, and her voice cracked. "Who's there, who said that?"

"My name is Althea, does that solve anything for you, are all the answers clear now? I didn't think so, so now I need you to wake up and listen, your family needs you."

"Who are you? What are you talking about? I was just at my birthday party then woke up here."

At this she stopped, her family, Jen, Paul, Cecil, the kids, oh God they must be freaking out. She was walking with Jen, then... She remembered the sound as the rock came slamming down on Jen's open mouth, cracking teeth, the cold splash of the water as she rolled her, still alive, and tied to a brick into the creek. Then, Lilly, and the monster, the deal. It was all coming back now, the deal. Her or Lilly, and she did it, she gave up her life for her daughter's future. But where was she now? She was supposed to die.

"I don't understand, am I dead? Why can't I see, what's happening?"

"You were, quite dead in fact. You see, no one can come to this place without first passing through the veil of death. Lord Seanchara completed the harvest as is his role, then brought you here, to us. In his wisdom he knows how to bring us to our best self. I will admit, we are all thrilled you made the right choice. There are many here waiting for you. But first, you must see."

As her disorientation faded, she started to feel more grounded, more herself. With that return to self, came the traits that made her so successful and such a force to be reckoned with no matter what the arena. Her wit, her curiosity and fierce independence, but most of all her ability to set a goal and bring it to fruition. She spoke into the darkness.

"Wouldn't that be easier if you turned on some lights. I am not sure what you expect me to see in the pitch black. Wait, does that mean I am back from the dead?"

"That's what quite dead means, isn't it?"

"Just stop, that doesn't make any sense."

This time, the voice sounded from directly in front of her. "There she is, there's Bets."

She reached out her hand in front of her and the voice was behind her.

"Always in charge, aren't you, sis?"

Now, off to her left very far and soft. "Not here, you're not."

Bets spun to her left, listening for some kind of movement, had to be some kind of trick. She felt the tip of a fingernail, light as a feather, dragged down the right side of her neck from ear to shoulder and she spun, reaching out for whomever just touched her, and the voice spoke from in front of her again.

"I need you to understand something, Colleen Elizabeth Milburn. Right now, in this moment, you have a choice to make. You can go back to sleep forever, or you can let go of this false sense of control and embrace real power, real control over the world around you and in the process do some real good in the world. Not just self-serving success, but real good. You can become part of something bigger than you have ever imagined."

"Mercer," Bets whispered.

This time, the voice was just behind her right ear. "Yes, sister, Mercer, our home, our mission, our true family. A name unknown to the world outside the family, except through a select few. But there is not a land where our influence has not reached, because there is not a land where corruption and oppression have not reached. When things run their normal course, you would be given all of the background on our family and mission before being awoken to your gift and brought to your power slowly a little at a time.

"A decision has been made, that given the circumstances, your lineage, your inherent stubbornness, and what is apparently a fondness for you on the part of Lord Seanchara, your awakening will take a different shape. Our elders have asked me to present you with a choice: join our mission and begin your awakening right now, or we can return you to your gentle sleep where you will spend eternity in the embrace of the infinite."

"Did you just say that my choice is join your group or die? What kind of cult bullshit is this? Comply or die? And you are acting like you're good guys? If my memory serves me, that sounds like the speech of the oppressors, not the beacons of freedom."

The soft giggle that came in response seemed to come from all around her at once.

"Under most circumstances, that would be the case. You are not most circumstances, you are a descendant of both the Milburn and Wilcothe lines, your grandmother's family is a direct line of blood relation to Mother Mercer herself. You have also already proven that you have no issues with bending morality or legality when it suits your needs. Lord Seanchara looked into your mind and soul and declared that the cleansing of death and awakening would be sufficient to bring you to the path. Even with all of his wisdom and power, Lord Seanchara is the harvester of Mercer, and the guardian of the path, he is not the final say here, nor is he even involved after the initial harvest. You may live another one hundred years and never lay eyes him again. We revere him, but he is not a god or ruler. Simply, he is a powerful ally to us and has the ability to read minds and spirits as easily as you may read a child's book. You have many advocates among the sisters here, but there are also some who felt like your powerful lineage, combined with your personality would lead only to disaster, so this compromised was reached.

"You will not be brought on and awakened over the normal period of weeks or months. You will be given the choice: join us in our great work and begin the process of becoming a Mercer woman, or return to dreamless slumber."

"If I stay here and join you, can I return home, can I see my kids, my husband?"

"I am afraid not, I know it doesn't seem fair, but the damage of losing you has been done, and it would only be made worse by your reappearance. Bets, you murdered your sister-in-law by bashing her head in with a rock and throwing her alive and helpless into a creek, then vanished. Not only have the police found her body, but in the course of the investigation they have turned up your lover and will undoubtedly unearth your other infidelities and many transgressions involving your business. Do you think it would be a good idea to just go walking back up the driveway like a cat returned from a night out terrorizing the neighborhood in search of mice?"

Bets began to cry. "Cecil, Lilly, Steven, I need to see them, please, I can explain to them what happened, I can explain everything."

She felt a hand touch her cheek and instinctively pulled away, the hand found her cheek again, the woman speaking obviously right in front of her; this time, Bets did not pull away. The touch was soft, the fingers warm against her skin. They felt long and slender, the tips slightly calloused. The hand cupped her cheek gently, then that soft voice, again, so close to her now.

"Bets, as of right now, you are missing, and your sister-in-law was found murdered. While the police did uncover the apartment where you kept your lover, communication with your lawyer is privileged and they cannot go any further. Fortunately, we have a friendly face inside the police department, and they aren't making that information public yet, or informing Cecil. So as of now, you are the potential victim of a sadistic killer, and everyone is hoping for the best, but it's been long enough now that they aren't overly optimistic. How long will that continue if you come walking back in now after more than a year and claim you were taken by a magical monster who told you about a secret pact and before he kidnapped and murdered you? But you felt like it would be a good idea to beat your sister-in-law to death with a paving stone before you left?

"During the ensuing trial, not only would your family get to see you on trial for a brutal murder, but they would also get to meet Jason, as well as witness all your other transgressions. Please, Bets, believe me when I say. This is the only option for you right now."

Bets wanted to fight, to defend herself, to come up with a hundred reasons why, but she knew there was no point, she was not being judged, that part was apparently over. Now was just the time to move forward however she could. She reached up and touched the hand upon her cheek, stroking the smooth skin on the back of it and leaning her face into the palm. She had no idea how starved for human contact she was. Had she really been asleep or dead for more than a year now?

That couldn't be true, her body would have begun to rot, or at least atrophy beyond use. She focused on the feeling of the hand, grounding her, connecting her in this endless dark, to whatever this new reality was. She took a deep breath and released it.

"OK, I am ready. What's next?" The hand was suddenly withdrawn, and she felt a little sadness at its absence.

"Just what I said, Bets, first you need to see. Take a deep breath and focus on the sound of my voice, we are going to start slow. Modern fiction is very close to the truth, there is one energy that makes up all of existence. This energy, we call it the divine energy of creation, flows through and in all things. You can feel it every day, and have for your whole life, the spark of life that makes you who you are. While anyone can feel it, and some people can even manipulate it at some level, while under duress or unconsciously. In order to truly understand and interact with it. You must pass through the veil of death and be brought out the other side. There is something about the process of death and rebirth that allows one to truly control the energy of creation. It may be barely noticeable at first, a slight vibration, in your fingertips, a hum at the base of your skull. But if you breathe and search for it you will find it, waiting for you to plunge your hands into it, manipulate it as you would clay. Shape it to your will."

As the voice continued, Bets fell into a rhythm of deep breaths, she was no stranger to meditation or visualization. Nor was she a stranger to the idea of one unifying energy that made up all creation. She was a celebrated fantasy author and nowhere was the idea of unified energy more prevalent, outside maybe Star Wars fans.

As she listened, she sat up tall on the slab, her spine straight, she stretched out her arms, first in front of her where her fingers reached in the dark. She focused on the sound of the woman's voice and spread her arms wide, taking in a breath. With it came the slightest vibration. A tingle of something, her muscles being flooded with blood and oxygen after being dormant, but there was something more there. Something bigger, no, something deeper.

"I can feel you reaching out, Bets, that's perfect, keep going, just like that. With every breath out, extend your circle a little further, with every breath in, listen to what the energy is trying to tell you. Let it describe for you the world around you. Let it tell you its secrets."

Bets followed the voice and slowly, a picture in her mind began to form, a stone table, like an altar, in the middle of a stone floor. She was seated upon it, this was not a clear picture, not like watching television, more like a blurred image, a flash, then she pushed the air out of her lungs and pushed her senses further. There, a hint of a shape.

Don't get too excited, she told herself. *Just focus.*

"There are four candles at the four compass points in this chamber, Bets. I want you to search for them, find them, breathe, focus, find the candles so you may see the truth."

This time she could feel more inside that voice, it wasn't just the sound, there was power in this voice, this woman carried real power in her. Bets breathed out again, knowing her goal, to see the candles, was important, but at this moment, that was almost secondary. She needed to see the woman's face, to know her guide. She pushed further, and when she drew in the breath this time the picture revealed more than she expected. She was seated on the slab in the center of the room, rough stone floors, but in front of her, just a few feet away was a beautiful woman—tall, slender, pale, her white hair long over her shoulders and framing a face that appeared not much older than Bets herself. What startled her was the mirror image of the woman just behind Bets, dressed identically, her head bowed. Bets tried not to falter in her focus and let the truth flow over her.

"Twins!" she shouted, fearing her outburst would cause the image to fade but it did not. "There are two of you in here."

From behind the second voice, identical to the first. "Good, now find the candles, we are tired of sitting in the dark, and if you can determine we are twins, then you can get some lights on in here."

Bets continued expanding, feeling confident now, instead of big exaggerated slow breaths, she focused on a rhythmic in and out, her circle of perception expanding a little each time. She tried not to get distracted as the twin from behind her moved around the slab where she was sitting and stood next to her sister. A couple more breaths and she saw them, four large white candles, each in a wrought iron holder, high up on the walls. The one behind the two sisters was above a great wooden door, the others were simply hung on bare walls.

"Found them."

"Good."

Both sisters spoke in unison, then the one closest to her continued. "Now, light them, light them so that we may see each other and begin in earnest."

Bets stammered, "I, I am not sure." She was cut off.

"Sister, a shape shifting God-form capable of teleportation, and reading minds, pulls you out of your life only to kill you and bring you back from the dead, and lighting some candles is where your faith runs out? Focus on the candles, but now picture a small flame in your mind. A charm like this works because of your manipulation of the energy of creation, nothing else. Breathe, focus on the flame, now pull the energy in the room into you, and hold it, breathe out a little and again, release nothing, but pull more into you. Think about the feeling when you are trying to orgasm, that small golden filament in your mind, growing brighter and hotter with every breath, with every stroke until you crash into the inevitable peak. This is no different, pull in the energy and hold it, focus on the flame while you see the connection between the flame in your mind and the wick of the candle glowing brighter. The peak is unstoppable now, those candles will light. When the power is hot enough, just vibrating though your very core, let it go, send that flame down all four filaments, feel the release, just like your orgasm as the flames find their targets and light the candles."

Bets was lost in her words, in the sound of her voice, seeing the flame, feeling the energy build and build, then, just as she had described it hit. Like the most powerful orgasm Bets had ever felt, only instead of the waves of pleasure focused inward, this was a great expulsion of energy outward, down the paths she saw in her mind. She saw the little flames fly down their paths and all four candles ignited. Bets collapsed over onto the bench as the room lit up, her eyes stung as she felt four hands rolling her onto her back. She squinted up into the faces of the women as they held her in their arms, she felt spent and exhilarated and terrified.

The sister cradling her head, brushed her hair away from her face. "Welcome home, Bets."

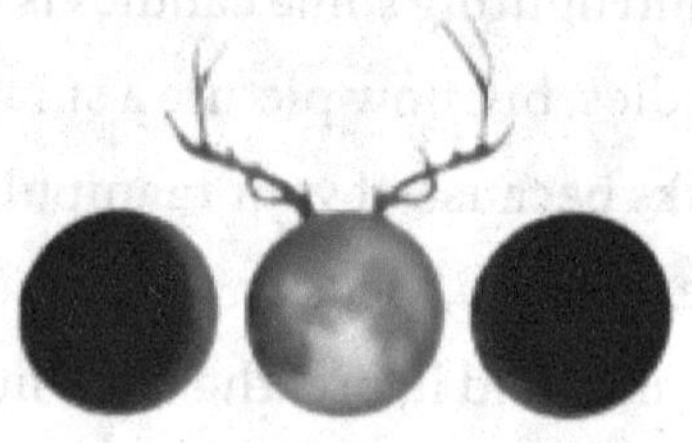

HISTORY WITH THE TWINS

Soon after her awakening, the sisters, Desma and Althea, although she still could not tell which was which, walked her down a short, institutional, hallway to a second room. This room had none of the archaic and primitive construction of the room where she was awakened. It looked very much like a corporate break room. Tables and chairs, a well-furnished and spotless kitchen, everything you would expect. A sign hung over the sink, "Clean up after yourself, we are all mothers here."

The walls were a pastel pink and on the one opposite the sink hung a whiteboard. Several columns of words were written in a neat hand. It only took her a second to realize one column was a grocery list, the other a cleaning schedule. Diane - Monday, Ashanti - Wednesday, Desma - Friday.

One of the sisters brought her a plain white robe to put over the light gown she had awoken in. The other warmed up a bowl of strong broth and a bit of bread, and sat it on the large table in the center of the room.

Bets slid the robe on and asked, "So is this some kind of initiate or neophyte robe? Do I get cooler clothes the more I learn?"

The sisters laughed in unison, and Bets could feel their laughter roll across every cell, like her body was flooded with laughter.

"No, but you didn't exactly arrive here with a suitcase, and we didn't have anything spare lying around in your size."

Bets glanced between the two sisters, both well over six feet tall, and giggled like a child. "What was that? What just happened to me was like I could feel my soul laughing when you two started. Like I had no choice but to laugh."

"That is very astute, you could not have helped it without a lot of warding and some very real experience with emotional hypnosis. Desma and I both possess a gift that allows us to influence people's emotions with our speech. Kind of a forced empathetic response. For most of our lives before coming to Mercer, we believed that Desma could only provoke calm and serenity, and I could only provoke rage and violence. We discovered after being here for a while that we could both effect either, and when we speak in unison it can get very intense, very quickly. Together, we could make the strongest man fall in love, or jump off a bridge, we could cause a riot among librarians or calm a war zone."

That made total sense to her, having felt the power of that laugh, and now, at least until they got up, she knew who was who. The broth was bringing her back to life fast, her natural curiosity piquing.

"How long have you been here at Mercer? How did you get here?"

"We have been here for many years, and we came here much as you did, harvested by Lord Seanchara, although we knew him, and his bride, Elder Valkyrie, by different names then. To us they were The Stag of Red Mountain and the Mother Moon."

"So, you were both forty?" It hardly seemed possible; these girls looked barely forty now. "You were forced to choose?"

Althea seemed confused for a moment, then nodded. "The sacrifice."

Desma finished the thought. "No, Bets, we did not. There are many ways to come to Mercer. There are some things you need to understand. Every single person alive is affected by and can act upon the divine energy. Some people can even manipulate it to an extent. Either unconscious under duress or through great practice and intentional work.

"Some families, all of them direct descendants of the first Mercer witches, have very specific requirements or rituals for deciding how and if they will come to Mercer. Our father's family are all familiar with the lore and many are gifted from birth. They choose members almost at random and summon Lord Seanchara in an elaborate ritual, lasting days. Our mother was a Wilcothe. They gathered at a small church on Red Mountain once a generation. Lord Seanchara and Elder Valkyrie would come to the little church and choose four among them to join Mercer."

Desma paused, considering something unknown to Bets. Althea touched her arm and Desma continued.

"That was the way things were until our generation, when your grandmother Neeny and the pastor's wife, along with a couple of other people attempted to trap and kill Lord Seanchara and Elder Valkyrie, by manipulating her love for him. He made good on his promise and slaughtered every family member in attendance, except the two or three that escaped. Neeny among them. He had already made up his mind about us being chosen, along with two others. He was enraged at the attempt on his lie and had been slaughtering family members for some time when he got to us. He took us, one in each hand and slammed us together, using each of our bodies as a weapon to kill the other."

"Christ," Bets breathed, looking each girl up and down in the fluorescent light, searching for some sign of the trauma Althea described.

Bets started to speak, and Desma cut her off, "Nonsense, you have nothing to apologize for. Lord Seanchara does what is necessary to bring us through the veil as our best selves. While it was a fate I wouldn't wish anyone else to endure, it was exactly what was needed for us."

"As for the sacrifice, the Milburn family has their great bargain. Once a woman in the line turns forty, she is given the opportunity to either sacrifice herself to save her daughter or give up her daughter and continue her blessed life. The women of the Milburn line are potentially some of the most powerful in our great family. They are also some of the most troublesome. This is why Lord Seanchara demands the choice, the woman must prove she can put her own desires aside and be willing to die for another. If she sacrifices the daughter, they are brought to be raised among the Mercer women, to remove them from the influence of their mother's corruption. If the woman, like you did, makes the choice to sacrifice herself in place of her daughter, she will be brought through the veil and begin her life anew."

Bets thought for a long moment absorbing this. If she would have sacrificed Lilly to save herself, it would be her here now, eating soup with these women. She hoped she made the best decision for Lilly. In her heart, she knew she could not live with the thought of her daughter dying for her.

"So, Lilly was in no danger?"

"Other than passing peacefully through the veil and being separated from her family?"

"Okay, that's fair, it's a lot. What of the women who do sacrifice, like Neeny, who give him their daughters?"

"They either continue to sacrifice daughters or daughters of their line until they finally pass from old age, or they see the error of their ways and sacrifice themselves."

"Do they then come here? After they learn that is?" Something was tickling at the back of her mind. Something she should know. A puzzle that she has the pieces for but just hasn't assembled yet.

Desma shook her head. "Not in the way that you think. Once a woman has sacrificed her own child to prevent her death, Lord Seanchara would never permit their entrance into the Mercer family. If they choose again to give themselves when he returns to offer the bargain again, they die, as all do. But they are brought to a special chamber here, where they rest for eternity. Never to pass through the veil and join our family."

"Wait, my grandmother Neeny wasn't a Milburn, she married James Milburn, the preacher. Everyone called him Slim, but she wasn't a Milburn."

"She was. actually. Neeny was born a Milburn. But her parents had moved from their home long before she was born. She married your grandfather, a conman posing as a big tent revivalist. He was on the run from the law in two different states. So, they decided to move back to southern Illinois where her family was from. But since no one there knew them, he took her last name. Pretending he was the son of that wayward cousin who ran off decades before. No one was the wiser. The Milburn family had a reputation in the area for being healers and prophets already. It was easy for him to sell his con, with Neeny's knowledge of folk remedies and his charisma, they made quite a living.

"Not all who join our family are born to the direct lines. Many were rescued by our brothers and sisters. Brought here in death and given the choice to join in the fight. Especially the consorts."

Bets cocked her head slightly at the twins. "Consorts?"

Desma replied this time, "Most of the witches here among us, especially those who work in the field, are assigned consorts. Usually men, who have little, if any, affinity for our gifts, but are trained in protection, combat, politics, whatever the sister may need to aid her in her mission."

"Will I have a consort; will I be in the field one day?"

Althea reached across the table and grabbed her hand. "While it remains to be seen how your gift will manifest and how best it may serve the family, it would be highly irregular if both of those things did not come to pass. Especially given your family's reputation for warriors and generals. You have some big shoes to fill, Bets."

Desma snickered. "About a size ten work boot last I saw Dorothea, and of course it's impossible to tell what size Polly wears, she looks different every time you see her, size six high heel, size ten cowboy boot, and if she isn't walking around in Christopher's giant sandals as a goof once in a while she is missing out!"

That was when the puzzle pieces that had been rattling around her mind fell into place. Bets stared, her mouth agape. "Did you just say Polly? My Polly, my sister is here?"

"Well, considering she is older by a few years, she would probably say you're her Bets, and she hasn't returned here for some time, but yes. Your beautiful sister is counted among our numbers. Also, your aunt Dorothea, your mom's oldest sister, is here."

Desma was beaming at her and started to speak again when Bets jumped up and cut her off.

"Where are they? Why aren't they here? Please, Desma, Althea, you are sisters, I have not seen Polly since I was eight years old. I lost so much, can I see my sister? Please take me to her."

The desperation in her voice was as foreign to her as another language, she was nearly begging these women, who seemingly brought her back from the dead to take her to her sister who apparently had been alive and well all these years. She needed to see her, to know this was real and getting her arms around Polly would be the proof.

Althea squeezed her hand again. "Bets, sister, I understand, but Polly does not live here in Mercer. In fact, she is currently in St. Louis, she has been there for the last three years."

Bets stared in disbelief. "What? Where? Why? I don't understand, how could she be in my city and I not see her, why wouldn't she reach out to me?"

Desma gave her a stern look. "Bets, what exactly would she say? Oh hi, sorry when Grandma Neeny sacrificed me so she could continue her life as a charlatan's wife. I was reborn into a magical city and now spend my time crisscrossing the country saving the innocent and punishing the wicked. Oh, and our aunt is here too along with hundreds of other witches around the world, but please don't tell anyone or write about it!"

Bets stiffened up, as if struck, when Desma yelled the last three words.

She stood up from the table, her chair dumping over backward from the movement. She took a step back, she did not know what she was going to do, trapped as she was, no clue where she was or how to leave or even if she could. She would be damned if she was going to be talked to like a child for wanting to see a long-lost sister who was living her in own fucking city. She started to say just that when a voice boomed into the room from the open doorway behind her.

"Well, look who is up and making friends with the other kids already."

That voice, that was his, it was Seanchara. She spun around but the scene that greeted her made no sense. Through the open door in the hallway stood three men, the first and closest, was the tallest of the three, his head partially obscured by the door frame. Shaggy brown hair hung down to the collar of his perfectly tailored suit, but in his hands, he held the unmistakable walking stick, its black bird's eyes twitching as they shifted focus from Bets to the twins and back. Behind him to the right was a man, almost as tall as Seanchara, his bald head shining black in the fluorescent lights, he wore a silk navy button down shirt over charcoal pinstripe slacks, black braces matched his black wingtip shoes. In his well-manicured hands, he held a silver box, roughly the size of a toaster. To the left of Seanchara stood one of the strangest men Bets had ever seen, and she had spent the better part of the last twenty years doing speaking events and book signings in Cons of all sorts, all over the world.

This man was as tall as Seanchara, but his skin was ivory white, whiter even than the twins; his hair too, was completely white or grey, it was hard to tell in this light. He was wearing what looked like a homemade leather vest, worn and patched, over loose trousers with sandals. In his arms he was carrying what was obviously a small body, draped in a dark shroud. Bets stared at the body. Seanchara spoke again.

"Yes, witches, another daughter of Mercer has emerged."

He turned to the pale man carrying the small body. "Christopher, if you would, the third door on the left please and I will join you momentarily."

He then turned back to the three women. "Bets, I am thrilled to see you up and among the living, although I fear if you continue to tempt the fates with these Lewis twins, you won't remain that way long. Do try to stay alive long enough to prove me right if you would. Desma, Althea, I will join the consorts and complete the ritual and leave the future of Mercer in your capable hands. If you are going to be here a moment or two longer, I will send the consorts back down to say hello and get acquainted with our newest sister after they have fulfilled their obligation to that young lady. I am sure she will find Fredrick and Christopher delightful, and I know you would love to catch up with your cousin a little, perhaps Christopher will be kind enough to cook for everyone. Besides, won't that be good fun, the look on Dorothea and Polly's face when they realize that the guys got to meet her first. It will serve them right; I had just sat down to my supper with Elder Valkyrie when they summoned me right out of my chair. Farewell, ladies."

Seanchara turned and strolled down the hallway. Bets turned to face Desma and Althea, intent on apologizing for her outburst and hostility, when she saw them—they were holding hands and staring at the empty hallway. She stepped closer, and Althea's eyes returned to focus on her.

Bets moved close to both of them. "Are you okay? I am sorry about losing my temper, what's going on?"

After a couple agonizingly long seconds, Desma spoke. "We have not been this close to Lord Seanchara since—" she trailed off.

"Since your death?" Bets asked gently.

"Yes."

"Is that what he looks like? When he came to me, he was small, ape-like, and alien."

Althea answered this time, "Lord Seanchara appears as whatever vision is needed to accomplish his goals. When he appeared as the Stag, he was much larger, he would not have been able to stand straight in this room with a set of antlers wider than this doorway, cloaked in animal skins. The most common sightings by Mercer sisters are the form that you saw when you first encountered him. The form you saw today is generally only used when he harvests children or deals with consorts. Today appears to be both. He is exceptionally gentle where children are concerned, and he loves Christopher above all others. No one but him and perhaps Elder Valkyrie knows why. When they return, they will tell us more about how they came to be assisting Lord Seanchara with his duties today and why they aren't protecting Polly and Dorthea, or being protected by Polly and Dorthea is probably more accurate. But let's find you some real clothes and grab some supplies for Christopher to cook with. Can't have you meeting your new family in a bathrobe."

Desma grabbed a marker and scrawled on the whiteboard, *Gentlemen, make yourselves at home, we ran for supplies so we could pretend to cook until Sugar throws us out of the kitchen and does it right. Fredrick, please don't let him leave, it has been too long, and we need the company. Plus, we need you to get word to the ladies that Bets is awake.* Behind this, she drew a funny little smiley face and a heart. Bets could not help but smile.

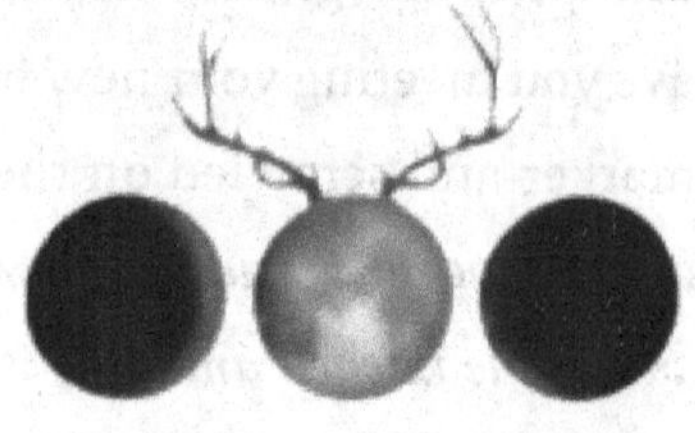

DINNER AND A FUNERAL

As they rounded the corner heading back to the kitchen, the smell of garlic and herbs almost took Bets off her feet. She put her hand on Althea's shoulder, and her stomach growled. "What is that?"

"That, Sister Bets, is Sugarfoot."

"Ok, well that didn't help much, but lord if he makes anything that smells that good, I am in."

Desma laughed. "Sugarfoot, or Sugar, is our little cousin Christopher. He is Polly's consort."

Bets slowed down a little. "Are they?"

"A couple," Althea finished. No, though no one can tell you why. Everyone can tell they are crazy about one another. But for whatever reason they refuse to admit it to themselves or one another."

Desma leaned in like a middle schooler with a secret. "I wouldn't mention it, though. Christopher is sensitive and protective about your sister. It wouldn't do to get on his bad side right off the jump. Besides, you do not want to miss out on family dinner!"

Bets followed the twins silently the rest of the way. There was a lot to take in, but this. She was about to have dinner with the person in the world closest to the sister she was sure was long dead and gone. She didn't even know what to ask. She had to admit this had made her more nervous than anything else so far.

They entered the little dining area to find the table set for five and the two men already busy in the kitchen. The twins set their groceries down on the counter and ran to their cousin. The resemblance between the cousins was eerie.

She walked to the other man. He was tall, dark-skinned, handsome, appearing fit, and a little older. Although how old Bets could not guess. He had taken off his suit jacket and rolled up his sleeves. Her immediate impression was refinement, elegant refinement. She extended her hand. "Hi, I'm Colleen, Bets, if you like. It's a pleasure to meet you."

He made direct eye contact while shaking her hand, his big brown eyes seeming to draw her in. "Fredrick Sapp, ma'am, pleasure is mine. Would you like to sit? May I offer you a cup of coffee or tea?"

He pulled a chair out for her, and his smile radiated a warmth that Bets immediately found comforting and disarming. "I would love a cup of coffee, but I can get it, Fredrick. If you like I can make you one as well."

Fredrick smiled that beautiful, earnest smile.

"Thank you, but I am afraid, by the time you find your way around this Lewis kitchen we may both expire for lack of caffeine, besides, if your Aunt Dorthea heard that I was letting you make coffee for me, she might take great offense. You see, she makes a cup of coffee that bears a strong resemblance to motor oil, so I always insist on making the coffee. I have told her for more than twenty years that it is something I take great pleasure in and if I let you make me one, she may find out that I would rather arm wrestle Lord Seanchara than drink a cup of the swill she makes."

Bets grinned so wide she feared her face might split.

A soft voice from across the kitchen, like the strum of an antique string instrument. "Well, that explains a lot."

Sugarfoot had broken away from his cousin's embrace and moved to her. He extended his hand; she shook it, amazed at how her hand disappeared into his. She had never met a man so large, he had to be seven feet tall. Broad across the shoulders and visibly muscular. His skin was as pale as a marble statue, and his eyes were so dark she could not tell iris from pupil. His hair was pulled back in a ponytail and tied with a strip of leather braided with beads.

"Colleen, it is so wonderful to meet you. You can call me Christopher, or Sugar, I am not partial to either. M and Dorthea are going to be so mad at us for getting to see you first."

"M?" Bets asked.

"Polly, like most everyone in or around Mercer, chooses to use an alias. It wouldn't serve anyone to be running around using the name of a girl who died thirty years ago when that girl still has family that may run across her in the normal course of their life."

Bets nodded, understanding. "What about Dorthea? Is she using an alias as well?"

The Lewis twins lowered their heads and snickered, Fredrick cleared his throat politely and busied himself emptying a grocery bag and trying hard not to look up from his task. Sugar looked around and rolled his eyes. "Thanks, guys, way to have my back."

Bets smiled and held out her hands questioningly.

"Dorthea is Dorthea, she keeps her own council on anything not one hundred percent related to Mercer business. She is a respected general and leader in the fight against the evils of the world. Even among the Elders of Mercer, who have seen centuries, the name Dorthea Milburn is spoken with profound respect. And more than a healthy dose of fear, by anyone other than the most powerful among us." Althea was no longer laughing, and Fredrick looked grim indeed.

Fredrick spoke in turn, "They are right, ma'am, your aunt, Dorthea, my sister witch for many years now, is a formidable adversary. She is skilled in many forms of magic. She has a mind as sharp as a razor and a spirit and body hardened by countless battles, and all well-earned jibes about her stubborn and gruff demeanor aside. Dorthea Milburn has probably saved more innocent lives than the rest of us combined ever will. She is the high-water mark by which many of us judge ourselves. We give her a bit of a hard time, but it is out of admiration more than anything else. Her commitment to the cause we serve is unwavering and her willingness to engage any enemy on any ground is known to all of Mercer."

Bets smiled at Fredrick, feeling an immense pride at his description of this family member, though she had never met her and until a few hours ago, knew nothing more about her than she was an older sister of her mom who died during childhood.

"Thank you for that, Fredrick." She reached out and touched the man on the shoulder.

"Your respect for her is obvious and that was important for me to hear. My life has just been turned upside down. I know all of you have been through it already, but I am still getting my feet underneath me, and hearing about all the good my aunt has done is good for me. I need to know all this craziness is worth it. I feel like I have been just accepting all of it because there was no way to not accept it, but somehow, having a goal, and having a standard set is what I need. Dorthea is the best. Then learning enough, being good enough, to one day stand next to her is the goal, and goals I can do."

Fredrick smiled that warm smile again. "Remember what I said earlier about arm-wrestling Lord Seanchara? Perhaps start with that as a more realistic goal."

The tension in the room faded with their laughter, and Sugar and Fredrick got busy cooking.

Sitting later over a plate of amazing roast chicken with mushroom risotto, Bets couldn't hold her questions any longer. "Christopher, I am dying to know, what is she like, M?"

Desma and Althea both tilted their heads in his direction, eager to hear how he described her.

"She is smart and tough, dedicated to the cause. She doesn't like to be idle; she is always starting a new project as soon as the end is in sight on her current one. So, she doesn't rest as much as she should. Her gift is based in glamour, and it makes it difficult for her to feel connected in real ways to people."

Bets asked, "Glamour?"

Althea answered, dabbing a touch of garlic butter from her lips with a napkin. "M can change not only her own appearance but how people perceive almost anything around them. She can alter your perception of reality to a near-infinite degree. You can be staring right at her, and she can shift and change her appearance so rapidly and effectively that you will not even be aware of the process, only of your confusion and inability to interpret what you are seeing. So not only will she look different every time you see her, but she can have you running through doors that lead only to walls, walking down empty sidewalks that are actually four lanes of heavy traffic. Fighting monsters that don't exist."

Fredrick chimed in, "Or worse, not aware of a raging Christopher headed right for you. Horrible way to go, one moment you're walking along looking at the pretty flowers then all of a sudden, you're smashed under the weight of an angry giant." He grinned at Sugar, who rolled his eyes and shoveled another fork full of chicken into his mouth.

"Does she know about me? I mean, everything?" Bets looked at Althea.

Sugar spoke up, "She does, she knows you are here and nearing the time of awakening. She is not aware that you are sitting here now with us. She also knows about what happened the day you were harvested. We had a case that brought us very close to Lilly, and as a result, she became aware of some things. Others she was informed by our social work team from the area. They let her know so she would not be surprised if things went a different way. It caused a bit of a stir if I have to be honest. She wanted to be here for your awakening, to be the one to mentor you and bring you into your gift. She and Dorthea went more than a few rounds over it. But ultimately Dorthea was right. M is too personally invested in being close to you, in seeing you, and connecting with you. There was no way she could be objective about the decisions that must be made during this process. We haven't spoken about it for some time, but I know she is always thinking of you. She very much wants to see you, to talk with you."

Bets stared at Sugar. "Is Lilly ok? Please, I know I can't go back, but is Lilly ok?"

Fredrick reached across the table and grasped her hand. "She is fine, those same social workers dropped her off with Cecil last night. Something happened to Kay's father, a very evil entity took control of him and made him try to hurt the girls. Lilly showed quite a bit of innate ability under duress and saved her own life through some pretty powerful magic before we got to her. She got to meet Dorthea, M, Christopher, and myself. Although she doesn't know who we are, or yet who the ladies are. But according to them, she was extremely intuitive about it and could tell there was a connection between them. "

"Todd, Kay, are they ok?"

"I am afraid Todd did not survive the ordeal, Kay will be ok eventually. Whenever the ladies here deem her ready to return to us."

Bets' head snapped to the twins. "The body, that was Kay, that tiny body you were carrying. Is she dead, what happened? Can you take me to her?"

Fredrick again squeezed her hand. "Kay will be ok, she will pass through the veil, just as each one of us did, and she will join us in our great fight. Kay was left orphaned; her choice was to live that life or to join us. Dorthea and M summoned and petitioned Lord Seanchara on her behalf and he accepted her into Mercer. The harvest is complete, and she will lie now in The Chambers of the Veil, until Althea and Desma determine it is time for her awakening. Once she is awake, you may see her, if the twins allow it. But to disturb her now would be disastrous. Hearing your voice, feeling your presence, even through the veil of death may draw her back before her time. Never does that end well."

Bets nodded her head slowly. So much had happened, so much to process. But more than that, she was different, all the fight had gone out of her. The stubborn streak, the obstinate bull-headed woman with something to prove, was nowhere to be found. In its place, a quiet curiosity, a steady fascination. She wasn't sure how she felt about that change yet. But at least she was alive to process and examine it.

The sound of a great bell pealing brought her from her contemplation, she looked at her companions, her mood still somewhat lighthearted. "Okay, is that some kind of curfew or meal signal?" she grinned.

Sugar and Fredrick jumped up and sprinted from the room and the twins were pulling her roughly from her seat. "What the fuck, Althea?"

"That's the funeral bell, a sister or brother has fallen and has returned home," said a very shaken Althea as they ran out of the room, pulling Bets behind them.

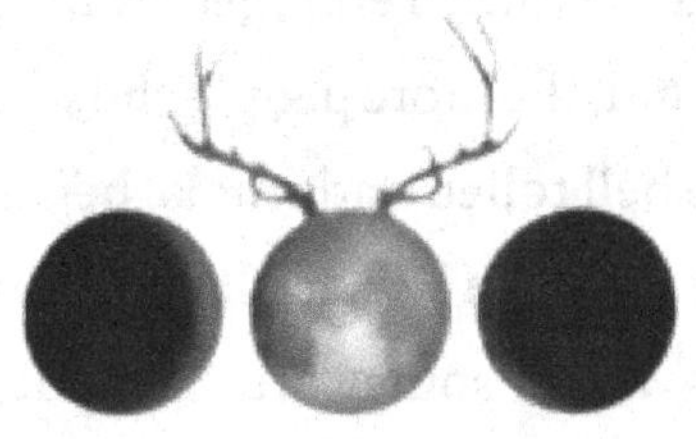

A Song for a Hero

The hallways were a blur as they ran, she lost sight of the guys quickly, but Desma and Althea let her keep up with them until they passed through a low archway and emerged outdoors in a large courtyard. Several buildings surrounded a central fountain and flower garden. She caught a glimpse of Fredrick as he rounded the garden and back out of sight. She pulled free of the girls and sprinted in that direction, the twins, a full six inches taller than her, passed her and kept running. By the time she caught up to the group, the men were standing in front of a group of older women nodding and speaking in low tones. She watched as they left the group and each took a place near a wooden A-frame.

The twins had moved off the side near another group of five or six older women. Bets hurried toward them, determined to remain as un-obtrusive as possible and just follow the lead of Desma and Althea.

Dozens more men and women emerged from various doorways. The more Bets looked around, the more people she saw. Just appearing from every direction as the bell tolled and smoke began to fill the courtyard.

Inside the wooden A-frame was a platform suspended by ropes, it hovered over a pit or well of some sort. Laid out, under the starry sky was a body, or at least it looked like a body, covered in a white sheet with beautiful floral patterns embroidered into it. Torches burned every few feet throughout the area illuminating everything with a shaky orange light.

A woman stood on a short stone block before the platform. She looked to be in her late seventies, she wore a loose-fitting, white robe and her long grey hair flowed down over her shoulders. Somewhere in the distance drums began and the flames from the torches shot into the night. The woman screamed, a sound full of rage and anguish. She dropped her robe, her naked body cast in firelight, covered in tattoos. She screamed again and rubbed what looked like a combination of ash and oil across her face and chest, as she did several of her tattoos lit up with a light all their own.

"Mathew Weems!" she called out, her voice raw and cracking.

"Mathew Weems." The screaming response from the gathered crowd.

She spun in a circle, throwing her hands into the air and screaming as she did. Flames shot from her hands and tears streamed down her face. "Brothers and sisters of Mercer, here in the Temple of the Mother, lies Mathew Weems. A warrior, a brother, a lover, and a friend. Mathew Weems."

An undercurrent of musicality cut through the obvious pain in her voice. This wasn't a eulogy, she was singing. Bets had never heard anything so tragic, so beautiful.

"Eighty-nine years, eighty-nine years, he served our family."

"Mathew Weems," the crowd responded in the same musical tone.

"Eighty-nine years, he saved the innocent of the world."

"Mathew Weems."

"Eighty-nine years, the enemies of the innocent fell beneath his blade."

"Mathew Weems."

"Eighty-nine years, he held the hands of the frightened as they faced their biggest fears."

"Mathew Weems."

"Eighty-nine years, he taught his brothers and his sons, the ways of our family."

"Mathew Weems."

She paused, catching her breath, and raising her hands to the sky.

"Now, our brave brother has fallen, protecting the ones he loved from a monster in the night."

"I swear to you brothers and sisters, in front of the Mother, in front of the Stag and the Mother Moon, as my love rejoins the Divine Energy in its great journey. I punished his killer, I boiled the skin from his body, I clawed out his eye, and I dug my hooked tongue into his brain."

At this, the rest of her tattoo work lit up. "Even now, as he licks his wounds in the belief that he succeeded, he succeeded only in leading me to his origin, to the power behind him. A power that will fall before me when I avenge my brave lover."

She looked down at Sugar and Fredrick on either side of the frame. "Brothers, please, help me, lower our brother into the eternal."

At this, Sugar and Fredrick rose, and Bets noticed both men had stripped as well. She thought to ask Althea later about the tradition but at the moment, she was enrapt. The two men untied great ropes, thicker than their arms, and began paying out slack. Their movements were so perfectly timed that the platform on which Mathew Weems rested lowered without tilting in the slightest.

The woman danced again on the stone platform. She spun circle after circle, her hands raised to the sky crying his name, tattoos glowing, over and over. "Mathew Weems, Mathew Weems, Mathew Weems, Mathew Weems." She stopped spinning her arms out wide, facing the pit, Fredrick and Sugar standing off the side, and she screamed one final time. "I love you, Mathew." She slammed her head back and howled to the sky as flames shot from her hands and into the pit. Years of love and trust and memories were carried on that sound and in those flames. Fire rose from the pit, a column of flame taller than any of the surrounding buildings. She searched for Fredrick and Sugar in the glare, scared for them, but they had returned to their kneeling position. Within moments the flames from the pit subsided, Bets watched as a small woman with short, wiry, hair helped the older woman down from the platform and wrapped her in the robe.

Bets turned to Althea and Desma. Behind them, above the crowd, she saw the silhouette of what could only be Lord Seanchara, bigger than any man could be, atop his head a great expanse of antlers, on his arm, a woman nearly as tall as him, but much slighter, on her head the triple moon. "The Stag and The Mother Moon," she muttered to herself as Althea waved her over. She glanced up again to the balcony where she had seen them, and they were gone.

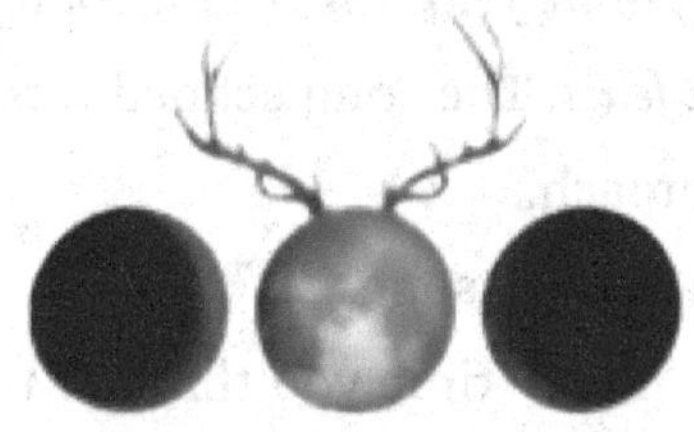

May You Never Forget His Name

I t could have been the understatement of a lifetime to say Bets felt overwhelmed. She was standing between Althea and Desma, in the courtyard of one of the most impressive buildings she had ever seen. She studied the walls, carved stone and wood, every inch of its enormous face covered in intricate designs. Faces, gargoyles, and detailed scenes depicting people and acts she did not recognize.

Movement caught her eye as Sugar and Fredrick approached them, the men had put their pants back on and carried the rest of their clothes. Groups of people milled around, but Bets noticed the looks as Sugar and Fredrick passed, everyone acknowledged them in some way or another. A nod, a word, a couple of stops for hugs. She could not tell if it was related to the duties they had just performed for the dead man,

Mathew Weems, eighty-nine years, he held the hands of the frightened as they faced their biggest fears. The song echoed through her mind as she watched the men approach.

She turned to Desma. "The song, it…"

Desma cut her off, "Every time you think of this moment, you will remember his song, his story. The spell she cast was not for him. It was for us, who may or may not have known him, to learn his name and what he did for the family and the mission. It also helps to start the grieving process for her and Bast. Every witch, every consort, in the Mercer family heard that song and we all know it now. It is part of our living memory, the bond that holds us all together."

Bets could feel the song flowing through her mind, becoming a part of her as Desma spoke.

"We know there is no afterlife. There is no heaven, hell, or great beyond. When he passed from this life, the spark that made that body into Mathew Weems fled this world and rejoined the divine energy of creation. The only way we know how to be eternal is to be remembered by the living. So, we sing their songs, we remember their stories, and they become part of the Mercer lore. His face and deeds will be etched into the great stone faces of the Temple of the Mother that you see before you, and we will sing his song for as long as Mercer remains."

Bets lowered her head, staring at the ground. She said nothing, only let the moment and the thought of Mathew Weems pass over her. She found that as she sang the song in her mind, she began to see a picture of the man. A young soldier on a boat being tossed around by waves, gunfire rattling in the distance. Older now, carrying a small boy over his shoulder as a barn burned in the background. She saw him in a big open arena sparing with a young boy, a boy with skin as white as snow, hands, and feet comically large, as he circled Mathew Weems looking for an opening.

She saw him slowly dancing on a bridge over a stream in the woods, moonlight shining on him as a woman feverishly pulled his clothes from his body in a moment of passion. More and more the waves of memory washed over her, and then, Mathew in a fight for his life against a shadowy form in a dark garage. The quiet determination as he tried to fight off the attacker. The pain, the sorrow, when he realized it was over, the sound of the stomps as the memory faded.

She swayed and would have fallen had strong hands not held her upright. She opened her eyes, red with tears and rage. She was looking up into Sugar's face. "Bastard, I hope he heals so that she can hurt him again."

A voice from behind, soft, but commanding. "Christopher, is that our new sister? Seems she got the full force of Hannah's song. Help her to me if you would."

Bets swayed in his arms, her mind a blur of images and emotions. Everything she had seen since she had awoken that morning, the last day of her old life, the funeral, the barrage of memories that were not her own.

Sugar led her on her unsteady legs toward a small group of people. Bets felt her legs go limp as her head whirled, like being dizzy drunk, waiting for that last big spin before you passed out. Only his strong arms held her upright. She found she could no longer see what was in the world around her. Only the memories of Mathew Weems, covering her mind in the fog of his long life. No longer was it just his accomplishments, but his entire life, his mother and father, the farm, the garden.

She felt something warm and wet swipe across her forehead, then a whispering all around her. Then a wind was blowing, pushing her head back. She heard a voice cut through the din.

"That's it, Ashanti, blow the fog away from her mind, keep going until she comes back to us. Feel the fog clear, Bets, you listen now, walk into the wind, I know those memories are powerful things, girl, but let

Ashanti clear your mind. They will always be there, but that's enough nostalgia for one day, love."

Bets focused on the feeling of the wind in her face and walked into it as she was told. Slowly, the vision of Mathew's memories began to fade. When she could finally see with her own eyes, she realized Sugar had been holding her up, standing behind her, his arms wrapped around her waist.

When she felt like she could stand on her own, she tapped him on the arm. "Thank you, Sugar."

Bets took a deep breath, she still felt Mathew's memories below the surface, but they were no longer overwhelming her. She looked at the two women standing before her. One was younger, possibly in her mid-twenties. The other was older, but Bets could not tell how old, sixties, maybe early seventies. They both wore beautiful robes, silks in crimson, gold, and bright blue. The older woman stepped close to her and handed her ornate walking stick to Sugar. She took Bets' face in both her hands and drew her close. Bets was shocked at the strength of those small delicate-looking hands. She looked into Bets' eyes, first one and then the other. The torchlight reflected in the woman's large brown eyes made it look as if her eyes were on fire. A moment, then two, it felt like an eternity. Then the woman released her.

"Much better now, young sister?"

Bets tried to place her accent but could not. "Yes, ma'am, thank you both." She nodded to the younger girl. "How did you do that? I, I thought I had lost my mind, I couldn't find my way through his memories."

"No, child, I don't imagine that you could. The funeral song is powered by the witch. You had the unfortunate timing of only being awake a few hours. No idea how to ward yourself or protect your mind from that kind of spell. Add that to being this close to one of our most potent sisters grieving a man she loved more than life. Mathew was not just her consort, they had been married for many years, and I suspect had been lovers since they were young. Even I took an emotional beating from Hannah's funeral song. That's part of the beauty of it, we not only share in his life so that he will live forever in our memories, but also her grief. We take much of it into our collective minds and spirits to share her pain and support our sister. It is one of the things that helps to bind us together, shared memories, shared grief, and shared joy."

The woman led Bets to a small ledge, Sugar, and the younger girl Ashanti, were close behind.

"My name is Niri; you will find many here who call me Mother Mercer as well. I want you to do something with me. I know our sisters had you light the candles this morning, right?"

"Yes, ma'am."

"Good, good. That saves us a step now. Bets, close your eyes, I want you to open your spirit up. Search like you did this morning. But do not search for a goal. Only to feel, to see."

Bets closed her eyes and began to breathe just like before when she was trying to get a picture of the room. Steady, in and out. It only took a moment before she began to see an image in her mind. A few feet in front of her, Sugar, holding Niri's walking stick. Ashanti was close by his side, staring intently at her. Niri on her right. Then further out a handful of people were milling about, all either watching them or slowly making their way to where they were sitting.

"Do you see us?"

"I do."

"Now, look deeper, with your spirit. You are seeing the physical manifestations of the Divine Energy of Creation, now look for it. Look at Christopher and see him as we see him. See the creator in him. See the power of all creation as it flows through him and gives him life."

It started slowly, in the blurry indistinct picture in her mind, the image of Sugar suddenly lit up. Dazzlingly white, with beautiful streaks of yellow and green flowing through it. She could still see him, but these colors and feelings flowed through and around him. She could see the lines of colors reach all the way to her chest, and when she focused on that line, she found she could feel him, his presence there. As she watched, in awe of what she was seeing, she noticed more lines extending from him and from her. Thin bands led away from her chest and further into her fields of vision. Three of them extended to the left of her. She followed them to their origin, or termination, she could not tell. Standing in a tight group watching her intently she saw Desma, Althea, and Fredrick. The twins shared a band that was the size of their torso. Each one also had a large band of brilliant blue and green that led back to Sugar. The colors coming from Fredrick were darker, rich deep red, and purple with streaks of brilliant white light. She felt herself grinning as she followed the light back to Sugar. She glanced at Niri and her breath caught in her chest.

The light passing through the small woman shined in every color imaginable, and silhouetted her in a rainbow image of herself, twice as tall. Bands of light shot from her in every direction, all sizes, and colors. Hundreds, thousands of them.

"My God, the connections, so beautiful."

Niri put a hand on hers. "Now look back at your connection to Christopher, feel it. Extend your feelings down that line until you can tell where he is and what he is doing without looking at him. Feel the connection and let it guide you."

Bets threw her head back and laughed. "Your voice, oh Sugar, that is beautiful. I can hear his spirit singing. I have never heard anything so incredible."

"So now you know why we all love him so much." Althea was standing next to Sugar with her arms around him.

Sugar grinned like the cat that ate the canary. "You love me because I am the best cook in Mercer."

Niri raised an eyebrow. "Careful, son, my paella has been causing divorces since before the American Revolution and Mama Rosie's birria once made a Senator run naked across the Capital lawn."

Sugar raised an eyebrow and bowed gracefully, his long hair brushing the ground. "Mother Mercer. It is more likely your beauty that has caused divorces around the world, and Mama Rosie gave that man neroli, musk, and devil's shoestring in his birria and told him he was a sasquatch running free in the great woods."

Niri shook her finger at Sugar like a scolding grandmother. "Don't you forget that, Sugar. You may be handsome, charming, a good cook, and a better singer, but you make me mad, and I will have my new friend here turn you into a cockatiel."

Althea and Desma spoke in unison, "But then you would have to argue with her sister about who got the cage."

The laughter from all around caused Bets to open her eyes, and she found that the images she was seeing in her mind had faded. Like a transparency overlayed onto the real world. But they were still there. She focused on them, and they became more intense, then faded back to barely visible.

"I can still see it, even with my eyes open, I can still see the energy there, I can still hear his spirit singing. Can I really turn him into a cockatiel?"

Niri put her arm around her and hugged her tight to her side. "That is a question I cannot wait to see you answer on your own. Now you have also learned why we don't let you drive for a while. It takes some time to incorporate the vision into your reality and we don't want you running anyone over because Fredrick started laughing and you got distracted by all the pretty colors. But that is enough learning for tonight. Let us join the rest of our family in the Hall of the Elders. Hannah needs our love now, and I am sure you have had your fill of new experiences for the day."

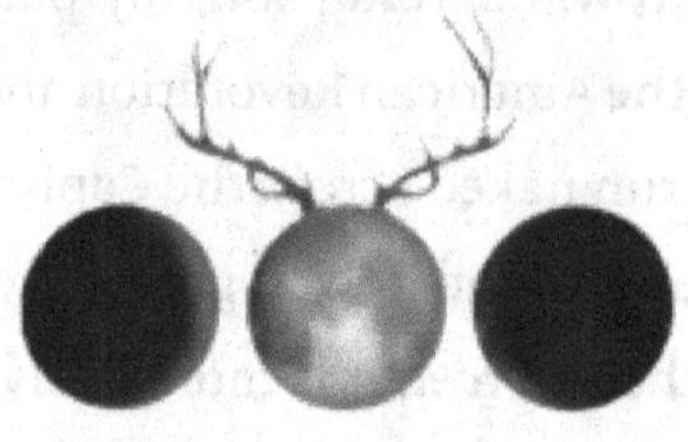

TEA AND CANDY

The dining hall inside the Temple of the Mother was one of the largest rooms in Mercer. Rows and rows of tables and chairs lined its great floor. At a glance, Bets estimated you could put more than a thousand in here comfortably. She had followed the procession into the room. Niri led the way, holding delicately onto Sugar's great forearm as he led her into the hall. Ashanti and Fredrick followed close behind. Bets herself walked between Desma and Althea.

A balcony ran the circumference of the giant oval room. Twenty-five, maybe thirty feet off of the ground. Bets could see many hallways, from the ground floor, and the second leading off into the building. There were people everywhere. Possibly one hundred, maybe more. Some sat in small groups at tables, some on the balcony, some milling about. Bets saw wine glasses and plates with various foods. She was reminded of the mess still to clean up in the little kitchen, she thought of mentioning it to Desma or Althea, but this did not seem the time. She would volunteer to tidy up when they were done here. That would help ground her a little. She could use a task, a job to do, and nothing like a little clean up to help center herself.

She came back to the moment as Hannah came walking up to their group. A flash of memory as Bets pictured Hannah throughout the years, the memories threatening to come rushing back in and over-whelm her again. She took two steady breaths and was able to push them back down.

The woman walked straight up to Niri and wrapped her in a fierce hug. Niri pulled the woman close and cradled her head on her shoulder. Bets could hear her speaking softly. "Hannah, I am so sorry about Mathew, he was the best of men. We owe so much to him, and to you. Please accept my condolences and whatever support we can offer."

Hannah pulled back; her fierce eyes red with tears. Bets could feel the anger coming off of the woman. It was jarring. She couldn't just tell the woman was angry, she could feel it, like it was pushing into her, making her angry. She wanted to track this man down and rip him to pieces, she wanted to hold him down while Hannah cut her pounds of flesh from him, one for every year of love between her and Mathew.

She jumped when Desma touched her shoulder. "Breathe, Bets, con-trol it or you'll lose yourself again."

Bets nodded at her, but there was no fear or confusion in the look this time, only the slightly dimming rage she felt at the man that had killed Mathew Weems, and the bond of grief she shared with Hannah.

When she refocused her vision, Niri and Hannah were standing side by side, staring at her. She bowed her head. "Apologies, I did not mean to interrupt. Seems I keep making a spectacle of myself tonight."

"None needed." Hannah was walking towards her. Bets allowed her vision to open a little, to see the energy flowing through Hannah and connecting her to the rest of creation. A deep rich blue emanated from her, with streaks of crimson and black.

"That was a neat trick for a witch that has only been alive for a few hours."

"I'm not sure I know what you are talking about."

Bets looked to Desma and Althea for explanation, but they just stared.

Hannah walked uncomfortably close to her, eyes locked onto Bets'. Bets had seen the power she wielded, the fire. She had felt the rage and energy coursing through this woman. Beyond that, she did not want to make enemies of people when she wasn't sure what she had done wrong. No one spoke, no one breathed as the two women stood staring. Bets tried to relax, to extend toward the woman all the love and goodwill she could. She had meant no harm and had no idea what was going on.

As she opened her vision, she could see lines of energy coming off Hannah, reaching toward her. Almost like tentacles they stretched and probed. Then the moment passed, and Hannah smiled warmly at her.

Bets saw the tendrils of energy recede and rejoin the light surrounding Hannah. She extended her hand. "Colleen Carter, ma'am, or Bets if you would like. It's a pleasure to meet you, my condolences on the loss of your husband."

Hannah pushed her hand aside and wrapped her arms around Bets. "Thank you. I know you have been through a lot today, wake from the dead only to experience a funeral before your first sunset in Mercer."

"Yes, ma'am, it has been a bit overwhelming."

Hannah took her by the hand, and led her to a nearby table, the group followed. All except for Ashanti, who leaned close to Niri and whispered in her ear, then walked off down one of the many hallways.

Everyone began to sit. Hannah motioned for Bets to sit next to her, across from Niri. Everyone else filled in places at the table except Sugar and Fredrick. Bets looked up at Fredrick and he bowed.

"Sisters, if you will excuse us, Christopher and I will see to tea service for everyone."

Hannah acknowledged him with a sad look. "Thank you, Fredrick. Christopher, you as well. Thank you for your service to Mathew tonight. He would have been honored to know it was the two of you who attended his body in its last moments. He loved you, boys, I think…"

She paused, collecting herself, steeling against a moment of grief. "I think, knowing you two were out there, doing what you do, was one of the main reasons he was okay with us retiring. Knowing that you were carrying on the fight, made him feel as if a small part of himself was still out there. Still protecting, still saving. Still doing what's right no matter the cost."

Sugar and Fredrick bowed their heads, both men fighting back tears.

Sugar spoke, his soft musical voice drifting across the noise of the hall. "The honor was ours, neither one of us would be the men we are today without Mathew."

"When it comes your turn to teach, remember what he did for you. For so many others. You make sure he lives forever, you pass his lessons on when your time comes to serve in the Temple, and you live long enough to get there. Now if you would not mind, I have a little teaching of my own to do here."

She glanced at Bets, who was staring wide eyed at the interaction. "And I would be so grateful if you could slip a nip or two of that Grand Marnier Cuvee Du Centenaire into my tea. I know Alpine and Stasis keep a bottle back there in the pantry where they think no one will remember it. If they try to give you the triple sec or that Gran Gala garbage you twist one of Alpine's ears until he coughs up the good stuff."

Fredrick smiled through the sadness in his dark eyes. "As you wish."

And the men headed off toward the back of the hall.

Bets started to turn to Niri, hoping to get some reassurance. Instead, she saw only concern there. Alone with these women now, Bets suddenly felt very small, very insignificant.

Hannah took a deep breath and released it in a slow stream. "Do you know what you did over there, Bets? Could you feel what happened?"

Bets looked back and forth between Niri and Hannah; she glanced at the twins, each looking grim faced and more than a little uncomfortable.

"I do not, I saw you standing there with Mother, I opened my vision up, just slightly. When I did, I saw the beautiful aura of energy surrounding and flowing through you. Then I could feel the rage and anger in you. Deep, searing anger. How badly you wanted to punish the man who killed Mathew, then I wanted to punish him with you. I could feel your rage, your pain, and I wanted to avenge it. I started to think of all the ways we could end this man. I thought that it was a side effect of what Mother Mercer said. Being that close to you during the funeral song before I knew how to guard myself or ward?" She looked questioningly at Niri.

"Yes, ward, that is correct." Niri reached her hand across the table and held Bets' hand gently, reassuringly.

Bets marveled at how openly affectionate everyone she had met so far had been. They hugged and touched, held hands. It was a physical closeness that she had never been comfortable with her entire life. But here, with these women, it seemed like the most natural, gentlest, thing in the world.

Hannah continued, "Let me tell you what we saw and felt and hopefully it will both put your mind at ease and explain my concern. I felt you reach out when I first stood before Mother Mercer. Gentle at first, the kind of clumsy exploration I would expect from a witch newly born. A bit rude perhaps as it was not passive reading, more of a probe. Think of the difference between noticing a pretty bird on your windowsill and grabbing it and pulling at its wings to see how it works inside."

"Oh Hannah, I'm…"

"Don't, it will take way longer than it needs to, and I have taken no offence, you just need to understand what happened so we can figure out what to do next. As soon as I felt you probing, a pulling started, I could feel you pulling at the energy around me. Specifically at the pain and rage in my spirit. When I realized what was going on, I just observed a moment as the rage and anger left my body, pulled into you. Almost immediately we could all feel it. You were getting larger. Not your body, but your spirit, the energy that surrounds and flows through you. You were pulling my pain and rage into yourself, and it was feeding you. Almost like a battery. The angrier you got on my behalf the more brightly you burned."

Bets looked between the two women. "Is that something bad?"

Niri asked, "Do you remember how you came out of it?"

"I am not sure what you mean, I remember everything. I was just angry for a second or two, then Desma touched me and broke my focus."

"Bets, you were in that state for almost a minute siphoning power off of Hannah. I signaled to Desma to reach through the trance to you and try to gently bring you out of it, so you did not explode and hurt someone or yourself. Ashanti put up a ward and shield so if you did, it would minimize the damage to the temple or those around who could not protect themselves like Fredrick or Christopher."

"I could have hurt someone, I am so sorry, I don't remember Desma saying anything. I don't understand."

Bets was completely lost again. In what seemed like the span of a day she had gone from a confident, savvy, warrior of a woman to this unsure, apologetic, crying mess. Maybe she should have chosen death when it was offered. Who had she become, what had she done?

Hannah turned in her chair to face her. "Listen, Bets, this isn't a gift we have never seen before, you are not the first witch by far to be gifted as a syphon and empath. Your sister is a tactile empath, she can read emotions through touch and is able to manipulate the fabric of reality in impressive ways. You aren't even the first syphon of this generation. We know how to train and teach you. We know what the framework of wards will work best to allow you to control it. We know how to teach you to focus its release. You will likely become a very powerful witch one day.

"But you cannot give in to self-doubt. You will be fine, we will be fine, everything will be just as it is meant to be. What we need to do is get you started training so that you aren't standing next to an angry woman at Starbucks and end up blowing the roof off the building. Not to mention the pain in the ass it is to get filled with every single emotion of everyone you come in contact with. That will get old very quickly. People's feelings are messy and confusing and that will affect your casting and spell work if you cannot control who you pull energy from and how much."

"Does it hurt the person I am pulling from? Did I hurt you?"

"You did not, other than pulling my rage from me and making me face my grief without the barrier of rage and revenge to protect me. But any therapist worth their salt will tell you that's a good thing. As far as hurting someone, I guess it might be possible to weaken them to the point where they cannot recover, I have never heard of it. But I suppose it would be possible. More than likely, you would over run your own warding and focus first and blow your top. Long before you could permanently drain someone. Remember, the energy of creation is infinite."

"So, what do I do next?"

Niri answered, "Tomorrow, the Council of Elders will convene and decide who will mentor you and what that training will look like."

Hannah interjected in a conspiratorial whisper, "For now, we enjoy our tea and some eye candy, the men are coming back."

Niri grinned. "Hannah, those are children."

Bets blushed despite herself.

"Mother, those are VERY grown men. But alas, you are correct. My husband's ashes are still cooling, and I am a very old woman."

Niri leveled a steely look at her.

"See, Bets, this is what you have to look forward to—being one hundred and forty years old and still being scolded by Mother."

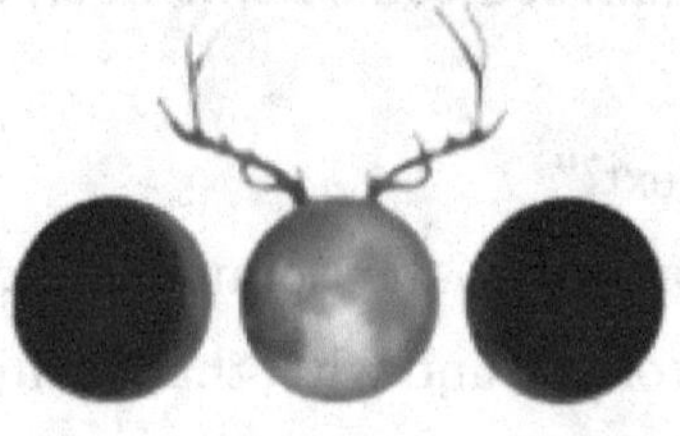

BAD BLOOD

The air in the courtyard of the Temple of the Mother was heavy, humid, the smell of incense and burning torches hung thick, and low to the ground. Bets was seated on a stone bench, in an alcove. Sugar sat beside her; his long legs stretched out before him.

Althea reclined on a bench, her head in the lap of a woman named Diane, whom Bets was introduced to in the great hall. The woman was polite and courteous, but Bets could definitely feel a coolness in her tone. At the moment she was stroking Althea's long white hair. Desma was sitting on a large round cushion, leaning against the alcove wall. Another pair, Charles and Malvika, where sitting on the bench opposite Bets and Sugar, sharing an orange. Charles was a slim man, no more than five foot five, bald with a finger width scar that ran from the corner of his mouth to his left ear, which appeared to be split in half. Malvika was tall, statuesque, in a green and black saree, with a braid of black hair so long Bets thought it might be taller than Charles.

"Sugar, I heard you say that you knew him, that you were taught by Mathew Weems?" Bets asked, leaning into him.

"I did, he mentored me when I first came to Mercer. He was a hand-to-hand combat instructor. He had such a gift for teaching and planning. That was probably his greatest strength in a fight. He could just outthink you, every time. I don't care who attacked him, twenty years ago, when Mathew was still in the field and training all the time. This man could not have gotten close and would have died quickly and probably painfully. Even Fredrick or I would have had a difficult time fighting with Mathew. He often beat me in sparring sessions up until I was in my early twenties. It was an honor to attend his funeral rites, for Fredrick and me."

Bets nodded in understanding. "Speaking of funeral rites, why did you guys strip? Is that part of the tradition?"

Sugar chuckled. "Only in a matter of practicality, Hannah's spell protected us from the heat of the flames, but it would not have saved our clothing. The flames are incredibly intense, incinerating the body in moments. We would have spent the rest of the night walking around naked, not to mention burning one of Fredrick's ties. Which would have been a true tragedy."

"How about you shut the fuck up and not worry about them until you know the slightest bit about what is happening here."

Every head snapped up. The woman who had been cradling Althea's head was now standing, heading toward Bets and Sugar. Bets was shocked, her head rocking back as if struck.

"I am sorry, I don't understand what you mean."

Bets could feel waves of anger and sorrow rolling off of the woman who was now walking toward her. She tensed, she was out of her element and confused, but she had also been in enough fights as a kid in a small country town to know when she was about to be hit. She started to rise off the bench when Althea slipped between Diane and Bets sat. Sugar put his hand on her leg, a signal for her to stay seated.

Desma had risen as well, Charles and Malvika looked on curiously.

"Diane, if I have offended you or violated some etiquette, I am sorry. I have just been trying to learn as much as I can and not be in the way. "

"Whatever, Colleen, you can play dumb, you can play eager and everyone else might buy it, but you're just like the rest of your fucked up family. You will show your true colors and one of us will get hurt. That's what you Milburns do."

She stomped off through the courtyard. Althea turned to Bets, who still sat, shocked and too stunned to even reply.

"Bets, I am sorry, I need to go after her and help her calm down. I will see you tomorrow. Desma, can you help her get settled please?"

Desma nodded gravely at her sister then turned her attention to Bets as Althea trotted off.

Bets held her hands up, trying to figure out what had just happened. Desma stood silently for just a moment, collecting her thoughts.

"Please try to understand, Bets. Mercer is filled with history, some good, much of it, tragic. Diane's tale is filled with tragedy. Your grandma Neeny murdered her brother Brad right in front of her. Her mother and father were killed on a mission led by Dorthea. While Dorthea did nothing wrong, it did not matter to Diane. So much of the pain of her life has been tied to your family. Now you have been brought through the veil and awakened and will take your place among the kinfolk here in Mercer. Even though many of the decisions you made in your life before here, show a distinct lack of character."

"Diane was very adamant in her opposition to your awakening. She felt, as did more than a few others, that you were beyond redemption. Ultimately the decision was not hers and the Council of Elders made a choice, and we are bound by it. But as you can see, Diane is not one to hide what she is feeling. For better or worse."

Bets did not speak for a few moments, when she did, she looked straight at Desma. "She is not wrong. I probably was beyond redemption. Do you know what I was doing when Lord Seanchara appeared to me? I was standing in my bathroom trying to figure out how to manipulate my loving and devoted husband into being okay with me having a lover half his age. When he told me what my sister-in-law was doing to my brother, torturing him for years, not only for her own enjoyment, but to prove she was somehow smarter than me. Do you know I never once thought about my brother or their children when I was smashing her brains in with that rock. All I could think about was the audacity of that second-rate bitch, thinking she was smarter than me. The only thing I did right, the only selfless choice I have ever made, was to die in place of my Lilly. I made it without hesitation and without the knowledge that there would be something on the other side. I just did it. Does that make up for a lifetime of hurting people for my own benefit? No, I know it doesn't, but for whatever reason, I have been given this chance to do the right thing, and I am taking it. I am sorry that she hates me, I don't want anyone to hate me, but even if I did not do the things she is angry at me for, I did so many others, that I am sure I deserve it."

As she blinked away the tears, she realized Fredrick was now kneeling beside her, she did not see him arrive during her outburst.

"Bets, I will make you a promise. There is almost no one in the ranks of Mercer that doesn't carry some kind of baggage. Many of us consorts were in the midst of dying horrible deaths when brought here by Lord Seanchara. So many witches were sacrificed or victims of horrible abuse. There are also more than a few, who were like you, unaware of the great bargain. Living their lives, not knowing that all their great successes were also blessings of the Mercer line. Desma, how long do you expect young Kay will be in the Chamber before her awakening?"

"A month, no more than two." Desma stared at Fredrick. "It might be a little soon for this."

"Perhaps, Desma, but I think it is only fair. Does anyone remember how long Christopher was in the Chamber?"

Malvika spoke quietly from her seat opposite Bets, "Two weeks, two weeks later this long limbed, clumsy thing with skin as white as snow and feet as big as clown shoes, was up and running. Hanging from the rafters and climbing everything he could get his giant hands onto."

"Bets, do you know how long you were lying in the Chamber of the Veil?"

"I, I don't know exactly, more than a year."

"Eighteen months, do you know why the long length of time compared to everyone else?"

"No, I don't."

"When Lord Seanchara deems you worthy of entry into Mercer, he makes two determinations at the time of the Harvest."

Desma spoke quietly, "Fredrick please, she may not be ready."

"With all respect, Desma, would you rather she carries that weight even a moment longer?"

Desma shook her head; Bets was surprised at this dynamic. She had initially felt that the consorts played a kind of subservient role. But that was clearly not the case.

"He first decides how you must die. The manner of your death is chosen to help you overcome the traits that he feels will be most detrimental to your life within Mercer. The second is how long you will lay in the Chamber to recover from that death, spiritually and physically. Kay, who is an innocent child, will lay for no more than a month. Died when Lord Seanchara gave her a kiss on the forehead, as fathers have kissed their daughters since the beginning of time. By the time she realized he was close enough to touch her, she was already dead at his feet. She felt no pain, no fear. Bets, you were dead for eighteen months. Why do you think it took so long for you to recover and pass through the veil?"

"I, I don't know."

"Have you noticed any differences in your personality since you were awakened, have you reacted differently to things than you would have in the past?"

"I think so, it's been a very long day."

"I know it has, but you need to know this. Whatever you were, whatever mistakes you made in the past. You can feel regret for them, you can see the error of your ways, but understand, whatever lived inside you that caused you to make those decisions it has been beaten, carved, chewed, and twisted out of you in whatever way The Harvester felt would be most effective. He would not have permitted you to walk these streets without first cleansing you of anything that could be harmful to our family and our mission. The unfortunate part is that one day, you will remember the lesson. Desma, he beat you to death with Althea. He saw your undying commitment to your twin as the one thing that might cause you to falter in your commitment to our mission and he used each of you as a weapon to kill the other to break that bond. How long were you awake before you remembered?"

"A few days, Althea took a little longer."

"Bets, my guess is your mind is still blocking out the way you died, but you will remember eventually, and when you do, you will realize you have already paid the penance for your sins. It is time now to move forward. To build your new life here in Mercer, with all of us at your side. There will be bumps in the road and heartache along the way. But you are here for a reason, Bets, a great purpose, in service to something far greater than ourselves. Those who question that will come to know the truth of you as you show them. They will come around. It is not our way to form cliques and hold grudges. Our mission is too important, and everyone here is dedicated to it, above all else."

Bets reached out her hand and Fredrick took it and squeezed it gently in his.

"Now, if you will forgive me, I must collect Christopher, and we must be on our way. Lord Seanchara is going to open the path for us, and we need to return to our duties, and you need to sleep. You are in good hands, Bets. We will see you soon."

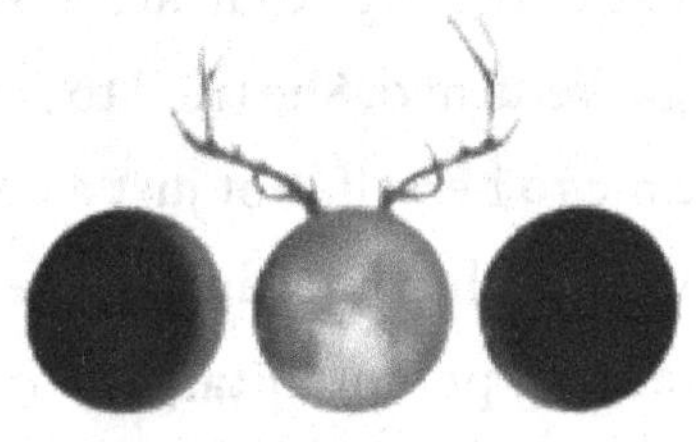

Ain't Nobody Got Time For That

D orthea sat at the little table in the back of the shop. M had just gotten back from her meeting with Beck and had jumped in the shower after getting Dorthea up to speed. The news about Coleen wasn't great but also was not entirely unexpected. Watching and keeping track as they did; Colleen had a lot of Neeny in her. Brash, bold, and ruthless. She was also tireless, and willing to do whatever she needed to in order to reach her goals. That could serve Mercer well. But now, M needed a break, they all needed a break.

Dorthea was not young anymore, and she was tired. The fight with the tether had been exhausting, then dealing with the fallout, the kids, and the summoning of Lord Seanchara. It was all just too much. She should sleep. M had a spare room, maybe she would forget about getting to a hotel and just crawl into that little bed and not come out until Fredrick and Sugar returned. She tried to remember the last time she had taken some time to herself. Not just a day or a few hours. But really just taken off. Most of the time, during their downtime, she was researching, either tracking potential targets or victims. Or, she was learning, studying in the libraries of Mercer. She was always finding ways to adapt what she already knew into something more. She had added layer on top of layer to her traps and bindings. As she aged and she became less interested in the physical aspect of what they did, she focused on making her magic as effective as possible and seeking to understand it in new ways.

She thought about Colleen's reaction when they showed her the libraries. The closest one to here was in Kansas. A small house, in a small town, tended to by a lovely couple, Darleene and Marvin Walker. A handsome Craftsman style home, with a wraparound porch, beautiful flower beds, an herb garden, a large upstairs suite that the couple rented out as a Bed and Breakfast. That explained the coming and going of random vehicles and visitors. It would not explain the closet in the back of the second-floor bathroom. Standing in front of this open closet, if a guest of the Walkers were to swipe a leaf of Holy Basil across the Ajna Chakra, pulling in the energy of creation, and focus their will on Afsha Karna, The Revelator Charm. The Revelator would reveal the keyhole. A small circle of blue light that moved every time it was used. The guest would only have a couple moments to act once the keyhole glows its blue light. The leaf of Holy Basil, a single drop of blood from the witch, and the name of their mentor written on a small piece of paper, are all laid on the keyhole before it fades.

When the doorway opens, it opens onto one of Mercer's vast libraries, or maybe they are all the same library, just seen from different perspectives. There have been times when Dorthea has been sure that she has felt other doorways, or even the presence of other witches in the room while she has been studying. But she has never seen or spoken to another person while in the library. The libraries, like so much of Mercer, are maintained by the magic of the Council of Elders.

Dorthea knew that one day soon, likely another ten years or so if things remained on course. She would be asked to take a seat on the council. It was customary with her age, and time in the field, that she would be offered a chance to return to Mercer full time. She knew that the roles of the Elders were all somewhat different. But for the most part they focused on teaching newer witches and guiding the mission. "One day," she said to the empty seat next to her at the table.

As she drank her cup of tea, she got up and walked about the small kitchen. She knew that this space was all Sugar, and it showed. Everything had its place. The only things not neatly packed away were her teacup and the open wrapper from her tea bag. She would have to put things back right again before lying down. She had no idea how long the guys would be gone, and she did not want to mess up his kitchen. She studied the walls, clean, white, tile over the sink and behind the stove, faded floral wallpaper everywhere else. The cabinets were all hardwood, freshly stained. The linoleum was clean but old and needed replacing. Maybe if she stayed a few days, she would replace the flooring as payment for room and board. She sat her teacup down and laughed out loud.

Of course, she could not even fantasize about relaxing, she was already coming up with work to do. It would be fun, though. She and M getting some real physical labor in. Moving furniture, ripping up the old flooring. Trips to the hardware store. All of it. It would be like they were family again. It had been a long time since they had acted like family. Colleagues, acquaintances, rivals, but not family. She craved that and had not realized how much until just now. Dorthea got down on her knees to inspect the side of the cabinet, if the cabinets were installed properly, and not overtop of the existing linoleum it would not be too difficult.

A cough from behind her. "He keeps the good snacks up high, where he thinks I can't reach them."

Dorothea jumped, banging her head on the little overhang from the countertop. "Shit!" She grabbed the top of her head, sat back on her rump, and then just lay back on the floor.

M rushed to her side. "Dorthea, are you okay? Oh God, I'm so sorry. I should have—"

Dorthea's laughter cut her off. She lay on her back in the middle of the kitchen floor, howling with laughter. M stood over her grinning as well. She had never seen Dorthea like this, and it was contagious. She was lying on the floor like a kid, her knees up, hands on her convulsing stomach as the laughter shook her from head to toe.

Eventually, she threw her head back and looked up at M, still standing over her, a mix of amusement and concern on her tired face. "Oh, sweetheart, I cannot tell you how bad I needed that."

M reached out her hand to help Dorthea up.

Dorthea scoffed at the idea. "You would end up on Sugar's table back there, and I would be right back here on my ass."

M rolled her eyes and instead pulled out a chair for her to sit on and slid the other one closer to Dorthea for her to use to get up. An action that took just long enough to be uncomfortable for both women.

Back at the table finally. "M, do you still have the spare room upstairs?"

"I was just thinking the same thing, maybe you could stay on a couple of days until the guys get back?"

"That makes the most sense to me. I don't have a next stop. Cordray was a lifetime project for me. Now he is gone. We know we need to spend some time figuring out where he came from and what the tether meant when she said her father was not Cordray. But for now, I need to update the archives about this and see what my next move should be."

Dorthea looked thoughtfully at her tea, long gone cold. "It is one of the things I've always been jealous of you for, you and Sugar. You two made a home here, a real home. You travel as much as anyone else, and you do so much good. But you have a place to call home, the shop, the apartment, Sugar's garden."

She gestured to the kitchen around them. "You have a cupboard and snacks in the highest cabinet. I have Fredrick and myself in whatever car we happen to have this week, and whatever dirty hotel room we land in. I eat like a teenage raccoon most of the time. Gas station snacks and truck stop fast food. I have a Love's rewards account, so I get free showers when we gas up. I'm just starting to wonder if maybe it's time to root down and have a home base. Somewhere I can call home. Hell, I can find a place with a mother-in-law cottage for Fredrick, so he doesn't have to hide his distaste over my disorganized mess of a life."

M was absently drawing a protective bind-rune on the tabletop with her fingernail, a soft, orange glow followed the tip as she did. "You know, St. Louis is centrally located, and real estate is pretty reasonable here and in the suburbs."

Dorthea raised an eyebrow at her. "You think this city is big enough for two Milburn girls, M?"

"I am more concerned about the state of the farmer's markets, tailors, and record stores with Sugar and Fredrick in the same place for long."

Dorthea smiled and rolled her eyes; she doubted you would find an odder pairing of souls than Fredrick and Sugar. But the affection and respect the men shared was evident to anyone who had ever seen them together. If you had ever seen them working, you would also realize what a better place the world was with the two of them in it.

Fredrick was a fantastic partner and despite their occasional sparring and ribbing, Dorthea had the utmost respect for his abilities, she felt truly safe with him, and that didn't come often in their work. But Sugar, that man was different. Terrifying in a fight, gifted as a healer and teacher, not to mention as a cook. He was such an interesting dichotomy. Nurturing, affectionate, and empathetic, but also capable of incredible cruelty and violence. It had been noted more than once, his loss of control in some situations and how difficult it could be to bring him out of that state. If she knew the Elders of Mercer like she believed she did, she guessed there had been at least one discussion on how to deal with Mr. Christopher William Lewis, should he ever go too far over the edge. She glanced up at M who also appeared momentarily lost in her thoughts.

"Speaking of Sugar."

M's eyes snapped back to the present from whatever reverie she was momentarily lost in.

"What about him?"

"What about the two of you? This is me asking, your aunt, and your family. You know I love you, M, and I know how dedicated you are to the mission, but I also want my niece to be as happy and fulfilled as you can be, given our life. The two of you are beautiful together and always have been. Everyone who knows you sees it. I just hope that you are giving yourself a chance to live your whole life."

M stared down at the table; she reminded Dorthea of a kid in a classroom called on when she hadn't been paying attention. "Thank you for worrying, I mean that. But Sugar and I, it's complicated." She held up her hands as Dorthea rolled her eyes at her.

"We are all complicated."

M cut her off, "I just know I love him. There could never be another man for me. I can feel him when we touch. Every emotion, every fear, laid bare for me when our skin touches."

Dorthea nodded, that empathy border-lining on telepathy was one of the things she liked least about working with M.

"But somehow, it has just never felt like the right time, it has always felt like once that starts between us, everything else will move back a row. Mercer, the mission, all that gets the volume turned way down on it every time I think about life in his arms. As much as I want that, I just cannot help but feel like that is not why I was saved. Could I live with myself knowing that somewhere a child or a mother in need didn't get the help they needed because I was taking a morning off to lie in bed with Sugar?"

"I understand that, and I respect it. I just don't want you to wake up like me one day. Alone, bitter, and too damn late to do anything about it."

"Thank you, Dorthea. I promise you not a day goes by that I don't think of what it would be like and how to make it happen and still fulfill the mission. One day I will figure it out. And I don't know why you are talking like it's too late for you. You are not that old, and you know, us Mercer girls live a very long time."

M knew what Dorthea meant, she just did not have the heart to approach it with her, not now. She knew that Dorthea and her first consort, Islam, had been very much in love. But like Sugar and herself, they put their feelings on the back burner. One day, after more than forty years together, something happened to Islam's mind. They never determined what it was, genetic, environmental, or some kind of magic.

It didn't matter. Whatever took over his mind so completely, forced Dorthea to have to make a terrible decision. Let him destroy innocent lives or destroy him. Dorthea did what was necessary. She tried to bind him, restrain him, anything she could do to stop him without killing him. None of it worked. Only at the last moment, as another Mercer witch was moving in to try and stop him. That's when Dorthea noticed the gun in his hand. She was merciful but decisive, and M knew she had carried that pain with her every day since.

Dorthea shrugged her shoulders. "You're right, maybe I will settle down, meet a nice boy, and try to pretend I don't spend most of my time fighting the evils of the world. Using arcane magic and hanging out with the world's politest and most dangerous man. Should be an easy sell, right? Let's not forget that I have no legal history, I look like I am in my fifties, but I am closer to one hundred. Oh, and occasionally I have to invite a terrifying ancient horned God, or his ageless Goddess bride over for tea to get things done. Now I don't mean to be a negative Nancy here. But the deck is stacked against us as far as things like this go. You can't really meet someone outside of Mercer, but even within can be dicey. I sometimes wonder if that's why the decision to pair us up with consorts was originally made. Just to give us a chance of happiness, or at least keep the rebellion to a minimum."

M grinned. "I don't know, Dorthea, seems like most of us would have been just as happy with a good dog or a goldfish."

Dorthea laughed. "True, but then we would have to learn to cook and ain't nobody got time for that."

Their laughter rang through the small kitchen. A sound that healed a part of both women that neither knew was broken. A reminder that everything was okay between them, that they would be okay. Soon, there will be three of them. The Lewis twins would surely bring Bets through the veil soon. Sure, she would have her own mission to complete, and she may not be able to return to St. Louis for a very long time, but they would still have each other.

The chime of Dorthea's cell phone interrupted their banter. "Probably Fredrick," Dorthea announced as she retrieved it from her pocket and laid it on the table hitting the answer button and speaker button in rapid succession. "Yes, dear," she said as sarcastically as she could manage.

"Dorthea." A panicked voice, quiet and rushed. "Dorthea, it's Rosie."

M shot upright and Dorthea picked up the phone. "Mama Rosie, everyone is looking for you, are you ok, where are you?"

"Quiet, child, no time. I am deep in the mission. Fellowship of the New Covenant. Kids missing from this church, I don't think it's the pastor, but someone close. Happens in every city, it's too much to explain. Noblesville, Indiana, we will be there in two days. Meet me at the Uptown Café on Thursday morning, six a.m. on the dot. Is my boy with you?"

"No, Mama, he is with Sugar and Lord Seanchara, escorting a new sister to the Chambers of the Veil."

"Okay, you have someone you can bring, do not come here alone, Dorthea, I am very limited in how much I can move without blowing my cover, and I don't know what's happening or who is doing this. I don't want you in any more danger than you have to be. But there is something bad on the air here, baby."

"Mama, I have M.M. Wildes here, she can come along."

"Okay, that will be perfect, you girls gear up, though. I don't know what you will be up against. Six a.m. Thursday, Uptown café. Be there, girls."

With that, Mama Rosie was gone.

"Shit, M. I was just thinking about taking a vacation and putting new flooring in your kitchen. So much for that."

M stared at Dorthea for a few seconds. "No disrespect, but we will be safer dealing with whatever Mama Rosie was talking about, than messing with Sugar's kitchen. I need to take a little time to get things squared away with the shop. I hired a new girl to mind the shop so we can keep it open while Sugar and I are out of town. She starts this week. Let me get her situated and get prepared to leave. You want to crash, then you can drive the first leg while I sleep?"

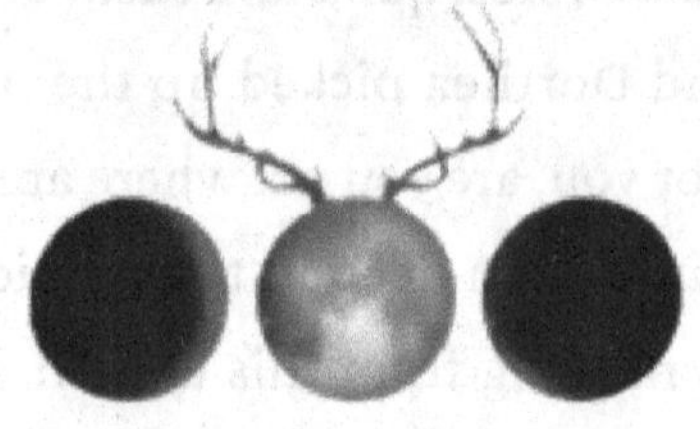

KOUTE VWA LIBETE A

There were many things Dorthea had witnessed in her long life in Mercer. Feats of will and power that defied all logic to the uninitiated, and some that even left her baffled. None of them held a candle to how Mama Rosie could walk through any room in the world without everyone present immediately falling to their knees. She was well over three hundred years old, but she did not look a day over sixty. In a sleek, royal blue dress, and white cardigan, with a matching wide brim blue hat, she cut across the dining room like she owned it.

Dorthea was one of the few people who understood the truth of Mama Rosie. Ezili Danto was her born name. A Hattian revolutionary, betrayed by her own people, scarred and mutilated by the jealousy and deception of her own sister.

Here she was, the personification of feminine rage, walking as gracefully as the wind through this small diner in Indiana, none of the folks here understanding that a goddess, come to life, just brushed by their tables on her way to get some coffee and eggs.

The small restaurant was filling up quickly at a quarter of six. Rosie was so very graceful, as if her feet barely touched the floor. She had the carriage of a dancer, long, lithe, and deceptively strong. Her hard flats barely made a sound on the wood floor. Dorthea smiled because she knew, as soon as Mama Rosie was seated and her legs comfortably out of view, those shoes would come off. It was an odd habit, but an endearing one. Mama Rosie never wore shoes unless it was absolutely necessary, and even then, looked for every opportunity to slip out of them.

Dorthea and M rose to greet her; Mama Rosie wrapped M in a hug so fierce she nearly took her off her feet. After a moment, she looked over at Dorthea, her eyes shining, and reached across the table, cradling Dorthea's cheek in her hand.

"Oh girls, I am sorry if I had you worried."

Dorthea held Mama Rosie's hand for just a moment before releasing it. "We had heard you had gone missing, we were worried, but now I am more worried about when Faith hears you called me."

Mama Rosie chuckled a little at the notion, she was fully aware of the combination of scolding and doting that was coming her way from Faith the next time they saw one another.

"Okay, let me get some coffee and eggs ordered, and I will tell you what is going on. We don't have a lot of time."

Once a large carafe of coffee had been delivered along with scrambled eggs for Mama Rosie, toast and bacon for Dorthea, and a bowl of oatmeal for M, Mama Rosie began to speak.

"I am not sure how much background you are going to need, but a big part of my life is finding potential family for Mercer. Not like the social workers, who are focused on the at risk or abused who may benefit from a life with us."

She spooned some more eggs into her mouth. "I spend most of my time looking for those who are already manifesting some signs of a gift. Who are either sensitive to or are already using the divine energy in some way. Most of them aren't even aware of it. Some see it as a sharpened intuition, or extraordinary luck. Strangely enough, the most tuned in sisters I find, are either in an evangelical church, or already practicing some form of witchcraft."

M raised an eyebrow. "In the church?"

Mama Rosie nodded. "Some of them, yes. It's no coincidence how the nine Charismatic Gifts of the holy spirit line up with what we do. Word of knowledge, increased faith, gift of healing, gift of miracles, prophecy, discernment of spirits, kinds of tongues, and interpretation of tongues. Those who are open to receiving the gifts are already tapped into the divine energy of creation, they just call it God, or the Holy Spirit. They cannot harness it or channel it the way you or I do, because they haven't passed through the veil of death."

"The resurrection," Dorthea spoke, her head down as she loaded a slice of bacon onto a wedge of toast.

"Yes, ma'am, I was not around then, but I know a couple ladies that were and that is the consensus, that the story of the resurrection was a man, known to Mercer as a philosopher and teacher, was brought through the veil by Lord Seanchara as a consort after his execution for sedition against the Roman empire. But let's not get in the weeds on this too much. Very long story, very short, I spend most of my time cruising churches, spirit shops, occult bookstores, those types of places, just feeling my way around. Might go months between contacts, then all of a sudden, bam!"

She slapped her hand down on the tabletop, causing the tables near them to look around.

"I will walk into a room and can feel the energy flowing through them, already see the faint lines of connections that they know nothing about. Sometimes all I do is take note of their name and location for them to be watched from time to time. It's not like I can approach a mother of three after Sunday bible study and ask her if she would like to die and be reborn into our weird ass magical family."

Dorthea chuckled. "You can say that again."

"But you know, sometimes, we have sisters just walking around living their lives without being as directly involved. Nurses, lawyers, police, EMS, politicians. Not every fight is a fight to the death in a dirty room over the lives of some poor kids. Sometimes the dirtiest fights are in the boardrooms as we struggle to keep greed and oppression at bay through more traditional means."

She stared into her coffee cup as if divining. Shook her head and continued.

"That is often where we find these sisters, the twenty-two-year-old CNA, living alone, spending her days off in Barnes and Noble, reading about candle magic and saving up for a new set of tarot cards, all in hopes of finding some kind of belonging. The church organist, who shows up every week to play, not because she connects with the message from the pulpit, but because she can feel something alive and real during the service that makes her believe in God with all her heart. The connected and sensitive are all around us. That is what put me on the path of the Fellowship of the New Covenant."

M raised her eyebrows. "I have heard of them, Sugar mentioned that they turned up in a couple things he was researching."

Mama Rosie nodded over her coffee cup, her dark brown eyes studying M intensely. M felt extremely naked under that gaze.

"You know, that doesn't surprise me. He is a smart one that Sugarfoot. Handsome too, I know my Fredrick thinks the world of him, and that is a hell of a reference in my book."

Dorthea and M knew that Mama Rosie often referred to Fredrick as a son, though there was no known relation between them. But it was Mama Rosie who brought Fredrick to Mercer as a small boy. No one but she and Fredrick, perhaps Seanchara, knew exactly what the circumstances were of her finding him. But Dorthea could remember the first time she saw him, being carried through the courtyard of the Temple of the Mother. Emaciated, pale, dirty. A consort carrying his skinny body to rest in the Chamber to await his awakening.

Mama Rosie continued. "I started hearing talk of this traveling revival. Everywhere I put my ear to the ground, people were talking. This pastor, Darrell Ray Miller, only preaches based on the teachings of Jesus, he doesn't discount or even talk about the rest of the bible. He just talks about the unending love and acceptance of Jesus. Love your neighbor, protect the weak, that kind of stuff, and it resonates with people from all over.

"So, I thought I would check it out. I met up with them at a service in Nebraska, out in a cornfield. Two hundred or so people come in and crowd under the big tent. His wife plays organ, and he comes out and just tries to make everyone feel loved and supported and talks about Jesus' love and acceptance. Then they sing and dance and pray all night. They lift people up for healing, they offer hugs and handshakes. He doesn't come down and lay hands on people, but he asks the congregation to do it.

"There is something real going on, as soon as the organ started, I could feel it. The divine energy flowing though the place amplified and concentrated. The things I have seen would be classified as real miracles if I did not understand the power behind it. Just a couple weeks ago, I watched a girl, an agnostic girl, mind you, just there to support her girlfriend who wanted to check things out. She got hit full blast, she levitated about four feet above the crowd for a full thirty seconds before coming softly back to the ground and being carried away. When I spoke to her, she claims to have seen a giant cosmic force, creating and destroying the universe.

"I joined up with them, traveling town to town, helping set up and tear down, tending to the congregation. That is the pastor's only rule. Anyone can travel with them, but everyone has to help as they are able. So, I am Sister Alice, from Birmingham, Alabama. A retired widow just on the road seeking solace after the death of my husband. I help organize the meals and keep track of provisions. They are incredibly generous and incredibly trusting. The pastor and his wife, in fact they might be two of the kindest, most genuine people I have encountered in a long time."

Dorthea rubbed her temples. "Mama, you said kids had been going missing, do you think this pastor might know what's happening to them?"

"I don't think so. That pastor may be somehow channeling a power he doesn't understand or somehow connected to it. But that man doesn't have a malicious bone in his body. As we travelled the group has grown considerably. When I first arrived, six months or so after they started out, the crowds would be a couple hundred people, and there were ten or fifteen people, including the Millers traveling with the Fellowship. Now, we are hosting crowds of a thousand sometimes and there are fifty people or more at any given time, traveling, helping. The ministry doesn't charge, they accept donations and use that to get us all from town to town and feed everyone, keep the tent and sound working. It isn't greed, I walked in on the pastor in his skivvies last week, because he was sewing a patch on the knee of his only pair of pants. I don't think they are at the bottom of it. Normally young kids, late teens, early twenties, wander in and out of a situation like this and I would not even bat an eye. But after a few events, I started noticing it was always kids that I had seen have a serious reaction to the energy flowing through the services. Every one of them was on my list of kids to either watch or approach about joining us in Mercer. I wasn't entirely certain until right before I contacted you. The girl I told you about earlier was there with her girlfriend, and they were completely inseparable. Alexis and Jenna, sweetest little couple, Alexis is a mile a minute maniac who should be under some kind of physician's care for her ADHD, if she isn't already.

"Jenna had not only been touched but was a serious conduit. You could stand next to her and feel it, and her connection was already very strong. I don't remember the last time I saw someone so tuned in to the energy of creation that had not passed through the veil. Especially someone who had not sought it out. She was only there to support Alexis. Anyway, she went missing one night. I felt something moving through our camp."

"Something triggered your warding?" M asked

"No, in fact it was quite the opposite. I don't sleep much, baby, I often just lay at night, and allow myself to fall as deep into my connection as I can. Just feeling, searching, reaching out for anything or anyone to make contact. I had the entire camp, about ten individual tents, fifty people or so, in my vision. Then I noticed a black spot in my sight. Just a shadow of unreadable blankness moving through the camp towards the tent shared by a handful of the kids. I got myself up and moving as fast as this old body would allow, preparing every defensive ward I could think of. Nothing short of Elder Valkyrie or Lord Seanchara should be completely invisible to me. But this thing was, if I had not been actively watching the camp, I would not even have noticed.

"By the time I got to the tent it was gone. I could not find it anywhere. I returned to my tent and searched as far as my sight would allow me and found nothing. The next morning Alexis was distraught, Jenna was nowhere to be found. They searched and searched. Her clothes were still there, but she was just gone. Alexis said they had laid down the night before. They share a sleeping bag, but Jenna had been warm and had just taken a sheet and lain down next to her instead of in the bag with her. I am telling you, girls, I got to know Jenna a bit and there is zero chance she just up and left Alexis, plus her friends had left after the first night and they had the van. She would have had to leave on foot, if that wasn't enough, you ever hear of a twenty-year-old just walking off without her cell phone, wallet, money, not even a bra, or change of underwear?"

Both women shook their head no, and Mama Rosie continued. "Damn right you haven't. Because that's not happening."

M leaned in closer. "Mama, if you don't think it is the pastor, do you have any other idea where to start?"

"As far as who, I have no idea. Someone who is identifying these kids the same way I am, which cannot be good. If they are tuned in enough to identify potential witches and consorts and snatching them away to who knows where. I can't imagine it's for any good reason. Plus, anyone powerful enough to block my vision, that's some real work. You can't just get online and stumble on a ward strong enough to hide you from my sight. No, that's not right either, this person was not just hidden from me, they were a black spot, a total void in the divine energy of creation and that just does not make sense. I need to consult the elders, but I don't want to leave here long enough to do that. I do have an idea of a location, I saw a pamphlet on a table the other day, and as soon as I read the name all the bells and whistles started going off. I am not one hundred percent certain that's where the kids are being taken, but there is something bad going on there and it needs looked at no matter what." She slid a glossy trifold out of her purse across the table to Dorthea.

"Kaskaskia Valley Youth Camp and Spiritual Retreat, Sponsored by Meadow Ministries," Dorthea read aloud. "I think I have heard of Meadow Ministries. Big player in the evangelical, prosperity gospel scene. I always pegged him for a hack, just in it for the money."

Mama Rosie agreed. "Me too, and that may be true. Meadow Ministries is a big damn business, he may not even be aware that his ministry sponsors this place. You know how that goes. These guys are the face on stage, the voice on the mic, they are rarely the brains behind the operation. But I cannot find any other clue at all. It is actually on your way back to St. Louis, somewhere in rural Illinois. I am going to stay with the Fellowship a while and see what I can find out, if you two can check out the camp at least we can eliminate one possibility. If I need to break cover here and head back to Mercer I will, but I want that to be a last resort. But for now, I need to get back, it's not like I am guarded or anything but if I am missing long that may look a little suspicious."

The women all stood together, Dorthea sliding the pamphlet into M's bag. Mama Rosie embraced them one by one. "You girls please be careful, text me on that number I called you from when you know something. Tell Fredrick I love him, and I will reach out soon. Please be…"

"Sister Alice." A soft, voice from behind her caused all three women to look that direction.

M looked over Mama Rosie's shoulder, a small pretty woman, her blue eyes, studying the group of women curiously. Next to her was a slightly disheveled looking man, in his late thirties. Shaggy, sandy brown hair, brown eyes, faded brown chinos and a baggy T-shirt.

Mama Rosie's face underwent a dramatic transformation that even M was impressed by, as she spun to face the speaker. "Brother Darrell, Sister Margarite, good morning."

She hugged them both and turned to Dorthea and M.

"Brother Darrell, Sister Margarite, this is my sister-in-law, Dorothy and her daughter, my beautiful niece Marianne. Dorothy was my late husband's younger sister you see, and we realized a while back on our weekly call, that we would both be traveling through here at the same time. Figured it would be a great time to play catch up."

Darrell reached for Dorthea's hand, then M's in turn, Margarite did the same. M thought she caught a sideways glance from Dorthea as she made contact with each of them. Knowing M's gift for reading emotions and feelings on contact.

"Ladies, it is so nice to meet you, I am sure I don't need to tell you what a privilege it is for us to spend our days with Sister Alice. She radiates God's love in a way I don't think I have ever experienced."

Dorthea put an arm around Mama Rosie's shoulder. "No sir, I would say there isn't a soul that knows her, that isn't aware of just how magical she is."

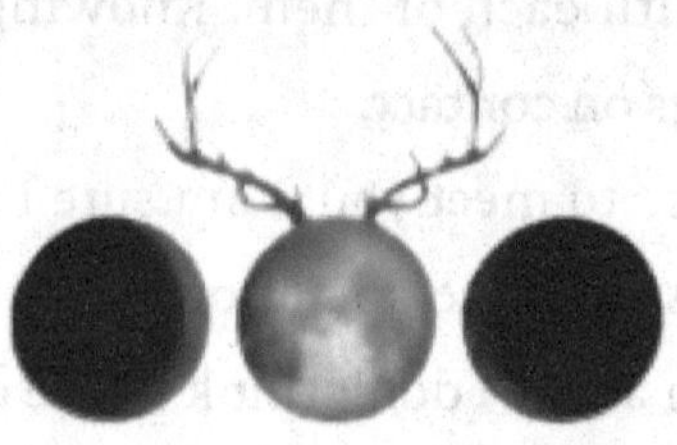

CARPENTERS IN THE HALLS

S he could feel Alexis wrap her arm around her waist and pull close in their sleeping bag. She didn't remember taking her shirt off when she got in, but apparently, they both had at some point. She could feel the heat of Alexis' small breasts against her back, as she snuggled tighter against her and sighed softly, grabbed Alexis' wrist, and pulled her arm further around her. Alexis slid the palm of her hand over her stomach, her hand left a trail of fire across Jenna's desperate skin.

They had been on the road with the Fellowship for a few weeks now and had been sharing a tent with two other people up until tonight. She was starving for Alexis' touch, not just the holding hands or stealing a kiss when they could. She needed to be touched, to be kissed deeply and hard, to feel Alexis' teeth and tongue and breath up and down her body. She needed her to hold her down and force orgasm after orgasm out of her starving body.

Alexis slid her hand down, her fingers sliding beneath the waistband of Jenna's sweatpants. Jenna rolled her hips urging her on. Begging with her body, *please, baby, please, I need you*. She reached her arm behind her, between them, and rubbed Alexis through her shorts. She responded by sliding her free hand through Jenna's hair, up to her scalp and pulled hard.

Jenna bit down on her lip to stifle the moan that threatened to escape. She felt Alexis' teeth on the side of her neck, nibbling under her ear. She bent forward and pushed back against Alexis harder, she grabbed the waistband of her sweatpants and pulled them down as far as she could in her position. She pulled Alexis' hand out from around her waist and guided it down the back of her sweatpants as she bent further.

She needed to be taken; she didn't care who heard what. She needed Alexis to own her body, to fuck her, hard. She felt Alexis probing, pushing into her.

Suddenly, her entire body was wracked with pain, a spike of fire drilled through her head. Her body convulsed and she vomited.

A voice carried on the pain, riding the line of fire directly into her mind. "Paula, sleep, you need your rest. So much depends on you, God has called you through the fog of sin and death. It is time for you to take your place at the head of his holy army, to lead his faithful as they heal the world."

Jenna writhed on the stone bed where she lay, screaming. "No, my name is Jenna, not Paula, you have the wrong woman. Please, please let me go, please."

She convulsed and twisted in agony and passed out.

Sometime later she awoke in the darkness. "Alexis, where are you? Please someone, this hurts so bad, where am I? Where am I?"

Jenna did not know how much time had passed; she could hear the voices nearby but could not see who was speaking.

"She woke again, sister?"

"Yessir, this is the third time. No one understands how or why."

"What do the seraphim say?"

"They are at a loss, they have yet to have a failure during the Ascension."

"I thought we have lost a few?"

"That was always due to an unperceived flaw in the mind of the chosen, never because they could not hold them during the process. In fact, no one has ever awakened before the command, even the most powerful among the ascended cannot force their way out of the process. It's unprecedented."

"Thank you for the update, I will pray for guidance."

"The Lord will provide, as he always does. Should I reach out to Bishop or the Carpenters to terminate?"

The man's voice rose precipitously. "You will do no such thing, the Lord placed his calling on this young woman and just because we have failed to fulfill our duties in this, does not change her being called to service. You will keep her as comfortable as possible. Perhaps if we have a conversation with her, help to alleviate some of her anxiety, the sisters will have more success."

"Sir? You want me to tell her what is going on?"

"I want you to do what you've been called to do, just like all of us. Just because up until now the process has not required you to engage with the chosen in order to help them ascend, does not mean that will always be the case. Remember the end goal here, sister, remember the revelations to come and what that will mean for us and for all of the ascension. Do you think Bishop or the Carpenters will be the face that the public sees? That is not their role in this, they are warriors, God's truly blessed and chosen soldiers, but they aren't going to be in front of the world telling them about the blessings and joy to come. That will be folks like you and me. If you cannot muster enough faith to explain our mission and role in God's plan to one young, and likely terrified little girl, then do you believe in what we are doing here? Are you ashamed of our work, sister?"

"No, no sir, I am not ashamed of my faith or my part in our sacred mission."

"Good, then get in there and get your arms around that child. She is probably terrified, has no idea what's going on. We are doing the Lord's good work, sister. Do not be ashamed or afraid, we are not working in secret because what we do is wrong, we are trying to protect the ascension from the evils of the world until they are strong enough to protect themselves, and it's closer every day. Largely because of the work you and the seraphim are doing here."

"Thank you, brother Jim. You are right. I think the secrecy and nature of our role in the Lord's plan sometimes clouds the fact that his cause is a righteous cause. I have been here, in these rooms for so long, nursing the ascension, I fear sometimes, I lose sight of the revelations."

"There is no need to thank me, sister. A shepherd guides and protects his flock, every single one. It is my role here. To make sure you feel safe and supported as you do the sacred work you do. Sometimes that means a reminder of the path and that the work is not the goal, the ascension is the goal. Heaven on earth is the goal, and it is you and so many others who drive us toward it every day. God loves you, sister; we all love you. I will leave you to your work."

Jenna heard nothing else in the darkness of the room where she was lying. She could see nothing, but the walls felt very close, she dared not explore. She had read the Pit and the Pendulum too many times to go crawling around in the dark.

Several long moments passed in the dark. From the side of the room opposite where she had heard the voices, she heard the sound of a door creaking open.

The same feminine voice. "Jenna, are you awake?"

She did not answer.

"If you are, shield your eyes, I am going to turn on a small lantern. You have been in the dark for a while and it will hurt your eyes."

Jenna closed her eyes and covered them with her hands. She heard the door open further and footsteps walked toward her.

"Open your eyes when you can, sweetheart."

Jenna slowly opened her eyes behind her hands, the light stung, but the relief from no longer being alone in the dark made it bearable. She squinted up at the woman in front of her. She was a short, thin woman with blonde hair. She was dressed in a white peasant skirt and a blue cotton top. She was starting at Jenna with pale blue eyes.

"Is that a little better?"

Jenna nodded her head and continued to squint up at the woman.

"Good, my name is Milly. I am sure you have a lot of questions. You will have to forgive me; things did not go according to plan with you and I'm afraid you have suffered needlessly because of my lack of preparedness. I am truly sorry for that, it is inexcusable. Can I help you up and we can get you somewhere comfortable?"

Even as hurt and afraid as Jenna was, she could not deny the need for some kind of comfort, her body ached, and her mind felt as if it had been hollowed out. She took the woman's offered hand and allowed herself to be pulled up. As she stood, she realized how small the woman in front of her was. Jenna was roughly five foot eight. It always made her smile because she and Alexis were exactly the same height. There was something so quietly electrifying about exchanging level kisses in public.

The woman in front of her had to be barely five foot tall, slight of build, and frail looking. Her wispy blonde hair was tied back tightly over her scalp, and Jenna could see how thin it was. This did not look like a healthy woman, in fact, her features, hair, skin and posture looked like that of a woman easily into her seventies. But looking at her eyes and smile, Jenna put her no older than twenty-five. What happened to this woman that made her age like this?

She swayed a little on her feet and Milly reached out to steady her. Jenna felt how slight the woman was. She was able to provide her with some balance, but that was about it.

Jenna could not say where the idea came from, if you had asked her a month ago, a year ago, hell, five minutes ago, she would have told you it wasn't possible. But in that moment, her arms on that woman's frail shoulders, hearing her words in her head. *Should I reach out to Bishop or the Carpenters to terminate?* She thought about Alexis, her friends at the Fellowship, she knew this woman wasn't in charge of whatever sick business had kidnapped her, but she was the only one in front of her.

When the woman turned to lead her out the open door, Jenna didn't hesitate, she just moved. She put one hand in between her shoulder blades, and she grabbed the woman's wispy blonde hair in the other, high up on the back of her head. She ran forward fast, pushing with all her body weight as she slammed the woman's small head into the cinderblock wall next to the door.

A sickening crack and a small exhalation were the only sounds made as Milly went limp in Jenna's hands. Jenna lowered her body as softly as she could to the floor. She stared at the woman's open staring eyes, soft blue, unblinking. She saw her chest rise slightly and fall again. A trickle of blood from Milly's forehead. Jenna looked around the small space for something to put over the cut, to limit the blood flow. She felt something wet against her bare foot and she stopped and looked back down at Milly.

Milly's bladder had let go and the woman had gone incredibly grey. She seemed to still be breathing, but Jenna knew none of this boded well. She felt the slightest twinge of guilt then it was gone, replaced by a swell of rage. These fucking people, whoever they were, had taken her away from her girl, away from her new family, and this bitch, had wanted to terminate her. Her anger only grew as she looked down at Milly's still form, she spit on her face.

"How did that work out for you?" she asked her unblinking stare. She wondered briefly if that crack combined with that weird, wide-eyed stare meant something important had broken inside the woman's brain. *Good,* she thought, *I hope it scrambled your shit forever.*

Seeing no weapons or phones, she checked Milly's shoes, but they were several sizes too small, and no good to her.

She took a deep breath and focused. *The most important thing right now is escape. Get to daylight no matter what.*

She grabbed the lantern and headed out into the hallway; her room was at the end of a corridor. Drab, brown carpet, well worn, showed the track in and out of the hall. The walls were the same block as the room as she was in but painted white. Fluorescent fixtures dotted the ceiling about every six feet, giving the hallway a bright but washed out, institutional feel.

If this was like any other building she had ever been in there had to be exit signs right, some kind of lighted emergency sign. They may be kidnappers and religious weirdos, but the building still had to be inspected at some point. She just needed to get out of the building before anyone realized she was gone. Even if she was out in the middle of nowhere, if she could see the sunshine, she could get free, she was sure of it. She was fast on her feet; she always had been a runner.

At the end of the long hallway, she came to a T, she put her back to the right-hand wall and sidled slowly up to the end of the hall, so she could look down the left corridor without sticking her head all the way out, or at least she hoped. She peeked as far around the corner as she dared, more brown carpet and white painted cinder block. She slid back a few steps and crossed to the left side. Moving slowly to the end, she could see a change in the intensity of the lighting from that direction but nothing else.

She gave herself a little pep talk, *You can do this, come on. One glance to the left then go, stay quiet, move fast. But don't look like you are sneaking, better to have someone who knows you aren't supposed to be there see you being casual but purposeful, rather than have someone who has no idea who you are, see you sneaking.*

She walked out into the corridor, a quick glance to her left, three doors, one on each side of the hallway, about halfway down its length, and a door at the very end. She turned back to her right. She nearly pumped her fist in the air in celebration, a flight of stairs led up just out of sight. But she could see obvious sunlight shining down them. *Go now!* she admonished herself. Walking at a quick but controlled pace she passed four more doors, two on each side. These were all classroom style, wooden doors with long vertical windows. All the rooms were dark. Okay good, no one to see her pass by. She started up the stairs quickly, resisting the urge to take two at a time. She crested the top and saw—across from the stairs was a small alcove, a wooden table with an old book stood in the center. Red tapestries covered the walls of the alcove. She looked to the left and the corridor went on out of sight. The brown carpet downstairs had been replaced with beautiful, polished hardwood floors. The white cinderblock walls were ornate wood paneling decorated with sculptures and paintings that she took no time to inspect. She looked back to the right, she could see the daylight from the door at the end of that hallway, no more than forty feet away. Salvation, out the door and she was gone. She didn't care where she was, out that door was better than whatever was waiting for her here when they found her.

She was only a couple of paces from the door when a shadow moved between her and the light. It took her a moment to focus and take in the details, she tried to keep her face passive. Wondering if she could make this person believe she was just supposed to be walking right out the door. Her heart sank as her mind put together the truth of what she was seeing. The man now blocking her path to the door, was not much taller than Jenna herself, unlike her, he was wearing only a pair of athletic shorts and nothing else. He had black hair, slicked back with something wet. He was slender, but obviously strong. His wiry arms and muscled torso were covered in tattoos. In the middle of his chest were three crosses on a hill. She continued walking toward the man, thinking, *Just be cool, pretend you are supposed to be there and walk right past him out the door.*

As she came nearer, she nodded at him and smiled her biggest, flirtiest smile.

Almost there, just a few more feet, just keep going.

She was almost even with him when he took one step to the side and stopped in her path, she looked at him and smiled again, hoping to play the confused but friendly damsel in distress.

His expression did not change, but he raised his hands in front of his chest, with his palms together in a praying gesture, and bowed his head. His dark eyes never left hers. She wondered for a moment if this was some kind of greeting, but before she could mimic his movement, he lowered his hands and turned them palm up, fingertips still touching as he rotated them.

Jenna was now genuinely confused, then a ball of blue-white light glowed in the bowl made of his palms. Jenna was transfixed as the ball of light grew to the size of a cantaloupe. Jenna tried to turn and walk the way she had come, before she could look away, an image came into view inside the ball of light, like a fortune tellers crystal ball from a cartoon. She gasped as the image clarified into her grabbing Milly by the back of the head and ramming her into the block wall. The image shifted, and Jenna watched in graphic horror as she lowered Milly to the floor and spit on her face. Terrified, she looked into the face of the man in front of her; he smiled, his teeth were dazzling white, so much so that Jenna believed they could not be real. He slammed his hands shut making her jump, then she started backpedaling and he waved at her. A slight playful movement, just the fingers on his right-hand waving, bending at the palm.

She turned and ran back down the hallway, she had to chance the other direction. She looked back over her shoulder, expecting to be struck down any second. But it never came, no alarm sounded and no sudden burst of pain from an attack. Down the corridor opposite where she went when she came in. She followed the hard wood until the hallway bent in a curve. As she rounded the corner, she froze. Several feet in front of her, leaning against the wall was another man, the same shape and size as the last one. He too appeared to be blocking the way out.

This man was also dressed in nothing but athletic shorts, he even had the same triple cross tattoo on his chest as well as all the others. The only difference she could see in her panicked state was he had blond hair and icy blue eyes.

"Hey, girl," he drawled the words out like he was singing them. She had never heard an accent like his before, kind of southern, but not really. Like someone who had never heard a southern accent imitating someone who did a bad imitation of a southern accent.

"I see you met my big brother, huh? Yeah, he doesn't talk much, but he still gets his point across, doesn't he? So, here's the deal, my name is Asher and that is my brother Levi, and the woman whose head you smashed into that brick… She was real special to us. I am afraid, even as pretty as you are, it's just not going to end well for you."

He stood up straight and started toward her. It was only then she noticed the hammer in his left hand. It was the largest hammer she had ever seen that wasn't some kind of medieval weapon. This looked like a regular carpenter's hammer. *Carpenters.* The thought made her blood run cold as she remembered Milly's words outside the room where she woke up.

Should I contact Bishop or the Carpenters to terminate?

He hoisted the hammer up to his shoulder and she saw the tension in his muscular arm. This man was easily capable of beating her to death with that thing. She turned and bolted back down the hallway, no idea where she would go now or if she would run into the other brother just around the corner.

She made it back to the stairway and stood for a moment, thinking. Maybe she could try one of the dark rooms, see if she could find a place to hide until she could come up with a plan. She turned back to the small alcove, remembering the tapestries, thinking there might be something behind one of them, or even a way for her to hide and wait until they went down the stairs to look for her. Before she could finish her turn, she screamed in pain and fear and surprise as the largest hand she had ever seen wrapped around her neck and she was hoisted off of the ground by her throat.

She did not know that people could be as big as the man who was now crushing her windpipe in one hand while he held her off the ground. She tried to cry out as he pulled her close to her face with a snap and screamed, "Blasphemer," before he threw her off of the landing and into the void over the stairs.

The last thing Jenna saw was the man's sneering face as she flew backward away from him as if in a dream.

"Damn, Bish, that was messed up even for you."

Asher was standing just off to the side of the alcove, looking down at the broken body of the girl at the bottom of the stairs. His brother Levi was silently approaching from the other direction.

"Asher, do not speak any more today in my presence. Clean this up. Security in the Halls of Ascension falls under your purview and your lackadaisical attitude and lack of discipline cost us dearly. If you had an ounce of decency or shame you would hit yourself in the head with that hammer of yours."

Asher glared at the bigger man. He thought briefly about smashing Bishop's oversized skull with his hammer. Bishop was tough, but not tough enough for both Carpenters. Another time perhaps, for now, Bishop was right. This was his mess, and he needed to wrap it up and be done with it. He would contact the reverend and see how he wanted this handled; first, he would check to see if the fall had finished the girl off or not.

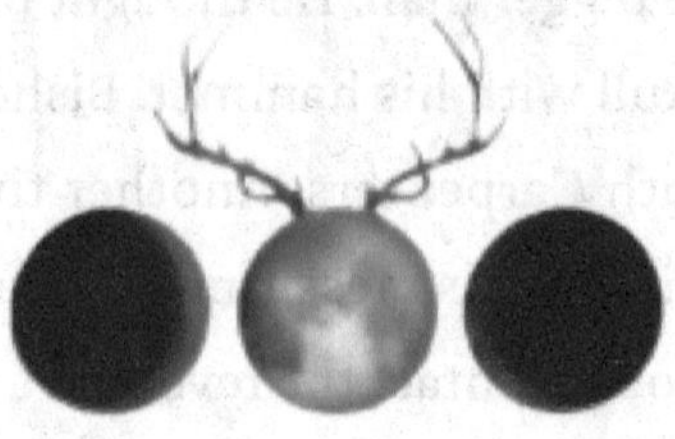

SPARE TIME

"**D**uke, do you see him?" Faith said in his ear bud.

"Yeah, Faith, I see him. This is that motherfucker that killed Mathew and all the rest. I can see how too, big bastard. Maybe bigger than Sugar."

"Did you call it in?"

"Yes, ma'am, the cavalry is on the way. Fredrick, Beck, Snow, Devlin."

"That's good, Dukie, no ego, and no mistakes."

Duke was leaning against the passenger door of his truck, looking across the street at the Spare Time Lanes Bowling Alley. "He has been making a whole lot of noise. Went after two more witches since we met everyone and stopped just short of killing both of them. Then went after Jackie and just knocked her out and ran away, but not before she got a good look at him. I think he is leading us here or leading someone. Maybe Hannah?"

He could hear Faith shuffling around for a moment before she answered. "I don't think he knows about Hannah, unless he has some serious help backing him up. She planted that idea pretty deep according to her. She and Bast are in Oklahoma and headed this way now. But I think we can get this guy, Dukie, we just have to be careful. You say he's big?"

"Yes, ma'am, he is as big as Sugar, maybe a little bigger. Moves like an athlete, we know he can fight. He took on Mathew and walked away, and Hannah said he was guarded against much of her magic. She was able to get through, but not easily. I don't like how public this is. Do you think he has led us here intentionally? Do you think he wants this out in the open?"

"Well, I don't think he is here to roll a few frames, but it doesn't matter. This is the first time someone has been in pursuit of him, instead of the other way around. We cannot miss this chance, we owe it to Hannah and Mathew, we owe it to all the family he has killed so far. I am in the lot of the bowling alley now; I will park and find a spot to see if there is a quiet spot to do this. What weapons do you have on you. In case I cannot bind him long enough for you to get him restrained. Have you called for backup, just in case?"

"I did, I reached out to Dorthea, she is out in the boonies somewhere with M.M. Wildes, she got me through to Fredrick. He was just returning from Mercer with Sugar. I asked him to drop him off and head to us. I would trust Fredrick with my life, but I don't care how dangerous this guy is, I don't want Sugar around. I have a Taser, a sap, cuffs and a .45. I don't want to use the iron unless I have to, I am legal to carry here, but this state isn't as friendly to defensive firearm use as some others. I have a drop piece in my boot I can slip into his pocket if I need to. But that can get messy. If we absolutely have to put him down that way, I can say he was trying to rob a sweet old lady and didn't realize I was with you."

"Hey, sir, you can save the old lady cra—"

The line went dead. Duke's stomach dropped, he did not hesitate to see if it was a technical issue but sprinted out across the busy street, dodging one minivan, and hopping the small ditch on the opposite side of the road. He slid between rows of cars headed for the side entrance closest to where Faith turned in at. A movement by the door of the bowling alley, he glanced that way, there he was, in the doorway, blocking most of the doorway. Was he waving, Duke turned and stared, Faith's car was just a couple rows up. The fucker was waving, no, he was waving a cell phone. Then he opened the back door of the bowling alley and slid inside. Duke ran to Faith's car; there she slumped over the wheel. *Please, no. Not her, not like this,* he thought as he slammed open the driver's door and reached in. He checked her pulse, good, breathing, pulse strong. Duke couldn't wait. He laid the seat back, lowering her into a reclining position, fished his twenty-year sober coin out of his pocket and laid it in her lap. A signal that he had been there and was on the hunt, should she wake up.

His phone buzzed in his ear, he tapped the button on his ear bud as he ran for the door, already knowing who was on the other end.

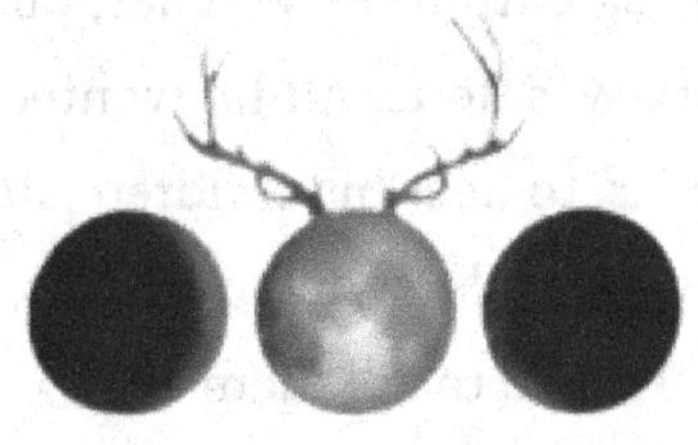

PHILIPPIANS
4:13

The setup had been too easy. After he awoke from his fight with the old witch in the farmhouse, the pain had been tremendous. Worse than the injury, the angel told him he had failed. He had not actually killed the witch. She used her demonic magic to fool him into thinking he had, then followed him back to the barn where she witnessed the angel rescuing him.

His right arm was raw and burnt from his collarbone to his elbow, and his left eye was torn up pretty bad. The angel had healed him a little. Stopping the arm from becoming infected and speeding up the healing process, but he was still a long way from whole.

But he had to pay his penance, the Lord's work had to be done, and he could not fail in his missions. Now the enemies knew to watch for him, they knew what he looked like and how he struck. He must make amends before he can go back to his family. The angel told him that she would keep his family safe from the witches, but he could not return to them until his work was done. All he wanted was to see them, to hold his wife in his arms, to hear his children laughing. But it was too dangerous, now the witches knew who he was, they would hurt his family to get to them. He had to kill them all.

So, he started laying a trail of breadcrumbs, leaving the devils alive for the time being. Most of the ones he went after did not seem to be as powerful as the old witch and her husband. He had been marking a very clear path before landing here. The angel told him that there were two of them headed to this little midwestern city. That they would be more powerful, but killing them would go a long way toward his penance.

He had spotted them watching him, earlier in the day, and led them here. This would be perfect. The crowd helped set the stage, but more importantly he needed the empty building next door. These monsters were smart and trying to stay hidden. They would not likely use their demonic powers in public or just try to kill him outright in front of people. They would want to sneak around. The angel had assured him of this. He laid his trap and set the plan in motion.

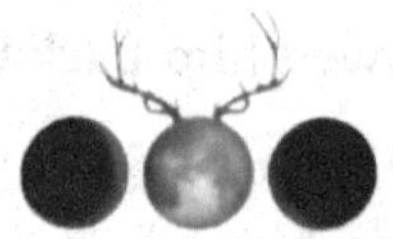

Duke did not speak; he simply tapped the answer button. The voice in his ear was deep and commanding even through the cheap earbud.

"Nice to see you finally joined me, I was beginning to think I would have to wave you over to get this started. It's rude to be late to your own funeral."

"Listen, I don't know who you are, but I can promise you, this isn't going to go the way you have it planned in your head."

"But it already has. I left a trail of half dead demons and their concubinus as bait, and you came running. You monsters think you can hide from the Lord's righteous wrath, but you cannot. I am blessed and privileged to be able to serve my God in the eradication of you and the other hell spawn, and I will not fail him."

The hiss of a door and the rush of sound in Duke's ear. The rowdy cacophony of a bowling alley. Balls rolling down polished wood, pins collapse in a thunderous display of physics.

Only a couple ways to play this, Duke thought. "You think you're on a mission from God? Look, guy, my friend you assaulted, she is a social worker, and I am a private investigator. You have multiple warrants out for your arrest, and you were spotted, so we were called to try to talk you in peacefully before the county sheriffs arrive and ventilate your big scary ass. You need help, brother, you are sick. We can get you that help. None of the people you have hurt were demons. A retired gym teacher, an accountant, a couple stay at home moms. Like you have hurt some innocent people. I know that if you believe in God, if you read the bible, you know that God doesn't want innocent people killed. Come out of that crowd and let's get you the help you need and get you home."

The noise of the bowling alley in his ear was deafening, but there was nothing else. Ten seconds, twenty, thirty.

"You and I both know there are no cops coming, Duke. This will be just you and me until I break your back and make you watch while I stomp the old bitch to death, a bone at a time. The only thing you get to decide is how long this takes."

Duke headed for the door of the bowling alley, he didn't like the idea of tangling with this guy with witnesses, but he liked the idea of this monster loose in there with innocent bystanders even less. Last thing he could allow was this big bastard getting all God told me to, on some innocent kids.

The chaos inside was disorienting, the music was blaring through old speakers hanging from the ceiling. Kids ran back and forth everywhere; the lanes were packed with families. Hearing the noises all around and through his earbud was almost too much for him.

In his ear. "Good to see you, Duke. So what's the plan? You going to wrestle me to the ground in here, flash your bullshit PI card and hope I don't fight back? How many people do you think are in here, Duke? One hundred, hundred and fifty? Enough you won't start shooting if I come right at you."

Duke spun on his heels, trying to take in all angles at once, this guy was big enough, he shouldn't be able to blend in with the crowd. Duke was walking along a wall, but he felt vulnerable. There were alcoves with lockers and doorways all along its length as far as he could see. A sign about twenty-five feet ahead of him hung above a door and read The 11th Frame, in bright yellow letters.

He did not like any of this. That guy could be in any of those alcoves or doorways and Duke could not see him until it was too late. This guy was just too damn dangerous to let him get the drop on him.

Duke shifted his path out to the middle of the floor closest to the seating behind the lanes. The big tables were where people gathered to eat and drink and wait their turn to roll. The frat house smell of pizza, cheap draft beer and sweat was nauseating. He scanned wall opposite, confident that this guy wasn't hiding among the families and teens in the lane areas.

"Smart move, Duke, staying away from the wall, gotta make sure I don't sneak up on you."

Duke spun around. *Where was this guy?* "So, since it's likely only one of us is getting out of this intact, what's your name anyway?"

"Duke." He dragged out the word. "Are you hoping to catch me monologuing? Maybe get me to reveal some weakness, or some information you can pass along to your den of butchers and perverts before you die? My name is Bishop, but what I am called isn't important. I told you; I am God's righteous vengeance. His living breathing sword of justice, and I will come for all of you. You will all pay for the sins and crimes you have committed against the innocent of the world. If you need a name to plead with, to beg for forgiveness as you die, you should call upon the Lord, perhaps he will judge you mercifully. I will not. But it doesn't matter, at this point, I am going to have to come to you, you've walked right past me twice."

Duke spun around, searching the crowd, trying to distinguish the guy's form.

"No, not there, the other way."

Duke spun and jumped back startled by a group of three or four small kids, no older than seven or eight, each with a handful of dollars, running past him screaming and laughing. On their way to some overpriced delight. The crash of the pins was starting to grate on his nerves. He had to wrestle back some kind of upper hand. The constant noise was making it hard for him to focus and not knowing where this guy was, how was he missing him?

"Wow, Duke, I thought you were going to kick one of those kids. Watch out, first graders on the way to the arcade are serious business, at least for sick perverts like yourself. Don't want to damage the goods, right?"

"What the fuck are you talking about? You weird ass, deluded asshole. You think I mess with kids? Someone has you all twisted up. But that makes sense, I have seen your dumb looking ass, and you seem like the kind of guy that would project his bullshit on to other people. You know who normally experiences the kind of psychotic breaks you're having? Middle-aged white dudes who are recently divorced. Is that what's happening here—your wife catch you watching porn and divorce you? Take the kids on the ground you might be a risk. With that size and temper of yours, I'll bet it took all of ten seconds for a judge to grant her full custody and a restraining order. You get to see them at all, or does she have some other guy playing daddy now?"

"You couldn't be further from the truth; my wife and children are home safe. Patiently waiting for me to return from killing you and the old woman. But since you want to play tough, let's play tough."

Duke looked toward the end of the bowling alley, where the concession stand, arcade and restrooms were. There he was, standing right in front of him. Thirty, maybe forty, feet away. Duke struggled to keep his features stoic. This guy was every bit six feet ten inches tall, a wall of muscle in cargo pants, solid hiking boots, and a hooded jacket. He was just standing there, staring at Duke. A wire ran from his ear to his hand where Faith's cell phone looked like a child's toy in that massive hand.

There were just too many people here, Duke had to get him back outside. He did not stand a chance trying to stay out of the guy's reach. He was just too tall; Duke could never get in and out quick enough to hit him and get away before the guy could counter. His only chance was to bridge the gap, get in tight, hope the guy wasn't used to working up close and inside, or even better off his back. Get a double leg takedown or trip and get on top of him, crush his hips, and go to work. But even then, odds were, someone would intervene and that could mean disaster for Duke. Getting pulled off, detained, arrested. Not to mention the possible complications of a black man tackling and beating on this big Captain America looking white guy, for seemingly no reason, in a midwestern bowling alley. What could go wrong there? He needed to get back out to Faith, see if she was awake yet. She could restrain this bastard, and they could get him locked away somewhere quick.

Duke locked eyes with the man over the heads of people walking past. "Listen, why don't we step outside and..."

The man bolted to Duke's left, towards the men's restroom. Duke covered the distance quickly, but when he hit the heavy wooden door, it did not budge. He pushed, once, twice, finally he drew back and drove hard with his muscular legs. The door frame cracked as he went tumbling into the room. He gained his footing and back pedaled expecting an attack. What he did not expect was an empty room. Two stalls with no doors, two broken, filthy urinals, and a hand sink that made you feel like you would be safer washing your hands in the urinals. But no big bad guy, no one at all. He noticed the carnival noises in his ear had stopped. He thought he had lost the connection, but then the man spoke.

"Neat trick, isn't it? Philippians 4:13, Duke. Now you had better hurry or you're going to miss the party. Don't worry, I will stop and pick up Faith on the way, I am sure she is still napping. Midazolam and diazepam are a rough mix. Hopefully, she didn't stop breathing yet. I mean, she will soon, but hopefully not until I have had time to make her pay for all the pain she has caused."

Duke ran out of the restroom back down the bowling alley, pushing people out of the way as he ran. "Why don't you leave her alone and just wait for me to get out there. She has done no harm to anyone, but me, I am exactly the type of motherfucker you are looking for. She is a fragile old woman, but not me. Come on, you big pussy, you scared to fight me, so you want to pick on a sedated old woman?"

"Fight you? Duke, this isn't about your ego or mine. God has commanded that you perish as punishment for your sins. I could not let either of you leave here alive, even if I wanted to. My hands are God's to command, and they will be ending both of your lives today. I am sorry if you were hoping for a different outcome. I understand, but this is the only path."

Duke heard the sound of glass smashing and the unmistakable sound of a car door opening in his ear. "Upsidaisy, there we go. Alright,

Duke, I'll see you next door. Hurry now, I get creative when I am bored and that won't end well for her."

Duke slammed out of the bowling alley door and into the bright afternoon sunlight of the parking lot. Squinting as his eyes adjusted but wasting no time running for the car. Off to his left his saw movement and looked just in time to the man, Faith over his shoulder like a sandbag, running into a doorway of the old office building next door to the bowling alley.

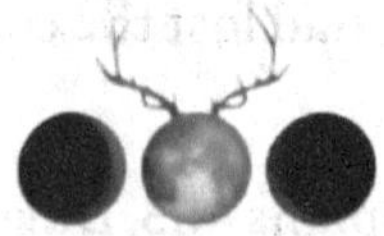

Bishop dropped the old woman next to the big window on the third floor of the office building. He had staked this place out earlier in the week and had been squatting here since. There was no one else around, especially on a Saturday, and this spot was perfect for what he wanted. The room was big, with hardwood floors and exposed rafters, with lots of pillars and half walls to hide behind.

He wanted to just kill her now, but he might need her to disarm Duke. If the man did not enter the room with his gun in his hand, he wasn't near as bright as he was giving him credit for. It would be foolish at this point for Duke not to try and shoot him. Duke had to know he could not win in a fight, and so far, only the women he had dealt with had any extraordinary powers. The men, while all capable, were just mostly normal men, trained to fight, but nothing special.

The old man had come the closest to besting him. That hammer would have smashed his brains out had he been an average height and turned to look at the opening door. As it was, he was so focused on killing the old man, that he never even looked back.

Nothing like the women, they all had some real evil in them. The old woman had literally boiled his skin and convinced him that he had murdered her. He did not like the idea that there were people capable of planting things in your mind that weren't true.

He hated to think of the kind of evils that would turn loose in the world if there were people running around that could just plant whatever false idea they wanted into your mind, and you couldn't tell the difference, without an angel, or maybe God himself, showing you the truth.

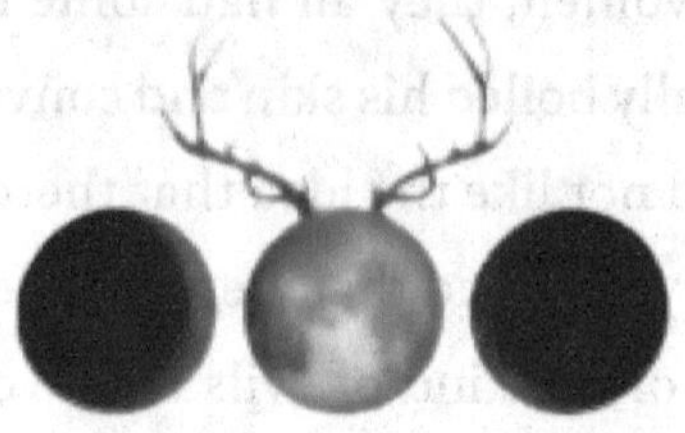

LET'S NOT TALK

Duke rounded the last corner at the top of the stairs, breathing heavy but ready for a fight. The door at the end of the hall was open. Duke slipped his M&P .45 out of the holster at his waist. Unlike most of the consorts, who did not carry, Duke carried everywhere. He grew up with guns, was comfortable with them, recognizing both their danger and value. He knew that this bastard would probably expect him to be armed and would try and ambush him to take away that advantage.

What he did not expect, was for Bishop to be standing out in the open. When Duke pushed through the door crouched, his pistol at the low ready position. The man was standing at the end of the long room, a big floor to ceiling window at his back, silhouetting him. He was holding Faith in his arms, close to his body, but the way the light was pouring in the window behind him, Duke could not see how she was positioned against the man.

"What are you carrying, Duke, a Glock? You don't seem like a Glock guy, but you can't always tell about people."

"Smith, want to see if my range time is paying off? Put Faith down and I'll see if I can end it in one shot, save you some suffering."

"Smith? Performance Center? I love those M&P Pros myself before the Performance Center upgrades. But I am a fan of iron sights. I never got used to optics. Anyway, you drop the mag, kick it to your left, rack the slide twice, then field strip that upper right off there. One button and a click, you know the drill. If you don't, I am going to pull her head off, Duke. Do you doubt I can do it? I promise I am strong enough. I will twist and twist and pull it right off. Or maybe you are thinking about taking the shot. Can you see where she ends, and I begin? Are you going to shoot into a shadow? Are you willing to take that to hell for all eternity, you shot her, your only friend, because you were too scared to face me?"

"No, see you got me fucked up, son. Your ego has you thinking some shit that isn't true. Those other guys you've fought." Duke dropped the magazine out of the M&P. "Matthew was a friend and a mentor, but Mathew was one hundred and twenty years old and had been retired for years. The rest of those guys, social workers, politicians, and teachers."

He racked the slide a couple times and ejected the shell, inwardly hating the sound of the brass hitting the floor. "You know what I do for a living?" He locked the slide in place, squeezing the trigger then sliding the entire upper mechanism forward, dropped the weapon in two parts.

"I catch and kill fucked up psychos like you. I am not an old, retired guy, a teacher, or a social worker. I am the guy they call when evil like you pops up in the world, and they need someone to make it go away. Put her down, and let's fucking go."

Duke watched, shocked as the man mule kicked straight behind him with his right leg and the big floor to ceiling pane of glass disappeared into the afternoon light and shattered on the parking lot below.

He sprinted toward the window, his only thought somehow reaching Faith before the thirty-foot drop to the concrete ended her life. When he was still about ten feet away, the man spun and threw Faith through the open window; then used the momentum of his spin to launch a roundhouse right hand that would have ended the fight right there had Duke not ducked under it sliding toward the window. A huge work boot slammed down on his right calf as he did, he didn't think it broke the bone, but the fire shooting up his calf was crippling all the same. He rolled onto his back and pushed hard toward the left. He needed to get up, and, on his feet, he could not fight this monster from his back.

"You mother fucker, I am going to kill you," Duke growled at the man as he turned a back summersault and rolled up to his feet. He bit back the scream of anguish and grief as he thought about Faith's broken body at the bottom of that fall, and charged in.

Duke slipped a jab and drove a hard right hook into Bishop's ribs, ducked the follow up right hand, then drove his forehead straight up into the man's bottom jaw. Duke was about six foot tall and on a normal sized opponent that would have broken his jaw, as it was, even with the momentum from springing up, it made just enough contact to make him step back a couple steps.

Duke shot low, attempting to get under the bigger man's hips and get him off of his feet. But even stunned from the headbutt, Bishop was still fast enough to dance to the right and connect on the side of Duke's head with a powerful punch that sent him sprawling headlong into the dust covering the floor.

"Duke, I am not going to lie, I did not see that headbutt coming. But the takedown attempt lacked creativity."

Bishop was slowly circling around him as he got to his feet trying not to let the damage from that punch show. He could feel the side of his head and face swelling already and his vision was a little blurry on that side.

"Oh Lord, get over yourself, sweetheart. You are big, that's all, if you were five-ten, you would already be dead."

Duke circled in the opposite direction as Bishop but inching in with every quarter circle or so, closing the distance, he was not going to rush in again. He had underestimated this guy's training.

Bishop paused in front of a short half wall, about four feet tall and six long. Obviously constructed as some kind of room divider. Duke continued to circle around him, when he got even with the wall to Bishop's right, Bishop rolled backward over the wall with no more effort than taking a step.

Duke again kept his face as stoic as he could, but watching this giant of a man, easily pull a half turn, reverse summersault over a wall. It just did not make any sense. He was reminded of watching Sugar. The similarities were just uncanny. The size, the athleticism.

Duke stalked forward, not intending to move all the way in on him, but to get him to react. Try to draw the big man into committing, he was just too dangerous to let him play counter fighter. Duke needed him to come for him and maybe he could catch him in a mistake.

Again, Bishop seemed to know what he was thinking, he danced backward in a smooth shuffle. Every time Duke started to close the distance between them, Bishop was on the move. Never striking but not letting Duke get anywhere close to striking distance. Duke would dart in; Bishop would step gracefully to the side. Duke faked a step to the left and spun back to the right to try and get close. Bishop just hopped back two or three feet and laughed.

"Frustrating, isn't it, Duke? I have killed and hurt so many of your people, now here you are. The big bad, the closer, and I have already killed your witch. Having stomped a few of you to death now, I am guessing, you guys are just the muscle and it's the women who are the evil behind it. Makes sense to me, Eve, The Whore of Babylon, Jezebel, Delilah. All of the problems really, are caused by women. At least now that I have killed yours, you can get a moments peace, before I send you to hell after her. Should I just drop you in the puddle I am sure she made? Or would you prefer for me to just leave your body up here for the rats?"

While Bishop was talking and circling, Duke finally had an idea; he would circle back toward Bishop. Try to maneuver his back against the little half wall again. He was willing to bet he would pull that same flip over the wall as last time. Only this time, while he was rolling and distracted, Duke would draw the taser on his left hip and light him up. He could fire the taser then hit the big bastard with everything it had until it brought him down.

"I thought you said before you weren't going to monologue. Honestly, I thought that it might end up being your only redeeming quality. You weren't going to talk much. But you haven't shut up yet!"

Duke took on a mocking tone and started flapping his hands around. "Oh, I am God's wrath, I am going to send you to hell, blah blah blah, Jesus fuck, you overgrown 'roided up prick. Come on with it already."

The positioning was almost perfect, Bishop was next to that wall in almost the same spot as before. *Here we go*, he thought. *Time to kill this prick.*

Duke darted forward with a right jab that was way too far out to land, he saw Bishop's legs backing into the wall. He inched a little closer, hands up in a high guard. Bishop leaned his body back to start the roll, and Duke dropped his left hand to his belt to unhook the taser. Bishop exploded forward, kicking off of the wall and launching himself the few feet between him and Duke.

He tried to get the taser up and was buried under Bishop's tremendous weight and momentum. He landed hard on his back with the monstrous man right on top of him. Duke pushed his hips up hard, trying to use the momentum to roll Bishop over. But he didn't budge. Duke tried again to move his left arm to get the taser out, but Bishop must have seen it or felt it because he trapped that arm even tighter. While Duke was trying to get his arm free and focusing on keeping Bishop close so the man could not start raining down punches, the big man reared his head back and slammed his forehead down onto the bridge of Duke's nose. It shattered in a crunch and a spray of blood. The back of Duke's head slammed hard to the floor, and he struggled to stay conscious. He could feel his arms moving but could not do anything to assist them. Bishop had tossed the taser to the side and Duke could feel him sliding up into a full mount. He knew if he was going to survive, he had to get his hands up, get his feet under him and drive his hips up hard. He could hear Bishop praying.

"Father, thank you for the strength to carry out your will, and guide my hands as they purge this evil from your sight. Amen."

He felt the first punch land in the middle of his sternum and felt the breastbone crack. The next punch to the jaw he did not feel pain as much as a disconnected thump and a further disconnection between his body and his consciousness. His vision was blurred in both eyes now, he could feel Bishop put his hand around his throat and push down hard, holding his head tight against the floor. He did not see him raise his hand to begin the punches that would smash his skull into the wooden floor.

He also did not see the knee crash into the side of Bishop's head as Fredrick him at a full run.

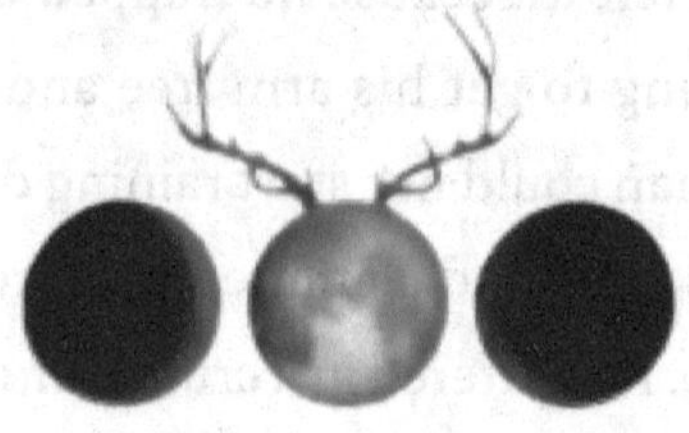

AGAIN WITH THE ANGELS

B ishop's head swam and he felt his grasp on the world slip as he rolled with the hit and tried to get his feet under him to face this new attacker. His vision was blurry, his eyes watering from the knee to the side of the head.

But it was like a giant, black bat turning a circle around him, was it dancing? Were those wings? The form spun close, and pain shot down Bishop's right forearm. He had instinctively thrown it up to block and something as hard as steel slammed into it. The throbbing pain was instant, and he could feel the blood running down his arm to drip off of his fingers and onto the floor. He stood and turned, determined to meet this new challenge in the name of God, to prove himself worthy of God's trust in him. As his vision cleared, he realized it was not a bat, but a man, almost as big as him. Dark skin, as dark as the suit he wore.

What looked like wings were the tails of his jacket and the two black batons he held in each hand as he spun.

He was sure his arm was broken but that did not matter, whoever this was. He would die just like his friends.

He started to say just that when he got hit hard from behind, a solid kick to the back of the head as Devlin connected. Bishop somehow managed to keep standing but stumbled forward. Which brought him into Fredrick's range and the man struck out again. Faster than Bishop could track, he felt the crack of the batons on the backs of each of his raised hands, breaking the small bones there. He tried to back away, bellowing in pain and crying out for God's angels to come to his aid. Devlin delivered a hard strike to the side of his knee, the leg caving in to the side in a completely unnatural way.

Devlin moved around him, in a counterclockwise circle, Fredrick circled clockwise. Bishop tried punching out at Devlin, thinking the smaller of the two men would be easier to incapacitate with a punch. But his leg would not support the move, and he had to pull back before it collapsed. As he turned, his salvation appeared to him. He saw the angel move into an empty supply closet; he did not understand how the other men did not see her. But it didn't matter. If he could get there, she could save him, she could heal him. She had done it before.

He started to run for the closet, his left leg buckling again as Fredrick brought a baton down on the back of his head. The blood splattered like a halo as Bishop fell to his knees. Devlin unleashed a series of punches to his head and face that crumpled the man as he fell unconscious. The last thing he saw before his vision faded to black was the angel staring at him from within the closet.

Fredrick whipped zip ties from his pocket. "Devlin, quick, get someone up here for Duke. I cannot tell if he is breathing from here."

Devlin leapt toward the open window, grabbing the frame at the last second and swinging out to grab the ledge of the next window, then working his way quickly to the ground in a gracefully controlled fall.

With Bishop secured and bleeding, Fredrick ran to Duke, who was lying very still on his back. He grabbed his wrist to check for a pulse. It was there, faint but steady. "Hang in there, Duke. Help is on the way; these girls are going to fix you up." He held Duke's hand, he could see Duke breathing, but his chest was rising unevenly. It looked like he had been in a car wreck. Fredrick was certain his sternum was broken. He heard the rush of footsteps and turned to call for Snow or Beck whomever came with Devlin.

What he saw instead were the zip ties he had used to bind Bishop, lying in pieces. He spun to his feet looking around wildly, hands already drawing his batons. Across the room he saw a door closing. He sprinted towards it. No way this monster was getting away, he hurt too many people. Fredrick wanted him to stand and account for his actions but had no qualms killing him to bring him to justice. He reached the door, counting two breaths and swapped the baton in his left hand for a modified bang stick. It carried a 9mm cartridge in a short handle. Just like its larger cousins used by alligator hunters, and for shark protection. All he had to do was press the end of the baton against something and push and it would set off the cartridge. There was nothing to absorb the recoil, so it was not pleasant to use. But it was effective. He would open the door and if Bishop charged him, he fully intended to pin him and push that into his eye and just be done with it.

He swung the door open, right baton leading the way left hand ready to strike. Nothing. An empty closet, four by four, no shelving, no doors, the walls did not give way when pushed and no ceiling panels. It was solid wood. This made no sense. Fredrick was confused. But he had been around the magic and wonder of Mercer since he was a small boy, and that was a very long time ago. There would be an explanation, or there wouldn't. Either way, they needed to save Duke and Faith.

He turned at the sound of Devlin's voice running up the stairs with Snow in tow. "Come on, he's over here. Sorry, Fredrick, we had to grab some supplies from the truck, the ladies exhausted their stash keeping Faith going. We are going to have to beat feet out of here, big guy. I don't know what just happened, but no one was paying a bit of attention to us at all, it was like they couldn't even see the building and now people are starting to notice us in the parking lot. Had more than a couple heads turning as they drive by.

"Get to Duke, get him stabilized. Snow, he is breathing, pulse is steady, but I am certain his sternum is broken, probably his jaw and orbital as well. Who knows what other kind of damage is lurking beneath the skin? How long before we can load him up and move him? They are both going to need long term healing somewhere safe."

Snow was kneeling over Duke with her hand on his forehead. Beck has Faith stable, but it took a lot out of her. Devlin, please help her get Faith into the car, then get back here with anything we can use for a stretcher for Duke, I will do what I can to put everything back in place so we can move him safely. But feeling around, he has a lot of fractures and bruising. No internal bleeding that I can feel, but you're right, Fredrick, his sternum is split nearly in two. What did he hit him with, a sledgehammer?"

"Might as well have been. What can I do?"

"Most importantly, make sure that bastard never gets up again. Then I will need you to help Devlin get him down. I can either float him down the stairs or keep his bones in place while you move him, I cannot do both."

Fredrick put his hands on her shoulder. "We will carry him, Snow. Just keep him alive. We need him for many reasons. But at the moment, we need to figure out how this assassin just walked into an empty closet and disappeared into thin air, five minutes after I caved in the back of his skull."

Snow looked up at Fredrick, eyes wide. "I have Duke, help Devlin. We have to get them the fuck out here."

Fredrick bowed. "Yes, ma'am."

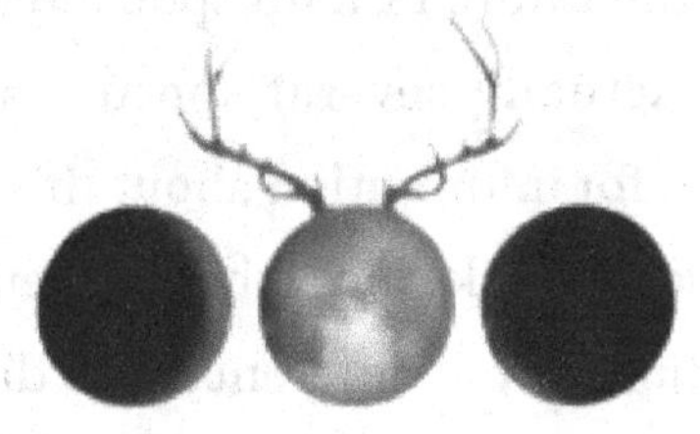

FINE AS FROG'S HAIR, RARE HEN'S TEETH, AND RIGHT AS THE RAIN

M was listening to Dorthea snore softly in the passenger seat of her Navigator. They had been going non-stop for days. It had been almost a week since their initial meeting in Todd Bryant's backyard and the events that had spun so much into motion.

They had located the Church Camp sponsored by Meadow's Ministries. There were actually several spotted across the Midwest. Dorthea had searched for information about this Reverend Jim Meadows. At a glance he seemed like any other big tent evangelical pastor. But Dorthea had noticed some differences, he did not seem to flaunt his wealth or prosperity, as they called it, all over the place.

He was obviously successful; his church had a very big social media presence and a considerable congregation. But you did not see him in private jets or expensive suits. In fact, he seemed to sponsor a lot of youth groups and charity organizations, several of these camps, urban outreach, food banks all over.

Seemed most of his efforts were with the poor, and not just the white poor of the rural areas, but he focused just as much on inner city and people of color as well. Seemed his generosity did not discriminate. It wasn't until Dorthea pulled up a video of one of his most popular sermons that she found what she was looking for.

M could not see the video, but she could hear it loud and clear.

"Brothers and sisters in Christ. While we gather here today in celebration of this amazing building we have opened here, this incredible opportunity provided to us by God's heavenly will, to feed and house so many of his children, who previously would have been out on the street. Let us look around, see the many faces in the crowds, understand these are all brothers and sisters in Christ. Know that there is no such thing as an outsider, or someone who doesn't belong in the family of God. We are one united family under his name. That is our mission, to bring everyone into his loving arms. For the only real threat to the peace and prosperity he has promised us on earth are those who will not open up their hearts to his message, those who attempt to poison our children with the evils of sin. That is where we must turn our watchful eyes, that is where we must erect our shields. That is where our soldiers must march in the name of God. We must protect the most vulnerable among us from a life of damnation due to the corruption of the non-believers. The time is coming family; the time is coming when our God will rain down his miracles upon this world. When he will reveal himself to all, believer, and non-believer alike. You must be ready to stand firm and hold the line when the time comes that God begins to cast out those who would stand against his will."

That was all either of them needed to hear.

Dorthea turned to M. "I have always said that if the White Christian Nationalists would give up the White part, they would take this country by storm. The only thing stopping them form completely taking over our government has been their continued embrace of racist ideas and refusal to disavow racist groups. If they were to combine with the black churches over their common ground instead of demonizing them, you would never see another non-Christian get elected."

Shortly after that, Dorthea found the camp on the map, it was only an hour or so out of their way back to St. Louis, so they agreed to go check it out before meeting back up with Fredrick and Sugar. Dorthea rocked her seat back and asked M to stop at the town closest to the camp so they could get a plan together and get their supplies in place in case things got messy.

She was almost in town when she got a call from Fredrick.

"Hey, Fredrick. Dorthea is napping, how did everything go? Are you guys back?"

"M, listen, I am on the run and don't have more than a second. Sugar is at the shop, but I got called out. Faith and Duke got into a bad scrap with a bad man. Beck, Snow, Devlin, and I made it in time. But both of them are hurt badly. I don't have time to give you all the details, but we are getting them to a safe house to heal for a while then we will head back to meet you two in St. Louis."

"Oh Fredrick, okay, no, I understand. Dorthea and I are checking out a lead passed to us by Mama Rosie. We will meet you there as soon as we can."

When she hit the button to hang up, she turned to give Dorthea a shake only to find the woman already awake and looking alert.

"In twenty years, I have never heard him anything less than composed. Even in the most stressful situations he never breaks. That was panic I heard in his voice. I don't like that."

M was wheeling the big SUV into a parking lot of a grocery store, closed now this late on a Sunday afternoon. "You think this is about Mathew?"

Like every other woman of Mercer, M and Dorthea had both heard the funeral song, that Hannah sang for Mathew Weems. Being so far away, it slipped into their minds as easily as remembering an old favorite tune as it came unexpectedly on the radio.

Dorthea nodded grimly, having once sang her own funeral song for a lost consort. "It has to be or are you telling me that within a week we come up against someone tough enough to kill Mathew Weems, survive Hannah's vengeance, and a completely different random run in that hurts Faith and Duke bad enough to scare Fredrick, of all people. Come on, I am not buying it at all. There is something going on here that we aren't seeing, M, something bad. Let's finish this little scouting mission and get back to them and regroup. I know you don't like Devlin, but we are going to need all hands-on deck for this at some point."

Fifteen minutes later, M pulled off to the side of the two-lane black top just fifty yards or so from the drive marked with a big white wooden sign. Kaskaskia Valley Youth Camp and Spiritual Retreat.

"Alright, what do you think, Dorthea, lost travelers blundering up the road? Or leave the car here and try to sneak in and get a look around?"

"I say we drive right up, no sense in sneaking. Worst case scenario there are people there, we apologize. So sorry, mom and daughter road trip you see. Just got turned around trying to explore the countryside. We will be on our way now. I think between the two of us, unless this is some extremist military compound disguised as a youth camp, we will be able to handle some overly enthusiastic church folk."

"Alright, fair enough. Let's check this out then get home as fast as we can. I want to gather the troops and see if we can get to the bottom of whatever is going on there."

The lane up to the campground was gravel, but well-tended. No patches of weeds or grass growing through it. The rock was even and deep. M wondered what kind of funding a place like this would have to have to maintain a driveway as long as this one, as well as it was maintained. Trees lined either side crowding the drive and added a claustrophobic feeling to the dimming sunlight. In the full bloom of summer, the forest surrounding the road was a sea of green and brown.

M and Dorthea had rolled their windows down and M had the car at a crawling pace. Dorthea had her eyes closed, senses extending, feeling with the energy at her command. The forest was a symphony of life. Layers and layers of colors and sounds between it all the energy that binds the universe coursed. In places like this it was less bands of connection between one life and the next; it was more just a flow of interwoven colors and lights among all the life here. Both women had spent much of their time in the cities over the years since becoming part of Mercer. But both had been born to a country family. Small town life, farm work, running in the woods. The fields and trees were home in more ways than one and on the rare occasions they got to visit places like this. It still floored them both how beautifully interconnected it all was.

"M, stop the car. Look, up ahead."

"I am seeing it too, but that doesn't make any sense. Have you ever seen anything like that?"

Dorthea was as well versed in the lore as anyone in Mercer, and she had never heard of anything like this. As the energy flowed through the forest it reached a point just outside the church yard where it seemed to crest and was then pulled into the area around the church. It was one of the most beautiful things she had ever seen. Like the church had some kind of gravitational field that was pulling all the energy toward it.

"No, I haven't, it's... I don't know what the hell it is. Like some kind of focal point. Look behind the church, what is that?"

There were great bands of energy flowing in and out of the roof of one of the long buildings behind the church.

"What is that, there are what—twenty?" M asked.

"Twenty-five."

Dorthea extended her senses, feeling for any sign of what they were dealing with. She could feel the waves of energy surrounding the church. She then fell deeper into herself. Closing herself off from her body as much as she could and allowing her consciousness to float along the energy. She felt herself pulled into the church ground, picking up speed at an alarming rate. This form of astral travel was unpredictable for any practitioner, and it was far from Dorthea's specialty. It wasn't like just picking a destination and then going there. You were releasing your hold on the physical and riding the flow of energy.

In this case it was starting to feel like a slip stream, moving faster, she could feel her spirit being pulled towards something that seemed to be recirculating the energy and pushing it out again in those big columns that crashed against the heavens and spread out in various directions. Almost like the great bands of connection she had seen on Mother Mercer. She broke her trance and returned to her body, not liking the out of control feeling.

"Alright, there is something crazy going on here. I've never felt anything like that. Let's take a quick look and get the hell out of here. I think we need to seek guidance on this. At the very least we need to contact the council and see if they want us to investigate further. But let's give them as much recon as we can."

They got out of the car and started slowly walking up the path, Dorthea readying a quick defensive charm to shield them both in case of an attack. M shifted her glamour to appear as unassuming as possible. Skirt, sandals, loose T-shirt, hair in a bun. From a distance, they could pull off the mother-daughter lost on a road trip, with no problems. Dorthea could hear M mumbling under her breath. She did not know what charm she was casting but knowing M, it would be exactly what the moment called for.

A few yards short of the church gate, just outside the area where the energy crested. They stopped short at the sound of a man's voice, slow and deliberate.

"Well, hi, ladies." From a small shed, just inside the gates, three men were emerging into the sunlight. All wore similar brown trousers, with white, short-sleeved, button-down shirts and brown suspenders. They looked like beardless, Mennonite cosplayers. The man in front raised his hand in a salute as they walked out to great Dorthea and M, obviously having no intention of letting them in the gate.

"How are you, gentlemen?" Dorthea asked, slipping effortlessly into her accent and cadence from her early life.

"As well as one could expect in this heat. How about yourself?"

"Well, fine as frog's hair, rare as hen's teeth, and right as the rain. If the Lord is willing, I'll fall asleep just like I awoke, on the right side of the dirt."

It was everything M had not to bust out laughing, how many times had she heard Jim Milburn, her grandfather, Dorthea's father, say the same thing.

"Well good," the man in the middle said, his mouth smiling, but his eyes flat and lifeless as a shark's. "You two up this way for anything in particular?"

"No sir, my daughter and I were just out on a bit of a road trip, you see. We went up to Noblesville to catch that big tent revival we have big hearing so much about. The Fellowship of the New Covenant. Well anyway on our way back down south, we thought we would just drive around a bit, do some sightseeing. My daughter was looking online for country churches, and wouldn't you know that the computer spit this place out. So, we thought we might come and have a look, being it was a Sunday afternoon, thought we might catch a bible study or something along the lines."

The men glanced at the women. Neither was dressed for Sunday service anywhere. The man in the middle shook his head. "Sorry, ladies, no service here. This is a youth camp and spiritual retreat. The only services are while there are campers and there aren't any here this week. I think the next batch is, what, Paul, two weeks from now, something like that?"

The man on the left, closest to M, nodded his head. "Something like that, yessir."

Dorthea smiled. "Well, then gentlemen, I do believe we will be on our way."

She leaned forward and extended her hand to each man in turn, all three of which shook it as she said to each, "Dorthea Milburn. Pleasure to meet you. Oh, and this is my daughter, Marianne."

M leaned over and shook each man's hand in turn, saying, "Nice to meet you," to each one.

When she backed away from the last man, she held a water bottle up to her lips to take a drink, Dorthea had not seen the bottle previously. In fact, she was sure M had been empty handed. When she glanced at the arm holding the bottle she saw a flash of black as one of M's many living tattoos shined through the glamour, its message clear. "RUN!"

Dorthea took only a moment to realize that was not a water bottle in M's hand, only the glamour hiding the truth of it. She knew as well what the charm was that M had been muttering as she spit a spray of concentrated poneratoxin across all three men's faces and turned to run for the car, screaming, "There's more, we have to get out, now!"

The smallest droplet of that spray was the equivalent of a bullet ant sting, and she just sprayed about eight ounces worth across the men's faces. Cries of anguish followed them down the driveway as the men rolled on the ground, no way to ease their suffering but death.

Beyond that, Dorthea could hear the shouts of other men and the stomp of boots on gravel. She looked back in time to see a man, in the same strange dress as the others, but younger and stronger built, rushing toward them like a football player. Intent on catching them and bringing them down. She spun and threw her hands out wide pulling the energy around her, she slammed her hands together only a foot or so in front of the man's grasping reach. The force from her charm slammed him in the chest and sent him tumbling backward. He writhed on the ground, holding his broken ribs and sternum, gasping for air.

M spun a circle around Dorthea, a baton in her left hand and her push dagger in her right. There were three more men closing fast. She heard Dorthea chanting hard, falling into her casting. Trusting that Dorthea would anticipate her moves, she focused her glamour and began a graceful dance of death around the men. With her glamour in full focus, she was able to make it seem as if she was teleporting at random. Attacking from both sides and behind.

The men wisely put their backs together in a triangle. It made no difference. M slammed on man in the ribs with her baton, then vanished. She struck the next man hard across the shins and he collapsed, screaming in pain. The last guy began swinging wildly moving away from the safety of his companions in the process. She slipped behind him driving the punch dagger into his kidney before spinning away and disappearing again before he even fell to the ground.

She appeared before the last man standing, he blinked, hesitating at the shock of her appearing directly in of him. She took advantage of his hesitation and swiped the razor-sharp blade across his forehead, opening a gash down to the bone. Blood poured down his face and into his eyes and he screamed and tried to run back up the driveway. M darted in front of him and slammed the baton hard into this right kneecap. He collapsed over his left leg and hit the ground crying and begging for mercy. The first man M had hit in the shins was crawling his way toward the man bleeding from the kidney, who had stopped moving altogether.

M stalked toward him, baton raised and slammed it down, weighted end first onto his spine at the base of his skull. She walked next to the man on the ground closest to her. Blood flowed from the wound to his kidney, and he had gone grey. He would not live long, but M did not want him to bleed to death slowly. She rolled him over and punched straight down, burying the dagger through his eye and into his brain.

The last man was back on his feet, limping on his broken right knee but trying to get away. Two fast blows to the back of his head ended his escape attempt.

M looked up at the end of the driveway. There were several more men headed this way, and she could see a couple more running out of the church. She turned to Dorthea who was deep in her casting, trusting M's ability to protect her so completely that she allowed herself to get drawn into the spell with all of her consciousness.

"Dorthea, there are a bunch more headed this way, we can break for the car. But they will be here quick. If you can hear me, it's time to move."

As the last of the column of several men left the gate of the church and they began sprinting down the lane, the first in line was suddenly blown into the air. The gravel under him exploding in a shower of shrapnel, tearing through the next in line. In succession, in neat rows of three, more of these explosions tore across the driveway. Working its way back toward the church. By the time the explosions and accompanying showers of rocks and body parts stopped. There was nothing left of the pursuing men.

"Holy crow, Land mines, you just conjured LAND MINES!" M was yelling in celebration as she dragged Dorthea back to the car. "Come on, we gotta go, if there was anyone in the county unaware of our presence before, they sure as hell know about us now. Let's go."

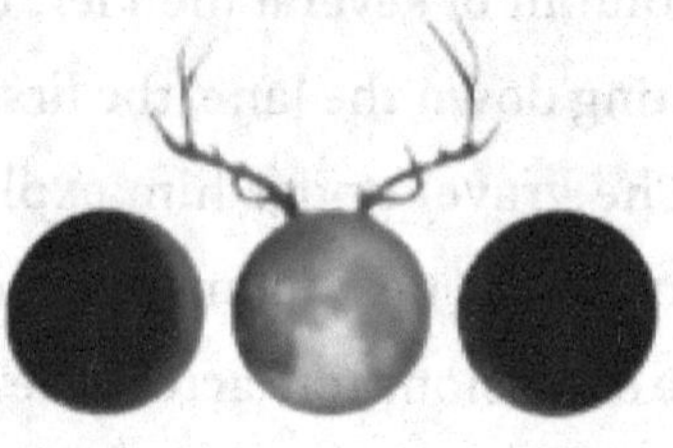

OURS OR THEIRS

M put a fast fifty miles between them and the camp before she risked stopping at a rest area. The sun was down, and there were only a couple cars parked in the lot. Two dozen semi-trucks were parked in the next lot, with a couple of big RVs sprinkled among them. She pulled as close to the doors of the main building as she could. She knew she was a mess, dirt and blood clung to her. She would hit the bathroom, clean up, and change best she could. They were only an hour or so from home, but she did not want to get any further without cleaning up. The last thing they needed was to get pulled over and her be covered in dirt and blood. She was exhausted, they both were. Dorthea was already sound asleep. The amount of effort it required to use her glamour in such an active way, combined with the physical combat and adrenaline dump, left her feeling hollowed out and weak.

She did not feel confident that she could hide their appearance from anyone should they look too closely.

A quick cleanup and change, then she could hit the next gas station for coffee and make the last sixty miles or so to home. She knew the people at the camp would not call the police, or at least not involve any law enforcement above their local department. Even then, she did not think that napping here, out in the open, would be a good idea. She had pulled a lot from her contact with the men at the camp. They knew Mercer, they knew what she and Dorthea were.

More than that, they were more scared of whoever was behind that chapel door than they were of them. Each man had been feeling something different, she got the impression none of them knew exactly the same things, but they all had snippets, little pieces of the puzzle.

The one thing that was crystal clear, and consistent. *Kill these witches or answer to the Carpenters.* The other things she picked up were so confused and fractured as to be impossible to interpret without some time and context. One man held a fear of angels, so deep it was bordering on panic. Weird for someone to be that openly terrified of an abstract idea. Another one was grieving a son lost recently, but he was not allowed to say his name out loud. Her mind was too exhausted to figure much more out.

She needed to get home, eat and sleep so she could focus on problem solving. One thing was for sure, there was more going on than they could see. Those men knew who they were, if not by name, then by their association, and they wanted them dead because of it. More than that, there was something in that church that scared them even more than going up against a couple of Mercer witches in broad daylight.

When M emerged from the rest area, stained clothes in a plastic bag, somewhat clean and not even a little refreshed, Dorthea was standing leaning against the driver door of the SUV.

"Hell of a day."

M nodded her head in reply. "Sorry, I didn't want to wake you, but I figured rolling around in bloody clothes was just asking for trouble."

"Nothing to apologize for, let me run in and pull myself together then I will drive a bit, and you nap. I will have you home to Sugarfoot before you know it. We can beg, bribe, or threaten him to make us a late dinner. Then we—" Dorthea stopped short.

M was only a foot or so in front of her, even in the dim light of the parking lot, Dorthea did not need her full sight to see how wrung out her niece looked. She reached up and brushed M's hair back from her face. "Are you alright, sweetheart?"

M shook her head, no more able to hide the truth from Dorthea than from herself. "I hate when I have to do that. I know that a lot of times, it's kill or be killed. When I touched those men, I knew two things. That they would not stop until we were dead; and even knowing what we were, they were more scared of what was behind that chapel wall than fighting us."

She tilted her head back to the sky. "I know that I did not have a choice and neither did you. But it never gets any easier. Even when they are bad, not like those guys, who seem to just be working for the wrong boss. But really bad. It's never easy, I never walk away, having killed and sleep okay. I am not broken; I don't want to quit. I just hate the fact that so many times, the only option we are given is death. Ours or theirs."

"You are right, I am not going to stand here and feed you some bullshit about how that is what separates us from the bad guys. I would bet at the end of the day, a whole lot of the people who have been hurt or killed at my hands wish it wouldn't have come to that. I doubt very many of them woke up and just decided they were going to be evil. It is insidious and comes on slow, you start moving that moral boundary a little at a time, for whatever reason. Money, acceptance, desperation, fear. Then before you know it, the boundaries no longer exist. Maybe you have a couple hard lines you won't cross, but the more desperate the situation becomes or the more dangerous it is to get out, the more likely even those lines blur or disappear altogether."

"I know, it would be so much easier if they were just all monsters."

M closed her eyes and took a deep breath. Dorthea watched the tension run out of her shoulders and jaw. When she opened her eyes again, she said, "Okay, if you're going to drive, I will catch a couple hours shut eye. But after what we saw there and what they knew, I think we need to contact Mercer as soon as possible. Some deeper recon would be wise. My gut is telling me just to grab the guys and go back and see what they are hiding in there. But considering what Mama Rosie said, and the possible scope of this being funded by one of the largest and most well-respected evangelical ministries in the country. I don't think I should be making unilateral decisions on what is best for everyone."

"Let's regroup with the guys, check on Faith and Duke, have Beck get word to the Elders that we need council and see how it plays out. I think we need to get a warning to Mama Rosie as well. She might be in danger. Her preacher friend saw her with us, and a few hours later we pop up at that camp. It might cast some suspicion her way, especially if there were cameras."

"I think if there was footage of us at that camp, we would have already had Elder Valkyrie riding shotgun asking us how we could have been foolish enough to go viral blowing up a church gate and murdering about twenty people."

Dorthea shrugged. "That's fair, and don't forget about the spitting, you do have a thing for spitting, M. Not very lady like if you ask me."

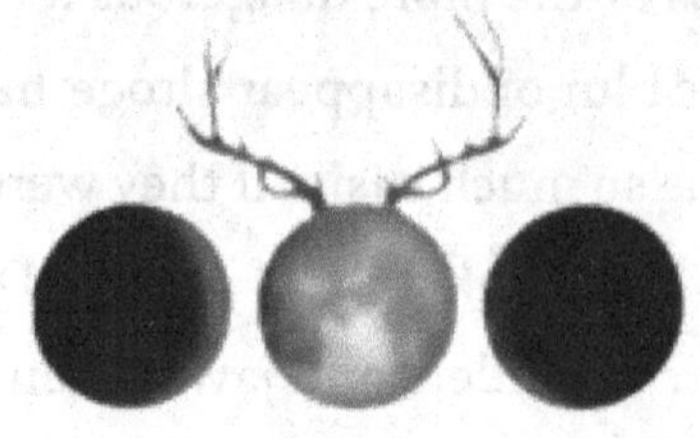

WE NEED A MONTAGE

"**G**ood! You almost stayed on your feet that time."

Bets leapt to her feet from her crouched position on the sand of the arena floor. She felt exhilarated. It had been almost two weeks since her awakening, and today she was getting to stretch both her physical and mental muscles. Her lessons had finally begun in earnest. They consisted of three parts, an Elder named Dinah had been overseeing the total of her training and teaching her how to focus and manipulate the Divine Energy of Creation. She had begun teaching her the basics of warding her mind against the kind of beating she took at Mathew's funeral. So far, she had managed to avoid another instance of siphoning like that, but she had also not been exposed to anything that intense.

Dinah also dictated most of her schedule. When she ate, what she learned and from whom, when she had free time to study or relax.

Everything. Giving up that level of control wasn't something that the old her could have tolerated. But since her awakening, she seemed to relish it. Just being able to focus on her goal of improving and learning and not having to feel like she was in control of every single aspect of everything around her. It was glorious.

Her physical fitness and martial arts instruction was coming from a man named Eugene. Eugene was short, slender, and wired tight with muscle. But this was not the body of man who spent time working on his aesthetics, this man had not studied himself in a mirror and looked for imbalances and targeted workouts to correct them. This was a body created by decades of training to be great at other things. The physique was a result of that hard work, not the goal. He drilled her every day, Yoga before breakfast, then shortly after her midday session with Dinah he would come and retrieve her from wherever they were, he always seemed to know and put her through a gauntlet of techniques and exercises.

Every day the session seemed based on a different martial art. So far, she had boxed, practiced Judo throws, wrestled, her favorite to date, and even spent an entire hour on the ground, trying to escape from Eugene, who was on her back with a chokehold locked on but not constricting. She hated that part. He said for now he was just assessing which direction her training should take.

In the evenings, just before she fell exhausted into her bed, he would come by for another session of Yoga. This one would be strictly flow, just dancing from one pose to another, letting her body guide her through what it needed.

Most of her time though, was spent with Hannah. Hannah was teaching her the hands-on dirt magic, as she called it. Herbs and roots, spit and blood, chalk and salt. Hannah was teaching her how to take what Dinah was teaching her and turn it into a practical reality. How to draw a protective circle and pull the energy of creation into it to prevent any magic from entering or escaping. Charms and spells which used physical components to focus the energy into specific results. After two weeks, she felt like she finally understood enough about it to know that she knew absolutely nothing about it. Which felt like a good starting place.

Today they were in the arena, Dinah sat on a bench peeling oranges and sharing them with Mother Mercer, while Eugene and Hannah were running her through a series of drills meant to teach her how to keep her energy focused for charms while dealing with physical attacks. Combat magic she supposed. Although she had noticed a particular lack of labels and naming among the women here at Mercer. Most things just were; categorization did not seem to be terribly important.

The idea seemed simple enough, Eugene and Bets ran through light drills with Escrima sticks. Bets loved the balance and beauty of the carved and burned wood sticks that Eugene had given her. He was constantly striking at her, she was strictly on defense, parrying and blocking. Occasionally he would rush her, knocking her off balance or bowling her over completely. All the while, Hannah moved around her, holding a white candle. Hannah would stop and turn toward her, then Bets had to cast her charm to light the candle while fending off Eugene. As soon as it was lit, Hannah would pull the flame from the candle wick and send the small ball of fire hurtling back toward Bets. She would need to get a defense up and in place before she was hit, all while holding off Eugene from either smacking her hard with a stick or pushing her over completely.

The first couple of fireballs smacked her hard, not so much burning her as popping intensely and stinging. Bets was reminded of those paper poppers she always got as a kid around the Fourth of July. Little white bags that you slammed against the ground, and they would pop and spark a little. Of course, all the kids threw them at each other as often as possible. It did not happen often but every once in a while, one of the big kids would throw one hard enough to snap against skin. That is what it felt like when Hannah's fireball hit her.

She had gotten surprisingly good at lighting the candle without getting hit by Eugene. After the third fireball hit her on the side of the head, making her wince, she tried to change tactics. When Hannah turned to face her, off to her side and about thirty feet away, Bets sent the fire charm out. This time, Bets felt like she had the timing down, she couldn't get her shield charm up in time, but when the little fireball came hurtling back at her, she rolled to her right just as Eugene swept his left arm out in a wide arc, stick aimed at the side of her head. She rolled under the attack and under the fireball and bounced back to her feet triumphantly. Eager to see the reaction from her instructors. Eugene was smiling at her, but said nothing, nor moved to attack. He just stood there. She turned toward Hannah to see what she thought of the maneuver. When she did, the fireball that Hannah had paused and held over her slammed into her chest with far more force than any of the previous ones.

Eugene offered her a hand to help her up. As she rose, Hannah spoke.

"Well executed, Bets, but I never had a doubt you could dodge a slow pitch. You have to get that shield up to disperse the energy or redirect it. A good shield charm can stop a bullet and use the kinetic energy in the impact as a weapon. Redirecting it at your will."

Bets nodded her understanding. She had felt rather clever in the moment, but again Hannah just highlighted how little she knew. She dusted herself off and turned back to Eugene to begin again. She caught movement out of the corner of her eye and risked a sideways look in the direction where Dinah and Niri sat. Ashanti had emerged from one of the hallways opening up to the arena floor. She was nodding and saying something to the two women. Then bowed to them and disappeared back down the hallway.

Dinah rose and approached smiling. "Okay, as much as I hate to break this up, we have good news."

Hannah raised an eyebrow.

"The meeting time is here; everyone is awaiting our arrival."

Hannah nodded. "Where?"

"The Garden Of the Gods, Lord Seanchara will meet us in the library in fifteen minutes and open the doorway to the place."

She turned to Eugene and Bets, who were watching the exchange curiously. "Eugene, I trust you won't mind if we steal your pupil for an hour or two of business?"

Eugene bowed at the waist. "No, ma'am. I am sure she will welcome the break from Hannah and I tormenting her."

Hannah hurried toward Bets. "Come now, we only have a few minutes, and you need to get changed, quick. Your room and back at the library entrance, changed and clean in ten minutes. Can you pull that off?"

Bets nodded her head and sprinted out of the arena.

Dinah looked at Hannah, an eyebrow raised in curiosity. "You aren't telling her?"

"No, she has been working hard. It will be a nice surprise. Let's see how long it takes her to figure it out."

Bets hit the door of her chambers at a full run, stripping out of her dirty workout clothes as soon as the door was closed behind her. A quick rinse off at the bathroom sink and she was grabbing clothes from the bedroom closet. As she did, her mind raced. What could be happening. Hannah did not tell her what to dress for, so she opted for the loose cotton harem style pants, a matching blouse, and sturdy strap sandals. She just assumed if there was something specific, she should prepare for Hannah or Dinah would have told her what was expected.

On her way out of her bedroom, she stepped back into the bathroom for a hair tie her braid had come loose while she was training, and she wanted to make it at least presentable on the way back to the library. She glanced in the mirror at her reflection. She stared in wonder at the woman looking back at her. What a difference a year can make in life, she remembered standing in her bathroom back in St. Louis, the day Lord Seanchara had first appeared to her, her fortieth birthday. She stared at her reflection in the mirror and the room around her reflection changed from the small wood and stone room in her chambers here in Mercer, to the big white and blue tile of her bathroom in the home she shared with Cecil and her children.

She blinked her eyes rapidly, her reflection did not. Her reflection was picked up off of the floor and slammed against the door by an invisible hand. Bets fell backward into the wall of the small bathroom, staring in horror and the scene playing out in the mirror. Lord Seanchara became visible, he held her head over the basin, and she started retching, her body convulsing. She could see nothing coming out of her mouth in the reflection, but she remembered the hellish feeling of maggot ridden flesh as she vomited it up. The searing pain in her head as the beak of his bird headed cane poured liquid fire into her skull. The reflection of her bathroom changed into a dark stone chamber where she hung, naked and bleeding, her arms tied to something in the middle of the room.

A man approached from the shadows, his arms were covered with blood up to the elbows. He launched into a series of hard punches to Bets' naked body. While she stood in her bathroom in Mercer, she felt the blows and screamed. Her ribs cracked, and her body swung on the ropes like a heavy bag. She gripped the sink, trying to stay upright as the memory flooded in. The pain, the humiliation, the days of torture. It all came flooding back, her death at the hands of Lord Seanchara.

Bets closed her eyes against the vision of pain and death in the mirror. She remembered her first lessons with Dinah. She took a breath, then two, focusing past the horrid tableau of memory. This was no different than protecting herself against the funeral song or warding against siphoning others' emotions. She focused on the wards she had constructed in her mind, pushing the power inward instead of building a wall around her mind. This time she built one against the horror of her own death. It took less than a minute for Bets to get herself under control.

Had she really been that terrible, had it taken a tortuous death to rid her of all of the horrible things that she had done? She trembled and the memories threatened to overtake her again. She poured her will into the wards in her mind. She did not want to repress or destroy the memory; she didn't know if she could even do that. But she needed to regulate it, right now.

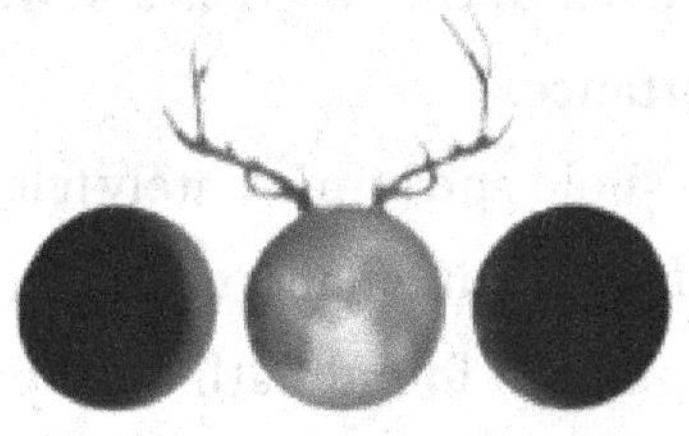

GARDEN OF THE GODS

Bets rounded the corner and came to the library entrance. The two massive wooden doors, every inch of their twenty-foot height and eight-foot width carved with intricate designs. Some faded by time, others appeared to be much newer. There were times, wandering the courtyards and temple, that she got lost in the decoration. It seemed to her that every day she was here she was able to understand more of the designs. More than once, she had walked by a carved stone and seen only a faint impression of a carving, but a day or two later, she would see a full ritual, spell and components detailed in the stone.

She wondered if she studied here long enough, if every surface would reveal some secret to her. Some memory or magic. Dinah had explained to her that like much of the magic surrounding Mercer, the spells, rituals, memories and knowledge carved into every brick, every wall of their home, revealed itself to the witch as she was able to understand its purpose and importance.

She crossed the threshold and immediately felt the pull, she had been in this room twice before and it emanated power from every direction, she opened up her sight and found path after path through the rows and rows of giant bookshelves. The room was much larger on the inside than the dimensions of its exterior would allow. When she was in this room, she felt so connected to the brothers and sisters of Mercer, like there was a part of all of them in this room.

Bets could hear them talking now as she rounded the next corner cutting between the rows on her way to the back wall, following the thread of connection between her and Dinah.

"Are we sure this is a good idea, this is a lot of us in one place outside of Mercer, if there is something insidious about, maybe we should be meeting here or only a couple of us attending. But..."

"Dinah, love please, go mother Bets or fuss over Bast. We are walking into one of the most protected and magical places on earth outside Mercer, not to mention Mother, Elder Alysse, and Elder Valkyrie. If there were ever a time when I would be okay with someone launching a surprise attack against us, it would be while I was standing in Stag's Grove, alongside Mother Mercer and The Mother Moon, his very bride. Can you imagine the hell that would be unleashed if someone wandered into there with bad intentions. The best thing that could happen is getting turned to dust on the spot. Getting caught between this lot isn't a fate I would wish on many people no matter their intentions. Well, there's Bets."

Dinah looked her up and down as Bets approached, her eyes narrowed then shot open wide and she rushed to her.

"Oh, sweetheart, are you okay? Come here."

She wrapped Bets in a motherly hug, pulling her in tight. Bets let herself sink into that feeling, smelling the sage and cinnamon smell of Dinah.

"What a time to remember, I guess there is no convenient time to remember something like that. Did you get your barriers in place? Can you hold it in check?"

"Yes, ma'am, it took me for a moment or two, I am still not totally okay, but I am hanging in there for now."

"Just remember, you don't want to suppress it completely, it will not work. But just regulate how fast and hard it hits you. Assimilate only as much as you can process. Just as important is that Lord Seanchara did only what was absolutely necessary to bring you through. I know it won't be easy should you come face to face with him as you remember. But he is the agent of change and growth, he did not make you the person that you were. He unmade that person so that you could become the person that you are right now."

Bets nodded, her eyes welling with tears. Dinah released her as Hannah approached them.

"Alright, enough of this. We have good news and bad news for you. The good news is you are going on a trip, a very, very, long trip. Although it will only take a moment to get there. The bad news is that it is meeting of the Council of Elders so you will have to listen to a bunch of old women prattle on."

"Why would I be invited to a Council meeting?"

"A couple reasons. We now know that the monster that killed Mathew wasn't acting alone, there was something powerful aiding and perhaps driving him to kill. Now we are hearing there have been some other developments. Bishop was cornered and somehow escaped again. There have been enough odd and disparate occurrences that Niri thought we should get everyone together to discuss them in person and perhaps put some pieces together."

Dinah leaned close. "We need to go, but you need to know a couple of things before we do. The doorway leads to a protected grove in a beautiful forest, we are safe. The path was opened and is guarded by Lord Seanchara, his wife, Elder Valkyrie, will be among the witches present. She is as ancient and powerful as he is, guard your thoughts. Especially where he is concerned, she is as devoted to him as he is to her, and she can be volatile. When you cross the threshold of the doorway, you will be stepping across thousands of miles in a breath. Block all of your senses. You must be an impenetrable wall, nothing can get in. It can drive you quite mad to be aware while crossing the distance. Just close yourself off and take three steps through the doorway. You will be fine."

"Dinah, if this is a gathering of the powerful to discuss these strange occurrences, then why am I going to be there? I can barely control my siphon most days and certainly won't have anything valuable to bring to the table."

"Nonsense, you are new to Mercer Bets, not new to the world. Besides, Niri wanted you there. Said it would be important to your growth to attend and when Mother wants something, we don't question. Now come on, in you go, just shut everything down and step through. We are going to be late to lunch."

Bets stood before the open doorway, she could see into the room beyond, it looked like a small office, grey worn carpet, institutional white walls, bad fluorescent lighting. All a very stark contrast to the beautifully ornate room she was standing in. She pulled in the energy of creation and focused on dropping walls over all of her senses. She blocked every possible input. No sight, sound, smell, feeling, anything. When she was completely closed off to the world around her and sure that nothing from outside herself could get in, she stepped through.

Before she could even open her eyes, she smelled the forest, green and lush. She could hear the murmuring of many voices, as well as the sounds of a living wilderness. The wind in the leaves, birds singing, something skittered through the undergrowth off to her left. She opened her eyes and was nearly driven to her knees from the beauty.

She stood in a large clearing, green grass nearly up to her ankles cushioned every step, trees towered around the perimeter, and she could not see past the first couple rows. This was a very serious woods, this was a wild place. She smelled the green of the woods, the wild musky smell of some animals, and food, no, she smelled meat.

She glanced around, taking in her fellow occupants, and she felt Hannah and Dinah step through. She turned to look at them and see the doorway. But there was only the two women and a pair of small birch trees, seemingly out of place in this grove. It appeared they had just stepped through the trees.

In the center of the grove there were more than two dozen people standing around a fire pit; she could see the smoke rising from the middle of the gathering. Niri sat off to the side in deep discussion with two women Bets did not recognize, one older black woman in what looked like a track suit, the kind favored by television mobsters from the nineteen nineties, the other woman was short, white, with a spiky haircut, dyed pink. She had multiple piercings and tattoos that Bets could see from where she stood. The younger woman was telling what was apparently an extremely exciting story, from how animated she appeared to be. Dinah and Hannah walked forward toward the group. Dinah grabbed Bets by the hand and pulled her gently along.

Bets recognized Malvika and Charles. They were standing with a brunette woman and a short but incredibly handsome man. He was smiling perhaps the most charming smile Bets had ever seen on a man so young. When Bets looked back toward the center of the grove, her path was no longer clear. A woman had appeared out of nowhere. No, that wasn't right. She had stepped from nowhere. Bets was sure of it, like the woman had stepped out from behind a tree or pillar, but there was nothing there for her to be behind.

She was tall, taller than Bets by a lot, her beautiful black hair was pulled back in a complex series of tight braids that crisscrossed her scalp and piled high atop her head in a large bundle. Bets thought they would probably reach the ground if she freed them. She was dressed in a loose wrap of some very sheer material that left almost nothing to the imagination in the bright morning sunlight. Every inch of exposed skin, other than her face, was covered in tattoos. It took Bets only a moment to realize that, like the walls and sculptures of Mercer itself, this woman was covered in spell work. Ingredients, phrases, equations, and drawings. This woman's body was a living, breathing grimoire. As Bets studied her, the woman spoke.

"I am not sure how to feel about being read like a page from a book, young sister."

Bets' eyes snapped up to the woman's face only to realize that she had no eyes, just empty sockets where they should have been. Even in the daylight, a soft red glow emanated from them.

Bets bowed her head in humble apology. "Ma'am, I meant no offense, and hope that I have caused none. I was simply struck by the beauty of your art."

She held out her hand to the woman, realizing who it is she was talking to, the stature, the eyes, this was the Elder Valkyrie, and Bets had just made a fool of herself gawking at her like a schoolboy with a crush on the teacher.

"I am Colleen Milburn, Bets if it pleases you, ma'am."

Elder Valkyrie did not take the offered hand but bowed her head. "It is good to finally meet you, Bets. I have been acquainted with your family for a very long time, for good and for ill." She let that linger in the air just long enough to make her point before continuing. "My husband was quite taken with you."

Her eyes glowed a little brighter and Bets could feel the intrusion into her mind, not a total invasion, just a brush. Enough that Bets understood that if this woman wanted to plumb the depths of her mind, there was nothing at all she could do to stop her.

"After he took the appropriate steps to unburden you of that incredible ego and stubborn streak."

Bets felt the walls she had built around the memory of her death start to collapse a little. Then Elder Valkyrie did take her outstretched hand and almost instantly she felt them return to where they were. Safely hiding those horrible memories from her consciousness.

"I just thought I would see for myself what material Colleen Milburn was made from. I must say, for someone so recently reborn, you are magnificent, sister. What a powerful witch you will be one day if you can survive whatever it is we are here to figure out."

Bets just stared at the woman, remembering Dinah's warning.

"The real challenge, is going to happen as soon as I step away. People are standing right behind me who have waited a very long time to see you. I just wanted to take my turn before they took up the rest of your day. Be well, sister, your adventure is just beginning."

With that, the woman disappeared again. Bets shook her head, trying to clear the surreal experience from her mind. She looked up and first saw Fredrick's smiling face, his bald head shining with a little sweat in the heat. To his left was Sugar, in his homemade clothes, his long white hair hanging down loose over his shoulders. He wore no shirt under his leather vest. Bets could see every muscle in his arms and torso. She beamed at him and started to walk toward them, intent on wrapping them both in the most ridiculous hug she could manage on the two giant men. She had gone a full three steps before she noticed the women standing between them, maybe it was seeing the familiar faces of Fredrick and Sugar made her oblivious to anyone else.

She froze. Her breath caught in her chest, and her throat convulsed. Next to Fredrick, an older woman, dressed like she was freshly back from safari, blue cargo shorts, a khaki work shirt and hiking boots. Her close-cropped grey hair, and a pair of spectacles perched on her head completed the look of comfortable practicality. But her eyes, those were her grandma Neeny's eyes staring back at her from that square jawed, tanned, face.

"Dorthea?" she whispered, then looked to the other woman, already knowing who this had to be. Her long red hair in a braid down her back, in a flowing emerald skirt and sandals, with a white sleeveless shirt. Tattoos covered her arms. The woman reached over and put a hand on Sugar's large shoulder to steady herself.

Bets began to cry, it was her, it was Polly, she had not seen her in more than thirty years. Her big sister, her hero, her idol. Stolen from her, and now, here she stood, and Bets was frozen to the spot. Big bad Colleen, unable to even move for fear that this was all a dream. Seconds passed with the three women just staring. Finally, Dorthea held out her arms to her, and that was all Bets needed to break the fear that held her paralyzed. She ran across the few yards to where they stood and when they met, both women grabbed her, embracing her, holding her. For a long while none of them moved, then finally Bets pulled back enough to look at both of them.

M reached up and touched her face. "I wanted to come to you, I promise you, I was going to burn down the walls if they wouldn't let me in. But when the guys got back, they told us they met you. I focused all my rage on them."

Sugar piped up from his spot a few feet away. "Bets, she chased me with a broom. It was terrifying."

Dorthea rolled her eyes at him. "You are damn lucky we weren't both there when you told her. I can do far worse with a broomstick than just batter you about a little. I have none of M's compassion or shame, Sugar."

Sugar held his hands up in surrender.

Bets' sobs relented enough for her to speak. "I need a drink, and maybe a place to sit down. If I do not, I am going to pass out. You are both just so beautiful."

She did not pull away from either woman enough to break contact. Still gripped by the fear that if she disrupted the moment, she would break the spell.

M led her to a row of stone benches closer to the fire pit. There was a spit over the flames with a suckling pig being roasted. Two grates of thick metal wire were suspended over the fire as well, each loaded with every type of vegetable that Bets had ever imagined. Bets' stomach lurched at the sight of the food and her mouth watered. She had been in the middle of an intensive training session when she was told to run and get ready for this adventure. Her body was sending distress signals, eat or die.

"Fredrick, Sugar, please tell me that is your work over that fire."

Fredrick bowed. "Yes, ma'am. Christopher and I arrived here yesterday afternoon to begin preparing for this conclave."

"Oh, lovely, I was training with Hannah and Eugene when they said go change clothes and get to the library. I am way overdue for breakfast."

Dorthea reached over and took Bets' hand. "Eugene and Hannah, let me guess, Escrima and fireballs?"

Bets grinned and nodded.

"So how did you fair? Did she stall one on you yet and knock the hell right out of you."

"Yes, ma'am. I got too clever for my own good and tried dodging rather than warding. Figured I wouldn't need a wall if I were nowhere to be found when the shot came in."

"A fine theory, until you realize Hannah has literally seen every trick in the book and could throw one of those little fireballs through an engine block without even trying."

M brushed Bets' hair back from her face. "Are you okay, sis?"

"I don't know, most days. I guess. Being away from Cecil and the kids is tough. Oh God, the kids, you would love them. Well, Steven is a little teenage-ery at the moment. Brooding, sarcastic, you know the drill. But Lilly, oh you would love Lilly. She reminds me of us when we were little. All teeth and claws."

Dorthea chuckled. "Yes, she is. You should be proud of her, Bets. She stood up to something pretty terrifying and saved her own life. She knew who we were, maybe not exactly, but she knew we were family. I have never felt a probing like that from someone not born into Mercer and trained."

"Oh, I forgot the guys said you met her. A case? Oh no, I forgot about Kay, how could I forget Kay was lying there dead?"

"Because you have had a lot going on, sis. Kay is fine, she is young and tough. The twins will wake her soon and you will get to see her as she starts her training and finishes her education. That case is part of the reason we are here today. There has been an odd confluence of events lately and we want to see if we can put together all of the pieces. I am so glad Hannah and Dinah brought you along. Will you sit with us? With Dorthea and I, while we eat and talk. We have a lot to catch up on."

Across the grove seated on the ground leaning against a tree. Elder Valkyrie, watched with her magical sight. She could see a great many things even without her eyes. She could see the Divine Energy of Creation, binding them together. She could see the connections between all of the living things in the grove, connecting them to themselves and to him, as this was his sacred place. She could see the Milburn girls, reunited and content. She had already put together the pieces of what they were here to discover; these events had been foreseen long ago.

The only option now was to play her part, to carry this out until the end, until her end. She could do nothing now to change what was coming. No, that wasn't precisely true; she could affect a great many changes, nothing was predestined, nothing was immutable or written into the laws of the universe. But allowing this to run its course would be to the benefit of all mankind. It was, after all, why she was created—to protect mankind.

Now it was time to fulfill her duty. It was a funny thing about fate. She knew that what she was about to do, over the course of the next few years, would bring about the paradise on earth that she was created to ensure. Thus, fulfilling her destiny. She was also certain that the path she was undertaking was not the path intended for her. But she was her own agent and always had been. All the signs were in place. If everyone here told their truths today, she was certain at least Niri and possibly Dorthea would put the pieces together and take the next step she needed in order for them all to see.

Niri's sweet song of a voice brought her attention back to the now.

"Sisters and brothers, please gather around. Let us find comfort in one another's company as well as the peace of Stag's Grove. Our friend and protector Lord Seanchara has once again allowed us the use of his sanctuary and garden for this conclave. First, I want to thank Fredrick and Christopher for what I am certain will be a wonderful meal; my mouth has been watering since the moment I stepped into the grove. I know you gentlemen were here overnight preparing for our arrival, and we all appreciate your work on our behalf."

A quiet mummer of appreciation moved through the gathered crowd. Every single soul in attendance was looking forward to the meal.

The crashing of branches and the sound of heavy steps brought everyone to attention. Bets looked side to side and saw several sisters rising to their feet. She could feel the pull of energy being drawn in as several spells were prepared at once. Niri's eyes narrowed, and Fredrick, Sugar, and the smaller brown-haired man rushed from their spots and surrounded Niri.

Just as Bast came crashing through the trees. Getis, Gmate, and Kephalos, the three magical dogs of Elder Alysse, were close on her heels, snarling and barking as they came. M, Bets, and a couple of others moved forward as if to help. They of course did not know Bast or Alysse's hounds.

With a leap and a twist, Bast jumped ahead of the dogs by an easy twenty feet, then turned, and mid-

jump kicked off the trunk of a large oak tree and launched herself at the dogs. All three scrambled to a stop and changed direction, now running from Bast, and she gave chase, crashing back into the woods around Stag's Grove.

"Oh, blessed children," Niri said. "Perhaps when our business is concluded we can all join in, I cannot imagine a more healing way to spend an afternoon than barefoot running through the forest in pursuit of pure joy, with no more care in the world than what game to play next." She winked at Dorthea. "What do you think, Dorthea, should we give chase, put our speed against Hecate's hounds?"

Dorthea lowered the shield she had been pouring energy into, grinned and waved a hand down her body, indicating her work shirt and cargo shorts. "Mother, I would be honored to, but Fredrick has already chastised me about getting my Sunday best dirty, and he would be beside himself trying to get the grass stains out of my clothes."

"Well, we must not make the job of keeping you presentable more difficult than I am sure it already is, and I have no constitution for a reprimand from Fredrick Sapp. I am a sensitive girl after all."

It was not long before the meal was served, goat and suckling pig roasted over the fire. Along with every kind of grilled vegetable and tuber Bets had ever seen. Plates of grilled flatbread were passed around along with pitchers of the coldest, cleanest water she had ever tasted. Several bottles of wine were passed around, along with a tea service. For a picnic in the woods, it was an incredibly elaborate meal. Once everyone was served and eating, sharing accolades about the food, and several remarks being made about the wisdom of letting such incredible culinary talent work in the field where they could be lost to bullet or blade of an enemy, Elder Alysse rose. Slowly, she walked the perimeter of the grove. All eyes watched as she stopped at the four cardinal compass points of the circle.

Bets struggled to see what she was doing and had no chance of hearing her words. Dorthea noticed her confusion and came to her aid.

"She is imbuing the circle of this grove with a little of her power. A drop of her blood and a touch of her focus will help to close the circle. If I am guessing, she is also laying a charm on all inside the circle. A charm of memory and insight called Mother's Eyes. It will allow whatever is said inside the circle to reach deep into our subconscious faster than it ever could, and allow you to access your memory and insight in a much more deliberate and effective way. This way as well all tell our pieces of the story today, the whole of it will piece itself together in the mind of each person. Similar to the funeral song but with much less emotional impact. When she finishes the last marker, you should feel the energy flow over you."

Bets shuddered a little, and M put her hand on her shoulder. "The guys told us you caught Hannah's funeral song full blast on your first day, though the veil that would have been horrible for anyone. On the bright side, you could not have been in better hands. Sugar, Fredrick, Mother Mercer, the twins. If you are going to get your mind invaded with no chance of stopping it, there are no better folks around to help you pick up the pieces."

"Honestly, it feels like that has happened a lot, just this morning, Hannah sent me to get ready to come here. I stopped in the mirror to make sure I didn't look like a homeless person. No idea where I was going, or who I would be seeing. While I am getting ready it hits me, my entire death at the hands of Lord Seanchara, days of brutal torture and pain. All in one shot. I was able to get barriers in place, but not by much and not nearly fast enough."

M smiled. "It gets easier after the first year or so, or at least the big surprises get easier to deal with."

Dorthea clapped her on the back like a car salesman showing off a great deal. "Besides, after coming back from the dead and learning that magic is real and you are now a witch, who has to go fight evil alongside a bunch of family members who were also dead, where do the real surprises even come from after that?"

Bets felt the wave of energy roll across the grove, heads lifted up from plates and conversations. But no one seemed concerned. Bets was a little nervous even then. Her mind had taken quite a beating over the last couple of weeks, and she wondered if there was a limit to how much it could take before it just broke.

Elder Alysse walked to the center of the grove. "Sisters and brothers, let us begin. Polly, Dorthea, since you called this conclave and have the piece of the puzzle closest to my heart, will you begin?"

M stood. "Thank you, Elder Alysse. There are things we have not encountered before. Or at least Dorthea and I have not, we hoped that by bringing everyone together to share their tales and thoughts we could put the pieces together, or at least be sure the Council of Elders has all the pertinent information. I will start with what I know, everyone seems to have a piece of the puzzle and will share it as it becomes relevant."

As M moved to the center of the grove, Bets watched with a certain degree of awe. She was no slouch at public speaking, but M was different, this wasn't practiced movements and patterns of a college educated lecturer or a trained debater. This was a confidence and grace that seemed rooted in something deeper. Dorthea leaned over and whispered in her ear, "If you close your eyes and focus on the connection, you will see what Elder Alysse did with that insight spell."

She did, and as M started her story the images began playing out in her mind, like watching a movie. She saw Leo Benson, saw Sugar in frustrated combat with the grotesque but dangerous man. She saw M finding and warding the children and the chaos as the older black woman bound Sugar to protect them from him as he beat a limp pile of gore relentlessly. She made a mental note to ask Dorthea what grease was.

She understood a little better what they were saying about her sister and Sugar, their love for one another was evident.

She saw the altar to the goddess Hecate, understanding now that Hecate was actually the Elder Alysse, she wondered how many more myths and legends would be attributable to the women of Mercer.

Alysse rose and addressed the group again. "I can promise you there is no connection between this monster and myself. But the appearance of another that escaped and the witchcraft present, not to mention the skill and vile will necessary to make grease. He was obviously aided by someone more in tune than himself."

Many heads nodded in agreement. As Elder Alysse spoke of the making of grease Bets was inundated with the meaning and what it entailed. She felt her stomach turn at the thought and was suddenly extremely glad that Sugar did what he did.

Dorthea was the next to speak, outlining the events of their battle with Cordray. Bets saw the images flashing into her mind as if it was her own memory. She cried when she understood Todd Bryant's fate. It was surreal seeing her beautiful Lilly through the eyes of Dorthea. She was filled with longing and pride at the strength and insight Lilly showed. She looked around the grove and saw more than one head turn her way as Dorthea described the events. M put her hand on Bets' shoulder, her smile too was mixed with pride and sadness.

Dorthea brought the question of the tether to the group. According to their records, the young girl was somehow bound to the monster, an unwilling accomplice eternally enslaved to him. But that was clearly not the case. She had revealed great cruelty and power and referenced a "Father" that was not Cordray, intimating that it was her who had enslaved him and that her father would come for vengeance if Dorthea hurt her. She went on to tell of their message from Mama Rosie and the ensuing meeting and fight at the church camp.

Niri rose from her seat and spoke again. "We know there are many things in creation that we do not understand. We have much evidence from our many years of memory and records that suggest that becoming part of our great family is not the only way to manipulate the Divine Energy. Even now sweet Bast runs through the woods and not one of us could tell you her origin, although most of us have witnessed her power in its full glory."

Niri turned a slow circle, taking in her audience. Her voice a flowing, musical cadence that enrapt everyone there.

"We have all encountered people and things that could not be explained easily or did not fall within our understanding. There is magic of many kinds all around us. To assume that we have some kind of a monopoly on understanding and harnessing Divine Energy would be folly of the greatest magnitude. If the monster Cordray was not the father of the tether, than we must be diligent, as any creator would likely seek out those who destroyed their creation. Even one as twisted and evil as the tether appeared to be. For the younger brothers and sisters among us, please keep this in mind as we navigate this peril. The archives are full of encounters with others whose power and origin could not be discerned. While we have never found an organization or group of our size and influence. There is nothing that would preclude it. The Witch Father has not been seen for more than a generation, but he made no assertion that we were the only creations to whom he gifted the sight. We will discern if these events are related and deal with whatever threat has presented itself. As we have always done. Duke, would you like to tell us about your encounter?"

Duke rose from his place next to Faith and Snow, who had not left their side since their encounter with Bishop. He walked with a cane from where his leg had been broken. He was healing. But even with the help of Mercer's greatest healers it was slow. In no other circumstance could a person survive the damage that was done to him and be up and walking just a couple weeks later. He told his tale. Starting with the calls from Mercer, the baiting attacks on Amber and Michael Dudley and the others.

Everyone present had heard Hannah's funeral song for Mathew Weems, they all knew what kind of monster they were dealing with. He was dangerous and highly resistant to magic, but he was not impervious. Once Hannah had unleashed her full power against him, physically and psychically he stood no chance and only survived because she wanted to see where he came from, to assess a larger threat if it was present. The same could be said of his fight with Duke, he was too much for Duke alone physically, but with Fredrick and Devlin he was severely injured relatively quickly.

The biggest concerns were his disappearing trick and the fact that Hannah had boiled the skin off of the right side of his body, torn out his eye and turned his mind inside out manipulating his thoughts. Somehow, he was recovered enough to get the drop on Faith and nearly kill Duke in a one on one, unarmed fight only a few weeks later. It should not have been possible.

As Duke began to tell the story of the chase through the bowling alley, Bets was looking around at all those gathered in the grove. Dinah and Mother Mercer sat side by side with Hannah and two others that she had not met yet. She turned to look at Dorthea, thinking to ask who the two women were. When she caught sight of Sugar, she stopped. Something seemed off with him. He was glaring at Duke in a way that she found unsettling.

"I was armed when I came to the third floor, he was standing in front of the window, the sunlight was behind him. I could tell he was holding Faith in front of him but couldn't see well enough to get a safe shot at him without risking hitting her. I had no choice but to toss my weapon. Thinking in an even fight, with Faith safe, I could deal with him. His response was to smash the floor to ceiling window and toss her out of it. I did not know that Beck and Snow had arrived at that time, or that Fredrick and Devlin were close behind or I would have waited to engage and the three of us could have finished him. As it was, I charged in, hoping to deal with him quick and render aid to Faith if I could."

As Duke recounted his story of the fight as he remembered with all of the precision and dispassion of a practiced courtroom witness, Bets could see the battle playing out in her mind. The size of this Bishop monster, of course reminded her of Sugar, that same build. Stranger than that, the way he moved, it was so much like what she had just saw in her mind when she saw Sugar fighting the man in the swamps. She turned and looked at Dorthea and Polly, hoping for an explanation. Maybe her mind was superimposing one memory over another or something.

Dorthea and Polly were both staring at Sugar, he was staring blankly at the tree line, obviously agitated but no one could really tell about what.

As Duke finished and Fredrick and Devlin recounted their sided of the tale, Sugar seemed to calm. By the time the group had moved on to M and Dorthea talking about the confrontation at the Kaskaskia Valley Camp, he was completely back to normal. Still, it made Bets more than a little uneasy, and looking around the clearing, it did not appear that she was the only one who felt that way.

With all the pieces on the table, Mother Mercer once again moved to the center of the grove and addressed all who gathered there.

"Sisters and brothers, it seems we are facing a new peril, and either a new peril with tremendous reach and power, or a couple of groups who have somehow overlapped their work to disrupt everything we stand for. So, the question now is how do we move forward. I ask the Elders to speak now on this matter as I propose a plan. I think it's wise to engage some of our stealthier sisters to put this place under constant surveillance. Perhaps we can ascertain a little more about them and their purpose, and how they have harnessed the energy of creation in such a manner. Perhaps we may also discover the origin of this Bishop monster, my entire body is screaming that these cannot be isolated incidents."

"Elder Alysse, I feel safe in assuming you will investigate the mystery in Louisiana?"

"Yes, Mother, that is my first stop when I leave here."

"Beck, Devlin, can you get as close to Meadow Ministries as you feel is safe. I feel like they are the key to this somehow. But they are a big organization with a very loud presence in the evangelical world and up until right now, never a single accusation of corruption or impropriety.

Even people who have left the church when they lost their faith, have nothing bad to say about the ministry or the man who heads it up, this Jim Meadows. Other than the fact that is kind of an over-the-top throwback to the old Jim Baker days of TV evangelicals."

This elicited several groans from the older sisters in attendance, many of them well remembered the evangelical craze of the eighties, satanic panic included. It did not make their jobs any easier. It wasn't the inquisition or the witch trials, both of which, Niri, Alysse, and Elder Valkyrie were present for. But it was still inconvenient.

"Brothers and sisters, please proceed with caution. There is a power behind this, and we do not know its limitations or its influence yet. Many of you do not recall a time when we have been up against adversaries that know who and what we are. But I believe that is the case here, and they have dangerous weapons at their disposal, as evidenced by this Bishop. Hold fast to your training, and each other, as well as the knowledge that our path is necessary and righteous. I want everyone in constant contact, Dinah and I will act as relays from Mercer. We will spread the word worldwide, no off-grid assignments, no unplanned leaves of absence."

She turned toward Elder Alysse who rolled her eyes and smiled. "Yes, Mother." She mocked playfully, but her love and respect for Niri was more than evident on her beautiful face.

Bets wondered just how long the two of them had been together, how many centuries had passed for them maintaining the mission. What kind of bond would you share after hundreds of years, maybe a thousand, in each other's company. Fighting, loving, grieving, celebrating.

Then she remembered she could see, she allowed her sight to expand and instantly she saw the bands of light as thick as tree trunks flowing from Mother Mercer through every being here, and beyond.

The connections between Mother Mercer and Elder Alysse were giant multicolored bands that swirled, and twisted, streaks of darker colors, sometimes ominously darker, shot through the band.

It was brilliant and beautiful, and it brought Bets to tears again. She felt M's hand on her back, rubbing gently, and she smiled up at her.

She looked around the grove seeing all of the connections between the sisters and brothers gathered. But more than that, seeing the connections to all of creation, the trees, the animals in the grove. She breathed in the fresh clean air and felt her own connection to the grove and the people gathered here grow. She opened her spirit up further and allowed her sight to broaden and found herself pulling in more and more of the energy she felt surrounding her. She felt reborn, rejuvenated, after the physical and psychological beating she had taken over the last few weeks, this felt like stepping out of a shower, clean and hot and ready for the day.

Dorthea whispered in her ear, "Bets, baby, put your wards back in place, you're pulling power from everywhere."

She startled out of her trance and turned to look at Dorthea, more than a little shocked and embarrassed. "Oh shit, sorry, I was just falling into my sight, looking at all the connections and it felt so energizing, so healing to be here with everyone, in this place."

"No need to be sorry, happens to all of us from time to time. That's why we are here for each other."

Bets focused on Niri speaking in the center of the grove.

"Sisters, the Council of Elders will convene in two weeks to determine the best course of action with the information we gather. I love you all, be safe and be well."

Murmurs of, "Thank you, Mother," and, "We love you, Mother," echoed through the grove as everyone began to rise. Dinah and Hanna were making their way toward where Bets sat with Dorthea and M.

M put her arm around Bets again. "Come on, sis, let's say our good-byes to the guys so they don't get their feelings hurt that they got no time with you."

Bets laid her head on her shoulder. "I know, we have to go, you have to go, you have a mission, and I have, more beatings to take at the hands of Hannah and Eugene. But I wish we could stay together; I wish I could come with the two of you."

Dorthea took her other hand in hers, completing the chain. "So do we, sweetheart, but we will be together soon again, as often as we can manage, I promise you that."

She looked at Dorthea, a genuine plea in her eyes. "Can you watch over Lilly when you can, can you keep her safe from all this evil circling around our family?"

"Every chance I get, Bets, I promise you that, if it was up to me, she would have Sugar and Fredrick as personal bodyguards."

All three women laughed, a sound that echoed through the divine energy of creation, and the ripple of it touched everyone Bets knew and loved.

Cecil at home doing dishes, started to weep, suddenly remembering a time he and Colleen were young, in their first apartment, they were cooking dinner together, singing, dancing, and just being in love. She was in this little sundress and was twirling through the kitchen and he picked her up and carried her to the bedroom. Hours later, dinner ruined from neglect, they ordered takeout and sat on the secondhand couch together and dreamed of their future.

Lilly and Steven were out in the backyard, Steven had been mowing and Lilly helping by emptying the clippings bags and stirring up the compost pile. As she was bringing the bag back to him, they were both reminded of how their mom used to work in the yard with them on the weekends, how much she loved her backyard, its flower beds and brick herb spirals. When she handed Steven the bag, she blurted out. "I miss her, I miss her so much."

Steven, normally quiet and standoffish with his sister on a good day, pulled her in for a hug and told her he loved her.

Paul, alone in his empty apartment, his kids, well what used to be his kids, now that their "real dad" stepped forward to sue him for custody and won. Had moved out six months prior and he had not been allowed to see them since. Set the cheap .38 caliber pistol down on the end table next to the half full bottle of vodka, maybe he would give it one more day before he ended everything.

Jason, tending bar, looking rundown and ragged, looked up at the door as it chimed, just for a moment he thought he saw her, strolling through, in a group of women. Just like she used to, entertaining friends or other artist types. Pretending like she didn't know him before excusing herself to leave early about twenty minutes before the end of his shift so she could be naked on the bed when he came in from work.

He hung his head a little lower when the group of ladies got close, and he saw the woman he thought was Colleen. He knew he was only a toy for her, but he just couldn't get over her, wouldn't get over her, and he would not stop looking for her.

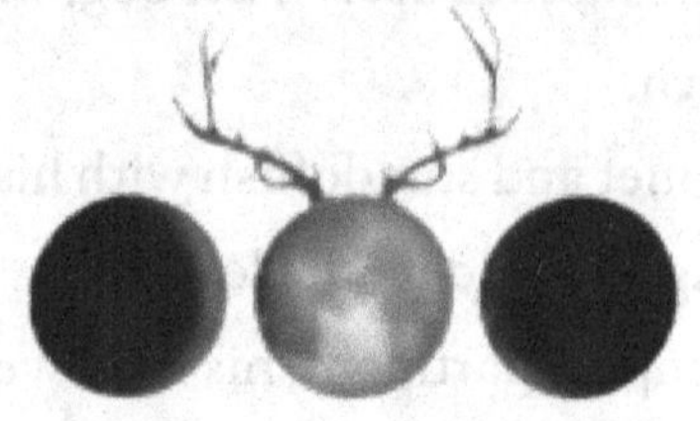

REPRIEVE, WELL EARNED

Bets walked with Hannah and Dinah back through the portal into the library at Mercer. She felt refreshed and full of love. She had lost a lot since the moment Seanchara had appeared in her bathroom and she grieved her loss every day. But today, she was really able to recognize what she had gained as well.

A sense of purpose, not blind ambition, or a lust for power. For the first time since she was a child, she felt truly connected to something, not just what those around her could provide her.

She missed Cecil and the kids with all her heart, but she knew she saw now the good she could do in the world, and it may never make the heartache of losing them fade, but it may at least provide some balance. As they reached the outer doors of the library that led to the courtyard, Dinah gently touched her arm.

"Bets."

"Yes, ma'am?"

"You have done well, sister; you are a sponge soaking up everything thrown at you without question. But you have also absorbed a lot of the last few weeks. I want you to take a weekend, today is Friday, let's reconvene Monday for breakfast at the Hall in the Temple of the Mother. But I don't want to see you before that unless it is in passing. No studies at the library, no sneaking training with Hannah or Eugene. Take the time, process what has happened. You have been through a lot since your awakening, and one of the most important things we can do, is to know when and how to step away from things and process. Should you end up in the field, like Hannah here, or M or Dorthea, the things you will see, the things you will find yourself forced to do, it is the only way to survive with your spirit intact."

Hannah spoke from beside her now, "Bets, part of your power as a siphon, allows you to heal and energize yourself by pulling the energy of creation into you and storing it like a battery. This can be used to power spells, charms, and wards, it can be used to heal wounds or keep you fighting long after you are exhausted. But like all things, there can be dangers. I will bet you feel fantastic right now, don't you?"

"Actually, I do, all things considered."

"Yes, you should be physically and emotionally spent right now. But you feel great. That's because we all felt you pulling in the energy of the grove. His grove. With all our combined power. Even Elder Alysse noticed, you caused the power on her Mother's Eyes, charm to weaken when you drew it into yourself. What I'll bet you cannot feel yet or cannot see is how hard the Stag himself is upon you. I can, and Dinah can. Your family may not have been able to, they are wise, but they are still young and haven't spent every day with you like we have. If you were to say, get into a conflict right now, or even a state of intense emotion, your reactions would filter and be affected by the power you drew from Stag's Grove. You would think and react just as much like

Lord Seanchara in his wild form as you would you. Does that make sense?"

"Yes, it does."

"It may seem like a benefit, and it can be, but you must be incredibly careful who you siphon from. You will take on their traits both spiritual and sometimes even physical. Imagine you've siphoned from Stag's Grove, like now, but in a bigger dose, undiluted by all of us sharing his space with you. Some unfortunate guy decides to get a little aggressive flirting with you at the gas station and instead of handling it like Bets, you handle it the way Lord Seanchara might handle a disrespectful lech. It might get messy, and you cannot disappear at will once the body parts have settled."

Dinah interjected again, "She is absolutely right, Bets, and we do not yet know the depth or impact of your gift, and you have a lot more to learn about even the most basic practical magic, but we can all see your heart, we know you want to be great one day. You want to stand among the elders and prove your value to our family, but I want to promise you a couple things. You were valuable to us the moment you were born. You are worthy of love and respect even if you spend the rest of your days lounging around here eating fruit with the twins and waxing philosophical about if The Witch Father should be a gendered construct or not."

Bets rolled her eyes and smiled a tired smile.

"My point is this, take your time, process what you have learned these last few weeks and today. Sit in your truth, apply what you have learned and allow it truly to become a part of you, not just another thing that you are going to be great at. Now go get some rest."

Dinah pulled her in and hugged her tight, she felt herself melt into her strong arms. It seemed everywhere she turned here, she was feeling that again, the bittersweet feel of that mother's love she was robbed of. Robbed by Neeny, but also robbed by Mercer, it was the Mercer pact that Neeny was so scared of that she continuously risked and sacrificed her own kinfolk to run from it.

"On Monday we will meet for breakfast, nine o'clock in the hall. By then, two things will have happened: you'll be meeting your consort, and Kay will have been awakened and introduced to Mercer by the twins."

Bets stiffened. "Oh, I hadn't even considered."

"What—that you are not special? You get paired with a consort just like everyone else, Bets. It is an important part of your life here. The only question left to answer is who and the elders are meeting tonight over cocktails to discuss it, and no, you do not get to have an opinion on the matter."

With this, Hannah and Dinah left her standing in the courtyard. Her body was buzzing with the energy she pulled from Stag's Grove and all the elders in attendance, her mind racing with new possibilities and questions, and heart very full of love.

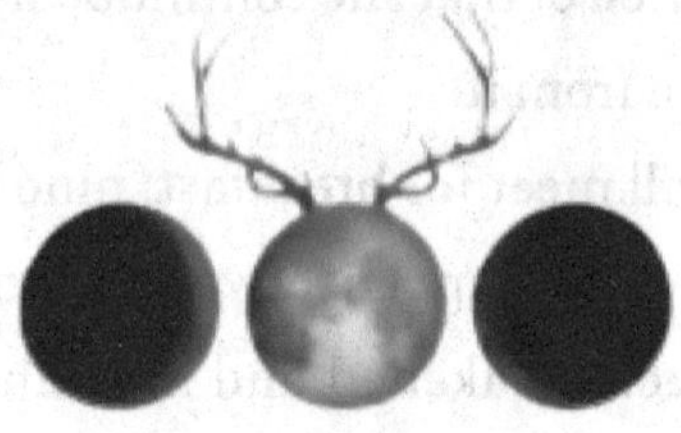

SECRETS AMONG THE HOLY

"**B**rother Darrell, do come in and join us. I am afraid we made ourselves quite at home here. I hope that is alright."

Darrell Ray had never seen Jim Meadows in person before, he knew him from TV and YouTube, all the other social media platforms. But he had never been in the room with him, nor had he ever imagined that he would be. Darrell Ray was after all, a small country preacher, who just happened to take his tent on the road, like so many small country preachers before him.

Following what he felt like was God's calling on his life. Then came Bishop, the terrifying giant, who claimed to be sent as a messenger from God and from Jim Meadows. Darrell Ray was skeptical but polite, then Bishop had told him so many things that no one but God could have known. Things like Darrell Ray's real name. Where he was from and why he and Margaritte, not her real name either, had hit the road with this traveling revival. Not that Darrell wasn't a believer in everything he preached. He absolutely was. But his conversion had come far after his crime.

He had been born Johnny Krotzer, and Margarite had been born Jenny Tewel, she had been married to Johnny's boss. She worked the reception desk at the garage that her husband owned. Johnny was a utility guy, changing tires, oil changes, tune ups, brake jobs. All the little stuff that kept the shop going while the other more experienced mechanics worked on the big jobs. Complete rebuilds, starters, alternators, computer work. That type of stuff. Johnny was never all that talented, but he was reliable and consistent and that's all Bob Sheets wanted out of him.

It had been love at first sight for Johnny, Jenny hardly seemed to notice him at first. But after a while, Johnny caught her staring at him from time to time. Then on Friday afternoons, Bob and a couple of the senior guys started taking off after lunch. Bob told everyone, including Jenny, that they were meeting parts distributors, wholesalers, and guys building race cars. Just the kind of networking that needed to be done to grow the business and keep the money coming in. Johnny heard a couple of the guys talking about it one day. The only networking going on was out at the Wildside Cabaret, out on old Highway 50. They were knocking off work every Friday at noon, then drinking lunch and most of dinner at the strip bar.

Johnny had been to the Wildside a couple times when he was younger, but it wasn't his type of thing. The girls were pretty enough, and would do anything you wanted if the cash was right, and they didn't think you were a cop. But thirty dollars and one completely unenthusiastic hand job later, he left feeling like he had traded his soul for a halfhearted orgasm, and he just never went back.

After hearing this and realizing it was just him and Jenny in the office, on Friday afternoons, he started wandering into her reception area after lunch. There usually wasn't much little stuff going on a Friday afternoon, everything was either done and picked up by noon or was a bigger job that would hold until Monday. At first, he just brought some extra lunch in with him and offered her some. Then one Friday, he ordered take out from the diner around the corner and got some for her as well. He had been watching her come back with food from there every couple of weeks for three or four months now and knew what she liked. He didn't even ask, just walked into the office with a grilled chicken salad, no onion, extra French dressing and sat it down on her desk. An hour later, he was straightening some tools on a shelf when she walked up behind him. He turned to look at her and saw she had been crying. She wrapped her arms around him and hugged him tighter than any woman had ever hugged him, at least since his grandmother had died.

"Five years. I have been eating there once a week for five years, and Bob still cannot remember what I get from there. Thank you."

Darrell knew enough about life to know that there was far more involved in that hug than a chicken salad. He also knew that falling in love with your boss's wife was a horrible idea. Even worse, being nice enough that your boss's wife falls in love with you.

"Darrell, I don't believe we have met yet formally, only through my proxy, Mr. Bishop."

Meadows rose to shake hands with Darrell Ray.

"That is correct, sir, what brings you down to the tents? I see you have met my beautiful wife."

"I have, brother, I have. The picture of hospitality. Why, she has kept us entertained for quite a while, hasn't she, Moses?"

The short, stoutly built man standing near the door of the tent nodded and agreed. Darrell Ray had never seen him before. Even shorter than him, but muscled, the sleeves of his blue polo shirt, with the Meadow Ministries logo on the breast, bulged out around his biceps. Faded tattoos visible against his dark skin.

"Well, I know you have a service to prepare for tonight, so I will get right to the point. Brother Darrell, our ministries serve much of the same purpose, bringing people together in the gospel and showing people the loving work of our Lord, each in our own unique ways. What I cannot express enough to you is that we need to not only continue our complimentary work but expand and strengthen the bonds between our two organizations. I will be frank and forgive me, darlin'."

He nodded a condescending look towards Margarite. "But I am aware of your circumstances, and your involvement in the ministry, so I will not spare the details for your sake. We are fighting a war, Brother Darrell. Not just against sin or the grinding progress of time. But a very real, very costly war. For a long time, people like me have been made aware of an organization, a family, they call themselves, of monsters. They are actually witches, devil worshipers. They are the embodiment of all that is unholy and sinful in the world. For years we have been working to hold their forces at bay. We fight them in the halls of justice, we fight them in governments around the world. We fight them in academia and entertainment. Just trying to protect our heavenly father's creation against these monsters."

Darrell Ray raised an eyebrow. "Witches? I am not sure I grasp your meaning, are you talking about the kids with the funny make up and tarot cards and crystals? Those witches?"

Jim raised his hand. "I know, I know, it does not seem possible, but I am telling you, they are hiding everywhere. Some of them are powerful beyond belief. If I had not witnessed their power with my own eyes on more than one occasion, I would not believe it either. But I promise you. They are very real. But, Brother Darrell, our God is also real, and a mighty God."

"Amen to that Pastor," Darrell Ray said with a smile toward his wife.

"I know you believe, Brother Darrell, that is why I am here. But I am not sure you understand yet. But you will very soon. When I tell you there is about to be a flood of miracles unleashed on our great land the likes of which hasn't been seen since Christ himself walked the earth. You are aware of the young folk who have gone missing from among your congregation?"

"I am, but I was told by Mr. Bishop not to interfere or report anything. He called it The Harvest."

"Yes, God's Harvest. He has been sewing his seeds for millennium and now, the time has come to reap. Every one of those beautiful souls has something in common."

"They were all struck by the holy spirit during a service here."

"Very good, Brother Darrell."

Darrell noticed the darkening of Meadow's smile. This is clearly a man who feels he is speaking to a subordinate and not just two men of God shooting the breeze. Darrell could hear the canvas of his tent rustling in the wind. His vision was narrowing. His body was telling him there was danger here. He listened.

"Brother Darrell, every one of those children of God has shown a certain sensitivity to the Holy Spirt that we need among our ranks. More importantly, these are exactly the young people that our adversaries target. You see, being open to interaction with the Holy Spirit, for the right kind of person, can leave them vulnerable to a kind of spiritual corruption."

"Like a possession?"

"No, nothing so obvious, although I am sure these witches are behind that atrocity as well. No, Lucifer grants gifts to his faithful, just like God. The main difference throughout history has always been that our faithful, those who are truly blessed by the Lord, usually see it in passive ways. Blessings of family, friends, and well-being. Occasionally you see the Charismatic Gifts being used actively, but generally even then. We open our hearts and when the Lord sees fit to provide prophecy or healing, he does. What makes these witches different is the pursuit of power. They are not content just living just and faithful lives and receiving God's blessings in his time. They want everything now, so through compacts with the great deceiver they are able to perform minor miracles and magics."

Meadows stood again from his chair. His face was turning red, and Darrell could feel a sermon coming on. He glanced at Margarite who sat stone faced.

"After consultation with minds far more pious and wiser than my own, and days spent in prayer, a possible solution was reached. We would approach this problem in a couple of different ways. To start, we need to make sure that everyone has an opportunity to experience God's love firsthand. Community outreach, in all its forms. As you probably guessed that is my primary function. We are building community resources, schools, and churches in places that most of the country likes to pretend doesn't exist. We provide low-cost alternatives to the horror of public education. Instead of subjecting your children to the mess of our underfunded and under supported public education system. We are providing free, or reduced tuition to our Meadow Ministries Education Centers. We set these up in major cities everywhere. Serving some of the poorest communities in the country. Children that would normally be left behind, now get a chance at a great education in a fully funded, fully served private school."

Meadows was pacing now, he was in his element, selling his vision. "The second part, and most crucial, is identifying these special individuals and showing them the power of God's love before they can be corrupted by the evils of the world. What we, and I say we, but it was folks far smarter than I, discovered, was that through focused prayer and seeking God's face, these special people can affect miracles. We have seen healing on a very real scale, we have seen people performing wonderous feats of strength as well as things I don't even have a name for. How do you think a man the size of Mr. Bishop moves undetected through your camp when he comes to visit? Do you think folks are so unobservant that they would not notice a man of his stature and visage walking among them?"

"Are you saying these special people, when they turn to God, they are given supernatural powers?"

"Blessings and gifts, Brother Darrell, blessings, and gifts. Miracles like you have never seen. But don't take my word for it. I want you to see it for yourself. What is your schedule for the upcoming couple of weeks?"

Sister Margarite spoke up, "We head to Indianapolis tomorrow morning. We are there for three days. Then back to Rockford, Fox Valley, Aurora, Decatur, and Pana. Each for a night, with one night in between, then a week off before three nights in St. Charles Missouri. Then we are back out to Wichita, Kansas after that. Not sure where from there but I could check the bookings." She smiled at her husband, who was looking at her with the same amazement he had been every day since the day they met.

"Perfect. Moses will give you the address of one of our youth camps, we have several of our most special brothers and sisters living out there. It is on your way back to St. Louis, so after your Pana engagement plan for the two of you to come by the camp. I think once you see the great works we are doing there, you will see exactly why I am so enthusiastic about this."

Darrell Ray rose and extended his hand. "Sounds like a plan, sir. Now if you will forgive me, it is only a couple hours until service starts here, and I still need to eat and spend some time in prayer before it starts."

Meadows held his hand and his gaze a bit too long for Darrell Ray's comfort. Again, he got the impression that Meadows wasn't used to, or fond of other people having opinions or needs that ran counter to his own.

"Of course, Brother Darrell, we will leave you to it." He turned to Margarite and offered her a polite smile, then walked out of the tent, Moses on his heels.

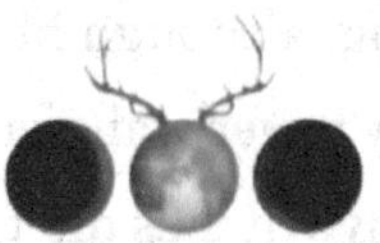

In the back of his Becker Automotive Design Cadillac Escalade, the reverend Jim Meadows was looking thoughtfully out the window and singing to himself. Once the car was down the highway from the sight of the Fellowship's latest encampment, he finally spoke.

"Moses, I truly do not understand Brother Darrell. I can see that the Lord put a mighty calling on his life, but for the life of me, I cannot understand what role he is meant to play. Clearly, he is important to the Lord's plan to wipe this modern day pestilence from his paradise. I just cannot see how."

"He is an odd one, sir. Do you think he lacks conviction?"

"He drives around in a twenty-year-old car and lives in tents to bring his message to the people. He probably brings more souls to salvation than all the preachers on TV, using just the words of Jesus himself. No fire and brimstone, no enemies at the gates. Just the words of Jesus and the holy spirit. And to top it off, he does it in an outfit that probably cost fourteen dollars from Goodwill. I don't think a lack of conviction is the issue. I think he lacks understanding and motivation."

"Sir?"

"I think he has yet to realize that there is a real threat. He hasn't seen it up close and personal like we have. Hasn't tasted the loss and grief from the damage these demons can cause. Perhaps, when he and the lovely Margarite visit the camp in Illinois, God will provide an opportunity for us to show them what we are up against. Speaking of, how go the repairs there?"

"Driveway and landscaping are almost done. Eleven dead, one will be soon, and one recovering, although he will likely need rehab for a long time and will probably never walk without a cane."

"Thirteen men, how many witches did they say there were?"

Moses flipped open a notepad he drew from his pants pocket. "Two, sir, one early to mid-forties, the other older, was the only description they got. Looks like they parked a bit back and walked up to the gate. Three men stopped them at the gate, those three were hit with." He flipped another page. "Bullet ant venom, sir?"

Meadows raised an eyebrow. "What does that do?"

"Most painful sting in the insect world, sir. A single sting can make you want to clean your ears out with a bullet. These three took the equivalent of hundreds of stings each. All centered around the eyes, nose, and mouth. Would have been a horrific way to die, sir. Apparently, the venom keeps the pain receptors open and firing long after they normally would have gone numb. So, no getting used to the pain, or your brain shutting it off to protect itself."

"Good heavens, Moses, how could someone be so cruel?"

"To be fair, sir, the new security supervisor, Lane, uh, Troy Lane, yes. Had given the order to kill both women. So, it's likely the witches picked up on that and went into kill or be killed mode. Video surveillance shows them all speaking amiably, then everyone shakes hands. After the younger one shakes hands with the last guard, a water bottle suddenly appears in her hands. She takes a big drink, spits it in the guard's faces then they take off running. The guards immediately dropped, screaming, and dying. It is terrible to see. The current theory is the younger one may be able to read minds through touch. Neither was in our data base, but we are adding all the details."

Meadows waved his hand gesturing Moses to finish up the recap.

If Moses was bothered by this dismissive gesture, he did not show it. "From there, reports are not as reliable, camera at the other end did not catch a lot. One guard showed intense trauma to the torso, like you see in car crashes. Three more appear to have been tortured to death. Cuts, broken bones, then vicious death blows. Looks like they were cut and beaten over and over in the span of just a couple minutes. None of them appeared to have many defensive wounds on them. Finally, five more died in the driveway explosions. Mostly shrapnel from the gravel."

"Only two of them?"

"Yes, sir."

"Well, make sure they get the repairs done straight away. We cannot have visitors with a driveway destroyed."

"Yes, sir."

"And Moses."

"Yes, Reverend?"

"Let's be sure if the good Lord should open any doors for us to further our cause. We make sure to run through them."

"Yes, sir."

Meadows fell into quiet contemplation for the remainder of the ride. He was used to managing a lot of moving parts, it was just part of his life now. He was beginning to feel like a couple of them were going to need some special attention. The sisters work with Bishop and the others was beyond miraculous. But their adversaries had proved once again just how dangerous they could be. That was two missions in a row that Bishop had nearly been killed. Perhaps it was best if he wasn't their only resource in that area. Maybe they should start to mold some others by that same means. He would pray on it. It never failed, when he sought the Lord in prayer, he made his will clear to Jim Meadows.

He could remember a time when his works had been based solely on faith. He believed in God's love and grace and had faith that his divine plan was always in motion and always what was best. He had lived his life on that notion. Then one day, not so many years ago, that all changed. Believing in God's divine plan was no longer a matter of faith. Miracles were no longer abstract ideas or left up to interpretation. God had chosen him, among a dozen or so others, to reveal himself, be it through some unconventional means. But he revealed himself, nonetheless.

Reverend Meadows some days wondered if having to have faith wasn't somehow better. It was easy to believe in a God that showed you his power in a tangible and undeniable way. It was different having his most favored angel reach out and put their hand on your shoulder and guide you through every step.

Either way, the time was near. The Harvest was reaching its crescendo, and when that happened the Revelations would begin in earnest. Oh, happy days indeed.

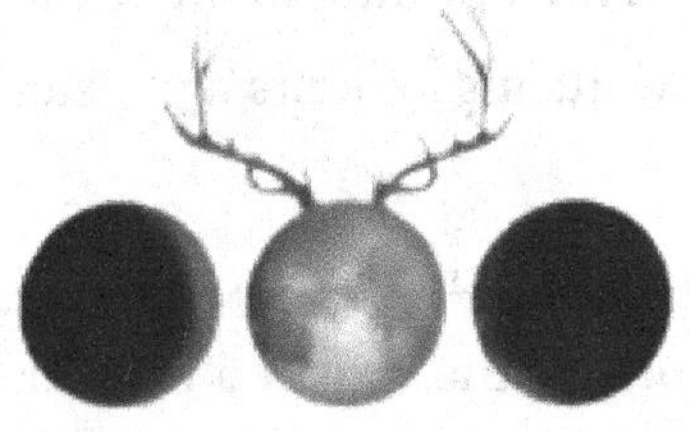

FROM ME TO THEE

The group gathered around Dorthea; this was a critical step for an operation like this. Not many witches could sustain the focus and will that it took to anchor a group this size. Not many witches were Dorthea Milburn. She was one of Mercer's great generals, not only because of her brilliant mind and dedication to their mission. But she was one of the few who were capable of binding and connecting a group this size to one another.

Once the ritual was complete, Dorthea would be able to use the interconnectedness of the divine energy to monitor each person in the group, communicating with them and relaying their communications to the group. With this connection she would coordinate their attack. The witches surrounding Dorthea chanted their incantation while she worked at a bowl of crushed amethyst, damiana herb, and a single drop of blood from each person. The simple rhythm of the chanting increased in speed, Dorthea pulling in all of the energy she could and forcing it into the bowl, its ingredients a physical manifestation of the connection.

When she felt the connections were at their peak she began. She ground a small amount of the crushed crystal, herb, and blood into her forehead, in the center, taking no notice as the shards of amethyst broke the skin. She turned first to Fredrick kneeling at her left and ground a small amount into his forehead as well, then pushed her head into his, whispering, "Me to thee, brother, thee to me." Then turned to Mama Rosie at her right, transformed from the sweet church going Sister Alice into her true face, the fierce Ezili Dantor, her red eyes shined, Ezili je wouj. She swayed to the rhythm of the chanting, but could not form the words, her tongue being cut out by her lover Ogun, to keep the secrets of the Haitian revolution before her rebirth into Mercer.

"Ke ke ke ke ke ke." Was the only sound coming from her as Dorthea ground the mixture into her forehead and pressed against her, whispering, "Me to thee, sister, thee to me." And the connection was formed.

Dorthea continued around the circle, M lost in her chanting, her image constantly shifting, tattoos, hair, eyes, all changing as she rocked back and forth. Sugar, naked to the waist, his muscled torso shining with sweat. Hannah stood with Bast, the calmness in Hannah's eyes belied the inferno raging there, she had tracked her husband's killer to this part of Illinois then lost him. The thought of being able to tear him apart had her rage filed to a razor's edge. Beck, Snow, Devlin, and Joy. When she came to Jo, standing beside her sister Joy, Jo backed off and hid behind her sister. Joy waved her off. "Better not, sister, some wild stuff in that head of hers, she will be where we need her, she always is." Dorothea nodded and moved on, understanding.

Each time she sealed the connection she began to feel their anxiety, their belief in what they were doing, their fear, their rage, their eagerness to do the right thing. If she extended her feelings down toward any given person, she could see and hear through their minds.

Once she had completed the connection with everyone in the circle, she made her way back to the car and sat in a circle she and M had imbued with power and began the process of assimilating all this new input. Feeling down each beautiful strand of light to see the spirit at the other end.

She pictured the place in her mind like a trailhead in a vast forest. She stood in the middle of the lush clearing, beams of light extending down each trail connecting her to the person at the other end.

Her sisters would be able to control the flow of energy and thought back to her, it was likely the consorts would not. They could not see what the witches saw, they were not used to extending or blocking the flow of energy and she would likely be bombarded with everything that comes into their mind.

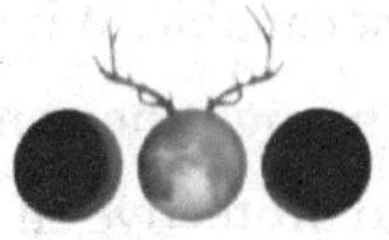

M began to lay out the plan for the others.

"We know from recon that there are over two dozen young people being held in the chapel of the church on the property. It doesn't appear to be fortified, only guarded. There is a great amount of energy being pulled into that chapel by something or someone. The connection is one of the largest concentrations of the energy of creation I have ever seen. We do not know what is causing it or what effect it will have on us, but we know those kids are all lying in the chapel in some sort of stasis. The property is fenced, but nothing we can't walk right over. It wasn't designed to withstand a siege or anything, just a little protection against kids doing kid stuff and the occasionally coyote, sniffing for scraps, or deer eating the landscaping. Even being sneaky there is no way they won't see us coming. We will hit them right as the sun is setting."

The group turned their heads at once in the direction of the cars. Dorthea stood at the top of the little rise. Each in turn felt the connection to her come alive as she began testing her spell, touching each mind. Seeing through their eyes, hearing through their ears, showing them images from one another. It was a disorienting process at first. But quickly they became used to the intrusion.

The energy and focus necessary to maintain all these connections at this intensity was extremely taxing. She felt the lines of connection between her and each participant. The spell work clinging to the physical components and amplified through their intention. There were very few witches in the history of Mercer who could manage this feat. Dorthea was by far the most capable. When the battle was joined, she would direct and advise. Through the connections she was also able to strengthen the wards and protective charms cast over the consorts. They were generally the most vulnerable and the first into the fight. They would protect their sister witches with their lives. Any one of them would lay down their life without hesitation, not only for their sister witch, but for any Mercer witch. While the witches of Mercer were powerful to a one, there was also ways in which they were vulnerable. M was a capable and competent warrior with powerful glamour. But in the heat of an extended battle her resources could be depleted. Powerful castings take time and focus, that is hard to do during hand-to-hand combat with trained opponents. Mama Rosie could be terrifying in a fight, but her powers as Ezili Danto took time and concentration and her victims had to be within earshot for her to be effective. That left her vulnerable to physical attack. The consorts were vital to the success of the mission, and they were family. It was Dorthea's privilege and honor to act as general on this mission, she would do everything within her considerable power to bring every single brother and sister home alive today.

Dorthea spoke into the minds of every gathered. "Snow, Beck, Devlin we need you moving in from the woods to the west, try to get between those houses and as close the back of the chapel as you can. They have moved the kids into the basement there. Hannah and Bast will move up to take the guards in the gate shed then right up the front doors if possible."

Everyone looked at Hannah, standing with Joy. Jo and Bast were both sitting in the dirt. Jo's dirty blonde hair hanging in her face. They were each drawing circles in the dirt, first Bast, then Jo. The women would then stare at each other and repeat the process. Clearly communicating in some way, but no one other than the two of them could understand how.

"We do not want a death toll here unless it is necessary. The best estimates put the number of people in the total compound at about one hundred. Joy and Jo have been watching for days."

Jo looked up from her drawing and eyed Dorthea suspiciously. Her lack of connection should have made it impossible for her to know she had been mentioned but that did not appear to be the case.

"The rest of us, we are the diversion and protection. The most important thing here is to give Snow, Beck, and Devlin time to get in and get the kids out as cleanly as possible. Hannah and Bast have the most raw fire power so they can run right up the front door and cover your exit. Amber and Mike Dudley will be waiting with the vans and will roll right up the front drive behind you as soon as they get the all-clear. We cannot risk anyone being able to get to the vans so we need to draw as much of their numbers out to fight as we can. I know that you all know how to deal with the threats that may come along. Joy has seen them training, drilling maneuvers in the woods. These guys look like Amish cosplayers, but make no mistake—they are trained. Plus, it is highly likely we are going to run into Bishop. He was tracked to this area of the state, then lost. It makes sense that this would be home base for him. It's only an hour or so from where Duke and Faith encountered him, and he somehow escaped after what should have been fatal injuries. No ego in this one boys and girls, if he pops his big ugly ass up, I want as much muscle on him as possible. Do you copy me on that, Sugar? This is not the time for ego or revenge. We need it done."

Sugar's grim expression did not change, but he nodded his understanding.

"Malvika, can you and Charles lead David, Daniel, and Joseph right through to the eastern wall? Make as much noise and as big a threat as you can."

Charles unfurled a large canvas roll with a flourish. On it, laying in neat rows, were hundreds of small shiny objects. Dorthea knew what they were, small mechanical insects, flying, stinging, biting nastiness. Charles invented and designed these little monstrosities and Malvika, acting as an artificer, gave them vicious purpose. They could swarm like wasps or hornets and devour like scarabs. Even she did not like to watch them unleashed. But no one who had seen them could deny the terror they struck in their enemies' hearts.

"Joy, can you and Jo sew some chaos around the place?"

Before Joy could answer, Jo began making an exciting yipping sound. Everyone turned to look her way. Jo was tall and skinny, all knees and elbows. She was wearing a dress that appeared to be made from woven vines and leaves, decorated with shells and beads. She was standing with her back to the group, staring up into the face of the largest canine any of them had ever seen. Its fur was yellow with black and brown spots and streaks, like a hyena, its head was shaped vaguely like a wolfhound. The mouth seemed too large for the head, and it could not close it entirely with the snarl of teeth sticking out. It stood almost four feet tall at the shoulder and closest to six at the top of its small, pointed ears. It had two horns growing straight back, like a ram's, on top of its head. It stood over Jo, growling, its maw full of crooked teeth only inches from her face.

M said aloud, "I guess Bast is ready."

Before Dorthea could finish her instructions, Jo leaned up and whispered in Bast's ear, the giant head tilted to one side in a manner that would have been comical were it not for the terrifying visage of Bast in this form. Bast growled low and angry, then lowered its head again. Hannah and Joy stepped forward at once, thinking Jo had somehow angered Bast, who could be very unpredictable in this form, only for Jo to smile back at them, leap up onto Bast's great back and cling to her. Before anyone could protest Bast took off in a shot, straight into the nearest tree. They did not collide with it, only passed through the trunk as if it did not exist but did not emerge from the other side.

Joy and Jo were sisters and woods witches. They came from a long line of rugged folks, living off the land, scratching out a living in some of the most hostile environments in North America. As such they had a deep understanding of the interconnectedness of nature as a manifestation of creation. In Jo, who was mostly non-verbal and only communicated in limited fashion with Joy, seeing Bast in her most wild form was like watching her wildest fantasy come to life. Bast, who was essentially a child herself, must feel somehow connected to Jo.

Dorthea continued, "Well, nothing to be done about that, I suppose. I hope they stay safe."

Hannah turned to look at her. "Dorthea, Bast is nearly invulnerable in that form and with Jo she can now move through the interconnected tree root systems like taking a train to another station. She is also fairly certain the caused the death of her father is here. I don't think being safe will be the issue, I think keeping it from turning into a slaughter might be harder. Joy, can you come with me up to the front of the gate and clear the path for the three musketeers over there to bring out the babies?"

Joy moved a little closer to Hannah. "Yes, ma'am, would be honored to. I am sure you are better company than my sister anyway."

Dorthea's voice in their head. "Okay everyone, let's do what we came here to do, there are people here who need us."

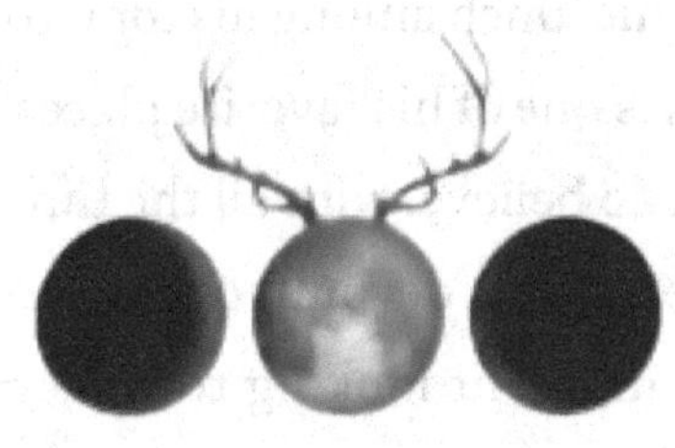

A PICNIC IN THE GARDEN

"**W**ell folks, have you ever seen such a sight?"

Darrell Ray and Margarite were standing on the second-floor balcony of the church, overlooking the whole of the Kaskaskia Valley Youth Camp and Spiritual Retreat. By their estimation, it was in fact one of the most beautiful places either of them had ever seen. Just past the four long bunkhouse-style buildings that made up the bulk of the structures on the property. A steep drop into rolling hills of forest. In the distance, the Kaskaskia, a small river, but full of life and history.

Margarite laid her head on her husband's shoulder for a moment, staring at the setting sun over the river and trees. "Reverend, I know this may sound silly, like the fanciful musings of a schoolgirl. But in my heart, I have always wondered if there aren't places on earth where God occasionally visits, just to sit in peace among his own creations. Like a gardener, taking a picnic lunch among his tomato plants. If that is true, then I am certain this is one of his favorite places to visit."

"Sister Margarite, I do believe, with all the time I spend around folks who claim to seek God's face, devout people, pious people. Folks who spend every waking moment looking to discern or fulfil some part or another of God's great plan. I have never heard one of them contemplate, even for a moment, if perhaps the good Lord has his own favorites among his creations. But I think you're right. I think if more people sought to see this world through the perspective of the creator, we would live in a better world. We may never understand his divine will, but I can only hope that somewhere in that plan, he gets to spend a little time marveling at what has grown from his holy seed."

Darrell Ray did not speak; he simply pulled his wife a little closer to his side. Staring out into the distance. It was a good visit. They arrived early this morning and had spent the day with Reverend Meadows and some of his team. They had seen the quiet Moses a time or two, plus some strangely dressed men who kept to themselves and did not respond when Darrell Ray said hello. Reverend Meadows informed them that they were members of the original congregation of the church here on the grounds. All of them had stayed on after Meadows Ministries had taken over. But recently they had been attacked by a group of witches and had lost several of their brothers to the cruel hand of the adversary.

They were given a tour of all but one of the buildings; that one, Reverend Meadows said, contained private quarters for some folks who stayed here year-round. Ground keepers, cooks, maintenance crew, that kind of thing. All in all, it had been a surprisingly wonderful experience. Darrell Ray was forced to rethink his initial opinion of the reverend. Maybe he had judged too quickly, letting his own prejudices cloud the truth of Reverend Meadows.

After a few minutes, Darrell Ray noticed a glint, a reflection of light off of something metal or glass off in the woods, just a little way off of the churchyard, beyond the big fence. He stared for a moment, trying to discern what he was seeing. "Reverend, is there supposed to be anyone outside the fence over there? I am pretty sure I just saw someone moving through the trees."

They all stared for any sign of movement. Darrell Ray saw it again. Like a white ghost, moving silently tree to tree. He started to point it out when Reverend Meadows' phone rang.

"Yes, what? Where? Can you tell how many? Okay, we are coming down now. Get the men together. You know what to do. I will see you downstairs."

He grabbed the Millers by the shoulders. "Come on, folks, unfortunate timing. But there seems to be a large group headed this way. People have been spotted moving through the woods from every direction. I am afraid we are going to come under attack. Let's head downstairs fast. Brother Darrell, can I ask you to come with me, to help direct traffic and join us in defense of our church?" Before Darrell Ray could answer, Mosses came running up with two of the strangely dressed men. They grabbed Margarite. The taller of them said, "Ma'am, can we escort you to our safe room downstairs in the back of the church?"

Darrell Ray leaned over and kissed Margarite on the lips and pulled her tight to him. "I am sorry, love; I could not live with myself if I could have helped and didn't."

"No apologies, you are the best of men, Darrell Ray. Go, do God's will, and return safe to me. Until you do, I will pray for all of us." She turned and gestured to the tall man. He nodded at the reverend, and they trotted off with Margarite in between them.

Reverend Meadows grabbed Darrell Ray by the arm, and ran back up to the observation deck, Moses followed close behind, carrying a black duffel bag. Once on the deck, near where they were before overlooking the property, Moses pulled out three radios with headsets. "Gentle-men, these will connect you to our men on the ground, from up here we can see everything, Troy Lane and I will cover the east and north sides, if each one of you will take the south and west sides, we should be able to help direct people to where they are needed most."

"Reverend, would you mind taking the west side overlooking the bunkhouses? We are heavily dug in there, but I expect that is where they will hit us the hardest. To an outsider, it will look like the most vulnerable target. Brother Darrell, the south side is pretty open past the gardens, there isn't much cover there, you should be able to see well. Just call out the identifier red block. That is the group working over there. Other than that, use a clockface for directions, and if you need more men, overrun is the keyword. If we are taking significant losses give the fallback command and they will all retreat to the nearest safe spot. There are several bolt holes and other such places they can get to in a hurry should they need to escape. These people are extremely dangerous, and I cannot stress this enough, magic. They have unusual powers, please try to remain as calm as you can when the crazy starts. Lives depend on your cool head."

With that, Moses handed Darrell Ray a radio and a pair of field glass-es. "Power on the left, volume on the right, mic is voice-activated, yes, that means we will all hear everything you say. So, keep the line clear unless you're giving directions or calling out enemy locations. Pray quietly, distractions can be deadly."

"Guns?" Darrell Ray asked solemnly. "I don't like the idea, but I grew up hunting and this is a solid vantage point. If you have a rifle, I might be able to push them back, give your men an extra second or two if they need it to get to safety."

Reverend Meadows put a hand on his shoulder. Inwardly, he knew that was a sign that Darrell was coming around to the idea. By the end of the day, he was sure he would have him securely in the flock.

"There will be a couple out there, but for the most part, I have only seen guns be effective against these people once or twice and that was a sneaky shot from hiding. They have some effective means of neutralizing guns, some of them nasty. I have seen whole magazines fire off at once. Shredding the guy holding it. Sometimes they just won't fire. Sometimes they fall apart. They know they are vulnerable to gunfire, so they take them off the board, fast."

Moses nodded in agreement. "The Reverend is right, plus it would immediately draw their attention to you up here and we don't want that. But I like the way you think."

Darrell Ray nodded. "What about Mr. Bishop, is he here? Seems like he would be handy in a situation like this."

Moses smiled. "You have a knack for this, Brother Darrell. We are trying to locate him right now. He was on the grounds earlier today, but he keeps to himself and comes and goes as the good Lord wills it. Keep my men safe and lead them well, Brother Darrell. Our flock is yours, protect them."

He ran off around the west of the building; Reverend Meadows close behind him.

Darrell Ray stood on the balcony overlooking the southern portion of the property. He saw the men of red block pouring out of their bunkhouse and the chapel below him, it looked to him like twenty-five or thirty men moving amongst the trees. He rolled the volume up on the radio and listened to the silence in the earpiece for a few moments then said. "Brothers of Red Block, my name is Darrell Ray Miller, I am watching from the tower and will offer what help I can. May the Lord bless and keep you all, Amen."

Reverend Meadows voice on the line, "Amen, Brother Darrell, brothers and sisters, we cannot fall this day, mighty are the righteous and faithful."

The first explosion came from just out of Darrell's sight over to the east, he closed his eyes against the sound. He knew the front gate was in that direction. He had no time to think as he saw figures sliding through the trees. "Red block, from my position center of the southern of the chapel. Two o'clock and ten o'clock, looks like about six on each side, and two hundred yards past the first line of hedges."

Darrell watched as several men scattered in different directions. His eyes swept across the tree line and the open field, searching for any sign of movement. To his right, streaks of fire shot across the field, forcing several of the brothers to dive for cover as the ground exploded around them. He saw all of the men scrambling away, though. So, none had been seriously injured. "Red block, two o'clock, someone throwing fire and it's hitting hard when it lands, be careful. Looks like only three in that direction, two men and a woman, I can't see where the fire is originating from, proceed with caution."

He swung his glasses to the west. "Red block, ten o'clock. There are eight of you headed that way, if you split three and three and head out around that pair of oaks in front of you and the other two take the middle you can box three of them in between those trees. I have seen nothing out of them offensively. Stay low, and they won't be able to see all of you coming." Darrell heard screaming coming from the east and another explosion from somewhere else on the church grounds. He muttered a silent prayer for Margarite and looked back down at the men he was charged with protecting. Three of them were lying on the ground as a tall muscular man with no shirt ran past the rest of the group and cut back to the east. "Moses, Reverend, one just slipped past the lines, big guy, no shirt, headed around the east. At least three men down from him."

Back to the west, Darrell saw all eight of the men from red block were pinning down two people, and binding their hands, while the third lay off to the side, face down in the dirt.

It looked like they were holding up, God was good.

As he swung the glasses back across the field his blood ran cold, several figures all in dark robes and carrying various items—staffs and clubs. He could see the energy glowing all around their weapons. They were charging straight toward the walls of the chapel. Darrell did not hesitate. "Red block, over run, twelve o'clock. Ten enemy combatants, running straight at the walls of the chapel."

Within moments, Darrell heard a cheer erupt from the men below him, and the invaders stopped their progress, seemingly confused. Two men, one black haired and one blond, both shirtless and covered in tightly corded muscle and tattoos, waded into the fight. Both men carried what looked like oversized framing hammers. They led the way as the men of red block jumped in behind them. Watching them enter the battle was awe-inspiring, they danced through the crowd of monsters with a grace unlike anything he had ever seen. Their great hammers spinning and twirling, dropping any enemy that came within reach. So complicated and well timed was their dance, that no enemy could touch them. Darrell saw fire range out across the field more than once, but it found no target. An explosion of dirt and leaves blow up very close to the blond man. He spun a tight circle to the left of the person who attacked him and launched his hammer straight at the person's head. He saw them crumble beneath their hooded robes and muttered a silent prayer for their soul. Evil or not, all God's creatures deserved redemption and salvation.

The rest of the hooded figures began to scatter toward the tree line again. Obviously retreating. *Cowards*, Darrell thought to himself. *Run away and never come back.*

The sound of the explosion from the other side of the building brought Darrell back to the moment. He felt the vibration through his feet as the building shook. "Margarite," he screamed as the realization dawned on him that she was somewhere in that building that had just suffered a hard enough hit to shake it under his feet.

Moses' voice on the radio, "She's safe, Brother Darrell, hold steady. Just a few minutes longer while we clear the grounds for stragglers. Everyone on every block, we are pushing them back everywhere. Clear the property, I want no stone left unturned, no tree branch unshaken. Go, report back in five minutes."

Darrell stood fast like he was asked. It might have been the longest five minutes of his life.

The Reverend's voice, low and cracking, no inflection, none of his usual bluster. "This is the Reverend Meadows, please rally at the back of the chapel near the staff entrance."

Darrell sprinted for the stairs, he had to see his wife, he had to see Margarite.

As he rounded the corner at the bottom of the stairs, he saw the devastation. A section of the chapel wall the size of a small truck had been blasted into rubble. Debris piled everywhere inside and out. He began to frantically look around for his love, his Margarite. He could hear people crying and someone was shouting directions. *Oh Lord, please, show mercy upon the injured,* he prayed. He was looking around for anyone he recognized when he heard her voice, the voice of his angel.

"Father, we ask that you take them into your arms and heal them, protect them, cradle them and let stand again amongst their friends and family if that is your will."

He ran toward the sound of her voice; as he rounded the corner, she was kneeling in another pile of rubble from the wall. A small girl, maybe twelve or thirteen, was lying on the ground. He could see the wounds on her small body, and it did not look good. She was bleeding from several places and one of her legs was twisted at an angle that just didn't seem possible unless it was severely broken. Two men of the congregation were working on her, trying to bandage, splint and stabilize anything they could.

He stood there in shock for just a moment before jumping in. "Brothers, how can I help, are there more injured that need attended to? I am pretty handy with a kit."

The older of the two men spoke, "Please assist brother Alfred here and this young lady." He nodded at Margarite.

Darrell jumped right in, wrapping pressure bandages. Margarite had her head bent over the little girls and he could hear her singing to her.

"And I will cherish the old rugged cross and exchange it one day for a crown."

He smiled in spite of the horrific circumstances, no matter what, Margarite was always true to who she was.

It was almost an hour later before the last of the injured were carried away by the brothers of the congregation there to some infirmary within the chapel. Darrell and Margarite were not invited to join the efforts to care for the injured there.

As the last gurney was carried off, Margarite threw her arms around her husband's neck.

"Oh, Darrell Ray, it was horrible," she spoke through the sobs, wracking her body.

"We were all huddled into one of the basement rooms when we felt the building shake, they must have blown their way in because it was only a minute or two later and there they were. In their dark robes and masks. They came for the children. We tried to fight them off but there was just too many. That man, Troy, he pushed me into a supply closet and had me lock the door from the inside. Still, I could hear it, the screams of the children, the sounds of them beating anyone who didn't cooperate, they were like animals. Preying on the weak and defenseless, laughing the whole time."

He held his wife close. "There were two men from the congregation, I have never seen anything like it. They both had big hammers, and they flowed over the fight like water just laying everyone low who got in front of them."

"These people, Darrell, how could God let people like this exist in the world?! We have to help Reverend Meadows and Mr. Moses and all the rest. These people are fighting every day to keep all of us safe against these monsters."

He kissed her on the forehead while she sobbed into his chest. "Let's get back to the Fellowship. We can talk on the road about what God may have planned for us next."

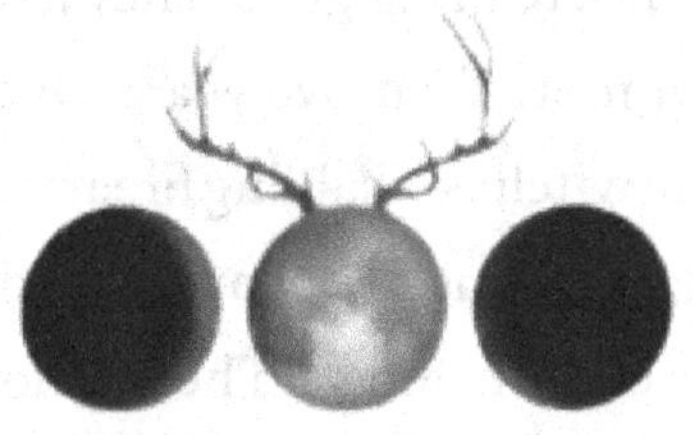

THIS MAN PLAYED FOR DEATH

Ryan watched as the woman leaped out from behind a large tree, her blue skirt twirling, her red blouse billowing out. She dropped to one knee before springing back up, moving in a wide, graceful arc around him and Jack. They had been watch partners and bunk mates for town years and trained hard for things like this.

Jack turned his shoulder at a slight angle to Ryan's so that from the front out to about one hundred and sixty degrees they covered one another. Ryan held a stun stick ready to hit this woman with what was essentially a bolt of lightning should she approach from his side. Jack had a riot baton in his hand, and a smaller taser on his belt. He also knew Jack had a snub nose .38 revolver in an ankle holster.

They had been told not to bring guns. They had been studying these devils and training for more than two years. Over and over, they were shown instances of the witches disabling firearms before the fights ever started or even worse, targeting the people carrying them with horrific spells. But Jack was stubborn and said he did not plan to use it unless it became an absolute emergency, but figured it was better to have a chance of survival if things went sideways.

Moses and the Carpenters drilled with them constantly hand to hand, and non-projectile combat. The message was always the same, you must be perceived as a non-threat until the moment comes to strike. Look inept, appear to be just a hired hand, a rent-a-cop, whatever you could pull off. Then when they had underestimated you and gotten within striking distance you unleash every trick in your arsenal and slay God's enemies on the field of battle, just like Samson, Joshua, and Benaiah.

The twirling dancing figure slipped behind a tree to Ryan's right, just ten or so feet in front of Jack, then appeared gliding from behind a tree to Ryan's left. Then the sound started, slowly, like a pulse. *Ke, Ke, Ke, Ke, Ke.* No, that wasn't right, it wasn't really a sound, it felt like it came from the woman and at the same time, like it came from inside his head. *Ke, Ke, Ke, Ke, Ke.* He squinted to try and focus on her, between the haze that had moved in and the sun setting, she was somehow hard to see. But that didn't make any sense. She was wearing a veritable rainbow of colors, scarves, head wraps, a big flowing skirt, and blouse. All different colors, she should have stood out like a sore thumb in the green, brown gloom of the woods around the chapel. *Ke, Ke, Ke, Ke, Ke.* How could that be so loud in his head, was Jack hearing it, he should ask. *Ke, Ke, Ke, Ke, Ke.*

No, why does he care what Jack thinks, Jack was supposed to be his best friend. His brother in Christ, a warrior of the Almighty. *Ke, Ke, Ke, Ke, Ke.* But what did he do? Less than a day after Ryan told him that he thought *Ke, Ke, Ke, Ke, Ke*, he was falling for Cathy, that new girl in the cafeteria, and wanted to take her for a walk around the grounds. Or maybe even invite her to sit with him at the next movie night. What did Jack do? The very next day, Ryan saw him *Ke, Ke, Ke, Ke, Ke*. Standing in the corner of the library with *Ke, Ke, Ke, Ke, Ke* Cathy, she was smiling at him. *Ke, Ke, Ke, Ke, Ke.* Jack, in his short sleeves, rolled just perfectly over his muscular arms. *Ke, Ke, Ke, Ke, Ke.* Jack, with his hair always exactly where he wanted it to lay. *Ke, Ke, Ke, Ke, Ke. Ke, Ke, Ke, Ke, Ke.* How could he do that? He was supposed to be Ryan's friend, *Ke, Ke, Ke, Ke, Ke* he knew how much he liked Cathy, but no, he could not let Ryan have anything, *Ke, Ke, Ke, Ke, Ke* he just had to go and ruin it. Had to go be handsome and charming and make her smile like that. *Ke, Ke, Ke, Ke, Ke.* It wasn't fair, *Ke, Ke, Ke, Ke, Ke.* She should only *Ke, Ke, Ke, Ke, Ke* be smiling for Ryan, not Jack, to the devil with Jack. He should *Ke, Ke, Ke, Ke, Ke* turn around and stick this *Ke, Ke, Ke, Ke, Ke* stun rod on the *Ke, Ke, Ke, Ke, Ke* side of this neck and cook that stupid tattoo right off of him. *Ke, Ke, Ke, Ke, Ke.* That is exactly *Ke, Ke, Ke, Ke, Ke. Ke, Ke, Ke, Ke, Ke* what he should do. *Ke, Ke, Ke, Ke, Ke.* He was turning to do just that when he felt the barrel of Jack's revolver touch the base of his skull. Then he felt nothing else.

Jack pulled his handkerchief out of his pocket and wiped at the blood and gore on his face and forehead. *Ke, Ke, Ke, Ke, Ke.* He was finally rid of that leach *Ke, Ke, Ke, Ke, Ke.* Ryan, he knew it was Ryan that had been *Ke, Ke, Ke, Ke, Ke* taking his snacks from his dresser. *Ke, Ke, Ke, Ke, Ke.* Well not anymore, now to go *Ke, Ke, Ke, Ke, Ke*, find Charlie. Charlie cheated at checkers the other night *Ke, Ke, Ke, Ke, Ke*, when they played in the cafeteria. *Ke, Ke, Ke, Ke, Ke. Ke, Ke, Ke, Ke, Ke.* He slipped the revolver *Ke, Ke, Ke, Ke, Ke* into his pants pocket. *Ke, Ke, Ke, Ke, Ke.* No longer the *slightest* bit concerned about *Ke, Ke, Ke, Ke, Ke*, the black woman *Ke, Ke, Ke, Ke, Ke*, dressed in the strange clothes, *Ke, Ke, Ke, Ke, Ke*, dancing from tree to tree. *Ke, Ke, Ke, Ke, Ke.* Or that weird sound in his head. But he was going to go *Ke, Ke, Ke, Ke, Ke* have a talk with Charlie, and *Ke, Ke, Ke, Ke, Ke* maybe with a few other low-down cheats when he was done with Charlie.

Ezili Danto, Mama Rosie, as she is now known, danced through the opening in the trees. Her bare feet gliding through the woods, her true home. Her head, shoulders, and hips rolled in a sensuous dance. Her eyes glowed a fierce red. looked thoughtfully at the body of the guard lying face down in a puddle of leaves and bloody dirt. She then cast a glance at her adopted son, Fredrick, as he moved with an eerie similar grace through the trees toward the chapel and his meeting with Devlin and the others. She turned her head up and sent the message to Dorthea, of her position and Fredrick's, then danced back toward the trees, certain there were more soldiers there to hear her song.

Edwin and Dylan knelt at the center of the clearing, fully aware of the danger their role carried. Each had a tactical rifle mounted on a small tripod, their only cover a haphazard arrangement of leaves and branches meant to serve as a crude sniper's blind. It was supposed to give the illusion of incompetence, and it did. They were the bait, and they knew it. The rifles did not even have any ammunition as the witches storming the church were known for making it explode in the magazines. But their position was carefully staged, anyone coming straight at them would have to walk down one of two paths. The first one, the obvious trap, was a straight bottle neck of about one hundred yards of tightly packed trees with one clear path in the line of fire of the rifles. The second one, better hidden but still plain to see was on a different angle at about forty-five degrees left of the main trail, this one appeared camouflaged and a safe route by which to flank the shooters. They were to remain in the firing position, visible but appearing to be trying to hide, when an enemy approached down the flanking path to attack, they would pass a series of bolt holes. Trap doors, camouflaged in the forest floor. The men inside these bolt holes were armed with various weapons, lethal and non-lethal alike. All of the trap doors opened away from the trail head, so that they only had to opened a little for the people inside to spring their traps. This made defending against the attacks even tougher as the witch would be past the trap door before, they opened. Two lined each side of the trail, with two men each inside.

Edwin spotted the man first, dressed in a brown robe of some sort, he strolled right down the path like he had nothing to worry about. Edwin did as instructed and pretended not to notice the man walking toward them down the side trail.

Just a little longer, he was almost to the first set of bolt holes.

The man stopped. He slid the weird robe thing from over his shoulders and laid it out on the ground. Then he stood up and turned around and walked away.

Edwin whispered to Dylan, "Did you see that? What was that about, just threw his coat on the ground and left?"

A small clicking sound drew their attention back to the trail. It looked for a second like the jacket or robe was moving, like breathing or something. A woman walked into sight on the same side trail. She as dark complected with long black hair and wearing a wrapped dress, like you would see Indian women in. There was no pretending now, this was getting weird. Edwin spun to shout a warning, but before he did, the woman lifted her hands. The clicking grew louder and the robe on the ground lifted three feet in the air before falling back down and revealing a cloud of some sort, shining, whirring, like hummingbirds, no, rounder, sturdier. He was staring at the cloud when all hell broke loose. Streaks of brown and gold broke off from the main cloud and shot toward the trap doors, pouring in. He could hear the clatter of what sounded like metal legs. A light glowed around the woman and seemed to flow through the cloud as more and more streaks flowed toward the trapdoors.

It only took another moment for him to hear the screaming, screaming didn't do it justice, wailing was more the answer. He backed into Dylan, who stood frozen. The woman smiled at him and with a little gesture of her hand, more streaks of color came swarming off of the cloud and headed toward them, he slipped and fell trying to untangle himself from Dylan. Before he could make it back to his feet, the clicking sound became a roar. Then the first of Charles' constructs, powered by Malvika's magic, landed on him, and began to tear into his flesh, and the clicking was overpowered by his own screams of agony as they stripped his flesh from the bone while he writhed on the ground.

Malvika walked the trail toward the piles of what was left of the men who had been camped as bait on the trail. Her constructs flowed out of the traps behind her and swarmed about her legs as more and more joined their brethren. As she passed by the bodies, nothing but bone and fragments of clothing, she said, "And the angels will throw them into the fiery furnace, where there will be weeping and gnashing of teeth. And the righteous shall shine like the sun in their father's kingdom, anyone with ears to hear should listen and understand."

The last of her children joined her as she walked away, Charles already directing her to her next target, and laying out another group of children for her to command. By the time this day was done, they will have feasted greatly.

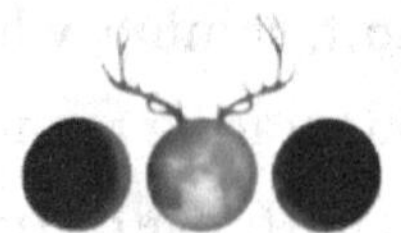

Bishop took off at a sprint; the first demon he had encountered had posed almost no challenge. He knew what was at risk, the brothers of the congregation were falling fast and if he could not turn the tide, Reverend Meadows would have no choice but to reveal the Ascension before the time. He would not fail again, twice he had been outfought by these devils. Today he would prevail, or he would die.

Sugar did not have to ask if it was the right guy, he watched in horror, unable to help as the bastard broke Daniel's back and dropped him in a heap at his feet. Sugar landed two quick punches to the head and throat of the man he was fighting and did not even wait to see the man drop before he took off after Bishop.

Fredrick and Devlin had given Sugar all the info they had on Bishop, he was able to get a little out of Duke, but Duke did not remember most of the fight. He knew he was as big as him and very quick on his feet. Had extensive training and knew how to use his size to his advantage. He also appeared to be utterly ruthless. The bastard had dropped right out of the tree and landed behind Daniel like a cat. Before Daniel even registered what was happening, he was in the air and broken. Bishop had grabbed his hair with his left hand, slammed his right fist hard into his temple. Then picked him up and wrapped him backward around the nearest tree. Sugar would not go down so easily. This man wasn't just here for a fight, a reluctant solider in a cause he may or may not believe in.

No, this man, this Bishop, this man played for death, and Sugar would oblige him, for the damage he has caused.

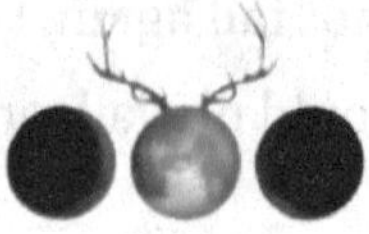

Bishop was running for the back of the chapel. He knew that would be the target; the seraphim were there with the faithful in transition. They must be protected at all costs. Flying through the woods, dodging between trees, and jumping fallen branches. He was reminded of the dream. Then he caught a glimpse, now, just like then. He felt the presence just off his left shoulder. Someone was running alongside him. Like a memory trying to fight its way to the surface. A face, pale white, long hair, a kid. Racing through the woods, playing, feeling free from any burdens or responsibilities. But that didn't make any sense, he didn't grow up in the woods, he grew up in Dayton, Ohio.

He shook his head to clear it and focus. One hundred yards and he could hop the back fence of the chapel and head off the ones trying to break through to where the children were.

He aimed for a gap between two silver maples, breathing heavy but feeling good in the work.

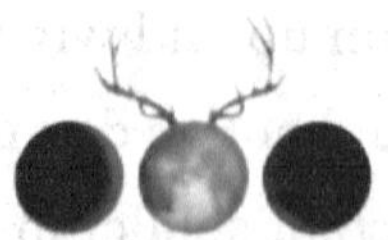

Sugar saw him running full out for the chapel and sped up. In his mind, he spoke to Dorthea. *I have Bishop, I am running him down, but if you can offer any assistance here, I don't want him to get to the church and Devlin before I get him.*

Before any response could come, he caught a movement out of the corner of his eye and spun to deal with this newest threat. What he saw was Jo, wild eyed and grinning ear to ear, riding atop Bast. Gore dripped from Bast's oversized maw, and Jo was splattered with blood. She had a strange looking twisted club of braided vines, a bloody mat of hair clung to it, wedged between two of the strands. As they ran up to him, Bast slowed, and Jo extended her free hand to Sugar. He reached for her, and she grabbed his hand and Bast sped back up. He ran as fast as he could trying to keep up with her, still holding Jo's hand. He wasn't sure what was happening, but he knew better than to think too much where sisters like Jo and Bast were concerned. He sped up, trying to keep pace. Looking forward, he realized they were headed straight toward a great oak tree. Its trunk more than five feet across. He saw Jo do this with Bast, but he did not understand the spell at work, he could not even be sure that Jo understood the working or the limitations. He had no idea where they would end up.

They hit the tree at a full sprint, or at least as fast as Sugar could run. At the last moment, he braced himself, knowing that slamming face-first into the tree at full speed could take him out of the fight, maybe for good. But instead, the world twisted around him. He felt his body being pulled, stretched, contorted. There was no pain, just a wild disorientation, no direction, no gravity. The only sensation was the feeling of Jo leading him, but it was not his hand she held on to. It was like she was dragging his very soul through the tree, through the roots, the trunks.

Then there was a blast of bright light, and he felt the wind blowing in his face as they emerged, still at a full sprint from another tree. Jo released his hand, blew him a kiss, and pointed to her right. She then used her knees, locked tight to Bast's rib cage to lean out to the left. They tore off in that direction. Sugar veered to the right and scanned the trees ahead. Off to his right, there he was. Sugar was now slightly ahead of Bishop and on a direct path to intercept. He caught Bishop just on the other side of a big tree. Sugar never slowed, he just blasted into him at full speed.

Sugar and Bishop hit the ground in a rolling pile of giant fists and feet thrashing. The collision was fast and violent and jarred both of them. Each man being a seasoned fighter, they struggled to use the momentum to gain the upper hand as they came out of the roll. Bishop rolled onto his stomach and stopped, feeling the other man go rolling on, he scrambled to his feet just as the kick to his ribs landed.

Sugar knew he could not let this killer get back to his feet. As he rolled to a stop, he twisted with the inertia and did a reverse somersault, landing on his feet, as the other man got one foot under him to jump up. Sugar kicked, every ounce of strength he could muster went into that kick. His shin bone connected solidly with the man's ribs. Feeling the crunch of bone, a smaller man likely would not have survived a kick like that.

As soon as the man hit the dirt Sugar was on him, two, three, four hard punches to the head as Bishop struggled to get some defense in place. Sugar was not having it. He pinned one arm under his knee and got his hands around the man's throat, determined that this time, he would not walk away, he would pay for all of the death, the destruction. He would make him pay for killing Mathew, for hurting all of those brothers and sisters. For the pain he caused Duke and Faith. He could not be allowed to live. Sugar slammed the man's head down hard on the ground then began to squeeze.

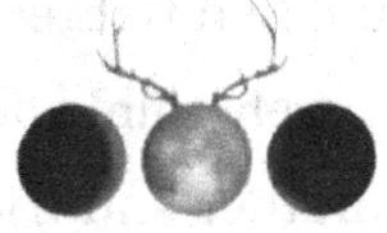

Bishop had never felt a blow like that, even when the man had kneed him in the head while he was killing Duke, that had rattled his cage, but given a moment to recover, he would have been alright had they not pounced on him and taken full advantage of his disorientation to completely overpower him.

This was different, he had thought since the man had rolled past him after the initial impact that he would be just as scrambled as Bishop, and since Bishop stopped first, he would get the upper hand. He had not anticipated the man could move even faster than he could, and foolishly, he did not see the kick coming. But he felt the bones breaking against the man's shin. He felt his whole body screaming in pain on that side, he felt the splinters stabbing him every time he tried to breath. Then he was rolled onto his back. The man straddled him, Bishop looked up at him, he looked like a ghost, like the angel had first looked when she appeared to him. All white, wreathed with long white hair. Naked to the waist, his pale skin smeared with blood and sweat. Then the ghost's hands were around his neck. He smashed his head down twice. Hard. Bishop looked up again. Why, who was this ghost, why did this face creep into his brain, like someone he should know, someone important? Some one long dead, someone beyond memory, in a place that Henry Bishop should not remember. But Bishop didn't remember him. Leroy did, Henry Leroy Lewis, that was his real name, not Bishop. He wasn't Bishop, who was Bishop?

The pale hands wrenched down tighter now, determined to choke the life from him. He could barely think, only to that night. The night the demon took their grandfather and tried to take them, the night their Granny B locked them in a closet, Leroy only four years old and his older brother Chris, no, no one called him that, what was it? She said, *The devil has come for us, boys, I can hold him off, but you need to call down Jesus, you have to.*

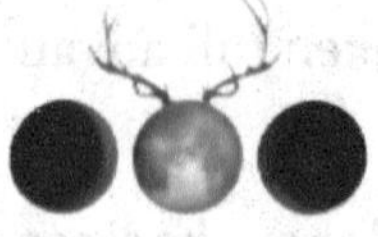

Sugar squeezed harder, Bishop's muscular throat constricting, cutting off air and blood to his brain. Just as Sugar felt the muscles start to go limp, Bishop opened his eyes and said out loud. "Sing, baby."

Only two people alive would know what that meant... M, who no doubt was headed this way, and... "No," Sugar breathed and leapt up from straddling Bishop.

He looked down at the man, struggling to breath, between the damage to his ribs and the crushing pressure Sugar had just had on his throat, it was likely the man wouldn't be able to breath on his own. It couldn't be, but there he was. The black hair, the blue eyes, his size, and speed, and that. The last thing Granny B had said to him as she locked him and his little brother Leroy in the closet. "Sing, baby."

Granny B had been dead and gone for many years.. He had told M, and it had been a secret code between them, a signal that it was time for him to fight his way to her. But she had only ever said it out loud one time and no one who had heard it survived the day.

But this man, this man who was his same size, who looked just like their father Dale. Who in his dying moments had uttered a phrase known only to them.

"Leroy, what the fuck? What is going on? How? They told me you were dead."

Leroy sat up and looked at him. "I, I don't know, I was at home with Amber and the kids. Then I just woke up a few seconds ago while you were trying to kill me. Sugarfoot, I watched you die, we searched for days for your body in the lake and never found you. You left me all alone. Are you real? What's going on?"

Sugar straightened and focused his thoughts again, feeling his connection to Dorthea.

"Dorthea, I have Bishop, I don't know what's happened, but he isn't who we think, it's my brother Leroy…"

A blast of energy slammed Sugar square in the chest. It felt like getting hit by a truck and he was thrown several feet back. Dazed, he looked back to where his brother lay broken on the ground. Standing just behind Leroy was a person, no, a thing that appeared to be made solely of white light. It had a human shape, but far larger than any human could be. He couldn't see any details. Just a silhouette in brilliant white.

Sugar struggled to his feet; he wasn't certain of what he was seeing, but he knew he needed to get Leroy and get out. He needed answers, and whatever this thing was it wasn't good.

The being glided rather than walked toward where Leroy lay. Leroy was scrambling backward, the pain from his injuries slowing his movements.

Sugar called out in his mind to Dorthea, *"Dorthea! Please, send everyone. There is some kind of monster here. I've never seen anything like it."*

He could only hope she understood. Despite his pain from the blast, Sugar ran to Leroy and stood over him, guarding him as best he could from whatever this was. Sugar drew his long curved knife from his belt and crouched low, ready to do what he could. The being, whatever it was, stood to its full height, it had to be more than eight feet tall and from behind it a pair of wings now began to extend out to either side.

Sugar stared in disbelief, unable to move or process what he was seeing. He only knew he had to protect his little brother until help arrived. The monster stretched its wings out and Sugar could feel what was coming, he could see the light at the center of its torso glowing brighter was its wings pulled back as if it would flap them and take flight. The giant wings swept forward, and Sugar tried to roll to the side. It did not soften the blow, but it did allow him to roll instead of just being thrown backward when the energy hit him again.

It reached down as if to grab Leroy. Even as big as he was, Sugar knew Leroy would stand no chance fighting back against whatever this was.

A blazing heat erupted near Sugars right arm as Hannah's fireball rushed past him and slammed into one of the giant wings. It reared up its head and unleashed a scream that rattled Sugar's teeth inside is skull and made him wish he was anywhere else. Before the being could flap its wings and send another blast of energy, a ball of pitch black enveloped it.

M, Sugar thought. He scrambled back to his feet, eager to seize the opportunity to get Leroy clear and safe while M and Hannah dealt this monstrosity. He had almost reached him when he saw the hand reach out of the darkness and drag Leroy in.

Leroy turned to look at Sugar, reaching out his hand. The terror obvious in his eyes, and his screamed for his brother.

"Sugar, don't let it take me."

"Leroy, no!" Sugar screamed as Leroy disappeared, dragged into the dark. Sugar dived for the sphere of darkness and a sound like bone snapping amplified through a public address system and a flash of light and the sphere of darkness, Leroy, and whatever that creature was, was gone.

Hannah spun on Sugar.

"What the fuck was that, Sugar? Why didn't you kill that bastard when you had the chance, you know what he did to Mathew, what he's done."

Sugar paid no attention to her, he walked straight to M, who was approaching, looking shocked and exhausted. Her shirt was ripped in two places, and she was bleeding from her shoulder. He inspected her wound as she stared up into his face.

"M, I'm sorry, I didn't protect you."

"Sugar, don't be dumb, this was a fight like any other, we all did what we had to do. Now, why didn't you kill Bishop? What happened and what the fuck was that thing?"

"M, it was Leroy. I don't know how, but it was him."

"Sugar, that's not..."

"Possible? Like anything is impossible, M. I am telling you, it was him. He looked me directly in the face and said it, M."

"Said what, Sugar?"

"Sing, baby."

Sugar turned and walked away, leaving M staring at his back, her jaw hanging open.

Hannah approached from behind. "M, he better have a hell of an explanation for what just happened."

"I am sorry, Hannah, but that was his brother."

"M, sweetheart, we have no way of knowing that. He hasn't seen his brother since he was twelve years old. We don't know what these bastards know about us, if they know half as much as they seem to then it would not have been hard for them to assess what kind of threat Sugar is and figure out ways they could slow him down."

"Hannah, that was his little brother Leroy. That man said something that only two people on earth know, me, and Leroy Lewis. No one else alive would understand the significance of that phrase to him. There was no doubt it was Leroy, what we cannot know now is how he came to be here and why he thought his name was Bishop and he was on a mission from God to kill us all."

Just then, the mental intrusion from Dorthea. *Everyone get back to the vehicles now, rally at the top of the road. The enemy is neutralized. I have Bast and Jo with me.* M turned from Hannah without saying another word, and walked back toward Sugar, who was kneeling in the dirt.

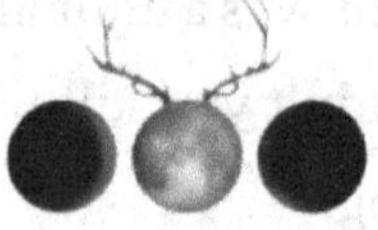

Dorthea stood at the end of the lane, out in the open. Devlin, Amber, and Michael sat on top of the van. Malvika, Charles, Joseph, and Fredrick were milling around quietly talking to David. M could see the sheet in the back of the van and knew that underneath it was the body of Daniel, David's brother.

Mama Rosie, now looking more like her matronly self and less like the personification of feminine rage, stood talking with Joy and Hannah. Bast and Jo were back drawing circles in the dirt. Sugar was sitting off in the grass on the other side of the road, his back to the group. M knew him better than anyone, and even she could not imagine what was going through his mind at the moment. She caught Fredrick's eye and indicated where Sugar was seated. Fredrick shook his head. He had no desire to engage with Sugar right now. Dorthea began to speak.

"The chapel was empty, Devlin, Beck and Snow searched. There is no one. The energy is still flowing through here. But the kids are gone, as are anyone other than the men of the congregation, acting as guards. But the children and whoever was holding them were gone. We did find a hole blasted in one of the walls of the chapel, not big but it looks like someone had set a charge against the wall and caved it in. We lost Daniel. Daniel did not have a sister witch, so I will escort him back to Mercer and sing his funeral song, so that his bravery and service to Mercer will be remembered forever. Thank you all. I am not sure how our recon, barely a week old, was incorrect and I am sorry we have gone through this and did not free the children. But we learned more and will continue to learn. Devlin, Snow, and Beck are going to remain behind for a couple days and tear the place apart. I am going to consult the council after Daniel's funeral, and we will see what they advise."

One by one, people started to drift away from the group to where their various vehicles had been parked.

M approached Sugar softly from behind. "Sugar, you coming back with me?"

Sugar did not look up. "If it's all the same, M, I want to stick around with Snow and Beck. Leroy was living here. I need to see if I can figure out what was going on. He was so confused, M. He had no idea where he was or how he got there. He was terrified. Then he was gone. The last thing he said was that the last thing he remembered was being with Amber and the kids, then he woke up here and had no idea how he got here or why I was still alive."

Sugar just stopped talking, he stared into the distance. The last rays of the sun silhouetting him. M did not ask him anything else. She knew what he needed and would let him have it without resentment.

She turned and walked back to their car. She would join Dorthea and the others escorting Daniel home.

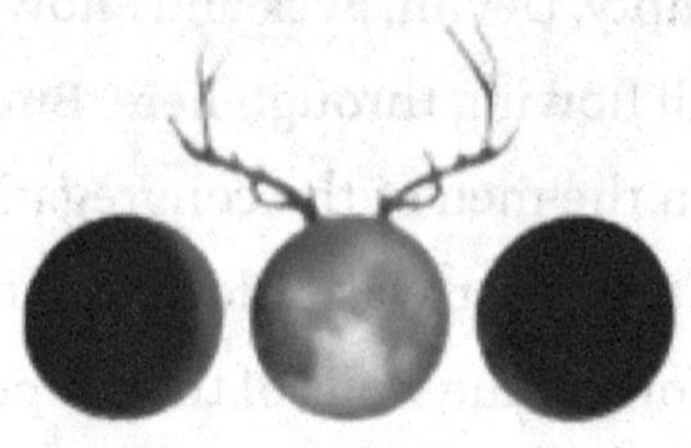

At What Cost

In his office at his home outside Nashville Tennessee, the reverend Jim Meadows was staring into an empty cup of coffee. His heart was heavy, he knew he had taken the right steps, he had followed God's will, but he could not help but feel the cost. He understood why, but it did not change that good people, people who believed in their cause and had believed in his leadership, had died, because of his choice.

A knock on the door brought him from his contemplation.

"Reverend?"

"Yes, Moses?"

"It's done, sir. All of the members of the Ascension have been moved to the new location. As you predicted, the Mercer witches came to the camp in full force."

The reverend leaned back in his chair and stared at the ceiling for a moment.

"Tell me, Moses, I am in no mood for dramatics."

Moses stared at the reverend. He did not react; he knew the reverend was under a lot of pressure and had been forced to make some hard choices. Moses was used to hard choices, men like the reverend had never been forced to choose the hard thing.

"Only four of the thirty or so brothers we left behind to put on the show have survived and they are in bad shape. Bishop was badly injured again. It appears his brother was at the battle and defeated him. Somehow he broke through the ascension. The Seraphim was able to retrieve him, but we have no idea what the process will be to restore him, or if it's possible. We were able to get some good footage of the witches involved and how their powers worked. We are comparing known individuals and compiling new data."

"Dear Lord, all the men and Bishop? What a sacrifice."

"Yes, sir, if there is a bright side."

The reverend raised his eyebrows, unable to think of a single bright side to this mess.

"The Miller woman has already reached out and asked to meet with someone from our organization as soon as possible."

"Thank you, Moses. I appreciate the update."

THE TRIFORMIS

"H ey, Beck, did you guys drop Sugar back off in St. Louis?"

"Hi, M, yeah. Snow dropped him off on the way back through. She is meeting us tomorrow in Little Rock. But I talked to her earlier today and he wasn't with her then."

"Oh, okay, how was he this week? I have tried reaching out to him, but he hasn't responded all week."

"He was quiet, he tore the bunk house apart, we never found any evidence of Leroy being there. He found some clothes in a trunk in one of the bunks that were obviously his, but no sign the bunk was lived in."

M sped up a little, almost without noticing. Wanting to get back to him, to get her arms around him.

"He is pretty distraught, M. I don't know him well, more by reputation than experience. But I can tell when someone has been broken by something. He is not okay, M. It's not my business, but he is going to need some real healing from this. That's the kind of thing you don't just compartmentalize and move on from. Not in our line of work."

A moment of silence on the line, then Beck continued. "This was a hard one for all of us. Whoever is behind this, they leave those men out there as bait, Leroy included. Why would they do that? Why sacrifice your men, including someone as dangerous as that, not knowing what kind of force we would bring?"

"Best we can figure, they knew we were watching somehow and moved the operation before we could get there. We believe they were somehow watching, recording, to study our tactics and abilities or get some kind of proof of our existence. We got the Elders up to speed, but we have no way of knowing for sure. So, for now we will wait and watch. Unfortunately, every one of us that was there, now has to stay completely clear of Meadow's ministries."

"M, give Snow a call, she spent three hours in the car with him, she will have a better understanding of where his head is, I am sure of it. Getting people through trauma is her job, and she is damn good at it. If she didn't have him talking about his feelings twenty minutes into the drive, I will be completely shocked."

"Okay, thanks Beck, will talk soon."

The conversation with Snow went much the same way. He was quiet and confused about Leroy. Snow had dropped him off a few hours ago, she said he was surprised at first because he had forgotten about the new shop clerk and couldn't figure out why the shop was open when they got there.

M was about an hour away from the shop when she tried him again. He didn't answer, but if the new shop clerk was there, she should be answering phones as well minding the register. She tried the shop number, her heart growing heavy, her intuition ringing all the alarm bells.

On the third ring the phones connected, but no one spoke. The new clerk, Terry, Tracy, M couldn't honestly remember her name at the moment, and did not use the greeting she was instructed to. M, frustrated and already having a bad morning. "Hey, this is M. Is Sugar at the shop with you, I have been trying to…"

She was cut off. "Is that what you called him? Sugar?"

The voice on the phone was not the voice of the young girl, maybe nineteen years old, she had hired to run the shop while they were away. This was an older woman, much older from the sounds of it.

"Who is this? Why are you answering my phone, where is the person who is supposed to be working right now?"

"You mean my daughter, Elle? She is preoccupied taking her pound of flesh from the bastard that killed her brother Leo."

M's blood ran cold. "If you have hurt him, you bitch."

"Hurt him? We have moved well past hurting him. Now we are divvying up the pieces among us, who gets what and for what purpose. You thought you could just walk in my home and kill my only son and walk away like nothing happened, you thought you could bury my baby in the swamp and get away with it. If you get here fast, we can end if for you today as well and you won't have to grieve him long. If not, we will be back for you after you've suffered a little while, knowing it was your arrogance that got him killed. You know he called out your name while I was cutting on him? Polly, that is your name, right?"

M could not think, her mind frozen in the image of Sugar, bound to a wall rack like the children.

"He got quite bad there for a little while, kept saying… oh what was that… Sing, baby, yes, that's what it was. He has quieted down a bit now, though. Barely makes a sound when you hit him. Do you want what's left of the body when we are done, or should we just bury it in a shallow grave somewhere for the animals to dig up and parade around with his bones, like you did my baby? Alright, I have work to do, I hope to see you today, if not, I will see you very, very soon."

The line went dead.

M was crying, she had to focus, she tried not to think about Sugar, bound and tortured, that wouldn't help him. She needed help, if these two were strong enough and smart enough to get the drop on Sugar, she would be hard pressed to handle them alone, walking into an ambush. Beck, Devlin, and Snow were halfway to Little Rock, she would be at the shop in thirty minutes and couldn't wait hours for them.

She tried Dorthea.

"They have him." She cried into the phone.

"Who? What? M, what are you talking about?"

"The witch, with the Hecate altar, it was Leo Benson's mom and sister. They have him, Dorthea, at the shop, they are killing him, have killed him. I can't get there in time."

"Okay, baby, breathe, we are two hours out, maybe a little more. Fredrick and I can help."

"I can't wait that long, Dorthea. I have to get to him. I have to help him. I cannot lose him like this, not without telling him."

Dorthea did not need M to explain to know what she was saying, to understand the fear that now gripped her niece. "We are right behind you, how far away from the shop are you? Focus, M, how long?"

"Twenty-six minutes."

"Alright, I am going to hang up and call everyone I can get on the line. We will have backup and healers on the way. You aren't going to lose him, but you are going to war, M. Do not let the fact that they have the man you love cloud that fact. You have been in battles before, and this is no different. We are right behind you, as fast as we can."

Dorthea was right, this was not her first fight, far from it in fact. She had her kit in the back of her SUV, batons, blades, did she have poneratoxin? She had her necklace, filled with a nasty paralytic. One touch of that would shut your whole nervous system off. She had her glamour, and her warding, the shop was hers, that was her place. There was nowhere on earth she was more powerful than standing in the home she had built for them. The home they had built together. She could not fail him, not now, he had lost so much. She had to be there for him as he had always been there for her, and when it was over, when she put these hateful poisonous hags in the ground. She would love him, she would love him without restraint, without care or caution. She would love him like he deserved to be loved, and she would allow him to love her. She had touched his skin, she had felt his heart in hers, she knew that he loved her, that he would follow wherever she led. She would never deny herself or him again.

M pulled her SUV over to the curb two blocks up from her shop. She gathered her supplies, weapons, spell components, a small charm made from a lock of his hair and hers and sealed with a drop of blood from each of them. With a word it would come to life and lead her to him no matter where he was. She had not heard back from Dorthea or anyone else. She was on her own.

M approached the shop; she knew there were at least two of them in there. *Through the front door or up the fire escape, fire escape.* There was a ladder hidden behind a trellis in Sugar's garden, she could slide right up in and through the window on the second floor into his bedroom. From there she could glamour up and slip right down the spiral staircase into the shop. Find them and hopefully get the drop on them before they realized she was there. She would need to move fast and quiet, but she could do it.

She slipped around the side of the shop; it was daylight, but M knew most of the windows in the interior rooms of the shop actually looked out onto the property, it was all part of the glamour spell she cast on the building every month to maintain it. She noticed no changes in the building as she moved around. She did not extend her vision or senses to feel for him or them. She did not know how in tune these women were to the energy of creation and that would be like lighting a signal fire if they were watching. As it was, she was well warded and guarding herself against leaving any kind of psychic trail. She hopped the fence and slid through the garden, behind the rose trellis and found the metal rungs of the ladder. Up quick, she found the window to his room and slid the little hidden latch that unlocked it from the outside. As silently as she could, she slipped inside.

M slipped the locator charm on its chain around her neck and slid it down her shirt, so it touched the skin above her breastbone. She pushed it against the skin and whispered, "Surask Ji." Immediately, she felt the pull, he was close, and more importantly he was alive. The charm could not find the dead.

She followed its pull across his cluttered and eclectic room toward the hall; she stayed as close to the wall as possible to avoid the creaking floorboards in the center. As she approached the stairs, she heard two distinct voices, they were arguing about how much of the herbs and oils, supplies they could feasibly take and use before it went bad or dried up, and if using supplies that she had procured or prepared would taint their work considering how much she would hate them for what they did. M focused her glamour, pulling in all of the energy she could muster. She also prepared a concussive wave, she would slip down, hit them hard then be on them with her blades. She drew both blades out from behind her back. She would carve these women alive for hurting him.

Quick and quiet, down the spiral staircase, as she made the last turn, invisible to any onlookers, she heard the older woman. "Did you feel that?"

The younger girl looked around. "Feel what, a disturbance in the force Obi Wan?" And cackled at her own cleverness.

"No, smartass, I think she's here. I can feel the pull, something is sucking up a ton of power, like a great beast breathing in all the air in the room. You are out of touch living up here on your own, aren't you, Elle?"

"Man, fuck that, I am doing what I can, do you have any idea how hard this is? Being sent away, being apart from the family? But here I am, doing what needs to be done for us to survive. More than I can say for you."

"You'll watch your tone with me, girl."

Good, M thought, *distracted and only one of them powerful enough to even feel a shift but not identify it.* The younger of the two women was standing with her back to the stairs. She could not see the older woman, but the younger girl was exactly how M remembered her. Short blonde hair, shorts, and tank top. Fit, but not muscular.

Telekinesis wasn't M's strong suit, but she knew she could hit hard enough to take them by surprise, give her a fighting chance. She didn't know precisely where Sugar was, but the shop wasn't that big. Two main rooms of store front, a living area and kitchen and bathroom behind the counter, along with an extra room that housed a small gym and open floor. There was an unfinished basement but the charm on M's chest was telling her he was close by.

The time for thought was over and if there was one thing she had learned from training with Sugar, when violence was the only answer, death comes for the hesitant. Do not puff or posture. Act quickly and decisively. M swung around the center post of the staircase, skipping the last four steps to land softly just behind the younger girl. She released the stored up energy into a blast of concussive force directed at where she thought the older woman was, and she rammed both of her push blades through the younger girl's back just below the ribs and into her lungs. She squirmed and thrashed for a moment before M twisted the blades and yanked them loose. Then the blonde dropped in heap at her feet.

The older woman had been hurled into a corner bookshelf, which collapsed under the force of both the energy wave and her impact. Books and decorations lay scattered across the floor. As she struggled to rise, M stepped over the body of the young girl and advanced toward her. Keeping her glamour in place the woman could not see M approach as she rolled to her feet and rose. M was struck at how much she looked like the younger woman, even for a mother and daughter the resemblance was damn near twins.

It didn't matter to her at all, these women had hurt her love, and she would make them pay for it. She readied her blades for an attack, she would dart in, take the woman's throat, eyes, and heart in a moment then find him.

A movement to her right caught her attention as a hand reached out for her, and she heard "Xechoristos" as a fine mist covered her face. M felt a panic wash over her like nothing she had ever felt before. She could feel her glamour disappear as she was cut off from the energy of creation. M had been a part of Mercer since she was given as a sacrifice at twelve years old. The divine energy of creation and the connections it formed between her and all living things had been the foundation her entire reality had been based on, and in a flash, it was gone. She felt nothing, no connection to her magic, no glamour. Nothing. She spun with her blades striking out at whoever had just attacked her, but the owner of the hand had already moved out of reach.

M spun a tight circle, blades extended as she tried to get her bearings in a room now devoid of her glamour and a world no longer connected to her. Against the back wall of the shop, the shelves were all torn down and knocked over, and a wooden X was hung on the wall in their place. Sugar hung there, his naked body bloody and slack. He did not move or make a sound, his head hung forward and his long hair was black with blood. In front of him was a very old woman, even old, the resemblance to the other two women was undeniable. She looked like an older twin.

The second woman rose from the piles of debris at the bookshelf, laughing. "Ahh, there she is. I'm glad you could be here to meet us."

There was an odd resonance in her voice and as M tried to place it, she heard it come from behind her. "You are going to pay for that."

She turned back to see the youngest of the three back on her feet. That same voice pouring out of her mouth, but again with the layers of age somehow over top of it.

The oldest woman, propped on a cane hobbled toward her from the front. She twisted side to side, trying to get her back to a wall so they could not get behind her, but cut off from her magic, she would have to fight. She didn't know how the youngest was back on her feet, those wounds should have been fatal, but it didn't matter, she was the closest target. M leapt the few feet toward her, ducking low, but coiled so that when the inevitable block came, she would shoot straight up and bury her knife in this bitch's throat. She would tear it out with her teeth if she had to. She was going to get him down, get him safe no matter how many times she had to kill these women. Her jump was caught short by a blast of cold air that knocked her onto her back. M rolled a back somersault and came to her feet. Her eyes darted back and forth between the three, looking for an opening, a weakness.

Again, the voices came from all three mouths at once, a chorus of the same voice, affected by age. "Well now you've found me, what will you do? Kill me, like my sweet boy? Bury me in the swamp? No, I don't think so. I think you're going to watch as I carve off the parts I need from your boyfriend here, then I will start on you."

M tried to jump at the middled aged woman on her left but was hit from the front by a wave of fire that singed her hair and blistered her face and neck. She cried out and dropped her blades, trying to put out the flames as her clothes caught fire.

This time mocking laughter came from all three mouths at once. "Stupid girl."

She felt herself lifted against the wall. The younger two had approached, chanting, and a powerful and unseen force suspended her two feet off of the floor, her entire body was pinned to the wall. She couldn't lift any part of her body, she couldn't draw her baton, she couldn't reach for her poison necklace. She couldn't feel the divine energy, she cried out again, not only in pain and frustration, but in fear. What if in being cut off from the energy of the universe, she did not join her love in the eternal journey of creation and destruction, what if her portion of the energy of creation somehow became trapped here, without him.

She screamed in defiance as the old woman drew a blade from her belt, long and thin and already bloody from its work. She spit curses at them, none of which held the power that she could have hurled at them only moments before. Still, they laughed, the old hag pointed the long blade at her and a flame erupted from it, searing agony into her flesh as it burned its way across her abdomen; what remained of her shirt caught fire and added to the pain. The smell of burnt flesh and burning clothing filled her nostrils. She threw her head back, praying that she would hear his beautiful voice once again, but knowing the truth of the universe, there would be no second chance, she would die, he would die, and the great potential of their love would die with them.

A rushing sound filled her ears, like a tornado in the small room, and a tearing like fabric being ripped apart by hands strong enough to rend the universe. M opened her eyes against the pain and despair to see Elder Valkyrie, The Mother Moon, appear behind the old woman. She wrapped one hand around the woman's head and the other around her throat, her pointed nails digging into the woman's flesh like the talons of an eagle as she pulled in opposite directions. Blood sprayed her face and she screamed, a sound of rage and power as she ripped the old woman's head off, snapping the spine and dropping her twitching body to the ground. At the same time, Elder Alysse appeared next to the middle-aged woman, hear hands weaving a pattern in the air in front of her. "Kano komatia," she screamed, releasing the power with the gestures. The woman fell apart, arms, legs, head, separating from her torso as she fell into a bloody pile on the floor.

M hit the ground hard now that the spell holding her against the wall was broken. The youngest girl screamed and tried to run, but her path was blocked by Niri Agash, her eyes cast to heaven, her hands stretched out wide, the woman was caught as if in a web, her body frozen in place. Niri chanted, "Motini amhet alehu, sheritwa yibelali, Motini amhet alehu, sheritwa yibelali, Motini amhet alehu, sheritwa yibelali." With each repetition, the woman drew in upon herself, appearing to dry out and shrivel until she fell, an empty husk where a woman had been just moments before. With a delicate sandaled foot, and toenails painted the soft blue of a morning sky, Niri stomped the head of the dried shell, crumbling it to dust as she passed on her way to where M lay, gasping in pain.

As Niri and Alysse gathered over M, Valkyrie was kneeling in front of the rack where Sugar hung. M could see her head bowed, blood still dripping from her braided hair onto the floor. M reached out her hand, trying to speak his name, trying to get someone to take him down, to tell her he was alive so that she could die at peace.

Niri took her hand. "He will be safe; she is summoning help. Lie back, love, you will be together soon, I promise you."

The agony ripping across M's abdomen was too much for her, and she faded into a welcome blackness. The last thing she saw as she did, was Lord Seanchara standing in the middle of her ruined home, her beloved Sugar held in his arms like a baby, as he cried over him. Then she saw nothing else.

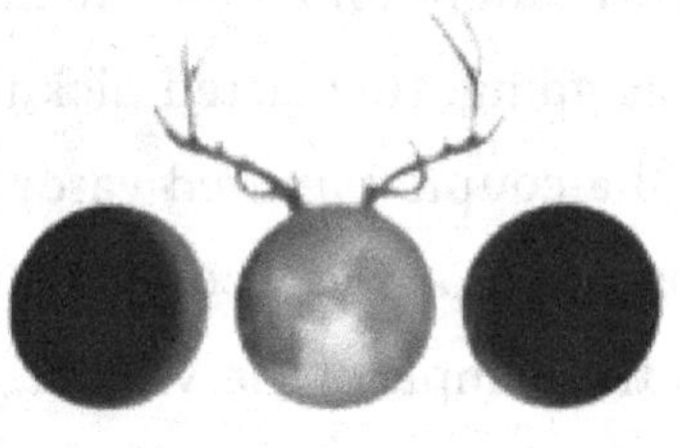

YOU!

"Sugar, come on keep up, you're going to miss your surprise."

"Kay, if the surprise is for me, how can I miss it? Wouldn't that mean it is just something that's happening that I might be surprised by?"

Kay was a few yards ahead of him and turned to give him the kind of impatient look that only an almost fourteen-year-old girl could manage. Sugar no longer walked with a cane and his physical wounds had mostly healed. He still struggled through some of his workouts, but that was mostly conditioning from six months of respecting his limitations and letting his body lead the way during his healing.

He had no idea why Kay and Tren, another teenager brought to Mercer this year, and Kay's likely consort, had excitedly come to his room at the ungodly hour of seven a.m. on a Wednesday morning. But apparently there was a surprise in the dining hall he just couldn't miss.

Tren had run ahead, but Kay was dragging behind with him, teasing him, goading him on. He had been training quietly the last three weeks. Trying to avoid the watchful gaze of Snow and Dinah who had been overseeing his care. He thought for a moment about showing Kay just how that training was going. He started picking up speed a little at a time, they were still a couple hundred yards through the winding cobblestone path from the massive doors of the hall that opened up onto the courtyard of the Temple of the Mother. He would wait until it was a straight shot to the doors, then give her a surprise of his own.

It was a brisk morning, and the morning air felt great against his skin, the leaves were just starting to turn. He had no idea where Mercer was actually located, he knew that seasons changed here, but he wasn't sure if they had to. He noticed the trees along the trail, at any given point you could see redwoods interspersed with eucalyptus and river birch, spotted with the occasional evergreen. None of these should exist in the same climates alongside each other. But it was all part of the beauty of Mercer.

They rounded the last corner in the trail that led to the courtyard, and Kay turned to tease him again about being so slow. By this time, he had caught up dramatically and it was only a few quick strides, and he was right in front of her. Kay startled at the speed at which he made it to her, and he didn't stop. He scooped her up over his giant shoulder like you might do with a toddler and took off in a run.

Kay squealed with surprise and mock indignation but couldn't stop laughing as he ran across the courtyard with her weight no more slowing him down than carrying a bouquet of flowers.

He made the doors of the hall and slipped in with Kay still over his shoulder. Both of them laughing as he sat her down and spun around. The table closest to the door was laid end to end with food: fruit, cheese, big plates of scrambled eggs, bacon, sausage, ham. Two big trays were filed with toast and biscuits.

Tren stood, grinning at the head of the table, as Bets, Althea, Diane, Desma, Snow, and Dinah filed in from one of the interior doorways.

Sugar turned to Kay. "What is this?"

"Sugar, it's your birthday breakfast." Her grin took over her entire face. "Tren and I cooked everything. Okay, almost everything. Ashanti made the biscuits and grits, and Elder Dinah made the gravy. But other than that, Tren and I did everything."

From behind him, Niri spoke, "Happy birthday, Christopher. Come in, let's eat, I am an hour late on my morning coffee and you know I will get mean if I don't get some caffeine in me."

Later, seated around one of the big tables, everyone had eaten their fill and sang the praises of the young sister and brother who had coordinated this and done the bulk of the work, to bring them all together and celebrate him.

Bets reached across the table and took his hand. "I spoke to Dorthea; she and Fredrick send their love. They are out on a time sensitive mission. But want to check in soon."

"Thank you, Bets, has there been any change with her?"

"No, Sugar. I am sorry, not yet. But Snow hasn't given up on her, she is using some of the same magic that preserves us as we pass through the veil to keep her body safe while her mind rests."

He noticed she didn't say "heals" because she should have been long healed by now. No one could explain what happened with M. For six months, she has lain in healing, her body nearly mended. She had no head trauma they could discern, but for some reason she just would not wake up. No one could figure it out. Not even their most powerful sisters could find a way to touch the part of her that made her who she was and prompt her to wake up.

They all said the same thing, there was an impenetrable wall around her consciousness and so far, nothing had broken through to wherever she was in there.

There were many hugs and claps on the back as the group filed out after breakfast. The kids started cleaning up and left Sugar alone with his thoughts. Everyone here knew the pain and regret he was filled with. The very real possibility that he had missed out on years of love and happiness over some imagined obligation to a rule that didn't exist. It wasn't the mission, how many sisters and brothers found love while still fulfilling their mission every day. Did it complicate things? Of course it did? But for some reason, they held onto the belief that the mission had to come first.

Maybe they both knew that the love they felt, if allowed to grow, would eclipse even their mission. Or maybe they were just both cowards, so scared of loving and being hurt that they ran from their best chance at real happiness and used their mission as an excuse.

Sugar wanted to lay his head on the table and cry. But he would not, not here in the Temple of the Mother. He would go back to his room and train and study. He would get his body and mind back to its razor edge and he would get back in the fight, otherwise what was it all for, all this loss.

But first, he would go by her room. He didn't see Snow at breakfast; he would box up some food for her and use that as a reason to go by and pray at her bedside. He would sing to her and kiss her forehead and tell her he loved her as he had almost every day since he could walk again.

Box of food in hand he walked down the hallway toward her room. He could hear voices through the open door. Elder Alysse, he stayed a respectful distance back. The room was small, and he knew the enigmatic Elder rarely visited Mercer and he did not want to crowd her. So, he sat on the small bench outside the room and listened to the conversation unfold.

"I was fortunate, I stumbled across a chamber underground in Louisiana and realized it was Diana. We thought she had died; she had been missing more than one hundred years. As soon as I understood what she had done, it made sense. It just took us too long to realize where she was headed. She always was a vindictive bitch. I cannot imagine how long it took her to perfect the Triformis ritual. Essentially becoming a triple Goddess, the maiden the matron and the crone. As soon as I told Elder Valkyrie, she knew how to deal with her. We could have killed them one at a time for eternity and never actually killed them. Have to kill all three at the same time to actually stop the Triformis. That's why she sent the youngest version out from the other two. Hard to kill all three if they aren't in the same place at the same time."

Sugar was nodding his head in the hallway; he didn't remember much from the day he was attacked at the shop. Seeing the new shop clerk, then the other older women, then nothing but blinding pain as they carved, and cut, and beat, and burned. He didn't even know until weeks later that it was over that monster Leo Benson. He had no idea why he was being tortured, only the suffering.

"So, when Dorthea called and told us what was happening, we gathered the three most powerful sisters we could find to deal with her. It felt a little deus ex machina but I just happened to be standing next to Mother and Elder Valkyrie when the call came in. Fortunate timing, I guess, and you and the big one can claim to be two of the only people alive to be rescued by the oldest women alive."

Sugar's heart stopped in his chest as he played that word over and over in his mind.

You

THE END

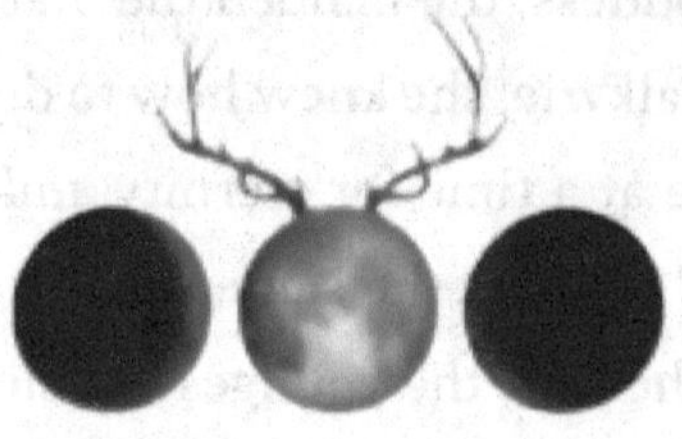

EPILOGUE

M ducked behind the small counter in the old office building. She could hear the dogs coming, growling, snarling as they smelled their way through the darkened building in pursuit of her. She knew Sugar was right around the corner and headed to her. Her lungs burned and her legs were nearly numb from the pain of running. She felt like she had been running for days. She was so tired she couldn't even remember how they had found her. Some kind of magic, she had never seen dogs like this.

They looked like the largest German Shepards she had ever seen, but the heads were too large for the bodies, with almost human faces, save for the fangs.

It sounded like six or seven of them coming down the hallway, their claws clacked on the old broken tile floor.

She pulled herself in as tight as she could, her baton was gone, as was one of her push daggers, she didn't know when she dropped them. Blood ran down her arm and soaked the leg of her pants as she knelt.

She couldn't tell if the wound was a scratch or a bite, not that it mattered. Heat pulsed through it, throbbing in time with her heartbeat, and her arm refused to move as it should. Something was very wrong, but she had no time to dwell on it now. She needed to get back to Sugar, to get her arms around the man she loved. She needed to stand back to back with him and wipe out whatever these monsters were and then track down whoever sent them.

She heard the door behind her splinter just as the dogs rounded the corner in front of her. Sugar, her consort, her lover and oldest friend, came flying through the remains of the shattered door and leapt over the desk into the pack of howling fangs and claws.

M made it to her feet and started a charm, a repulsion to try and deflect some of the dogs off of him, she knew if she could just give him a second's reprieve from facing the whole group at once, he would likely have them all dead in moments.

Nothing, she focused on the feeling the divine energy of creation as it pulsed through her and it was gone. She was cut off from her power, from her connection to all of creation and to her greatest weapon. She screamed in frustration and tried to leap the counter to help Sugar fight.

Her legs were frozen in place, no matter what she did, her muscles would not respond. She screamed again as the dogs bore down on Sugar. Six, ten, she couldn't count them. He stood in the center of the room, long bladed knife in his right hand, a steel riot baton in the left, a whirling dervish of death to any of the beasts that strayed too close.

His long arms and graceful frame kept the dogs at bay for a few moments, the couple that ventured too close finding death as he spun as circle through the room. But she could see as they moved in the dogs slowed, some blocking as the others moved around the perimeter of the space. Trapping him.

"Sugar, get out, get safe," she screamed over the sound of the monstrous animals.

He said nothing, only continued his dance of death through the room. Blood splashed in the air as he dispatched another with his baton when it couldn't move away fast enough because of the crush of dogs behind it, filling the space.

As one the dogs surged, several charged low from all around him, as even more leaped at his face and throat from every direction. M heard the cracks of the batons and shrieks of pain as Sugar fought back, but she could do nothing to help as he was dragged down under the writing mass of teeth and fur.

M screamed his name over and over as she heard the dogs ripping and tearing at his flesh. *Not again.* Her mind wailed, she could not lose him like this, not after all they had been through together.

Frozen in place, unable to reach into her power, M watched helplessly as the writing mass of bodies settled and quieted. The dogs all turned to face her. She thankfully could not see the body of her love. She didn't want that to be the last thing she saw before death. She thought of him, at play with Kay and Tren, while she healed at Mercer. She thought about the feel of his pale skin and hardened muscles as he wrapped his arms around her and held her to his chest.

She opened her eyes, bracing for the dogs to charge while she remained frozen in place. But instead, they sat still, unmoving. Behind them, a figure slowly rose. It was Sugar—his hair was gone, his head was shaved nearly down to the scalp, and he was dressed in some kind of tactical gear. She said his name, "Sugar?"

He did not answer, only stared at her with his eyes so dark they were nearly black.

"Sugar, baby. Hey, come on, help me. I am stuck. I cannot move and I cannot feel my magic. Please, baby."

The pleading in her voice grew more insistent.

Sugar cocked his head, as if listening.

Like a dog hearing its master's voice, she thought to herself.

Faster than she could really register he jumped the row of dogs in front of him, vaulted over the counter, and grabbed her around the throat. She tried to scream, to beg for him to stop, but his giant hand had wrapped all the way around her neck. She reached behind her back for her last push dagger. Sugar shook her like a terrier with a rat in its mouth. Her body rag-dolled as he shook her back and forth. She was scared her neck would break.

She couldn't speak or scream, just hung there by her neck as he squeezed tighter.

He pulled her up and close to him, held her face right next to his, screamed an incoherent bellow of pure rage and hate and slammed her hard down onto the ground. Her skull cracked against the tile floor and something in her back cracked loud enough to be heard.

She had no time to assess the damage before a flurry of punches crashed into her face, and darkness swallowed her.

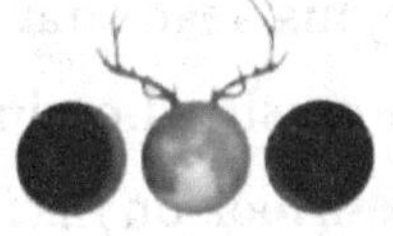

M woke, lying on a blanket in an endless field of green grass. She was staring up at the stars. A voice, soft but very masculine, spoke behind her.

"I told you, Polly, daughter, there was more misery on the horizon if you returned."

"I just wanted to do the right thing, to help people, to love Sugar."

"I know that's what you wanted, and it is noble, but to turn down an offer of rest and peace. To deny the opportunity to spend your eternity without the pain of loss and betrayal that is sure to come."

M rolled and tried to get to her feet, to find the Witch Father, to protest, to beg him, if necessary to stop the nightmares, to let her live out her choice in peace. She found she could not move; she struggled for a moment angry now at the constant theme of paralysis and hopelessness that has taken over her subconscious since her fight with Diana the Triformis and subsequent time unconscious. Struggling against the hold on her, she screamed in anger and twisted hard. That's when she heard his voice in her ear.

"M, you're safe, just breath, love. I've got you."

She opened her eyes and looked up into his beautiful face. He was on his side and cradling her in his arms, whispering soft reassurances to her.

"Fuck."

She slammed her head back against the pillow and his arm in frustration. She was still shaky from the dream. As she looked up at him, she could see the image of him, his head shaven, his eyes a soulless glass like the eyes of a shark, as he crushed her throat and slammed her to the ground. The cold emotionless look on his face as he beat her to death. She turned away from him and pressed her body against his, needing the warmth of his touch, feeling his concern and love for her through the contact with his skin. But she could not look at his face right now.

"The dream again?" The question was soft.

"Changed it up a little this time, this time it was giant mutated dogs, who killed you first, then you came back from the dead and killed me. Before I was again chastised for wanting to continue living my life."

He did not speak, he knew there was more she needed to say, but he would not push. That had no effect on her. When she was ready, she would say what she needed to say.

"How did I get here, Sugar? How have I become this weak quivering mess of a woman, when just a year ago, I would go to war with anything or anyone? I cannot sleep an entire night because I have scary dreams. I haven't taken on a job or mission in months. Other than you and Bets, I have had almost zero contact with anyone. Hell, even Dorthea has been pretty scarce."

She pulled his arm tighter around herself. "I just feel so damn useless right now."

Sugar hugged her tightly and kissed the side of her neck gently. "M, you are about a year out from some serious trauma. You thought I was tortured to death in our home, you were tortured and cutoff from all of your power, then, you met GOD. Who tried to convince you for six months to give up the fight and has been sending you nightmares ever since."

"Still."

"Still what, M? This isn't the movies; you don't get to have your guts cut out and burned and your whole world turned upside down and pop back up in the sequel with no scars to show for it. We are damn lucky the elders didn't pull you out of the field completely and keep you home. You just need to be as patient with yourself as you are with everyone else, M, you'll recover. We both will."

"It's bullshit, Sugar."

"What is?"

"That you get to be the pretty one and the smart one."

"It also isn't fair that I am the better cook, but we all must live in our destiny. Trust me, if I could tan, just once, I would give up all of it. Now, you want to make the coffee, and I will start breakfast."

"Maybe in a while."

"You want to stay in bed a little longer while I get the day started?" She pushed back into him and pulled his hand over her breast.

"Why don't you stay a while, I can think of something I need more than another nap. Then you can make me breakfast."

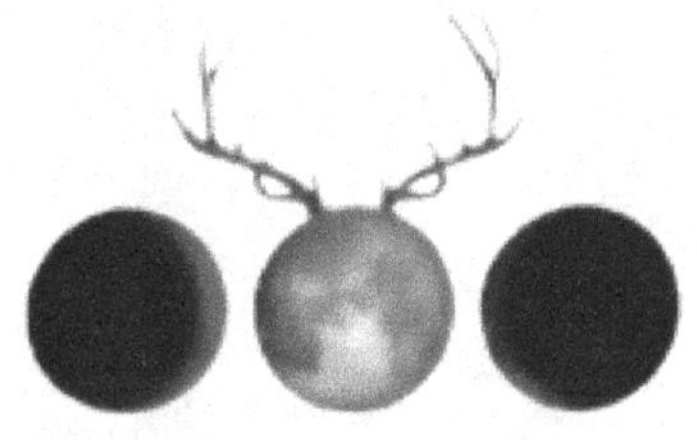

ABOUT THE AUTHOR

Punk rock bastard son of country folk healers and big tent evangelicals. Neo-Pagan and keeper of the Aging Elvinian Psycho Vaudvillian Vibration. D.O. lives in the Midwest where he experiments with taming wild animals with string band instrumentation, and roasting meats between writing novels.